THE LEGEND
OF DAGAD TRIKON

THE LEGEND
OF DAGAD TRIKON

Grégoire de Kalbermatten

daisyamerica LLC

Published by daisyamerica LLC
P.O. Box 545, Bronx, New York, 10471, USA.
Book design by: www.dimensions.at – Vienna, Austria
Cover design by Richard Payment – Vancouver, B.C.
Printed in the USA by King Printing – 181 Industrial Avenue, Lowell, MA 01852

The Library of Congress has catalogued the daisyamerica hardcover edition as follows:

de Kalbermatten, Grégoire.
The legend of dagad trikon / Grégoire de Kalbermatten.
p.   cm.
ISBN: 1-932406-01-8
1. Mythology—Fiction. 2. Spirituality—Fiction. 3. Lost civilizations—Fiction
4. Kundalini—Fiction 5. The Goddess—Fiction 6. Hidden treasure—Fcition

First US Edition 2006
10 9 8 7 6 5 4 3 2 1

GRÉGOIRE DE KALBERMATTEN

THE LEGEND
OF DAGAD TRIKON

TABLE OF CONTENTS

FOREWORD TO
THE LEGEND
OF DAGAD TRIKON

F iction is a convenient way to invoke shapes of possibilities. These may be scattered in the cosmos or hidden within us. We write fiction to channel our curiosity, our hopes or fears; we write to test the borderline with the unknown side of reality. Science fiction is therapeutic — it tells us we can do more. Can we imagine 'philo-fiction,' a world where philosophy would tell us that we can be more? In both cases fiction explores potential changes in the life of man.

This is not as crazy as it may sound. Evolving world cultures tell us, intriguingly enough, that common themes on man's perfectibility have surfaced repeatedly in philosophy, literature, and art, generation after generation. Yet, many in the brave world of modernity are convinced that the man who searches for the meaning of his life is wasting his time, is just a fool.

Too often, we are only busy with our day-to-day lives, caring about what we can own. We think that's all there is to it. But there are moments, all too rare, when we wake up and care to find out who we are, who we could become.

Once upon a time philosophers were those of us who indulged in the disturbing habit of raising fundamental questions. Let us pick it up this trail of philo-fiction at a time of twilight, when established certainties appear tenuous. Can those of us who are still curious discover somewhere deep within our unconscious, some cognizance of the meaning of the now mostly forgotten mythologies? Can we make sense of the riddles posed by scriptures and prophecies through millennia of trials and tribulations?

Carl Gustav Jung, the Swiss psychologist, asserted that we could. William Blake said we should. Much of his visionary work can be seen as challenging the exclusive primacy of Reason that comforted the eighteenth-century thinkers and the 'reasonable people' who followed them. It needs imagination to escape the scaffoldings in which reason imprisons our minds.

My tribute and heart-felt gratitude goes to Alan Wherry, my publisher and editor, who brought to this project enthusiasm, precious advice, and steadfast support. He made this book possible. Thanks to Maureen Goodman for proofreading, to Kingsley Flint for reviewing the manuscript, to Richard Payment for designing the jacket, to Radhika Rao Gupta for editing, to Dara Tittjung for designing the content and to Nira, Bea, and Alex for their comments. This work is dedicated to the master and mother, Shri Mataji Nirmala Devi, to her compassion, knowledge, and wisdom.

Gundelfels am Rhein, March 21st 2005

THE LEGEND
OF DAGAD TRIKON

On the Trail
of an Ancient Secret

I t was four o'clock in the morning: the moment of daybreak, when partygoers head home for bed, when streetwise cats try their luck in trash cans and poets seek inspiration in the early dawn.

A greenish light cut streaks across the Cairo sky. When Jonathan first saw the small monkey perched on the branch of a nearby acacia tree, he thought that the cute little visitor was pleading for food so he threw it a banana. Jonathan had a lot on his mind and it certainly wasn't the monkey that was bothering him. But, in his wildest dreams, he could never have guessed that the pleasing of this particular monkey was about to change his life. He yawned and went inside.

Jonathan O'Lochan, Counselor of the Embassy of the United States of America in Egypt did not find the moment propitious. With a mug of fresh-brewed coffee in his hand to help him start the day after a troubled and sleepless night, he glanced at his surroundings. The balcony overlooked a garden and birds were already chirping through the early morning mist. The Counselor's residence was an old colonial villa in the center of Cairo, decorated with white stucco and surrounded by a small park. It was conveniently located in Tibbanah Street, and from the balcony one could see the dome of the Blue Mosque, founded by Prince Aqsunqur Al-Nassery in

1347 AD. In quieter times Jonathan would sometimes go there and enjoy the mosaics of Muslim art on its walls. For reasons of security the Administration had wanted to relocate him to the confines of a walled compound and he had fought hard to be allowed to keep this little oasis of calm. He shrugged as he peered through the mist at the Egyptian security man standing at the gate. The thought crossed his mind that maybe one day a guard such as this might empty a machine gun into his belly.

Indeed, the day before had seen yet another bloody terror attack on the streets of Jerusalem. He wondered how it was that there could be so much hate in the Holy Land, where so many prophets, even Christ himself, had walked and preached the eternal brotherhood of man, It was so hard to build peace and so easy to trigger conflict.

Jonathan was an American scholar, fluent in Arabic and Urdu. He had been instrumental in improving relationships between the USA and the Islamic countries. Cementing a peace process between Israel and its neighbors had been a cornerstone of this policy. Yet with this latest atrocity, the gunning down of the Prime Minister of Israel as he was leaving a peace rally, it seemed to Jonathan as though history had moved past an invisible line, one that should never be crossed, and with fateful consequences for all. After all, the First World War had started with a few gunshots, when the heir to the Hapsburg imperial throne was assassinated in Sarajevo.

Forcing aside these gloomy thoughts, he took a deep breath, absorbed the freshness of the early hour, and noticed the morning dew that carries promises for the new day. He sadly remembered the idealism of his youth and the words of the prophet Isaiah engraved on the circular wall of the Sharansky steps on East 43rd Street in front of the United Nations Headquarters in New York: *"They shall beat their swords into plowshares and their spears into pruning hooks. Nation shall not lift up sword against nation. Neither shall they learn war anymore."* Such had been the dream of the founding fathers of the United Nations but it all sounded somewhat naïve now; unfortunately, the reality had so far turned out to be very different.

"You've been ages out there on the balcony, what's up?" His sister Tracy greeted him with a dreamy voice, hair falling in her face, as she emerged half asleep from the guest bedroom. It was so good to have her with him on a visit from home; she was a comforting presence who helped him face the stresses of these dark days.

"I am struggling with my thoughts, dear sister, those stubborn enemies," he answered lightly, not wanting to voice his worries. He took a shower, had breakfast, and left early for the office.

The line that Jonathan had long defended for the US Middle East policy, *'no peace without justice,'* was blurring rapidly as the State Department became overrun by damage containment and, irrespective of the consequences that would entail, an apparent willingness to do business with Israel at any price. Jonathan's attempts to focus American policy back to a *'just peace for all'* had largely failed and the thought depressed him. He had the troubling impression that the senior Embassy staff did not want him here any longer: they were so often at loggerheads. He felt helpless and humbled.

"God please, take us out of this mess," he muttered under his breath as he was processed through the security checks at the Embassy entrance. "The only one I have been able to help since I was posted here is the monkey who turned up this morning in my garden," he thought as he grabbed the top layer of faxes and memos in his in-tray.

During the emergency meeting called at the Embassy in the aftermath of the assassination, his Ambassador stated that the peace process would continue as before and he deliberately, it seemed to Jonathan, played down the impact of the tragedy. Counselor O'Lochan felt irritated and increasingly cranky: he just couldn't see the usefulness of cultivating a state of denial. He had been intemperately vocal in his disagreement with his boss – never a good strategy for a diplomat, and his observations had been abruptly dismissed.

"The motto of my country is *e pluribus unum*, 'out of many, one.' How is it that America, a country whose citizens come from so many different nations of the world and who live there in relative peace and harmony, a country that is always trying to do the right thing, always ends up on the wrong side of the fence, being blamed for most of what goes wrong in the world?" Diplomacy was a frustrating job, thought Jonathan.

More to the point, what could he, Jonathan, do about it? He had entered the diplomatic service to play a part in expressing the solidarity of his country with the other nations of this world. Was he going to find himself spending most of his professional life in fenced-in compounds, surrounded by Marines and bodyguards? Maybe he should just forget about all this and find a better-paid, less-stressful job? Such questions had been the source of his sleepless night.

Only one prospect cheered his somber mood: he had a meeting planned for that evening with his dearest friend, Lakshman Kharadvansin, an archeologist, who was in Cairo after a short visit to southern France. He would come with his cousin Lakshmi Vani after an eventful exploration that had taken them deep into the Sahara desert.

A month ago Lakshman had sent Jonathan some artifacts of potentially earth-shattering archeological importance that he had discovered in a remote desert location. He knew that Jonathan had access to CIA facilities and that he could count on his discretion.

Preliminary results of carbon dating were astounding: the objects, indicating outstanding artistic and technical sophistication, dated back some ten thousand years. When informed of their age, Lakshman had pleaded on the phone that, for reasons he said he would explain later, at this stage he did not want the archeological or any other authorities to become involved. He could hardly contain his excitement and this was indicative of something most exceptional, thought an intrigued Jonathan, because Lakshman was normally rather circumspect, not given to exaggeration or displays of superfluous emotion. Lakshman did not want to talk in detail on the phone but had promised to tell him everything when they next met.

More surprises came in. The day before, Jonathan had received a rather beguiling fax from his friend. Lakshman had sent him copies of a few pages from an old manuscript that he had found in a remote abbey in the south of France. He had highlighted a passage of the text entitled Chronicles of Provence, the memoirs of the Count de Provence, one of the great barons of the kingdom of France in the Middle Ages. The faxed pages related a strange event.

One Christmas Eve, the Count and his escort, were traversing a dense forest, seeking to find refuge from a fierce snowstorm. Suddenly, a lone knight barred the way; he was guarding a bridge over a small river and wanted to extract a tribute from the travelers. The knight's mantle was in tatters but, from the cross adorning it, the Count deduced that this grim figure had once belonged to the order of the Knights Templar. Foot soldiers from the Count's escort attacked the bold challenger but were swiftly repelled. The Count, in no mood for fighting on such an inhospitable and holy night, reported in his memoirs that he had addressed the lone warrior thus:

"Greetings, my friend, don't you have more holy work to do on the eve of Christmas than to extract a ransom from the Count de Provence? Behind me are five of my best archers. They will easily put a term to your insolent pretense. But, you seem noble and brave. Tell me who you are, what is your errand, and I shall spare your life."

The knight did not expect such courtesy and thus responded sadly: "My lord, my name is Renaud. I lost my family, land, and honor and I have resolved that I shall perish here or take a ransom. Hear the sad plight of a lost knight. Years ago, when we were young, my friends and I went to the Crusades to find the traces of our Lord Jesus in the Holy Land. We, in the order of the Temple, wanted to free his birthplace from the presence of the infidels and to prepare the conditions for his return. I wanted to defeat those who are cruel and false, but in the process, I myself became cruel and false. It was my original intention to fight evil and to spread goodness but in the process I killed fair and gentle people and became infused with evil myself. It is a great enigma that in desiring so much to do good, I did so much wrong."

"This may be true, but the mystery of sin is the human condition, there is no answer to this paradox," responded the Count with an emerging sympathy for the knight-turned-robber.

"There is, sire," responded the knight defiantly, and he added unexpectedly, "I threw my sword at the feet of the Archangel Michael and asked him to take away my sins. He told me my sins would be washed away if I could unveil the mystery of Dagad Trikon."

To Jonathan's frustration, the text stopped there. Lakshman had not sent any more of the story of the encounter between the Count and the knight. The words 'Dagad Trikon' had been underlined and there was a single comment, written feverishly in the margin: "Jonathan, some of the Knights Templar knew about my discovery. Wait until I am back. This is so big!"

This cryptic reference to the tale of the knight robber had whetted the diplomat's curiosity. Why had Lakshman bothered to send him this piece of archival material?

His cousin Lakshmi Vani had spent the afternoon on a shopping mission to the Khan Khalili bazaar. Comprising an array of shops dating back to the fourteenth century, the bazaar is renowned for its indigenous character and for the magnificent variety of gold and silver works, embroidered clothing, leather goods, and hand-carved woodwork to be found there. The shopkeepers and taxi drivers of Cairo are as sweet as Turkish delight but twice as sticky, and a shopping trip could easily result in a huge bill. But Lakshmi was not easy to persuade, and she'd returned with only the items on her original list. She was particularly pleased with her purchase of a fine example of an onyx statue of the sacred falcon Horus, the tutelary bird deity of ancient Egypt.

The evening brought a welcome relief from the oppressive heat of the afternoon as she hurried to find Lakshman on the terrace of the Sheraton Hotel. He had obtained a table by the Nile, where he was now relaxing while awaiting the arrival of his friends. The colossi of stone watching over this ancient river in the gray mist were no longer sphinxes or pyramids; now, their names were Intercontinental, Meridian, and Sheraton. The reflection of their lights, dancing on the surface of the river, signaled that these were indeed the temples of the modern age. At a nearby embankment, tourists were boarding a cruise ship where they would enjoy fine Lebanese food, the breezes of the Nile, and the traditional skills of a belly dancer. In the Sheraton, the waiters served scented mint tea and gorgeous Arab pastries that explained perhaps the plump contours of the ladies from Cairo's high society who were gossiping at a nearby table. The cousins ordered two fresh limejuices. A strong bond of friendship had brought Lakshman and Lakshmi together since early childhood. The cool of dusk provided a pleasant and relaxed atmosphere. While they waited impatiently for the arrival of Jonathan O'Lochan, they chatted happily and reviewed the events of the past weeks.

Lakshman and Jonathan had been friends since their time at the School of Advanced International Studies in Washington D.C., after which they had followed very different paths. Jonathan had pursued a career in the U.S. Administration whereas Lakshman, having graduated in archeology, had specialized in that discipline. Somewhat unusually, Lakshman was a European child who had been adopted at the age of eight by a rich jeweler in Mumbai. He could now afford to follow his passions and had enough money to do what really pleased him. The information he looked forward to sharing with Jonathan carried more than its share of excitement.

Over the past few years Lakshman, with the help of his cousin, had focused his attention on some ancient Sanskrit manuscripts that contained descriptions of lost civilizations. His research had led him to explore the temples and pyramids of Egypt. In the temple of Abidos, which probably dated from the time of Seti I, he had discovered a beam, between two high columns, about twenty feet off the ground. The original overlaying panel bearing Egyptian hieroglyphics had crumbled and fallen away, revealing an even older panel behind it. This older panel contained carvings of unknown origin, many representing flying chariots, figures on flying horses or geometric figures and numbers that, after some further investigation, appeared to correspond to flight trajectories. With this information, Lakshman had identified an area in the midst of the desert that seemed to be the hub of what he was forced to conclude, after much double-checking, reluctance, and skepticism, was the origin of the flight paths indicated on the beam.

He had decided to travel to this location in the Sahara and had invited Lakshmi to join him from Mumbai, as Lakshman valued his cousin's resourcefulness and enjoyed her company too. Now however, he confided in her a strong sense that he was under surveillance. He was certain too that his computer files had been searched and after discussing the matter together, they decided not to trust anyone except Jonathan.

Lakshmi had a light brown complexion that she had inherited from her mother, and lustrous dark hair. Her face was gently sculpted, well proportioned, and slightly round. Her eyebrows were thin and well groomed. She had a small and delicately fashioned nose and her slender figure, wrapped in shyness, exuded great charm. But all the gifts nature had given her paled in comparison to her eyes. They were, liquid, shaped like long lotus petals and shone with shades of green and blue. For those who knew her, she didn't always have to speak, for her eyes could express what she felt far better than words.

Lakshmi, for her part, had pursued divergent interests, having studied bioscience and ancient religions. She too didn't fit into a convenient stereotype and, like her cousin; she was able to enjoy the best of all cultures. At a Mumbai party, for example, she would be one of the few women still dressed in traditional fashion, looking beautiful in a silk sari, or she might be found on a beach at sunrise, offering flowers to a sand statue of the elephant-headed god Ganesh that she had molded artistically by hand. She was, at the same time, a modern woman, who excelled at horse riding and flying aircraft. Lakshmi's perspicacity and stamina were precious to Lakshman, who enthusiastically involved her in his research. This latest archeological venture seemed to be the most promising to date; indeed it had the unmistakable potential to be the high point of his archeological career. Together, they reviewed their recent discovery.

As they approached their destination in a rented Fokker plane, a spectacular sight had greeted them. A huge mountainous complex arose before them. They were surprised to find curved canyons and chiseled peaks and they admired three protruding monoliths that glowed in the sun with a fiery red hue. This ragged landscape was an otherworldly sight: in the midst of these ever-shifting desert sands, such a dramatic arrangement of rock took their breath away. Lakshmi slowly lowered the plane as she searched for a suitable landing place. Lakshman was completely engrossed by what he saw, as their descent revealed more and more details of the spectacular landscape unfolding beneath them. He sensed the rich archeological promise of the place and his eyes were lit with childlike wonder. Lakshmi landed the plane on an unusual flat granite table that afforded a suitable airstrip.

They were surprised to find no mention of this particular mountain system on their topographical maps and it took them some time to realize that there was something extraordinary in the fact that they had managed to reach this place at all, equipped only with hunches derived from the Abidos temple. After a few days of searching, they had found grottoes and chambers that had traces of ancient human dwellings. They had then begun to explore the labyrinth of caves and corridors leading to the bottom of a canyon. They were soon rewarded: they found pieces of artifacts which, when examined by Lakshman, revealed the existence of an ancient race who predated the ancient Egyptians.

They found inscriptions that at first baffled Lakshman. However, with growing excitement and after a number of failed attempts, he successfully deciphered a few with the help of a table indicating a connection to Egyptian hieroglyphics.

He discovered that these long-extinct people had called themselves the Avasthas and that they had known this desert mountain site as Dagad Trikon.

THE WHITE MONKEY
REACHES OUT IN CAIRO

E ach day in Dagad Trikon brought its share of new discoveries. It greatly intrigued Lakshman that he was the first person to discover the vestiges of what clearly had been an impressive civilization. He was an accomplished archeologist who had worked on numerous sites all over the world. Yet nowhere had he come across a mention of this civilization, with two exceptions: on the single scroll he'd found in New Delhi and in the Chronicles of the Count of Provence.

This was particularly baffling because what he had discovered so far pointed to a civilization that was highly sophisticated. "It's utterly incredible that here, in this age of satellites and space rockets, I should be the first to chance upon this extraordinary site," thought Lakshman. For a moment he saw himself on the cover of *National Geographic*, then, laughing at himself, he went back to work.

There was simply too much to do, too much to discover. From carvings on the walls of caves hidden deep within the fissures of the Rock, they became aware of the last days of the Avastha civilization and of how they had recorded their knowledge on special scrolls. In an imposing grotto, an explicit bas-relief depicted how ten major scrolls had been dispatched by riders on winged horses to the four corners of the earth. This was consistent, Lakshman noted, with the discovery of the flight trajectories in the Temple of Seti I. Guided by the text and by sheer good luck, they unearthed two liturgical weapons left behind in the calcified bottom of an area named the Alwakil fields by the Avasthas. The weapons were small and engraved with signs or symbols; Lakshman could only decipher their names.

Thus, he was able to bring back to Cairo and later identify the Avastha sword called Glorfakir and the shield called the Sadhan, weapons that had been molded in an apparently unknown metal. That night they had set up camp in one of the caves they had just explored, falling into a deep sleep almost immediately and dreaming quasi-hallucinations that seemed to reveal hints of Avastha life. Visions of ancient splendor visited them, accompanied by haunting music; they heard rumors of lost battles and the dying gasps of fallen heroes; they had glimpses of noble, beautiful, and elegant beings; they saw sad faces that whispered softly to them in an unknown tongue. These dreams revisited them every subsequent night at Dagad Trikon, the name they now knew for certain this place had been known by in those far-off ancient times. It was unnerving that their dreams were so vivid and so real and they would often wake up feeling dazed. There was something lingering here that was unique ... a power to which they both seemed to be acutely sensitive.

Lakshman and his cousin had become very tired. The heat at noon had been unbearable and they were almost out of water. There was still so much to discover but they knew they would have to leave soon. More questions were raised than answers found. Although they had found the weapons, adorned with intriguing inscriptions and symbols, they were, for some unknown reason, unable to remove the sword from its sheath. When taking the hilt of the sword in their hands, the cousins had an antsy sensation, as if it were softly buzzing with a compressed energy. Although they had discovered the existence of the scrolls, they still knew nothing of their present whereabouts. Insidiously, it seemed as if they had experienced a magnetic pull from the Avastha world, as if they were being coerced on to a path of inquiry, unwittingly inveigled into a script written by someone else.

After four more days of increasingly feverish work, Lakshman had deciphered an inscription relating to a casket that was symbolized by the emblem of a feather. It was accompanied by a map, which, imperfect though it was, seemed to indicate, by way of a prophetic prediction, the route to be followed by this specific casket. He speculated that perhaps the wealth of information was because this casket contained one of the most important scrolls of Avastha lore. When comparing the text and the map, Lakshman deduced that the casket was deemed to travel through what would subsequently become known as Europe and that it would finally be found in an island of ice and fire, draped in the aurora borealis, far beyond the warm seas. In fact, all the indications pointed to the island now known as Iceland.

However, after this momentous discovery and in the short time available to them, the remainder of the exploration did not reveal anything else of importance. Lakshman wanted to pursue further inquiries, to follow the amazing threads of discovery he had picked up in Dagad Trikon, indeed to find out more about the weapons and scrolls before being obliged to hand them over to unknown academics in an unknown museum. His reluctance to go public was strengthened by his strong intuition that he was being followed and that his computer files had been searched.

This was why Lakshman had flown to Marseilles at the invitation of a scholar and friend who specialized in the medieval writings of the so-called heresies that had flourished over many centuries in southern France. He sensed that this invitation was more than a fortuitous coincidence and wanted to check on his assumption that traces of this ancient civilization could not have been consigned solely to one Sanskrit scroll. He reasoned that if he had correctly deciphered the Avastha map describing the journey of the casket with the symbol of the feather through Europe, then there should be some reference, hidden or otherwise, to the Avasthas somewhere in Europe itself. Meanwhile, Lakshmi stayed behind in Cairo to record the minutest details of their expedition on her computer.

The trip to the abbey of Roquebrune had proven successful. With the help of his erudite friend and continued good luck, Lakshman had come across the reference in the Chronicles of Provence but he hid his jubilation because he had promised Lakshmi that he would keep their discovery a secret.

Now Lakshman was back in Cairo and ready to relate the story as he understood it to Jonathan. As he sat with Lakshmi awaiting Jonathan's arrival, he said:

"Lakshmi, you are well versed in the history of religion and aware that the Catholic Church and the king of France launched fierce persecutions against those in southern France who wanted to follow a free path of spiritual inquiry. The Pope let loose Simon de Monfort and the barons from the north who, naturally, were keen to dispossess the southern lords from their lands on the pretext of suppressing the heresy. Later on, the king wanted to seize the wealth of the Order of the Temple, which had long since turned corrupt. Therefore, as in other parts of Europe, it came to pass that the knowledge of ancient mysteries and sacred rites was wiped out, together with many gentle people who had died with their secrets intact. The destitute knight Renaud was probably one of the last of the mystic knights."

"A few allusions in scattered manuscripts here, some references in mysterious minstrel songs there, not much to go by," interrupted Lakshmi, grinning dismissively.

"Wrong, my dear, dead wrong!" exclaimed Lakshman happily. "I was able to trace in the archives of the nearby cathedral of Albi the report on the trial of the knight Renaud de Cormorant by the Holy Inquisition. Just listen to this: he was a close follower of the knight John of Jerusalem who wrote a book known as *The Book of Prophecies* and he had confessed to the inquisitors how it was that he had become a heretic. Guess what! The event happened in the Great Mosque of the Umayyad in Damascus. Can you imagine? You know, it is my favorite place in Syria. The Umayyad Mosque is a converted Byzantine basilica. It has a wonderful ambience, majestic, and peaceful – I visit it whenever I can. Renaud was hiding in the small mausoleum of John the Baptist, within the basilica, I mean, the mosque, as he received a mystical initiation at the hands of a magus from a far eastern land. It is amazing that I could find mention of the name of the Rock because… "

"Hi, Laksh and Laksh!" So engrossed were they in their conversation that the cousins were startled by the sudden appearance of Jonathan on the Sheraton terrace. He had come up on them from behind, accompanied by his sister Tracy. Lakshman gave an involuntary shudder. He had met Tracy a couple of times in the past and had become fond of her, but it had been his expressed desire and intention to see Jonathan alone. Jonathan noticed Lakshman looking somewhat hesitantly at Tracy and said, "Don't worry, Tracy is absolutely reliable, she's my sister and I'd trust her with my life. She's seen the artifacts you sent me, and, well, I told her you might be on to a big story. But she saw them at first by mistake," he added sheepishly.

"Well, okay, but from now on let's keep this strictly between the four of us," responded Lakshman whose annoyance was quickly melting under the imploring smile of the young woman.

"What's going on, Lakshman? First you send me this cryptic fragment of a medieval manuscript, then these incredible objects; what exactly did you find out?"

Lakshman leaned towards his friend and related in a lowered voice what he had found in the temple of Abidos and his subsequent flight into the desert. He spoke with a calm but intense conviction about why he thought these were such important discoveries. He recounted details of how they had explored the Rock and what they'd found there. He also spoke about the separate references to Dagad Trikon he had uncovered in France and India and ended his account with a whisper of warning: "Yesterday, when I returned to my hotel, someone called and hung up when I answered the phone although apart from Lakshmi no one knew I would be staying there. As weird as it may seem, since I picked the trail of the Avastha fortress in an ancient Sanskrit manuscript in Delhi, thanks to help from Lakshmi's scholarly friends, I have a certain and unsettling feeling that I am under surveillance."

"Well, I assure you it's not us, because I would know about it," said Jonathan half-jokingly. "But if you need some protection, tell me because we can help. Believe me, I had to fight hard to keep the background to your discovery secret. Our research people carbon-dated the one piece I gave them – not the weapons, of course: I kept them at home as agreed. The laboratory is intrigued because the drinking cup is the oldest recorded human artifact they've seen and they believe that the metal it's made from appears to come originally from an asteroid. The agency in Langley asked me to prepare a report for the Oikos Project but I managed to convince them it was too early to reveal this discovery."

"What's the Oikos Project?"

"I, well… confidence for confidence, this is also a classified subject."

"So? You got my classified story."

"I know." Turning towards his sister he said, "Why don't you tell them?"

Tracy was glad to oblige, having been immensely impressed by the account of the cousins' achievements. "Oikos started three years ago, and was driven by some arcane corner of the National Defense Agency, but the guys at the State Department managed since to transform it into a multinational enterprise because otherwise it would have made no sense to them. In a nutshell, the analysis of new threats to public security shows that in the coming decades, widespread conflicts will come from clashes of belief systems, the growing scarcity of natural resources, and the frustration of the majority of the world's population, the poor, who perceive that their prospects of receiving a fairer share of the Earth's wealth are increasingly diminishing. The scenarios indicate more natural catastrophes, a backlash to globalization, more divisions, separatism, and intolerance; there is a medium certainty that this will lead to more wars but of course, it need not necessarily be so. This is where Oikos comes in."

He continued, "Oikos means 'the house' in ancient Greek. It is a research project to identify whether there can be a common set of rules to manage our global house and, if so, how to apply more effectively certain shared values that go back to the core of ancient traditions, religions, and belief systems. Actually, I am now working for the American secretariat of the project."

"So you found my stuff by mistake?" said Lakshman, grinning doubtfully.

"Well, as Socrates said, 'we know enough by now to know what we don't know,'" responded Tracy, as she repressed a smile. "There is a huge chunk of history that is missing from our books. We are looking for the basis of common purpose, a common understanding between nations, a knowledge-based integration of belief systems to counter the rise of fundamentalism in various religions."

"And you think there's a possibility that we could get some clues from the Avastha scrolls?"

"Your discovery of Dagad Trikon is fascinating as it could potentially bridge the gap and persuasively link mythology to history. This is the core of our interest, if indeed there has been a glorious past, a Golden Age, a time of deeper knowledge that was lost according to many accounts, we would like to know on what belief systems it was built. It could help the international community find a sense of common purpose and shared values, and this is precisely the main driver of the Oikos Project."

"Frankly, Tracy," said her brother, "some in the Administration still believe that everything would be fine if the rest of the world would just roll over and adopt the American way of life, but many do not share this naiveté, mostly because of the growing problems of our society at home… "

"… Let alone the fact that the model is too wasteful to be transferred to the global scale," interrupted Tracy.

"You're joking," intervened Lakshmi, somewhat sarcastically. "You mean to say that Americans have at last discovered that getting rich is not enough? If so, they are truly ahead of the rest of us. Maybe if you'd let other people get rich too, we'll reach consensus on this a few centuries from now."

Jonathan continued with a wink at the fiery Lakshmi. "Well, it was on this basis that a group of Congressmen and senators managed to mobilize financing for Oikos. Then they persuaded major countries and leading scientific institutions worldwide to join in. We established the universal orientation of the project and we've already had quite a lot of progress, but so far we've kept it out of the U.N. and away from the media, because the territory is so unknown: there is too much sensitive information involved and no guarantee whatsoever of success. So if you agree, Tracy will personally follow up on your discoveries at Dagad Trikon, to see whether they fit with some of the Oikos findings, but she would never mention anything about it without your express consent."

"Okay," replied Lakshman after a brief moment of reflection, "I'll keep you posted, but I need your help. Please keep the weapons secure for the time being. It seems I'll have to go to Iceland if I am to follow up on the main clue we uncovered. Do you have someone there who could help me with preliminary research?"

"No problem, Laksh," replied Jonathan coolly. "I'll fix it with the Agency in the name of the Oikos Project. As a matter of fact, I have already arranged a security clearance code for you, so that you can be assisted through any of our embassies anywhere in the world."

"Don't tell them too much, please. I feel very unsure about this. Without finding the scrolls, we are nowhere. If we find them, I bet their content will prove to be of great strategic significance, I mean, they could bring revelations that some governments would like to control and we don't want secret services meddling in it, not yet, not now... I sense danger in this. I might be running into big trouble."

"Laksh, this is precisely why you should accept Jonathan's offer of support," said Tracy encouragingly. "If you don't pick up this trail soon, then others will and at the moment the whole thing is so exciting and still exclusively in your hands." Tracy trusted her brother's friend. Lakshman's Indian upbringing had given him a tranquil determination and the capacity to stay cool under stress but she was quite sure he also had the guts to push further into the unknown.

It was at least another hour before they agreed on a course of action. Lakshman confirmed his decision to head for Iceland, the island of ice and fire. Jonathan gave Lakshman and Lakshmi special cell phones so they could connect with each other on a secure line from anywhere in the world and so the friends parted with promises to keep in close contact.

Jonathan had had a full day. It had started with his early-morning worries about the state of world affairs, had continued with frantic consultations at the Embassy, and was later enriched by the extraordinary account he had heard from the two cousins. Obviously, he'd never thought that there could be any relationship between such unrelated questions as the rising specter of war and terrorism and the legacy of a lost civilization. He had no expectation either that the prayer he had uttered that very morning would be answered. However, the most extraordinary moment of his day was still awaiting him.

On the way home with Tracy, Jonathan stopped off to buy some Lebanese food at the fast food shop on the corner of his street. Its jovial owner usually provided the latest rumors and the wittiest and most recent political jokes against President Mubarak but the seriousness of these days kept even him uncharacteristically quiet. Jonathan and Tracy sat on the sofa together, and as they ate their meal of humus and kebabs they watched the news on television. There was an outpouring of grief from all parts of the world over the recent assassination. The two of them didn't talk much because what was there to say? Jonathan was exhausted by his lack of sleep the previous night; depressed by the current turn of world events, and he resented his Ambassador's short-sightedness.

The diplomat in him felt that he could not defend the newly emerging policy of 'papering over the cracks.' He kissed Tracy good night and went to bed early. Normally, in such trying circumstances he would have found it hard to turn off the thoughts running around in his overactive brain but mercifully he was soon fast asleep.

However, what followed was more than unusual. Indeed, it came to pass that the messenger who had come that very morning returned the self-same night.

Jonathan slept deeply, sinking into an abyss of total nothingness and the empty silence filled him with a sense of ethereal detachment. What followed was more than unusual. Indeed it came to pass that the messenger who had come that very morning returned the self-same night.

Suddenly, it was as though a movie had started up in his head. He saw a small white dot that approached his forehead in a zigzagging movement. As it came closer, it took the shape of a small white baby monkey, which reminded him of the morning visitor to his garden. Then, oddly enough, he thought of the soft toy monkey his younger brother Michael had had since they were kids. The monkey came even closer, approaching slowly and with a noble gait. It then became clear from its face that it was, in fact, a very old monkey, with eyes that shone with faultless wisdom and a reassuring touch of tenderness. It seemed to wait for Jonathan to introduce himself, or so thought Jonathan – but perhaps that was because he was a diplomat. So he said ceremoniously, "Pleased to meet you. My name is Jonathan O'Lochan and I am from the United States of America."

The monkey responded courteously, "Pleased to meet you too. As a matter of fact, I have been looking for you. People call me the white monkey and say that I come from China but really I was born in India where my name is Hanuman. However, I also have another name that is more familiar to humans from the western lands," he added somewhat mysteriously, without offering any further clues. Jonathan was intrigued, captivated, and curious to know more.

"What would that name be, and what brings you to this part of the world, sir?"

"'*Intuition*' is the name with which I visit many of the human race. Now they see me and now they don't."

At this point Jonathan recalled that he had heard the name Hanuman before. Lakshman had often spoken to him about certain mythologies and how he was trying to elucidate some of their meanings through his archeological pursuits. The Ramayana was one of the great epics of the Hindu culture and Hanuman was one of its main characters, the heroic monkey and adviser to the god-king Rama.

"I know you are much distressed, and rightly so," pursued the monkey in a voice filled with compassion." I have come to you at this time in my appointed function: I am a messenger, a bringer of tidings and hope from above. Your world needs radical change, a change for the good. What is needed is to go back to what is sometimes called the Golden Age, or rather, to make that age return because, of course, there is no going back. So the need is to return, to return to oneness, and the re-building of human souls."

This unlikely exchange continued in the same curiously ceremonial tone for some time. Then, all of a sudden, a baffled Jonathan saw that the monkey had become huge and that he himself had somehow disappeared, but he then realized that the white monkey was carrying him on his back into a different dimension of time and space. When they stopped, somewhere in the vast emptiness of his slumber, the monkey suddenly became small again. Hanuman unfurled his tail, a very long tail indeed, which then wrapped itself repeatedly around Jonathan. The feeling was protective and soothing. Then Jonathan thought he heard the white monkey whisper, "Travel now through this long tail. It speaks of the days before, to announce what will come in the days to follow."

Then Hanuman came even closer and disappeared inside Jonathan's head, or so it seemed. What followed did not seem coherent at all, but it was a dream and dreams are rarely coherent. Jonathan was swept away on a reverberating fantasy, on a stage without a background, full of theatrical surprises, where characters and situations were introduced one after another. He had a fright when, for a few seconds, the muzzle of the monkey suddenly transformed into the face of a powerful lion. Then he saw the heroic monkey in a variety of settings: being greeted by a celestial princess who was looking downcast: she was a prisoner in a lush garden, surrounded by ugly and heavily armed female guards. He next saw the white monkey torch a great city with his huge tail ablaze with fire, traveling through the air, carrying with him a boulder covered with grass and full of plants and flowers. "This is really an account of the feats of Hanuman in the Ramayana. This is what he is reported to have done, Oh my God, I can't wait to tell Lakshman," he thought, full of admiration for Hanuman and marveling at the wonderful fresco unfolding before his eyes.

He then saw the white monkey on the flagstaff of a war chariot looking protective in the midst of great slaughter. Then, with astonishing agility, the monkey jumped down, turned towards Jonathan and, winking, told him, "Verily, I am Hermes Trismegiste and Mercury." These were the names given in the Greek and Roman mythologies to the messenger of the gods and, indeed, Hanuman now appeared in the likeness of a handsome human, carrying the caduceus of Mercury. By now Jonathan was too dumbfounded to properly follow what was going on and he found himself totally absorbed in his own feelings and reactions.

The monkey had an endearing manner about him. Jonathan realized that in the presence of this visitor he felt like a small child, and he found himself hoping with all his heart that Hanuman would like him. For Jonathan, being in the proximity of Hanuman had the effect of casting a sharper light on himself and he sensed his own flaws more clearly. However, Hanuman's presence was soothing and Jonathan now felt protected and loved.

But the manifestation was still unfolding and in the next image the monkey was beaming the theory of relativity into the brain of Albert Einstein, who, at the time, was playing with soap bubbles in his garden. Thereafter the ever-transforming Hanuman flashed a truly angelic form of such brilliance and untold splendor that Jonathan closed his eyes – it was too much to bear.

Things then are never quite what they seem to be. A despondent American diplomat, who in the morning had expressed a prayer of anguish for those who had failed to build peace in the world, had received a most surprising answer. He had been visited in the evening by the high lord Hanuman, the white monkey, son of the wind, master of great magic, teacher of healing, prince of alchemy and healing, messenger from the unknown, bringing biddings from the gods and revelations to those men and women of the modern era who were still capable of listening. Jonathan's spirits soared: someone had heard and answered his prayers. He floated for a while in a sense of detachment and total comfort, without realizing he was at the very beginning of an extraordinary journey.

CONTACT
WITH DAGAD TRIKON

As Jonathan was borne along in his dream by Hanuman, the thought came to him that Hanuman was simply a manifestation of the heavenly messenger of divinity that had been portrayed differently in various cultures throughout the ages. Indeed, Hanuman, Hermes, and Mercury all expressed the same qualities of a single divine persona, one that brought pearls of insight to the human conscious mind from the universal unconscious. This in itself was a powerful intuition. Jonathan thought cheerily, "This means that a common pool of knowledge links us all, despite all our differences. There is hope for the Oikos Project after all."

Jonathan was transported, in a manner whose meaning and significance he could not yet understand, to a faraway time and place where he witnessed the Dagad Trikon legend, thus connecting to the remote rock location that Lakshman had so recently discovered. Jonathan saw the darkness of his sleeping state evaporate and the dream state seemed to become reality again. Or was it the other way around? He didn't really know what was happening, just that he wasn't flying any more and that he seemed to have shrunk or, more likely, the white monkey had become suddenly gigantic. The monkey's unfurling tail enlarged to become a huge screen that materialized slowly from the heavens. It contained images, sounds, smells, and movements that filled the senses. Jonathan found himself in a four-dimensional movie, floating in a vision while following the narrative of a lost age.

Next, he was airborne on the back of a giant seagull, which surprised him because they were so far inland and such a long way from the sea. The seagull flew toward a rock in the midst of a desert, which first appeared in the distance as a high reddish cliff with ominously impregnable vertical walls.

The great Thalassean navigators of ancient times had always suspected the existence of a formidable rock somewhere deep within the barren emptiness of what they called the vast Hasara desert, beyond the faraway reaches of earlier Earth. The few desert tribes, who would sometimes visit the water hole of the small and remote oasis of Kaal Ben Muzur, knew of this mythical mountain and they considered it a place of powerful magic. They called it *'the hidden triangle'* in their language. The name suggests, as with all the really good things on earth, that it was indeed a little hard to find. Indeed, until Lakshman and Lakshmi's recent discovery, no travelers had ever found this place. Now, amazingly, Jonathan was visiting it in his sleep and was about to discover, through the visual narrative brought to him by the white monkey, the history of Dagad Trikon itself.

As the seagull approached from above, the rock looked like a gigantic ocher triangle resting on a sea of sand. Jonathan was awe-struck, taken aback, for the rock was immense; its walls towered like formidable barriers whose height rivaled the greatest cliffs of Africa. These walls formed a three-sided rim, a nearly perfect triangle, which completely sealed off the interior from the outside world. The immensity of the rock was visible only because Jonathan was flying so high. The triangle contained a whole world within its high walls. Jonathan thought its ocher color evoked the mountain that the indigenous population of Australia knew as Uluru but this structure was considerably larger.

They flew onwards towards the center of the rock and saw that this massive tableland was made up of numerous canyons and corridors, with occasional large openings that allowed the golden rays of the sun in at appointed hours of the day. Successions of high peaks, separated by narrow and deep valleys, dwarfed the skyscrapers of the New York that he knew so well. It seemed to Jonathan as if aspects of the Grand Canyon and the skyline of Gotham had been rolled together to create this unique geological construction. The seagull eventually landed in a central valley.

Suddenly the seagull was gone and Jonathan now found himself alone and even more immersed in the vision. In the shady depths of the rock, the heat was always bearable. The rock walls displayed a splendor of multi-colored layers, from a muddy yellow to soft orange and peach. The skin-colored boulders and pillars varied from pink to brown to yellow. The walls of the canyons were made up of a series of rock layers, remnants of ancient mountains, seas, and riverbeds, many millions of years old. Varieties of fossils within the rock layers bore testament to the many stages in the development of life, from primitive plants to large reptiles and marine animals.

Jonathan was moving fast, as if he could fly. In some places the rock faces rose abruptly a sheer three thousand feet above the valley floor. The surface of the rock consisted of large flat tables of stone alternating with chiseled peaks. Huge stone arches linked the smaller gorges. The sun baked the peaks and the stone tables of the rock and filtered through to the canyon depths, where shade and moisture protected life on the valley floors. Here and there crystal waterfalls, underground springs, and a complete network of water canals alimented large ponds, pleasantly mirroring the greenery in the bottom of the canyons. A few dwellings could be seen perched on the cliffs walls, which could only be accessed by boat and steep winding paths that led up from the canals.

The smaller canyons that lay close to the edge of the three sides of the triangle grew deeper and more rugged as they descended and finally opened out on to the main canyon, known as the Gundaldhar Fault, which cut into the central plateau in three and a half concentric coils that led to a central mound at the very hub of the rock. Each coil was linked together laterally by narrow splintered gorges that converged toward the central mound. Jonathan had heard it whispered that the heavenly rulers had entrusted this mythical mountain complex to the scions of the early race, the elder brothers.

This earlier race had lived on earth before the advent of human civilization. The dwellers of the mountain were the remaining tribes, those that had escaped the tyranny of the darkness that engulfed the earth at the beginning of the rise of evil, in the period of the Great Schism. Avasthas were named differently in the languages of the later tribes of men but until Lakshman's discovery, no one in recent times knew of them.

Stupendous cliff villages testified to the building prowess of the highland Avasthas. Indeed, the canyons had many great caverns in their sidewalls, the largest of which had roofs of massive overhanging vaults of rock. These highland Avasthas had built their cliff dwellings in these recesses: villages with walls, circular towers, temples, and terraced houses embellished with spruce trees and little pinion woods. Access to these dwellings, hanging a thousand feet above the canyon floor, was difficult and secured through hanging bridges, tunnels, staircases, and corridors, hewn into the flanks of the mountain. The arrangement of houses in the cliff dwellings was intimately associated with the distribution of social functions. The population was composed of a number of clans or communities and each clan owned individual dwellings and larger rooms for collective use, a temple for ceremonies, and other enclosures for the storage of food. Fireplaces were located in the plazas or on the housetops. As a whole, these different rooms constituted the collective space that belonged to one clan and the ornamental style of the masonry of the adjacent houses expressed the distinct identity ascribed to each community.

The floors of the canyons were fertile and the rock dwellers brought their cattle there to graze. These openings provided space for the dwellings of the lowlands Avasthas, some of whom had built residences high up in huge banyan trees that grew in the Gundaldhar canyon but could be found nowhere else on earth. On many of the lower branches, wooden structures served as shady residences and food storage space for entire families. However, most of the lowland dwellers lived in the capital city, Shambalpur. There, the most wonderful stone architecture could be admired, carved into the reddish hues of the central mound.

And this is the legend that was unfolded to Jonathan:
Before the arrival of the Age of Dread, the water giver, Jaladhar, was said to have entrusted the Avasthas from Dagad Trikon with three leaves of various colors captured in translucent crystal stones, which together with huge underground water reservoirs, sustained life in the Rock. In exchange for his blessings they pledged to worship the water resource in its subtle form and to fight evil and its prince, using an array of weapons whose secrets were eventually lost.

At the time of its greatest bloom, the citadel of Dagad Trikon comprised forty-four thousand inhabitants. Legends of yore spoke of a mysterious force that maintained and supported the abundance of enchanted life in the Rock.

In these ancient times, when goodness still ruled the earth, divine beings resided in the Eastern mountain chains of Himavat, in the north of their land of predilection, the large and fertile plains of Bharatma. Only a few traces of these times remain except for hints within obscure legends written in the Sanskrit tongue. Originally the Rock was only a place of worship, a place higher beings would travel to with the speed of thought. Sometimes they could be seen on the mighty eagles of the Karudas type. They would, at times, gather in this special place to celebrate festivals guided by the position of the stars. These were times of great jubilation when a God would come from faraway Himavat and be worshipped in rituals whose richness and opulence were astounding. So much beauty was on display that these Pujan festivals recreated heaven here on earth.

No description of a Pujan festival could do justice to the magnificence of the event. There were many forms of worship, celebrations involving diverse rituals, hymns, and the recitation of magic verses. Large crowds of celebrants would remain seated on the ground for more than five hours at a time without a single movement and this was possible because the action and impact of the Pujan ceremony itself would be triggered deep within each individual. When played in the presence of a God, the harmonies of the Rasa music reached an altogether different dimension. They would be condensed into a dew of sacred sweetness that was absorbed into the brains of the attendees, who would enter a state of vaporous well-being, enjoying an ecstasy that comes with being entirely and completely in the present moment, the infinite now.

Through their worship, the Avasthas opened their hearts to the higher power and were drenched by an ambrosial experience. A voluptuous energy poured into the consciousness of the pilgrim, pushing him or her on a mighty journey into inner depths that would reveal exquisite architectures of insight and emotion, rivers of refreshing feelings, placid lakes of tranquility, and illuminating peaks of consciousness. The Pujan festivals invited the Avasthas to walk the paths of inner knowledge, the Deep Way within their respective souls. Untold power would be released when, collectively, they would reach the destination of this inward journey.

After the ceremony of worship, the revelers would take part in festivities, bubble with joy, and dance to Rasa music with merriment and laughter. The celebrations would take place in large caves, some fashioned by huge stalactite and stalagmite columns and decorated exquisitely with gems and precious stones that would sparkle with the vibrant glow of a thousand lamps and shimmering lights, like chambers in a multi-storied palace.

After each festival, the desert around the Rock would bloom for several years. In kingdoms and cities far away from the Hasara belt and even beyond the seas, all living races and species would enjoy the blissful moisture that permeated the atmosphere, carrying with it the vibrations that were released by the ceremony. The Thalassean navigators could tell the date of the Pujan festivals by the moods of the sea, for in those days the earth and all its creatures were in complete harmony. After each festival, every creature, great and small, each in its own way, enjoyed the energy emitted by the Triangle Rock.

And so it was, that for many millennia, the earth was a peaceful and joyful place and the Avasthas lived a harmonious existence within the great Rock, sending emissaries and navigators to forge alliances of trust and friendship with other Avastha kingdoms and with other species and races existing then during this First Age.

It was puzzling to some, in a world of goodness and harmony, how evil could exist at all and indeed how it was that it would eventually prosper, but when it finally manifested, after millennia of shadowy maneuvers, it caught the beings of the earth by surprise. Its rise was swift and terrible. In those ancient and terrible days, Avasthas from all over the world took refuge in the welcoming caves of Dagad Trikon whose grandeur befitted these princes of men. Soon battles were raging and a few exploratory expeditions of the forces of darkness almost reached the outer rim of the Rock.

The chief officials of the Rock, as portrayed by the screen contained in the tail of the white monkey, were Aslerach, high lord of Anor and Nizam of Dagad Trikon, and the wizard known as the Sand Keeper.

Aslerach was the commander of the warriors. He, the Nizam, had gray eyes that would shine like diamonds when he experienced the flow of the higher power or they would turn metallic when scrutinizing the soul of an enemy; enemies usually fled at the mere sight of him. Aslerach was a tall and commanding presence, a fearsome warrior, unrelenting in battle yet magnanimous in victory. How old he was no one knew but he had been a leader of the Aryan cavalry, back in the time when the hordes of Thanatophor had first been repelled.

For many ages he had been the archery teacher for generations of young Avasthas. The best archers in his army had such a remarkable mastery of concentration that with just the power of their attention they could direct their arrows accurately to their targets. Aslerach, the commander of the Triangle Rock, was supremely confident in the might of the Avasthas. He did not compromise with the forces of darkness but showed compassion for those that Thanatophor had lured or otherwise subdued. Thanatophor, the carrier of death, was the name given in the tale of the white monkey to the collective power that bound the negative forces together.

The features of the wizard called the Sand Keeper, whose real name was a secret, were known to very few because a hood usually hid his upper face. However, his voice was soft and persuasive, capable of many moods; it could cheer an audience with gaiety and humor or cut a foe like a blade of steel. He was widely revered as a teacher of the Deep Way, bringing the most promising amongst young Avasthas to the fullness of their inner power. He was a highlander and moved about in a network of vaulted chambers located in the center of a precipitous bluff two thousand feet above the fields of Shambalpur, which afforded a towering view in all directions of the Rock. He supervised the wide network of spies who brought tidings from the outer world. Secrecy was part of his art. He kept a squadron of Pushpak chariots in a large cave. These were the means by which the scions of the early race could fly at tremendous speed all over the globe. He often went himself on secret errands into the outer world, rallying alliances and firming up resistance to evil. Yet, of late, he had not left the Rock because the increasing strength of Thanatophor had become too menacing.

The true ruler of the ocher triangle was rarely seen. She was the High Lady of the Rock, whose power all worshipped but none fully understood; all they knew was that it stemmed from the very depths of the Triangle Rock itself. She lived in the most magnificent of all the caves, set in a wooded canyon connected to Gundaldhar. A huge spiraling stalagmite pillar sustained her residence. Ponds, spring waters, and small brooks maintained a pleasant coolness in her abode and exquisite perfumes, carrying specific messages and greetings from Mother Earth, were released through openings in the walls. The decoding of these fragrances was entrusted to children who had been born to parents who were expert in the Deep Way.

A dense wood patrolled by the Sheravalian Guard surrounded the large clearing before the entrance to the cave. The Sheravalian Guard was one of the marvels of Dagad Trikon. It was an elite company of young women who dressed in red lightweight armor of a special alloy whose secret composition has been long lost. Each had mastered the arts of war and was in telepathic command of a specific feline: tiger, lion, puma, cheetah or panther. The captain of the Guard was Erilie. She had long black flowing hair and was one of the few Sheravalians who rode a horse and not a feline. She could shoot arrows that would put an enemy into frozen slumber and when angry, with eyes aflame, she could, at will, cast a glance that pierced matter. Members of the Sheravalian Guard were athletic yet graceful and well versed in the arts of singing and dancing as well as in the arts of warfare. They were virgins and their chastity gave them complete protection as it provided them with an aura of purity that no ordinary evil could penetrate. This background, combined with their special military training, was the source of their extraordinary powers. However, on reaching the age of twenty-five, a member of the Guard would leave and marry.

A selection of boys and girls from Dagad Trikon were initiated early into the knowledge of the Deep Way whose purpose was to express a subtler energy although little was externally revealed. These children would learn how to focus their attention and to magnify their powers. Much of it had to do with the way they learned to strengthen the bonds between themselves and in how they interacted with each other. The sacred thread of the rakhi, which they would tie to each other's wrists during the harvest festival, was a bond that, once tied, opened the higher dimensions of deeper collective union. It secured a particular strength of togetherness between brothers and sisters. Significantly, in the Avastha language, the word for love and energy was the same.

The bonding of a man and woman was a source of great joy and marriage was one of the key rites in the culture of the early race. The marriage festivals were celebrated in colors of pink and gold, with music, processions, and dancing. At the appointed time, when a couple became one in Dagad Trikon, their union would bloom with the fullness of exclusivity and last for their lifetime.

They would join by mutual consent, following guidance from the stars and advice from elders who were knowers of the Deep Way. The newly married couple would be imbued with an intensity of love that made the pairing forever energy giving and enjoyable. It was thus that romance unfolded after the wedding, not before: consequently, children in the families of the early race would grow up confidently in the warm glow of love.

Such was the cardinal principle of Avastha culture. As children came of age, they sought to increase the potency of love in all its forms: respect, loyalty, friendship, brotherly and sisterly bonds, conjugal love, compassion, and devotion. The consequent emotional fulfillment left no space for material greed and the main value of matter was to express feelings of love and friendship, for the Avasthas enjoyed nothing more than giving.

As the story within the screen unfolded, it was explained to Jonathan that with the passing of the ages, the seeds of evil grew too strong in the outer world and the subtle balance that enabled goodness to prevail in nature and society was lost. Two demon kings served Thanatophor. The first, the devil Belzebseth, was the high priest of the dark cult and well versed in the art of sorcery. He was usually dressed in black and purple robes and had the ability to change his face at will. In his consistently sinister history, he had been known by many names. He was to become, among others, Belzebseth and Seth, the enemy of Osiris. The second, Hangker, was a titan of formidable powers compressed into a small shape, the commander-in-chief who led the onslaught of the evil hordes. While Hangker commanded the Azuric titans of the dark hordes, the Dark Council of the Necromancers, which comprised the ablest sorcerers and witches, seconded Belzebseth.

Eventually, Mother Earth herself rebelled against this onslaught of negativity and started to quake so much that natural catastrophes wiped out a number of the old kingdoms. Others survived and remained to fight the imminent Darkness. But some beings who could choose to do so retreated to other worlds. For a long time the Avasthas fought back and tried to hamper the process of decay but they did not succeed. The Darkness overtook them through the many devious schemes devised by Belzebseth. Hangker's troopers now began to defeat the Avasthas in open battle. Nonetheless, all the scouting expeditions sent by Thanatophor to access the Rock and to unfold its mysteries perished in the sands before reaching Dagad Trikon. Strange as it may seem, music was why this happened.

The Avasthas knew of the inner, intricate connections and connotations between the planets, musical instruments, the notes of the musical scales, and the seven component states of the psyche. Their music could ignite fires in seemingly spontaneous combustion or it could even bring forth the rains. They played specific tunes for particular functions, for example, to help the growth of their giant trees or to improve the milk yield of their cows.

Indeed, Avastha musicians were the only beings on earth who had mastered the secrets of the eleventh scale of the Rasa music. The meaning of this secret scale had to be understood: it carried a vibration of destruction that would throw enemy battle lines into blind panic.

They also knew how, with notes and beats, to engender courage and elation, or to create fear and despair. Their music was at the core of the defense mechanism of the Rock and the system worked in this way: in each of the three titanic monoliths emerging from the canyons' depths and towering above the stone tables near the center of the Rock, the Avasthas had carved a music station. In the event of danger, each station would project primordial sounds, known as the Bije notes. When mingled together, the sounds would cause the winds to whirl like a hurricane, creating a sandstorm around the Rock, which is why many names of fear were given to the dreaded music by the goblins of Belzebseth.

Thus, even the most formidable military expeditions sent by Hangker to discover the Rock could not reach or penetrate it. The story told how a few Azuric generals, who were titanic creatures, led devils, goblins, and men, mounted on giant lizards that were cross-breeds between the offspring of dragons and ancient sand worms. The beasts were immensely strong and resilient but the haunting tunes of the Rock music stopped them dead. Songs of doom, which sent whirling sandstorms against Hangker's hordes, slowly filled the air, hid the sun, and prevented them from breathing. Most of the soldiers and their steeds suffocated and became buried in the sands. Others somehow came in sight of the outer rim of the Rock, but then the Nizam unleashed a battalion of his crack troops, archers from his Household Guard, structured in six Yuva platoons, who were trained to fight in such sandstorms.

The army of the Rock Avasthas included many seasoned warriors but this leading battalion was composed of very young fighters. These warriors, in whose blood coursed the joy and vitality of youth, would create whirling patterns of deadly beauty as they wielded their weapons, singing terrible hymns of war that filled the enemy with fear. The Yuva platoons, like the Sheravalian Guards, had been trained in the arts of the Deep Way. Etakir, the leader of the Yuva platoons, had incorporated the accumulated knowledge of a thousand warriors before him into his understanding of the arts of war and so too had his friends Lidholon of Anor, the son of the Nizam, Aliskhan the Swift and Hanomkar the Strong, a tall and jolly fellow who was an expert in the beats of the Rasa music. From childhood the Deep Way had taught them how to bond psychically so that their strength would merge to form a formidable collective power. This force could be used by one and all whenever necessary. So, when the Yuvas were at war, their energy streams merged to form a thunderous river that swept aside all opposition like furious monsoon floods.

Gradually, however, the necromancers of the Dark Council accumulated shreds of evidence from the rare survivors of Hangker's defeated armies and became more determined than ever to somehow access or capture the hidden citadel. They were equipped with the power of far-sightedness and were rightly convinced that the hidden fortress held untold material and psychic treasures. Having taken many Avastha citadels on the eastern shores of the great sea, they had uncovered secret Avastha archives and obtained information through extortion and torture. Some of the Yuva spies who attempted to infiltrate the Dark Council narrowly escaped capture, but evil birds under the power of the Darkness had watched the path they took as they fled. After painstakingly examining the secrets that were spoken by the tortured mouths of those they'd captured and the details that his spies and troops had brought him, Thanatophor realized that he had to harness the awesome reserve of Avastha power that he knew was stored in Dagad Trikon. He wanted to obtain it at any cost because once he had control over it he would be a force that could not be withstood and could finally establish his global dominion.

At the bidding of his master and through terrible cross breeding and genetic manipulation, Hangker had produced a huge pterodactylian creature that could carry a fiendish devil equipped with the dark power of pestilence. Hangker thought he had created a beast capable of withstanding the defenses of the citadel and of defying the powers of the warriors protecting it. He worked even harder to make its rider, entering into a fierce tantric trance in which he brought forth some of his very own matter. He fashioned it with the blood of the Avasthas he had tortured, but even this was not enough. Thus, Hangker fused with Belzebseth who gave some of himself to Hangker, and the titan overlord then brought forth a force of unprecedented evil. In this way, the devil created heat and a foul stench that reeked of death. His very matter, it seemed, absorbed the sun's rays so that wherever he went it became darker. On the month of a red moon, Thanatophor himself, in the presence of Hangker, Belzebseth, and their chief lieutenants, urged the necromancer priests to release the huge bird and its ominous rider.

The fiendish devil was equipped with a micro ophtalir, a seeing jewel, so that Belzebseth, the maker of the ophtalir, could see what the devil would see and so spy on the mysterious Rock. They flew away in a pitch-dark night to avoid the piercing eyes of the eagles that had always been the friends of the Avasthas.

For weeks, this creation of Thanatophor flew over the Hasara and, finally, one morning as the desert lit up in the rays of the early sun, it closed in on its destination. The eagles nesting in the higher outer cliffs of Dagad Trikon saw the monster coming and raised the alarm. Sentinel archers sprang into action, mounted their eagles, and rushed to the defense of the holy Rock. But their arrows proved ineffective and failed to pierce its scaly body. The beating wings of the pterodactyl were as sharp as blades and the mighty eagles were unable to approach the flying monster. Thus, the Rock stood revealed to Belzebseth through the micro ophtalir.

As the pterodactyl circled before landing, Belzebseth had a breathtaking glimpse of the splendors of the Rock. The devil rider from the nether world lowered his altitude to provide a better sight of the Rock. The envoy from hell stared through the ophtalir at the three-and-a-half-coiled canyon, the cliff dwellings with their exquisite temples and fountains, the giant banyan trees, and the tamed flying horses. He caught sight of the preparation for the musical festival in Shambalpur whose objective was to create the sound waves that cast a protective musical spell on the sand dunes surrounding Dagad Trikon. Indeed, the protective spell was relatively short-lived and this attack occurred some time after the last festival so the effectiveness of the Pujan protection was at it lowest ebb. The wretched creature could not possibly fathom what it was to feel the wonder and awe that were laid at the Gate of Blessedness by the Avastha ceremonies. He had been conceived in a scheme of destruction, the perpetration of which was its only respite from the despair of existing.

The Nizam and the Sand Keeper wizard had been warned of the approaching enemy by a disturbance in the subtle energies. Indeed, because these men were strongly connected to the Deep Way, they were registering such disturbance in their beings as a rise in body temperature. At this point, by way of augmenting the narrative on the screen, Hanuman's voice filled the air as he explained:

"Every being emits a frequency of energy that registers on a spectrum ranging from positive to negative depending on the level of enlightenment of their soul. People who are captured by or aligned with the forces of evil tend to emit heat, which indicates the presence of negative energy. Those who aspire to attain a connection to the Deep Way, which is the path to selfhood, emit cooler vibrations. The Avasthas had this sensitivity because they were connected. Their vibrations were cool."

Even in his dream Jonathan felt at a loss to grasp the full implications of this. "Don't worry, Jonathan, you will come to understand all this at the right time," said Hanuman reassuringly.

Dagad Trikon was now on full alert. Sentinels everywhere had caught sight of the approaching flight of the massive bird of prey and its monstrous rider. In the canyons, war conches were blown, the Sheravalian Guard mounted their felines, the Yuva platoons rushed forward and, from the Music Tower, the waves of Rasa music rolled through the air in furious whirlwinds of sound. The Sand Keeper flew from the highlands on a winged horse to confront the devil above the peaks of Dagad Trikon.

The devil focused the ophtalir on him so that Belzebseth could recognize the enemy, but the wizard was a master of stealth and his true nature remained concealed. Nevertheless Belzebseth, who received the images from the ophtalir thousands of miles away, clearly recognized from the Sand Keeper's fighting technique that he was one of the higher Avasthas, one of the scions of the old royal lineages that Belzebseth thought had been totally exterminated. Fighting in mid-air with his superior wizardry, the Sand Keeper summoned and sent forth his flying discus. In a blinding flash of light the discus slashed through the monster as though its armor and body were made of fruit pulp, dissolving the very substance of the devilish rider whose shadowy remains returned to Hell's masters. The pterodactyl, de-stabilized by the phonic waves of Rasa music, fell to the ground. Such was the awesome power of the wizard of Dagad Trikon.

There, on the high stone table overlooking Shambalpur, the ferocious battle with the pterodactyl continued for some time.

Pumas and panthers encircled the bird, snarling furiously. At Erilie's command, they combined their onslaught with clockwork precision and launched attacks that were swift and penetrating. Harassed by the eagles and the felines, the giant bird emitted horrible shrieks. The spells-carrying arrows of the Yuva platoon further weakened it and by the time late-arriving members of the Sheravalian Guard reached the battlefield, the pterodactyl had been finally vanquished.

Alas, the final images the ophtalir sent to Belzebseth had revealed much of the secrets of the Rock. As it captured the shine of the magic discus that struck the rider of the pterodactyl, the art of the Sand Keeper was revealed. But the Dark Lord had seen even more. Esitel and Evenyl, the two sisters of Erilie mounted on their pumas, had both participated in the battle. Esitel dismounted, still perspiring from the fight and intrigued by a small object that had fallen from the sky, picked it up: it looked like a large jewel, was shaped like a binocular, and, unfortunately, its beauty was such that the innocent youth looked too closely at it. Even in those far-off days, curiosity was quite an enticement for the young. Erilie yelled at her but it was too late.

When her gaze met the sheer malice of the glance contained within the ophtalir, the power of the evil within it knocked Esitel off her feet. She became as pale as white linen and fainted. Seeing this, Erilie and Evenyl rushed to their sister and called Etakir. He and Hanomkar furiously smashed the sorcery of the object with their maces.

But it was too late. Belzebseth and his minions of the nether worlds, who'd gathered around him, had felt a raging surge of lust when they caught a glimpse of the astounding beauty of Erilie and her sisters as they fought the pterodactyl. When Esitel, off guard, had stared into his hypnotic eyes, Belzebseth had captured the beautiful maid using all his sorcery in the process.

More Yuva fighters had now gathered at the scene of the battle and they stood around the unconscious, lifeless body, silent and devastated. In the past none had even been able to penetrate their inner circle of psychic defense let alone overpower a member of the Sheravalian Guard. The fall of Esitel was a terrible omen and for the first time they knew fear. This was Thanatophor's first victory over Dagad Trikon. The Sand Keeper landed his flying horse on the stone table nearest the group. It proved hard to control and was further disturbed by the stench emitted by the corpse of the pterodactyl. The hood of the wizard's cape had fallen, revealing for the first time to most of the young warriors present an aquiline face, large black eyes, a well-proportioned curved nose, and a white beard. The wizard hastily dismounted and leaned over the body of Esitel.

Esitel's puma was growling feebly as Erilie knelt by her sister's side trying unsuccessfully to revive her. Esitel showed no signs of recovering, despite the healing touch of her friends. Nor, at first, did she respond to the ministrations of the Sand Keeper and his invocations of mantric formulae to call her back from the realm of the shadows. Eventually, she moaned softly and her body writhed, almost imperceptibly.

Aliskhan had suffered injuries from the claws of the bird; his bushy chestnut hair was stained with blood and his jaws were badly scratched. He stood pale and helpless next to the group and he was relieved to see that Esitel wasn't totally lost even though her limbs were lifeless and cold. Evenyl plaintively called to her fallen sister. Lidholon, an arrow still attached to his bow, scrutinized the sky in case another enemy would appear but only the eagles of Dagad Trikon were to be seen circling in the silence of the azure, high above their heads.

Etakir addressed the wizard, "Please tell us the truth, will Esitel return to us?"

The wizard, worried, spoke in a lowered voice, "Fate has been cruel to us today for malice has crept into the mind and the body of Esitel. This is the work of the demon kings who have marshaled the forces of evil and commanded powerful spells against us. She has been defiled, but the powers of our Mistress are unfathomable. Maybe she will be able to redeem her. We must carry her at once to the High Lady. Make speed."

The young warriors were much shaken. Aliskhan, his eyes suddenly filled with tears, struggled with his emotions. How could the enemy capture an elite Avastha fighter in this manner? Had the shadow of sorcery broken into the hidden Rock at last? But they moved to action at the command of the Sand Keeper. Carrying Esitel carefully in his arms, Etakir, escorted by Erilie, Evenyl, and their friends, rushed to the wooded canyon of the Lady of the Rock in a Pushpak flying chariot. The rest of the grim-faced Sheravalian Guards followed on foot while birds in the higher branches of the enchanted wood announced their approach.

The Yuvas warriors were normally not permitted to enter the wood of the Gundaldhar Fault, but this was an emergency. Dim and misty lights shimmered through the foliage. The foggy wood was a place of mystery as morning slowly broke; the forest canopy trapped the light of the afternoon in changing hues from hour to hour. Etakir and his party ran along the path, crossing small brooks covered with scented foam. Their path was shaded in a green and blue haze, observed at a distance by the deer and the felines. The wood eventually gave way to a spacious glade facing the circular wall at the end of the canyon where they could see the entrance to the cave of the High Lady of the Rock, the fabled home of all wonders. They had reached the mystical place that few Avasthas had ever visited, the abode that hosted the root source of the power of Dagad Trikon. They saw an armchair of stone on a patch of green grass before a small staircase made of three and a half steps of stone, which led to the entrance of the cave.

Erilie raised her hand to signal them to stop. They stood in a half circle. The young women of the Sheravalian Guard were totally crestfallen. Evenyl kept her hand pressed hard against her mouth to stifle her weeping while Etakir carefully laid the body of Esitel at the entrance step of the Cave of Wonders, mindful not to disturb the cobra that was its guardian. The Sand Keeper stayed close to Esitel and was able to ensure that her condition would not deteriorate further.

"We cannot pretend that this is not happening," whispered Lidholon hastily to his cousin Aliskhan, who was trying hard to compose himself. Aliskhan was still livid and sick with anxiety. "A spy of the demons reached the desert fortress, a member of the Sheravalian Guard has fallen, and now we are before the cave of mysteries. I fear the harvest of this day. See, here is the famous enchanted snake." He stopped talking suddenly. There was a pause. No one moved.

The cobra raised its hood and hissed softly. He was large in size and shiny, at least nine feet long. They were staring at the golden royal serpent, the sacred Uraeus, associated with the forms of the Goddesses throughout history. The serpent was later to be seen on the forehead of Isis and on the shield of Athena. The storytellers in Shambalpur narrated that sometimes the cobra would silently sneak into the grass and softly touch a visitor to the cave as he slid by. This was considered a blessing but was also a source of fear because when the sacred serpent touched someone, everything inside that person, good and less good, would be revealed in a flash of truth – and who wants to look inside oneself without first being well prepared?

The Avasthas respected serpents. While some snakes and dragons are subjects of Thanatophor, there are also those who belong to the sacred race. Serpents are ambivalent, spirals of mystical energies, like those mentioned in ancient mythologies such as Ananta for the Hindus, Quetzalcoatl for the Aztecs, Ophion and Chnoumis in antiquity, carrying in their undulations the secrets of divine energies and mystic transformation. But at this point the vision did not reveal the nature of the link between the sacred cobra and the High Lady. The Sand Keeper knew that she kept to herself the secret of the serpentine power that brings renewal and transformation.

Such happenings and more were seen and heard in Jonathan's deep mystic sleep. The white monkey had taken him to the very source of knowledge, the repository of all the treasures of the cosmos, at the confluence of his individual unconscious mind and the universal unconscious. Yet Hanuman knew full well that Jonathan would be unable to carry fully these revelations back into his conscious mind. Indeed, most men in the age of modernity have lost the power to connect with their own depths. Nevertheless, the all-knowing messenger, carrying Jonathan in his sleep, had decided to bring this man to the doorstep of the High Lady: she was the only one who could reconnect man to his higher Self and help him to face the menace looming over the coming third millennium of the era known in the West as the Christian age.

THE HIGH LADY
OF THE ROCK

T he brutal assault of the emissary of Thanatophor had been repelled but at what price? The survival of the Avasthas as a higher race depended on the integrity of their psychic defenses. If the mind of one could be captured, then suddenly they were all at risk. Many Avasthas were telepathic and the somber tidings of the capture of Esitel spread fast through the cliffs dwellings. Gloom settled over the inhabitants of Shambalpur. It was time to call on the power of last resort.

No description exists of the High Lady of the Rock because she is evoked in the tale as *'She who cannot be described.'* The Avasthas knew that her sight and presence were enchanting and ever yearned for an opportunity to appear before her. Her raised hand brought security, peace, and wisdom. Her soft and compassionate nature made it possible for visitors to walk near her abode without fear, for she was an Avatar, neither unborn nor touched by time, dwelling in her own splendor that was beyond the grasp of even the Avasthas. She had mastery over the Deep Way and could deliver its fruits. She could bestow the power of Angkura, the germinating power of renewal, and the state of Ananya, the oneness with the whole. Her mere presence was the core of the mystic shield that secured the Rock and protected the holiness of the Avasthas.

Etakir and his small band felt calmer now. The snake had vanished into the cave and they waited with intense expectation. Even in his sleep Jonathan could smell the perfume of rose that wafted in the air, and the silence now was total.

Moments later, alerted by the cobra who had fully realized the seriousness of the situation, the High Lady appeared. She was followed by Nirja, her lady-in-waiting, who was a proud warrior princess from the tribe of the sand people.

Some stories and songs have been preserved in the lore of the old desert tribes glorifying the princess with light green eyes and a face of dark golden bronze, whose complete dedication to her mistress was acknowledged even by the cobra king. When the High Lady, Mistress of the Triangle Rock, emerged from the jeweled cave, the young men immediately looked to the ground, for her luminosity was too dazzling, even for the eyes of the earlier born. In reflecting her brilliance the Uraeus shone like gold. The High Lady swiftly controlled her own radiance and invited them to approach.

As she eased herself onto her stone throne, Nirja solicitously placed a pillow underneath her and another behind her back. The mysterious ruler of Dagad Trikon gazed at them with a penetrating and reassuring glance. In a soft voice she said, "Come closer, children," and they sat in front of her some ten feet away. As she listened to Erilie's fevered account, her serenity was contagious and all became calmer. Those of the Sheravalian Guard who were the sentries of the wood had now joined them. Gently taking the lifeless body of Esitel in her arms, she chanted into her left ear many times the mantra "*Aham, aham, aham, aham.*"

Although she just whispered these words, the sound seemed to capture the waves of the Rasa music and rolled down the walls of the canyon with a mighty rumble.

She opened Esitel's eyelids in turn and stared into her vacant eyes. At that very moment, thousands of miles away, Belzebseth, who was reveling in the sight of his prey while probing in the fields of her innocence, was instantly blinded by a white radiance. The pain inside his brain was such that with a cry of impotent rage, he let slip his control over Esitel. The girl's consciousness immediately returned and she quickly regained the color in her cheeks. She opened her eyes, emitted a gentle gasp as she beheld the High Lady who held her in her arms. She sobbed softly as the High Lady tenderly consoled her, "Esitel, you are my child, your innocence is more powerful than any filth you may have seen or felt. You are precious to me and you shall be healed. Don't worry."

But the young warrior continued to sob desperately. The High Lady turned to the Sand Keeper, "Friend, in order to save my daughter, I had to reveal myself to the sire of the necromancers. From the shape of the three and a half coils of the Gundaldhar Fault that represents my symbol, he might have already guessed that he had found my dwelling but just now he had a glimpse of my very Self, that which he has sought for so long. Through many eons he has aspired to reach me to harness the immeasurable power of which I am the sole custodian. Now, with this latest trick he has succeeded in finding my abode. He cannot overpower me but unfortunately Dagad Trikon is now no longer impenetrable. This then is the course that fate has taken. Please summon the Circle of the Aulyas at once."

The faces of all those present became grave. "As you please, my Lady," answered the wizard, his voice shaking slightly. "The next full moon of Dhuljalal is indeed favorable. I shall invite them in your holy name."

The Aulyas were the great seers among the Avasthas and a meeting of the Circle of the Aulyas was a rare affair. They were selected from all races, were spread across all continents, and could be born into any family, rich or poor. They were best described as being at all times both fully alert and completely calm, a unique combination of spontaneity and inspiration. The path of purification to the status and state of Aulya was long and difficult and each aspirant had to pass through three stages of transformation and initiation into the Deep Way.

On attaining the state of Salokya, they would understand and experience the primordial secret of the world. On attaining the Samipya state, they would enter into greater proximity with the mystery, and on attaining the Sanidya state, they discovered and enjoyed complete integration with the revealed enigma of divinity. Having passed through these mystical gates, only compassion kept them bound to the earth.

Summoned by the Sand Keeper through the Deep Way, the Aulyas gathered a week later, but to emphasize the importance of the matter, the meeting did not take place in the great hall of Serapis, the elderly Councilor of Shambalpur, but before the stone throne of the High Lady of the Rock at the entrance to her cave. By the side of the throne, Erilie and two Sheravalian guards dressed in their lightweight armor unfurled the High Lady's banner, which was raised only for the greatest occasions: it was white with an ascending purple three-and-a-half coil rising within an inverted triangle.

As she took her seat, she looked thoughtfully at what she knew to be a historical gathering of the Circle of the Aulyas, for assembled before her were the epitome of all the races inhabiting the four corners of the earth, twenty-one in number, who had come to chart the path of their departure and equally importantly, the course of their eventual return to the world of human beings at the end of the Fourth Age.

In Avastha cosmology, the four ages constitute the cycle of history. In the Golden Age, the truth is known and Avasthas rule. In the Silver Age, misunderstandings appear and righteousness is weakened. In the Bronze Age, confusion and dissent emerge and evil rises; Avasthas are exiled. In the Iron Age, the Fourth Age of man that includes these modern times, the rule of evil spreads wide like a poison in the minds of men but the Avasthas plan to return.

Because of his prominence amongst the first-born, Prince Alhakim, of the House of Golkur, was the first to address the Assembly. Golkur was not one of the Avasthas' great houses, but the sons of Golkur were much respected as teachers of the scholarship and science of the earlier born. Alhakim had come to the Circle of the Aulyas from the land later known as Persia, from where his fire-worshipping forbears originated. He was tall and majestic, with black and silvery hair. He was a seer and a poet and those who knew him basked in the warmth of his heart. He ended his plea with the following words, "Hail again and again to our gracious High Lady. May She, the Benevolent, keep us under Her protection. O best amongst the knowers, I have related to you all matters pertaining to the scions of doom and we must now decide what to do."

Atha Glaukopis, the high priestess of Atlantis, rose from her seat. She had been brought by one of the Pushpak chariots from the island in the midst of the great Western ocean. She was held in high esteem by the Aulyas as one gifted with great foresight and as a well of deep wisdom. Her eyes, graciously shaped in the form of fishes, radiated a tender kindness and contained the depth of the ocean. She spoke with tears in her voice, "O pride of Golkur, my people have been won over by the enemy. Women have become inebriated by the taste of domination, taken control of our continent, and have ensnared their men, either by witchcraft or depravity. Some of the ancient spiders are born among them and few can escape their webs. There is no doubt that Atlantis is doomed. The Atlanteans no longer listen to wisdom. We all know the code of the Aulyas: we must respect their freedom of choice. However, I fear that our Mother Earth will soon shake off this burden but there is nothing that we can do about it. They have created their own fate, and before fate, even the Aulyas must bow."

Habimanyon spoke next. He was the youngest of the Aulyas, strong and brave, a splendid warrior in the spring of youth, fearsome and yet courteous and gentle in manner. He was a hero to his friends and doom to his foes. Habimanyon carried the chivalry of the land of Bharatma in his soul. Now he spoke, his voice quivering with indignation. "As I stand here addressing my illustrious peers, our great king and only ally in Bharatma, the High Lord Raghubir, light of the Aryans, has been forced into exile. His father, who exiled him has been bewitched by the intrigues of a palace maidservant. I cannot sense brightness in the future of my land for a long, long time. Indeed, I see clearly that, in two thousand years from now, I shall myself fall on a blood-soaked battlefield, betrayed by elder warriors that I have honored and served."

Aslerach of Anor, although not an Aulya, was attending the meeting because as holder of the office of Nizam he was the representative of the High Lady within the Circle. He responded, "Alas, dearest Habimanyon, best amongst archers, I fear you are right. I have sent scouts from the Yuva platoons to many parts of the world, as they are most astute at camouflage and spying. They reported to our Sand Keeper that all living species are losing the inner thread of love that binds them together and are heading towards disintegration. These are good tidings for the Darkness. Illustrious masters, we must ourselves take steps not to be engulfed by the coming destruction."

The Aulyas, in turn, related similarly how the slow and cold poison of the Darkness had entered the minds and hearts of so many beings and how they were at a loss as to how to reverse this trend. The Gods had departed. Mount Himavat was silent. The rulers of Bharatma had lost touch with the Deep Way and slyness had entered their hearts.

The Sand Keeper tried to console Atha Glaukopis because she foresaw the calamity to come on Atlantis and so, at the end of a long exchange under a moonlit sky, they turned again to the Mistress of the Triangle and invoked her with her secret names, imploring her for guidance. As her veil wafted gently in the soft breeze emanating from the jeweled cave, she spoke, "My whole body shivers with agony when I think that the beings created by the Highest One to enjoy the sweetness of love are instead willingly taking to the path of hatred. We must remain united and be resilient as we prepare for the subtle war against the rise of the devils. Be patient, for this hour and the next belong to them. Mother Earth will suffer much. But those who do good receive energy and those who do evil lose their power. And a time will eventually come when evil will be utterly spent."

The Sand Keeper asked, "O worshipful One, is there a way to avoid what is to come? Is there any way at all?"

The Aulyas strained to hear as the Lady whispered in a voice that was barely audible, "When the Highest One sends forms of Himself into this world, these manifestations are called Avatars. Only after the Mother Earth revolves another ten thousand times around the sun will the time of the return begin. During the Fourth Age of later men, in the land of Bharatma, on the beach of Nargol, the great Avatar of later days will call upon me to change the course of history and I shall rise as a living molten furnace of incandescent power. Thereafter, I shall inhabit my new resting places and men shall give me new names."

The Sand Keeper, with hands folded, asked again, "O Mother, High Lady, you know that in the lore of the first-born, a name contains the seeds of power. What is the name of this Avatar we must expect to come to awaken your awesome power? Who is this one who will come after such a troubled history so far down the long corridor of time? Please forgive me for asking but I know you are merciful."

The High Lady of the Rock looked with an affectionate smile at the assembly gazing at her in tense expectation. Slowly and almost inaudibly, she whispered the name and then, quickly and unexpectedly, rose from her throne. The audience was over. The Aulyas bowed. The Lady of the Rock vanished into the cave where Esitel was still resting, followed by Nirja. Erilie and Evenyl folded the banner. Hissing from the cobra signaled that no one was to ask further questions. The seers returned to Shambalpur and withdrew into the smaller Council Chamber.

Representatives of all the six great houses of the Avasthas that constituted the Council of Shambalpur had joined the Aulyas. The assembly was a splendid sight. Here stood Prince Chanta, the representative of the House of Kalabham, custodian of Urgaia, the spiritual force of the earth and of Angkura, its germinating power. The principles of his house were the very foundation of Avastha culture. The Lord Kriyafel Kurion of the House of Falkiliad was also in attendance. His house gathered the worshippers of Uragni, masters of the subtle fire and of the rules of action. It provided Shambalpur with most its architects, craftsmen, artists, and musicians. Philtalas, the ruler of the House of Elnur, was also present. His house had received from Jaladhar the power of Urjala, the mystical water, giver of energy. He was the father of Olophon, a young and valiant sailor admired by all. Among the heirs of the high lords he was the only one not to be the married for he was in love with a Sheravalian who was not yet of an age to leave the Guard. Thus, he would keep his feelings to himself. He had been biding his time for many years now. Ichwaril, sire of the House of Eleksim, was present too. He was known as the herald of Urvayu, the sacred wind and guardian of the rite of initiation to Ananya, the state of the great Oneness. He also officiated as the priest of the temple of the trident. Eleksim too had a vital role to play in the balance of the Avastha society for they were the custodians of the gentle art of love and of sublime emotions. Here too stood Udurlan, the sire of the House of Anor, younger brother of the Nizam and father of Aliskhan who could communicate through Urakash, the infinity of the ether. The sixth high lord was Isaprem of the House of Anorhad, which was the appointed carrier of Urtej, the light of transformation. The House of Anorhad was the least numerous of the great houses. Avastha culture was not generally much interested in material possessions; however, the Anorhadans completely shunned all materialism for the Lady of the Rock had bestowed on them subtle blessings and would always ensure that they would not lack for anything. Its elders were reputed to have the deepest knowledge and insights into the Deep Way.

When put together, the energy of the six houses could invoke the Lady of Grace, but this time she had already spoken and left them with a puzzle to solve. After some time, Lord Habimanyon broke the silence and asked, "We have much work to do tonight but before we proceed, let me, my lords, ask you this: what did you hear the name to be?"

Prince Alhakim said confidently, "I heard *Imam*."

Atha Glaukopis replied hesitantly, "I heard *Ma*, or *Mai*, or even *Mama*."

Rasmus, the Northern mathematician, had kept silent during the Circle. He could interpret the movements of celestial bodies and decipher the messages from the stars. To him, knowledge was a fluid relationship between certainties that he often projected in the sobriety of formulae or through the aesthetics of geometry. He interjected, "I definitely heard *Treya*."

"Well," said the Sand Keeper, with a rare hint of excitement in his voice, "it seems we heard many things... did she say '*Imamaitreya*,' I wonder? But we shall see, we shall see. Ten thousand years is a long time, even by our patient standards." The assembly nodded in unison: the temperature of their bodies had reacted well to the name. As mentioned, the Avasthas had a special sensitivity and coolness that indicated the presence of a being carrying great goodness; heat indicated the opposite.

Never again did any hostile force reach the Rock but, once revealed, the eventual demise of the hidden citadel was inevitable. Musically induced sandstorms barred physical access to the ocher triangle but the onslaught of sorcery never stopped. As their magic gradually weakened, the elders of Dagad Trikon realized that the days of the Rock Avasthas were numbered. The light in the leaves, which sustained life, dimmed and the springs of underground water began to dry up. The giant trees withered. The Avasthas began to die at a rate unknown in previous times. Children were no longer born in Dagad Trikon and the great banqueting halls in the proud houses of Shambalpur fell silent. The two commanding Avasthas consulted with the High Lady who explained to them in great secrecy where her next abode would be. They decided to arrange the withdrawal of their race and to carve the magic of the primordial notes of Rasa into the two weapons that had been forged in the early days of the Rock.

The Glorfakir was the weapon of the warrior. It was a sword of raw might and power that could cast spells and move matter. The Sadhan was the weapon of the wizard: it was a shield. Just raising it before an enemy could paralyze him. In addition, both weapons had much subtler properties that would be of great help to men and women of a later time. Of these properties, no word was said in the tale of the white monkey. These were in fact the weapons that Lakshman Kharadvansin and Lakshmi Vani would come to discover ten thousand years later in the Alwakil fields of the Dagad Trikon mountain.

The High Lady of the Rock summoned the Sheravalian Guard one final time before returning them to their families; she addressed the young women on many points precious for the mastery of the Deep Way. The Nizam had sent Etakir, Lidholon, Aliskhan, and Hanomkar at this time with a message for the dweller of the jeweled cave. Thus, by chance, the four young men also witnessed the words of parting. Although one of the wishes of the white monkey seems to have been to transmit the rare words of the High Lady, much could not be transmitted. Indeed, for what she had to say, words alone could not suffice, often failing to convey the essence of the deeper meaning that was absorbed only through the grace of physically being in her presence.

However, it is known that she said this much: "I am now leaving you and shall depart with Nirja. We shall follow the secret passage that runs through the deeper chambers of Mother Earth to a place that none can reach. Be brave and be prepared. Dark are the ages that soon shall be rolling down upon your world. The higher races shall disappear, people will lose the knowledge of the Deep Way, and they will come to lose their self-respect and to enjoy vulgarity. Men will behave like women and women like men. The brutal and ruthless shall rule and harlots shall dwell in untold wealth, their images worshipped by mindless throngs. Men will think they know better than women and all will make a virtue out of their weaknesses. The ignorant will show arrogance, the arrogant shall be ignorant. The earth shall quake and the seas shall rise. You shall endure all this and I bless you that you shall not be defeated. To find the path of the return, you need to find the narrow gate."

She then took a golden box containing red turmeric powder from the hands of Nirja and as the young men and women came forward in turn and knelt before her, she wiped away many a tear as she applied a red dot to the center of each forehead with powder from the box, while intoning each time in the language of the Aulyas, "To find the path of the return, you must first find the narrow gate."

Erilie was waiting in line. She knew she could not interrupt the ceremony, but there was a palpable sense of despair and grief in the air and she thought, "I must know, we must know the way. Otherwise she'll have departed and we will all be lost." Erilie had been partly trained by the High Lady herself and, because of this affectionate familiarity, she would at times dare to break with protocol. So even though she had previously been in trouble for this very thing, when it was her turn to kneel as the last of the guards to take leave of their mistress, she mustered all her courage and asked, "Please, Lady of Grace, tell us about the path and the narrow gate, for if you leave us now we shall all perish."

Everyone froze. Never before had anyone interrupted the High Lady during a ceremony and to displease her was dangerous. The few seconds of silence that followed seemed to last an eternity, and so they were relieved when the High Lady responded matter-of-factly and in a mild tone, "Erilie, you and all my daughters should follow the trail of the white elephant. And when you see him turning to the color of this Rock, then you'll know that he will take you through the narrow gate."

Erilie was always pleased when she heard the Lady utter her name. The sound of her voice enveloped Erilie in a feeling of bliss and love warmed her heart. Yet she soon realized that, as often happened, the Lady had spoken in Koan, a language often used by the Aulyas. It contained riddles that offered more questions than answers. She should have stopped at that and tried to find the inner meaning of the answer, but the captain of the now-disbanded guard felt how intently her sisters yearned for more light and understanding. She saw a mute plea to inquire further in Etakir's face. Also encouraged by the endearing tone of her mistress, she asked again, "Shining Mother, I beg you, will you tell us where to find the elephant?"

"All of you carry in you the youth of the scions of the earlier race," and in so saying the High Lady looked at the four boys of the Yuva platoon. "Hear what must now be said. There are two worlds on Mother Earth: the Inner World and the Outer World. In the age of goodness, the two worlds are united and many passages are built to facilitate movement back and forth between them. Mastery of the blissful unity is bestowed as the fruit of the Deep Way. But now evil has penetrated the Outer World, so the Inner World is receding to maintain its integrity. The gates are shut, the bridges collapsing. When the Outer and the Inner World are split apart, the evil of the Great Schism exerts dominance over the whole world. Only one door – one secret door – will remain to re-establish the link between the two worlds. But access to this door is well hidden, it will only be found after thousands of years have passed. This is the door guarded by the elephant."

She paused for a while. The young men had come forward and sat in the grass before her, alongside the virgin warriors. They listened intently as she continued.

"There is no escape from this fate. For many ages you will enter into this world in complete camouflage, not knowing who you are or even who you were in past lives. You will be entirely immersed in the world, exposed to its perils yet hidden from the spies of the Evil One. You will see empires rise and decay, spilling rivers of blood; you will see the great blossoming mushrooms of death and the twisting of human souls. Many misfortunes shall come to pass on the way to achieving greater purpose. Find the gatekeeper and accordingly you shall find the gate. Do not fear, for verily I tell you: one day you will return and take back from the thieves what is your own."

Then she rose in her majesty, a silhouette of shining light. All bowed before her. These were the last things that were ever said or known of the mistress of Dagad Trikon. When they raised their heads she was gone, and Nirja and the cobra had also disappeared.

"She said so little," said Esitel, crying softly. "She said so much," replied Aliskhan, his gaze lost on Dagad Trikon's peaks, which were now turning red in the sunset. "I hope we'll stay together," said Lidholon with a sigh. Etakir shrugged. He was a thoughtful, quiet lad, speaking little but well and when he did speak the Yuvas listened carefully. He kneeled slowly before the closed gate of the cave, closed his eyes, and said, "The laughter and song are dying in the chambers of the cliff dwellings. Behold the coming of our night; the sun has set on the days of honor. Valor shall faint, a flame flickering in the gushing wind of the gathering storm. Let us be faithful to the oath we gave when we first arose in the light of the Lady of Grace."

The assembled group of young people looked at each other, still feeling the lingering bliss associated with the presence of the High Lady, but they knew that in a few hours the feeling would be gone. They were now on their own.

Before leaving the Rock with their people for an unknown destination, the two overlords of the Avasthas, the Nizam and the Sand Keeper, led a farewell ceremony in which all the secrets, the lore and the legends of the earlier born from Dagad Trikon were recorded on magic scrolls and placed within ten caskets. The mood was one of grim determination. The hidden scrolls contained elements of the Grand Scheme that Adivatar the Almighty, Himself, the Unborn, had conceived for the third millennium of the Fourth Age of man.

The Avasthas had congregated in the Alwakil fields, a sacred place at the foot of the mound of Shambalpur. The poignant beauty of the hymn for the final farewell, piped from the music stations, filled the people of the Rock with pride and grief. The majestic eagles of Dagad Trikon took flight, never to be seen again. A long era was coming to a close, an age in which beauty and goodness had secured the happiness of all sentient beings supported by the Mother Earth. The path ahead was clouded even for the seers because it contained countless dangers, brutality, decay, and the penetrating onslaught of evil.

The gravity of the event filled the screen. The Avastha world was almost over. The Sand Keeper officiated in the centre of a vast altar surrounded by delicate temples hewn in the cliffs. By his side stood Aslerach of Anor, clad in the armor of Orichalc, the metal from Atlantis that could not be touched by mere mortals. He wore blue robes and a high-crowned helmet decorated with the black hawk wings. The helmet with its long cheek-guards hid most of his face. The mightiest Avastha lords surrounded him, carrying the crest mark of their houses on their helmets. The watching crowd kept their eyes fixed on them for this was an unprecedented sight. They could see Philtalas of Elnur, admiral of the once mighty fleet that the Avasthas maintained on faraway shores to keep open their lines of trading. His son Olophon, proud and tall, was standing next to him. He had spent the night catching up on the last news with his friends in the Yuva platoon for he was often away on sea errands. They had returned to the Rock the day before on a Pushpak chariot. They looked grim yet splendid, as befitted the heirs of such high lineages.

Serapis, governor of Shambalpur, opened the ceremony. His tall and thin silhouette stepped forward hesitatingly. He was a man of perfect courtesy, many secrets, and much power. He was perhaps more feared than loved because the easy-going people of the Rock did not understand the need for control by the first magistrate of the city. White hair cascaded like snow on his shoulders; he had reached the winter of his long age and suspected he would not survive long after the ceremony of the dispatching of the magic caskets. He stressed that while this ceremony heralded departure, it also promised a future return.

The congregation of Avasthas was silent and resolute. They knew how to ride the silver linings of the darkest clouds. Aslerach, overlord of Anor, addressed the assembly with a voice that echoed like thunder through the canyon, "O people of Shambalpur, all things created shall also pass and so it is with us. But the seeds of renewal and joy to come shall now be sowed, for our sorrow will also pass away. By the rings of Saturn and the discus of the Sower King, our Lord, I verily say to you that in the days to come, the Gift itself shall be bestowed on the children of ordinary men. They shall be consoled, counseled, and redeemed; they shall be merry and the whole earth shall bloom anew in an outburst of passion and joy."

Hanomkar began a slow beat of drums that was echoed by the walls of the canyon. Drums from the cliff villages responded, the music towers played their melody, the Sheravalians blew the great sea conches and the power that arose was awesome.

Aliskhan, who was known for his love of horses, was in charge of the stables of the Nizam household. He knew each of the horses intimately and each responded when he called its name. Followed by other esquires, he brought forward ten magnificent white stallions, in the likeness of the horse that Greek mythology later identified as Pegasus. Seven amongst the most accomplished knights came forward and bowed, greeting Aslerach with these words, "Farewell, Lord of the Avasthas and custodian of the Gundaldhar Fault. We shall do thy bidding. May the protection of the High Lady be upon us!" Each of them, knowing full well they would not see their own kin again, took a casket from the hands of the Nizam and mounted the winged horses while the Sand Keeper chanted mantric incantations.

The riders were clad in Orphean armor that would instill a deep amnesic sleep in anyone who happened to see them. The knights carried helmets topped by a star. Each star had differing numbers of points corresponding to the powers contained in each casket and each shone with its own unique aura. For instance, the first star of Kalabam with an orange-ocher aura had four points. The second star of Falkiliad, crowning the helmet of the knight Davidriel, radiated a golden aura through its six points. A ten-pointed wheel shone with a green-glowing aura as the star of Elnur on the helmet of the tallest Avastha. The next knights coming forward carried the caskets corresponding to the twelve-pointed star of Eleksim and the sixteen-pointed star of Anor; the latter looked like the discus of the wizard that had felled the winged devil. The points of the stars emitted their auras at different frequencies and with changing nuances of colors and intensity.

The throng looked on in amazement at this unique and magnificent spectacle, even for Avasthas who had always been surrounded by much pageantry and splendor. The colors corresponded to various energies and were important symbols whose meaning could not be understood by ordinary Avasthas. Then a rider clad in armor that seemed to emit the sun's light appeared and took the next casket. His helmet was adorned with the white wings of seabirds opening outwards and bore an Anorhadan sign in its center that was unfamiliar to the Avasthas: it was the sign of the cross.

The three remaining caskets were different in shape, more rectangular and certainly more ornate. These were entrusted to three amazons of the Sheravalian Guard, whose lightweight alloy armors were richly decorated. Their helmets, glowing like amber in the sun, bore straight feathers: one Sheravalian rider carried a white feather, another a yellow feather, and the third a blue feather.

The winged horses neighed forcefully and flew away, carrying their riders and the scrolls to their appointed places at the four corners of the earth where the prophecy would remain dormant for ten millennia. The final notes of Rasa music died when the last winged horse disappeared. All those who stayed behind fought back their tears; the children stood silent and grave for this was a farewell of loved ones. The entire crowd was filled with pride and sadness. They lingered there for some time, trying to absorb the fact that the end of the Rock Avasthas had finally come. Gradually they all dispersed in small groups.

It was in those ancient times that Mother Earth, the Goddess they later called Gaia, Demeter, Coatlicue or Bhoomi, intervened in what was to become history. She released herself from the dominion of the Lord of Doom. Thanatophor and his people had never met her as a deity, nor, as a matter of fact, suspected her existence as a being that could take a human form. Indeed she would reveal her personal form only to the purest beings. Thanatophor thought that Mother

Earth was a mere mass of mineral wealth covered by fertile soils and forests, good only for exploitation, conquest, and subjugation. Little did the creatures of greed know that she was endowed with awareness, understanding, and emotions, just like some of the beings she supported and bore. Nor did they realize that there was an intelligence controlling the precisely tuned rhythms of her life cycles.

It was through the fatal flaw of this ignorance that Thanatophor eventually lost control of the planet for which he had battled for so long. The loss of the subtle balances of goodness and the spread of abominations ultimately triggered Mother Earth's reaction. The volcanic explosion and sinking of the land of the Atlanteans sent gigantic tidal waves that flooded thousands of square miles of inhabited land. To keep control over the Thalassean navigators and the wealth of their trade, Thanatophor had erected his fortress on a cliff above the Western sea, which was thus exposed to the catastrophic sinking of Atlantis. His entire clan perished in the onslaught of the surging wall of water. The tidal wave destroyed almost every organized life form and all the traces of their passage on the earth in its path.

Thus spoke the tale of the white monkey. The link between legend and history could not be established. Men returned from Mount Ararat and gradually conquered the earth, chasing away whatever was left of all the higher species who survived only in the tales of the most ancient nations. The abandoned palaces of the Avasthas of Dagad Trikon crumbled and fell. The legend of the High Lady of the Rock, the memory of the grace and beauty that surrounded her, and the world of gentleness of the elder brothers died in the memory of earlier Earth. Millennia passed. The Gods occasionally visited the earth, sending aspects of their highest forms in an effort to lead mankind on the path of the return. Some of the Aulyas came back too but none of the ancient kings of the Avasthas ever returned. They knew it was just too hard to teach the Deep Way when the capacity to receive the subtle teachings had been lost.

Over the centuries, when great prophets such as Moses, Lao Tse, Socrates or Mohammed came and revealed the truth through their teachings, most human beings were not interested and would not listen. The few who could be persuaded to listen merely quarreled amongst themselves as to the meaning of these revelations. The accounts of these quarrels constitute history as people now know it. All the while, the magic was still strong deep within the Rock and even when, much later, men rode in flying machines, it still remained undiscovered, a place of long-gone legends, surrounded by a desert where none but a few could survive. Yet, it remained, waiting to be found, for legends never die when they carry the pollen of the flowers of Truth.

So it came to pass that, shortly before the third millennium of the Fourth Age of man, conditions ripened for the unfolding of an unexpected story. As the cousins discovered Dagad Trikon and Jonathan delved into his unconscious mind, fragments of the past were revealed again, but much was yet to be discovered and understood. The adventure started in the city of Cairo, that noisy and dusty metropolis on the banks of the river Nile, late in the second millennium in the age of Jesus the Christ.

Jonathan, sat up straight in bed, awakened by lingering feelings of sadness, love, and a pride that he had experienced in the parting ceremony of Dagad Trikon. A feeling of fear followed as he vaguely remembered how evil had overtaken the world. These impressions were intense but confused, mixed with a painfully strong recollection of the recent assassination, as if it was one and the same battle that was fought both in the hazy world of mythology and in the crude, harsh light of surrounding reality. Yet he felt a sense of hope that he could not explain. It was four o'clock in the morning and as he looked out of the window the night sky was slowly changing, light and color displacing darkness. The same cute monkey that he had fed the day before was staring in at him, perched on the same branch:

was it still part of his dream? Jonathan rubbed his eyes, looked again, and the white monkey was gone.

He lay down again, trying to remember everything he had witnessed but this proved impossible because the channels of communication between the unconscious and his conscious mind had not yet been established. He gradually fell asleep again and when he was to next awaken, he would be left with a diffuse nostalgia and yearning for the age of purity to return and with a strong desire to participate in the search begun by his friends, Lakshman and Lakshmi.

This had been one of the purposes of the white monkey: to forge the bond of a common will between seekers of truth and to trigger the courage to inquire about matters that most reasonable men think too huge to be answered.

EPISODE FIVE

THE ISLAND OF ROCK AND FIRE

Passing decrepit buildings and brand new mosques, the highway wound a gray zigzag path through the city like a large flattened worm. Lakshman and his cousin were on their way to Cairo Airport when he received a call on the secure cell phone that Jonathan had given him. It was Jonathan, trying to communicate elements of the vision he had seen when in the unconscious state. Both men agreed that his extraordinary experience was clearly related to the recent trip the cousins had made to the desert and their discovery of the Triangle Rock. They shared a premonition: that although they might have been looking for the legend, it seemed now that the legend was looking for them. It was a strange feeling, almost as if this adventure was forcing itself on them. The cousins both felt somewhat uncertain and wondered what exactly that meant, but Jonathan had now overcome his earlier skepticism and he affirmed his dedication and willingness to support Lakshman's research in every way possible.

Lakshman and Lakshmi took a flight to Geneva, where Lakshman's father owned a prominent jewelry shop on the Rue du Rhone. They spent the next months in Switzerland as Lakshmi had business to attend to at the Palais des Nations in preparation for a World Development Congress. In the winter the cousins launched a new jewelry collection designed by Lakshmi, of necklaces and bracelets made from Burmese precious stones. The collection's theme was the play of the chromatic harmonies between the textures of the stones and their settings in platinum and gold. It was a huge success with the jaded clientele of wealthy Arab and Russian customers who frequented the exclusive shops of genteel Geneva.

"It's all a matter of relationships, really," said Lakshmi happily, a comment that seemed equally appropriate to the theme of her collection and the search for the answer to the Dagad Trikon enigma. After the successful conclusion of their business launch, the cousins felt in need of a few days of rest and fun and so they went off to ski with friends in Gstaad. The group of young men and women indulged in constant flirtations but they pointedly left Lakshman and Lakshmi alone, assuming that they were already a couple. Hence, they rarely found the need to explain the true nature of their bond, which was more like that of brother and sister. Though both were single, good-looking, and desirable, their traditional Indian upbringing gave them a natural reserve that contrasted sharply with the lifestyle of their Western friends.

Lakshman, at this stage, felt it necessary to put some distance between Dagad Trikon and himself. Hence, he needed a break to ensure that he kept a cool head and to avoid being sucked too fast into a story so utterly fantastic and with such historical dimensions.

They left their happy party in Gstaad and drove to Verbier, a winter sport resort in Valais that had higher skiing fields. The snow had arrived late this year, and the ski slopes were deserted because the holiday season was already over. The enveloping whiteness was almost blinding as it echoed the shimmering sunshine. With a dark blue sky, almost violet in contrast with the powdery slopes, the conditions were perfect. They had a wonderful time and whether relaxing in the cozy warmth of their wooden chalet or racing on the fresh expanses of new snow, Lakshman's mind was gradually freeing itself of the huge problems of the quest he had embarked on.

The ingredients of the story were remarkable: the discovery of the Rock complex in the desert, the weapons of an unknown metal, and Jonathan's extraordinary dream, all of which pointed to the adventure of a lifetime. After each evening's *après ski*, Lakshman talked to Lakshmi about the implications of what they'd discovered and the possible future actions they might take. One part of him wanted to forget the whole thing, but the lure of a potentially epic quest was too strong. Although Lakshman had expressed the premonition he'd shared with Jonathan, they were completely unaware that an invisible net of Avastha magic, active over ten millennia had captured their curiosity and imagination. Finally, as they were leisurely basking in the sun on the terrace of the Ruinettes ski lift above Verbier, Lakshmi said forcefully, in a manner unlike her usual self, that he either had to forget all about the Rock and the quest or to follow his instincts without further prevarication and delay.

And so it was that Lakshman, after one final deliberation, put aside his nervousness and decided once and for all to go to Iceland and to take the quest to the next stage. He called Jonathan to request the support of the U.S. Embassy in Reykjavik to assist with various aspects of his investigation. He then called his parents in Mumbai and finished his business in Geneva. Lakshman checked some data at the Institute of Ethnography and, a few days later, flew to Reykjavik.

Lakshmi, having kissed him goodbye at Cointrin airport, flew back to Italy. The consulting firm she worked for had insisted that she return to assist the Indian delegation to prepare for an important conference about to take place in Rome. To refuse would have meant losing her job and, at this stage, she could not afford that. She left with a heavy heart, sad that she wouldn't be able to accompany her cousin on such a crucial phase of the search.

The first thing Lakshman did in Iceland was to treat himself to a Nordic breakfast of fresh local salmon and herring at a fine hotel. Then he wandered down to the harbor to a smoky tavern of fishermen and ordered an alcohol-free beer. The place was noisy and dusty but, on his many trips, Lakshman always made a point of seeking out local flavors. He heard sailors talking excitedly with tourists at a nearby table about the unusual hyper-geothermal activity under the huge Vatnajoekull glacier. The largest in the country, it stretched over thirty-two hundred square miles and a volcanic eruption was anticipated imminently.

The next day Lakshman visited the Icelandic Glaciological Society, which had alerted the authorities on the impact of climate change on the island. This group, entirely composed of volunteers, surveys the size of the country's three hundred odd glaciers and then files reports. It is believed that there have been glaciers on Iceland for the last few million years. Yet, because of warming temperatures, climate models predict that by the end of the next century, Iceland will be virtually ice free. They confirmed that the pressure building under the Vatnajoekull was going to release an exceptional explosion. Wondering whether his search had any connection to the imminent volcanic eruption, Lakshman spent the first few days studying options for pursuing what, at this stage, seemed a rather hopeless investigation.

However, the very next week, progress came unexpectedly fast. A CIA colleague alerted by Jonathan had conducted research and provided Lakshman with potentially useful information. Investigations in the Icelandic national archives had brought to light records of an obscure myth that appeared both relevant and interesting. A thousand years before the modern era, a Viking drakkar had landed in Iceland carrying a mysterious treasure that was said to be the subject of great awe and dread. Rebel Vikings who had fled to Iceland had taken it from the temple of Thor and Odin at the court of the Norwegian king. The object looked like a small treasure chest and bizarrely, all those who had tried to open it had perished slowly, consumed by progressive internal burns. Because it was clearly under some evil spell, they eventually decided to bury the chest under a glacier in the hope that it would never be found again.

Then, introduced by his contact to the National Institute for Geomorphology, Lakshman came across another compelling discovery. Playing with computerized models, the local geologists suspected that the tectonic shifts and recent volcanic activity under the Vatnajoekull glacier were caused by the emission of strong telluric waves or vibrations emitted from a specific point at the rim of the glacier. Lakshman became further intrigued... was this a clue to the possible location of the casket? Certainly it seemed a good point to begin a search for it.

As dusk fell that same evening, Lakshman suddenly realized that he was being followed through the narrow lanes in the center of Reykjavik; he wryly noted that his stalker wasn't very good at stalking. Yet the feeling of being under surveillance was very unnerving. A freezing wind was blowing and he was in no mood to play hide-and-seek, so he turned around, walked straight up to the shape in the dark behind him, and asked with barely concealed irritation,

"May I help you?"

"No, it is I who must help you," the voice replied, curtly and authoritatively. "Go to your hotel room and I will meet you there." The stranger, his face concealed by a Nordic hood, vanished into the night and Lakshman was too startled to give chase.

A couple of hours later, a strange conversation took place in Room 272 of the Hotel Loftleidir. "If I may say so, you were rather foolish at the Institute. It is quite possible that people there realized the true purpose of your investigation." The tall man emitted fiery glances from under thick eyebrows. He had noble features, high cheekbones, and a short well-trimmed beard. "I know what you are looking for, but no one else should," he said menacingly, seeming somewhat upset.

Lakshman was startled. "I beg your pardon, but what is it you think I'm looking for, and more to the point, who are you and what business is it of yours?"

"I'll get straight to the point for there is no time to lose. I am the heir of the wizard of Hllidarendi and I was instructed to wait for you. You are on the track of the most fabulous discovery of this dying millennium, and it will decide whether the next one will thrive or not. Your intuition is correct: the Vikings did hide an important piece of the riddle of the Dagad Trikon prophecy under the glacier and it is this object that has now triggered major volcanic disturbances. The time of its revelation has come. I myself cannot retrieve it because only an ordinary human can open the casket, although all those who have so far attempted it have paid with their lives. This is the dilemma. Besides, I fear, I am being watched too. So it falls upon you, my friend, to retrieve the chest immediately, before the eruption – there is simply no time to lose. So please hurry, the pressure of the magma is building up. Here, take this map," he said, taking a piece of paper from his coat pocket. "It shows the entrance of the glacial cave that affords access to the wall where the casket is enshrined."

Lakshman looked frightened and was dumbfounded. "Wait a minute! You follow me around in the dark; you walk in here claiming to be some sort of wizard, inferring that you aren't a 'normal human being.' You have the nerve to ask me, a complete stranger, to go and risk my life by running straight into the perils of a possible volcanic eruption and to retrieve the contents of a casket? Give me one solid reason why I should if it's that dangerous? And who is watching you anyway?"

"Please believe me, I come as a friend and one whom you need more than you can possibly understand. I know that you have accessed the Rock of Dagad Trikon that the sages of the past revered. Have you not unearthed certain weapons there? They could not have been found if this was not meant to happen. I honestly do not know why you were the one fated to find them, but to me, what you have discovered is already proof enough that you could be the one we have been waiting for. The casket must be unearthed and opened by a mortal man. If my wisdom doesn't fail me, you are that person although, as I said, none have succeeded in the past. But, if the volcano explodes, the casket will be lost forever, and with it our chances of finding the other elements of the prophecy."

"Do you really believe the impending eruption of the volcano has anything to do with the casket? This sounds like nonsense to me!"

"Well," said the visitor, with a touch of humor in his voice, "maybe it isn't nonsense. Icelandic volcanoes have their way of interfering with history at the appointed time. May I remind you that in the second half of the eighteenth century a volcanic eruption on this island pushed so much dust into the atmosphere that it changed the entire climate of Europe? In the ensuing harsh and freezing winters, the French peasantry was catalyzed to rally in the cause of the French Revolution."

"So, the King of France lost his head because of an ill-tempered Icelandic volcano?" Lakshman was bewildered. "That makes no sense and has nothing to do with the object of my research." The visitor lapsed into silence, staring intensely at Lakshman. He then said, icily, "It has everything to do with it. Only modern men in their monumental idiocy have lost the perception of the intimate bonds that tie us to nature. The earlier races understood this very well."

"Do you really believe the myth about the Vikings and their casket?" asked Lakshman abruptly. At first it seemed that he'd encountered a madman, but the detailed references to his investigation and the power and integrity of the stranger's convictions were most persuasive, which compelled him to review his earlier notion. How could this man know about his expedition in the Sahara desert?

How did he know so much about Dagad Trikon? The stranger dismissed the question with an impatient flick of his hand. His penetrating green-grey eyes were at once gleaming. "Storytellers, novelists, and mythmakers all need fiction to speak about reality. Some of them are old seers who revived legends from the past to warn about the future but that future is now rapidly becoming our present. And to answer your question, the Viking story is no myth: the casket will burn all those who aren't authorized to touch it."

Lakshman felt more than a bit lost but his visitor continued patiently.

"The Dagad Trikon scrolls have been placed around the world by the Rock Avasthas themselves. They were truly magnificent lords of knowledge, a combination of goodness, wisdom, and strength never to be seen again in any race, but they too have disappeared. However, they never conceded defeat, and despite the fall of the world into lower consciousness, these people, belonging to the highest of the earliest race, believed in a path of redemption that was available to all men and women.

Now listen carefully. The caskets contain a comprehensive prophecy to help mankind uncover the plot of the collective principle of evil, the one some humans call Satan. The clash was foreseen to occur during the first century of the third millennium after Christ. It could wipe out most living beings and involves the power of nature, Mother Earth herself."

"So, for example, volcanoes also have a role to play?" asked Lakshman incredulously.

"Yes, also volcanoes. Volcanoes or earthquakes are not the only calamities that are happening now. A long time ago, evil beings discovered that Nature itself was reacting to certain behaviors of the human race. They never forgot that lesson, which of course was lost on human beings. They have maneuvered for a long time so men would unknowingly trigger the awesome destructive powers of nature by insulting her very essence. Now, Mother Earth is angry; the climate is changing, and the destruction of the human race is at hand and may, in fact, have already started."

"Just a minute," interrupted Lakshman. "What do you mean by destruction? Is this some sensational news one might read in the tabloids? You mean destruction with a capital D, like in the Apocalypse, like in a Hollywood movie? I don't understand the meaning of your words because movies have an ending but life always goes on regardless, one way or another."

The visitor nodded approvingly. "I must say, you are quite right. Destruction is always part of a larger process. For example, you need to break the egg for the bird to fly: by breaking the eggshell you destroy it and at the same time allow new life to the bird. I suppose what really matters is to be identified with the bird rather than the eggshell. The breaking of the egg, death and resurrection, this is the message of the great Easter feast we are celebrating soon. But even now I fear the storm coming upon us. The mission of the Hllidarendi is to reduce the scope of destruction, to minimize its impact, and to help alleviate human suffering. Indeed, if Mother Earth reacts to evil, she also reacts to good, and so perhaps, we can still stop this. There must be a way, although right now I do not see it. I believe that whatever auspiciousness and magic these caskets contain they must all be found for their full and awesome powers to become manifest. Perhaps if the ancient vibratory magic can be reawakened, then the flame of Man's higher spirit can be rekindled – but simply reading the contents of one or two scrolls won't do the trick. We are fast running out of time and I only know the location of three of the ten caskets."

"Really? And where did this one come from?"

"The Vikings stole the Icelandic scrolls from a Norman monastery they pillaged in the year 1050 AD. The tradition of the monastery reported that it was the gift from a holy virgin who came on a winged horse. She gave it to a hermit, a holy man, during his sleep. He later became the founding abbot of the monastery. Unfortunately, after the Vikings pillaged the monastery and killed all the monks, no one really knew for sure where the casket actually originated. However, Avastha caskets cannot be kept by unauthorized humans, let alone be opened by them. Thus, this casket became a source of terror to its Viking keepers who had tried in vain to open it to take possession of its supposedly precious content. To save themselves from the curse of the Avastha wrath, they brought the scrolls from Norway to this island where all the sagas were born, but *'they'* know about it and are closing in."

Somewhat anxious now, Lakshman muttered in a low voice, clearly impressed, "Who are *'they'*?" he asked.

The Hllidarendi's face became gloomier. He drew his chair closer to Lakshman and suddenly, squeezing his arm firmly, by way of emphasis, spoke in a deep voice that was vibrant with intensity.

"*'They'* are those who would break the body and the spirit of man. We must withstand them or this age will be utterly ruined. If they succeed, goodness and love shall pass away. To fight this last battle, all the evil ones who ever lived before have come again. However, they have incarnated this time with new names, new methods. Indeed, they no longer attack innocent people through demons as in the ancient days. They have now perfected better ways. In these times they can enter a person's mind and slowly infect it with a brew of cunning, evil, and malignity. Through gossip, rumors, and whispers in the shadows, the evil ones enter through human ears as murmuring souls. They enter through the eyes to attack our innocence. They have found many ways to attack the citadel of our body and I will not name them here.

In their ignorance, many good men and women alive today have lost their will, have lost their way, and have been led astray in utter confusion. I sometimes marvel at the cleverness of the devil's tricks. Malevolent beings have also incarnated in human form. These events have been predicted and announced in all the great prophecies and in the great books of all the world's religions.

The Evil One wants access to the elements that will allow him to unravel the Prophecy of Dagad Trikon: he hopes foolishly to prevent it from being realized. You see, my young friend, this prophecy carries the seeds of his final doom and of Man's redemption. He fears that the Rock Avasthas may return just as he has. In the past, they always eluded him... old scores to settle... I cannot tell you more now. Go tomorrow and find the casket, please." The glance of the strange visitor was now beseeching. "I have told you what you need to know for now. I will contact you again. Now, I must go. Remember that this whole thing is not under your control."

"Story of my life," said Lakshman, shaking his head derisively. "I will do as you ask for this indeed appears to be my errand, although I cannot say that I have begun to understand it. So promise me, strange Sir, that one day you will explain everything I need to know."

"I shall... patience... I shall. I do not begin to know why such a task has been given to you but it has. Dire times shall come to pass but you must face them if you are to claim the powers of the weapons you unearthed." The wizard opened the door and looked around. Before vanishing down the deserted corridor of the hotel, he hissed hurriedly, "Beware of the raven!"

Lakshman slumped back in his armchair, his ears still ringing with the words, "... those who would break the body and the spirit of man." A cold and deadly fear gripped his chest. He felt utterly lonely and realized that he still did not even know so much as the name of his visitor. He felt irritated with himself that he had not managed to obtain more information from this strange and extraordinary old man.

As he tried to remember what the man had said, Lakshman grew more intrigued than ever. He had come to Iceland without much hope of finding anything, ready to turn back and to give up the whole thing, but now his search had progressed beyond all his expectations. On the other hand, it was hard to make sense of what his strange visitor had said. Lakshman's famous curiosity had been awakened: perhaps the only sensible way forward was to make an honest attempt to find the casket. He stared at the map the older man had left behind. This was his main, possibly only chance to find out about the prophecy. He studied the map intensely until late into the night, while also following the breaking news on television: an eruption was imminent and large numbers of residents living in vulnerable areas were now being evacuated from their homes.

The next morning was crisp and sunny and Lakshman headed toward the corner of Iceland that is entirely at the mercy of natural forces. The Vatnajoekull, which is larger than any glaciers in the great mountain ranges of Europe, sits on an active volcano, home of ice, water, and fire, none of which can be controlled by human will or science. He decided to avoid the coastal road and hired one of those sturdy Icelandic horses with a fluffy brown mane. He took a circuitous but more discreet route through the highlands. The horse was hearty and Lakshman found that his own mood was improving. He whistled an Irish folk song to dispel the anxiety he felt about his dangerous destination. He was not a volcanologist and did not feel particularly safe at the prospect of walking into the core of a potential cataclysm, but he had come this far and did not contemplate turning back now. He wanted, above all, to put his hands on the precious yet much-feared casket, which could otherwise be destroyed forever. He passed by the big stones near Burstafell and onwards through rolling hills covered with grassy pastures and rich green moss. He traveled through the high fells, rocks, and fast-flowing brooks, until gradually the great empty space of the highlands opened on to a more desolate landscape. Here and there crimson-hued extinct volcanoes kept a vigil on his solitary journey. Tortured shapes of black lava punctuated the desolation of the stony desert, thrown into relief by the white walls of the huge glacier on the horizon.

Lakshman stopped whistling and suddenly felt very much on edge. Other than a couple of sheep grazing between the rocks, he was alone, and yet he experienced a strong sensation that he wasn't. The sun had faded and grey clouds brought a heaviness to the air as the daylight dimmed. Lakshman gingerly led the horse down a path on the rocky cliff, which marked the parting between the American and European tectonic plates, into a valley where a lake filled the rift. At a crossroads near the inn of Walaha, he looked up and noticed a raven circling in the winds high above the cliff. The thought flashed through his mind: "Beware the raven," the wizard had said. That bird is spying on me, Lakshman thought, and he tethered his horse in front of the Walaha Inn, went inside, and bargained hard with the innkeeper as he downed a hot coffee. Minutes later, he slipped out of the inn by the back door and drove off in the four-wheel drive Grand Cherokee Jeep he had just rented from the innkeeper. Meanwhile, at the front of the inn, now perched on an old barn gate, the raven kept watch on the horse.

Lakshman turned on the car radio. Geologists now knew that the imminent eruption of the volcano under the glacier would release a cataclysmic flood: two hundred cubic meters of water per second, a huge wave rolling towards the nearby Nordic sea. The Icelandic navy kept fishing vessels well away from the area most likely to be in the way of the tidal wave. The imminent breaking of the ice cap and the subsequent flood from the ice cauldron was the first news item on all channels. There was very little time to spare. He accelerated and drove as fast as the road permitted. One hour later, by means of a winding country road and some cross-country driving, Lakshman arrived as close as possible to the base of the lowest ice plate of the

Vatnajoekull and continued the rest of the way on foot. He skirted the police security checks and the hordes of journalists who had come from all over the world to watch the impending eruption. By now, the tension in the air was palpable and large flocks of birds, including ravens, were flying away from the region of the glacier. The earth started to shake, and a deep rumbling, like the growling of a monstrous beast, came from beneath the glacier.

Lakshman was absolutely terrified; his mouth was dry; his hands were sweating. He pictured horrible things happening to him, possibly even his imminent death. He fully realized that he would have to complete his business in a matter of minutes given that his very life was at stake. He allowed himself a maximum of half an hour to discover the casket; if he did not, he doomed the quest to failure. Indeed, the violence of the expected geological activity would definitely seal access to the casket or even destroy the casket altogether. If he stayed any longer he would perish too, along with the casket. He panted: "I must do this, it's crazy but I must do it. I cannot turn back now." He hurtled forward, running as fast as he could.

Fortunately, the map was precise. Lakshman reached the bottom of the glacier and hastily put on two voluminous pairs of heavy-duty Icelandic cod fisherman's waders. He entered the ice cave at the location shown on the map. It corresponded to the epicenter zone at the source of seismic disturbances identified by the computerized projections made by the Institute. The ominous sounds of cracking ice became louder. He could hear and feel the muted rumblings of the volcano deep underground. The ice was melting and really hot water, with a strong sulfuric stench, flowed past his feet.

Lakshman rushed as fast as was possible. "As I forgot my swimming shorts, that old guy better be right," Lakshman muttered wearily in a vain attempt at keeping his spirits up. He struggled in the strong current of the rising, near-scalding hot water. The ice tunnel now turned towards the left bank of the glacier, and through the eerie blue light Lakshman saw the wall of the mountain's flank. The stench of sulfur was unbearable now and the steam was suffocating. The hydrologic response to the underground volcanic activity was building up.

Coughing furiously and with eyes smarting, Lakshman frantically explored the surface of the rock before him with his bare hands, conscious as he did so that one stumble in the searing hot torrent would be the end for him. The earth vibrations increased to a new intensity and he experienced a surge of absolute terror. Just as he was about to turn and run away, he saw it, glistening in the glow of his lamp. With a jolt of surprise, he saw some old masonry work in the stone at the rim of the glacier's side. Digging under the surrounding crust of stone with his knife, the explorer-archeologist soon exhumed an object that looked very much like the prized casket. Now knee-deep in violent whirlpools of the unbearably hot water and screaming in pain, he sped as fast as he could to the exit of the ice tunnel, climbed onto firm ground, and rolled over and over in the snow in a vain attempt to soothe the pain in his legs.

Moments later, as he gunned the engine of the SUV and raced away, the rumbling of the glacier increased until it became utterly deafening. Lakshman looked over his shoulder just in time to see the first jet of molten lava explode from the earth. The jeep continued on its way unnoticed as police helicopters, journalists, and even a flock of ravens, high in the sky, watched a mile-high geyser of steam, hot water, and ash explode from the earth.

"I promise that's the last time I get scalded under sixty feet of packed ice and snow," a shaken Lakshman muttered to himself as he drove back along the coast in the direction of Reykjavik. His legs hurt badly but he proudly caressed the casket lying on the front passenger seat, feeling a pleasant tingling in his hand, quite forgetting that many had perished just for having dared to touch this very special object.

THE CASKET OF THE
WHITE FEATHER

L akshman stopped the jeep on a rocky peninsula above the Atlantic Ocean and took a deep breath. Apart from the wind, the sun, and cormorants, he was completely alone. He changed into the clean clothes he'd brought with him in his backpack. Despite slipping on a pair of pants with the greatest care, the pain from the burns on his legs was excruciating. In the far distance, he could see the glacial flash flood rushing over the outwash plain to the sea. The air was filled with a rumbling that sounded as if a thousand horses were galloping past. A plume of dark ash and steam from the volcano was slowly spreading like a bloated nuclear mushroom. The sight was awesome, yet it captivated him only for a moment. His attention was inexorably drawn to the casket in his hands, on which he now gazed with a mixed sense of anticipation and incredulity at the enormity of the feat he had just pulled off; he just could not believe his amazing good fortune. He spread the remnants of his waterproof waders on a moss-covered mound nearby, and sat with his legs outstretched and the casket on his lap. Somewhat to his surprise, it opened without difficulty and a silvery wisp of smoke wafted out and swirled around his body. He immediately experienced a strong sensation of being infused with the strength and courage to face any future difficulties, whatever they might be.

He peered into the box and gazed in wonder at three parchment scrolls made of a soft papyrus-like material; he sensed that they were the apparent source of the energy he could feel coursing through him. To his amazement, whatever the power emanating from the casket was, it quickly, as if by magic, healed his red and blistered skin.

A strange peace washed over him, a sensation similar to that which he'd experienced when he had discovered the remnants of the Avastha settlements in the inner canyon of the Rock. At that time, and despite the overpowering heat, he had felt fresh, cool, and foolishly happy. Without understanding why, he felt now, as then, a great fondness for the Avasthas.

As he touched the first scroll, the Avastha script shone brightly. Blinded by its sudden brilliance, Lakshman momentarily closed his eyes and, in so doing, his attention involuntarily turned inward. The light did not subside and he went into the whiteness, which expanded and illuminated the space in his brain between his eyebrows. It was as if he was melting within the purity of this whiteness and his sense of inner well-being deepened and coursed through his limbs. A tingling rushed upwards from the bottom of his back to the middle of the top of his head and back down again, bringing a relaxing sensation to the muscles throughout his body.

Initially, the white light was cool and intensely brilliant, but soon it began to rearrange itself into a column that encircled his spine. There was no mental activity. He was just seeing and, without effort, he felt a powerful and sudden moment of recognition.

This column of whiteness was defining both the core of his identity and the channel of his destiny where all options, all exchanges between possible futures would be decided. The whiteness was most intense at its center. He found that it dimmed when his attention moved to the edges, either to the left or to the right, toward uncharted territories.

Outside the tranquil splendor of that inner central space, he felt with a blurred sense of unease, the presence of two other dimensions. The central channel, rising from his sacrum to the top of his head and beyond, was surrounded on the left by a blue glow that ebbed towards the color of night and on the right by a yellow glow that carried a dynamic and solar splendor. The blue territory teemed with fuzzy visions and furtive shapes, like a living tapestry. He resisted the temptation to explore this myriad of memories. His curiosity moved towards the right, into the yellow glow, ripe with the promise of knowledge and the prescience of things to come.

Contrary to the earlier feeling of safety he had enjoyed in the cocoon of whiteness, Lakshman became momentarily gripped by fear and anxiety, which came rushing at him like a train on a collision course.

Sensing that his refuge lay in the whiteness, in the calyx of the present moment, he nudged the ascending movement of the energy from its core. However, the channel seemed to become blocked at a narrow lily-shaped gate that seemed to be situated in the middle of his forehead. He found that trying to push through the gate brought on the beginnings of a headache. The vision of a cross of light flashed before his consciousness. He then fell back into the blue haze and began to distinguish clearer images; he realized that the scrolls were conveying their content through telepathic messages.

Lakshman had indeed struck lucky. The casket recovered from under the ice cap of the Vatnajoekull was the one carried initially by the Sheravalian Amazon with the white feather on her helmet. It contained three scrolls that were central to the understanding of the prophecy left behind by the Avastha overlords, the Sand Keeper and the Nizam of Dagad Trikon.

Lakshman now understood the way in which the Avasthas had planned to reveal their prophecy: the content of the scroll would download telepathically to the brain of the one who was granted access to the casket, the authorized witness. He thought that each casket probably contained elements of the Dagad Trikon legend. With a heightened sense of alertness, he began absorbing the first of the scrolls that contained the opening of the Kem Heim Saga, the Tale of the Return. Gradually, it related scenes from the ultimate days of the proud inhabitants of the Rock. He witnessed the Rock at the time of its last days, still clad in splendor, facing the attack of the pterodactyl and its fearful demon rider. He admired the grace of the High Lady of the Rock; he observed the healing of Esitel, the meeting of the circle of the Aulyas, and the farewell ceremony of the Avasthas. The appearance of the Sand Keeper did not reveal his identity, however, because, as usual, his face was hidden under the cowl of a hood.

What was being uncovered was the whole story that the white monkey had brought to Jonathan in the dream, but unlike Jonathan, Lakshman witnessed it in a fully awakened state. The content of the story was now precise and crisp, and in this form, it cast a much sharper light on the scenes that Jonathan had visited in his deep dream.

It showed the dignity and sadness of a people whose time had come, a people forced to leave that last earthly island of truth, goodness, and beauty, in the midst of a decaying world. Lakshman watched the proud departure of the Avastha riders, adorned with their star-crested helmets and mounted on their winged horses, as they set off to distribute the scrolls to the four horizons.

They first sped towards Mount Uluru, the red rock in the middle of the continental island known today as Australia. The second and the third flew towards the shores of the Eurasian land mass, to the areas today called the Middle East and Europe. The fourth fled towards the island of Great Britain in the great western ocean. The fifth flew beyond this ocean, over the continent that would one day be called America and landed in a rift valley of breathtaking beauty, the Grand Canyon. The sixth flew towards countries known today as China and Russia. The seventh departed for the highest mountains of the planet, specifically to Mount Kailash, perched in towering splendor between India and China.

The most beautiful of all the visions then came into view. It was of the three young Sheravalian Guards whose helmets sported three feathers with colors that corresponded to the zones of consciousness that he had discovered in his telepathic vision. The Sheravalian Amazon carrying the blue feather turned south and flew beyond the Tropic of Cancer to an unknown destination. The Sheravalian with the yellow feather flew towards the island of Japan. Finally, Lakshman saw the Amazon who carried the radiant white feather and who had been the custodian of this very casket.

He saw her dismount a winged horse and walk toward him. He could only catch sight of the brilliant eyes darted at him; her face was concealed by a golden helmet. She came closer and leaned over him. He felt a sense of comfort and protection flowing into his breast as the vision disappeared.

Lakshman was completely fascinated by his strange exploration. Somehow, the blue light seemed to contain the past and the yellow light the future. The blue zone corresponded to the emotional area, the yellow zone to the intellect, and the white corridor between these two spaces represented the channel of change and evolution. As the glow turned from blue to yellow in the spectrum of an accelerating time continuum, the Kem Heim Saga prophesied that the high beings from the First Age would have a last chance to manifest upon Earth, during the third millennium of the Fourth Age of Man at the time when evil would have almost completed its task of perverting the human race. Like other ancient beings, the Avasthas would return at that time, but as human beings.

In the Avastha belief system as in Buddhism, reincarnation was an element of the Grand Scheme that applied to all races and species.

It was a support to man's evolutionary potential: a human being could incarnate again and again in order to cross steps of awakening and initiation and perfect the movement of his or her own spiritual ascent.

Some of those races, for example, dwarfs and nagas (serpent people), were ambivalent and could potentially serve either good or evil. They, would, in modern times, also take a human form.

For instance, the dwarfs belong to a steady race that is adverse to any change and hence did not evolve much during the course of millennia. They grew a bit in size over many thousands of years but their behavior remained unpredictable. To this day they are ethically neutral. They hesitate to side with righteousness because they want to be on the winning side, no matter what, no matter how high the ultimate price. They are meticulously tidy, very organized, and love decorating their balconies with flowers. They like mushrooms and it was they who first discovered hallucinogenic substances. Above all, dwarfs love gold and keep it in vaulted caves buried deep below their polished streets. Perhaps they have grown in arrogance on account of their riches but arrogance is always the path to a fall. Their deep love for their mountains, hills and dales, for their emerald lakes and snowy water rivers may no longer be enough to protect them.

Nagas, now reborn in modern times in the human race, are harder to fathom, as they are shifty, seductive, and duplicitous as well as unpredictable. Nagas were renowned for being particularly shapely of form and for emitting a strong attraction, as Lakshman now discovered for himself. He felt momentarily helpless and experienced a loss of energy as a very pretty naga girl moved towards him. He could barely resist the hypnotic spell of her magnetic eyes as she came closer. It seemed to Lakshman as if she was attempting to enter into his forehead. Summoning all his will, he retreated into the blue of night, towards the back of his head. This was a dangerous move but how could he have known?

Indeed, he had unwittingly entered the zone where the servants of the Darkness – demons, ghosts, golems, and goblins – could be revealed in a blue spectral light. As he saw their ghostly shapes advancing slowly, he realized that they too would, in these times, come back either as humans or as haunting humans. Through a haze he suddenly saw six Dark Riders galloping towards him in a swirl of grayish dust. A creeping dread overcame him as these shapes projected a formidable sense of hostile power. Yet he immediately sensed that the Casket of the White Feather was delivering important information about the enemy. He strained to see it well.

The Riders were six of the seven Deadly Sins, who must ride together for maximum impact. Lakshman wondered where the seventh one was. He did not know then that the answer would only come to him much later. He presumed that the seventh was present, but riding under a cloak of invisibility, which would make him the most dangerous of all. Which one of the seven was equipped with this power? Lakshman did not have the time to find out. He started sweating: his hands were wet with perspiration and fear gripped his heart but fortunately the Riders did not see him and raced by without a pause.

Behind the Riders, in the depth of the night, he now sensed a more sinister darkness lurking at the extreme of the color spectrum. The domain of evil, under the command of a veiled king, emerged from the abyss and pushed ever forward hordes of creatures wrapped in doom. Lakshman correctly guessed that the veiled demon chief was Belzebseth. He could just about make out the huge marching army of Thanatophor encroaching through a penetrating, enveloping gloom. In witnessing what appeared as holographic projections, Lakshman realized that foul creatures had no memory of their origins, no purpose of their own. They wholly dedicated themselves to spreading the lifestyle conducive to the dominion of their master. The assignment given to these subjects was to create the kingdom of the Mlechas, creatures of abomination, in order to welcome back the formidable devil Thanatophor, the Overlord of Darkness.

Without transition, the telepathic message brought forth a vision of a crowd of humans. In a derelict warehouse in a down-trodden suburb of a Western city, pulsating music thumped out at near-deafening decibel levels. Scantily dressed young women sashayed and pranced through a grayish blue haze of cigarette smoke and strobe lighting. Mankind here had become a sadomasochistic sect. Table-strippers mingled with men and women on the dance floor. In this place there was only one game: that of predators and prey. To the prey, the paying customers, this was all fun, their idea of enter-tainment. They saw themselves as cool and hip, an elite. The hunters and their game strove for the pursuit of sensations and pleasure. Little did they realize that they were being moved, like pieces on a board, with one objective: their subjugation to the will of one whose existence they remained completely unaware of.

It was Belzebseth's plan to attract the appetites of men and women into addictive engrossments, to pull their attention away from spirit into matter. He shrewdly understood that men and women are easily captured when bound by the web of their own desires. Belzebseth wanted to ensure that Mankind's destination would be a slavery of many forms: slavery of the senses, bondage of tortured emotions, and cravings. In so doing the demon king was serving well the design of the ruling devil Thanatophor: let human consciousness regress, let it not be permitted to rise in freedom, to soar ever higher towards the bliss of the Spirit. The ultimate challenge of the Devil to God is to deny Man the chance of evolving into his highest potential as foreseen in the Grand Scheme of Adivatar.

Lakshman found himself in the middle of such a party. A multi-plicity of drugs was changing hands; there was abandon in the air, bred of apathy and lust. Violence was always near the surface as drug dealers protected their turf or made incursions into the territories of others. Craving for the most extreme sensations from sex or from cocktails of drugs and alcohol, the shadows danced and edged along, down the insatiable twin paths of addiction and perversion.

Lakshman hastily pulled his attention away from this modern update of that old abomination, slavery. This enslaved crowd had masters whom he did not want to meet. He promptly turned his attention away from the back of his head towards the right of his awareness spectrum, searching in its golden glow for the return of the Avasthas. Their bright images seemed molded in liquid amber as they fiercely attempted to dispel the shadows emerging from the left side. They were struggling and did not achieve much success.

An advanced scouting party of Avasthas was to prepare for the return of the ancient race and the opening of that blessed central passage. A number of them, cloaked in secrecy, had already arrived within the human race by the time Lakshman's mind had deciphered the living content of the scrolls. Stealth was their protection and they were thus known as the Stealthstars. Those Avasthas of the Triangle Rock who had now returned as Stealthstars had a faint memory that they were somehow different from other men and women. Unfortunately they didn't know how or why. Their purpose, however unclearly they understood it, was to emerge from this human waking slumber in the search for their true identity. Through the manifestation of their true nature and inner powers, their will was to free human beings caught in the middle of great and countless dangers.

The panorama now opened wider: the sun, carried somewhat implausibly by a huge and friendly monkey, rose above an orange desert. Lakshman saw the Avastha cavalry advancing slowly to the poignant tunes of the Rasa music, cacti blossoming in their hoofprints as they passed by. The sun's rays glinted off their splendid armor, illuminating their banners, unfurled high above the spears. He saw the colors of the great Houses, orange for Kalabham, yellow gold for Falkiliad, emerald green for the clan of Elnur, red for Eleksim, and blue for Anor. The advancing lines of riders marched grimly and purposefully to fulfill the grand scheme of Adivatar of which this specific scroll did not speak.

Yet, when Lakshman's attention turned to the left, to the battle-field lines of their enemies, the Avastha cavalry looked hopelessly outnumbered. To a muffled rumbling of drums, a huge horde was advancing upon them. Leading it, the six dark horses and their six Riders of pestilence surged again in his vision. They had grown in size and Lakshman knew they were coming to reap the fruits of their work, a harvest of death.

Then, in a brutal apparition, the commander of this vast army, Hangker, the other deadly king, came forward. He was bedecked with crown, bracelets, and jewels. Lakshman stared at the face: pale, inhuman in its icy meanness and with two pale eyes that seemed to pierce right through him. Lakshman was forced to avert his own eyes from the sniggering wickedness in front of him. A surging terror made his heart pound furiously, for never before in his life had he confronted such evil. With a jolt, he interrupted the vision and closed the lid of the casket.

There were many unpleasant things to be seen in this Pandora's box, and he seemed to hear a woman's voice whispering, "Not all that is unknown is divine." He opened his eyes and breathed deeply. The day had advanced and the sun's light had taken on a golden intensity that seemed to set the scant vegetation afire. The moss around him looked like yellow flames erupting from the black volcanic earth and he felt again the strangeness of this mysterious country. Still sweating profusely, he could somehow sense a weird attendant presence. He hastily looked around to confirm that he was still alone. In the distance, he could still hear the roar of the volcano and the flash flood rushing through the cracks of the melting glacier.

Lakshman had thought that he was alone but you never know in the weird and wonderful countryside of Iceland. A few hundred yards away stood a large, strangely shaped rock. It was a night troll, petrified since being caught off guard at daybreak a thousand years ago. Its mind was of course greatly numbed but it had felt a scorching pain when Lakshman had read the scrolls. The released magic of the Avastha Rock was too much for it to bear, being a rock itself. Its silent, piercing shriek traveled through the nether world and was heard by a chief lieutenant of Hangker, Gorschkak, the Northern Titanosaur who was busy at that moment stirring up greed and Mafia violence on the streets of modern-day Moscow.

Shaken by what he'd seen, Lakshman decided that he needed a break from the casket. It was time to return the jeep to its owner. He reached the Walaha Inn under the approaching dusk and was much too tired to continue his journey back to Reykjavik on horseback. With the casket placed in the innkeeper's safe for the night, he dined on the fresh wild salmon he'd promised himself earlier. He ate ravenously; such was his hunger after the exertions of the day. He then retreated to a cozy wooden bedroom on the first floor and immediately fell into a deep and dreamless sleep.

He awoke bright and early the next day, breakfasted in the hotel dining room on fresh herring fried in oats and mustard and hot, newly baked bread that he washed down with several cups of freshly ground coffee. The publicity leaflet on the bedroom writing desk explained that the Inn was located at the point where the American and European continental shelves meet. The meeting of the tectonic plates seemed to Lakshman a propitious location to venture further into the story released by the Casket of the White Feather.

He retrieved the platinum casket from the hotel safe and a moment later, in the privacy of his room, was about to open it again. However, when it came to it, Lakshman sat on the edge of his bed for quite some time, staring at the casket and trying slowly to stifle a

fear that was welling up inside him. He considered the casket carefully. He decided that he would not allow himself to be captured
or ensnared by the visions within, for, after all, he always had the
option of closing the lid and escaping from what he found inside.
Eventually, his intense curiosity drove him to open it once again.

He opened the second scroll of the Kem Heim saga and closed
his eyes. At first he registered a most enchanting message in the space
of consciousness defined by the white aura. The second scroll revealed
the chief purpose of the Casket of the White Feather: to reveal the
corridor of inner knowledge, hidden within man around his spinal
column, and how to progress along this central channel towards the
residence of the Self. This teaching was imparted in words of great
eloquence.

Gradually, Lakshman felt that his inner space in the area
embraced by the white light had become hollow. A soft and cleansing
breeze was blowing through it and he heard notes of heavenly music.
It was a flute, unmistakably, and to his astonishment he himself had
become the flute. Before this moment, it was as if he had been as
a solid piece of wood. Now, as bamboo, a new-found and blessed
hollowness in the core of his body changed everything.

The notes of the music were soothing yet elevating, each of
them tuned to a specific frequency, a particular tone of delight. In
the music of his being he realized the many aspects of his own
beauty and how much he had to share with others, how much more
he was capable of giving to the world. This Rasa music would heal
the nations of the earth and bring about a common understanding
of beauty, love, and oneness. There were seven holes in the flute and
seven centers in his body that generated the main notes. The first
one was below the base of his spine at the bottom of his torso. Five
more were embedded in his spine, one more being in the middle of
his head behind his forehead, and the seventh one was just above the
top of his head. He had always appreciated and enjoyed listening

to music but he had never suspected that he could actually be the music.

He innately understood that he had discovered something of vital importance: a key message of the prophecy had just been delivered. It concerned the untapped inner potential of man, a store of blessedness that he had just briefly experienced to a point where he now felt elated and enlightened.

It was all to do with this breath blowing through the flute. The breath was carrying the feather. Yes, this was the meaning of the feather: to learn how to be gently carried by the higher power of the breath. He was the feather and also the breath that carried it. He felt the wind blowing on his hands and arms. This blessed condition lasted for a time before softly fading away.

It had become clear to Lakshman that the central corridor of whiteness was the path of initiation. Accessing it had something to do with reaching an equilibrium point between the lateral pulls from the blue and yellow zones, a balance between feeling and thought. The purity of whiteness was the message of the Casket of the White Feather. He felt it deep within himself, yet this passage was narrow, hard to find, and easy to block. It suddenly dawned on Lakshman that the mission of the Avasthas was to keep the passage open for all human beings. It probably led through the gate of the Elephant and would restore the bridge between the Outer and the Inner Worlds.

Lakshman felt jubilant. In this inner corridor of whiteness he had indeed solved one of the riddles of the legend; he had found the passage that would bring back the Oneness that existed before the Great Schism. Mankind as a whole is meant to rise, not just a few gifted or meritorious individuals.

Then, unexpectedly, he was brought back to his discovery in the Alwakil fields of the desert fortress. Lakshman had a sight of the weapons he had discovered at the desert Rock as if they had a role to play in accessing the inner lightness, the blessed condition of the White Feather. It was made clear that he had to deliver them to the returned Avasthas. Unfortunately, the scroll did not reveal the time of birth or the whereabouts of the Stealthstars. Lakshman came to realize that the scroll would not identify those to whom he was supposed to deliver the weapons. In keeping with their name, the Stealthstars themselves remained hidden.

Secrecy was required because the corridor of whiteness was under attack, surrounded on all sides by spies, the ongoing aggression of powerful enemies who were preparing the imminent onslaught of Thanatophor. To make the point plainly, the vision offered by the magic scroll shifted and Lakshman's vision penetrated a network of underground caves, deep within an inhospitable mountain that he could not locate in time or space.

He intruded briefly and found to his horror that he had landed at the Dark Council of the necromancers and witches of Belzebseth. The witches were in session, deliberating ways and means to identify and entrap the returning Avasthas. They assumed that the Avasthas had returned to the human race very recently and that they were therefore either children or young people. So, they reasoned, this was the right time to catch the Avastha children before they could fully express their powers. However, the witches were greatly frustrated at not being able to recognize the Stealthstars, their parents or the families into which they had been born.

Lakshman recovered from his initial fright as he realized that he was invisible to the assembly he was spying on. By listening to the deliberations of the sorceresses, Lakshman was able to understand their strategy, which was a straightforward two-pronged attack.

Children were the targeted victims. Firstly, the female servants of Belzebseth would attempt to break up families: adultery, separated couples, and divorces were seen as optimal means of destroying or emotionally weakening the children. Secondly, the attack would target the children themselves and push them into the kind of behavior that would unquestionably be harmful. A young, good-looking witch croaked, "We must get at the couples because, without finding the parents, we cannot reach their children. Let us seduce the dear husbands; we have many tricks for that, and their susceptibility to seduction is the weakest link in the family." At this, all the witches burst out into a conniving roar of laughter.

However, it turned out that, despite their well-organized spy networks, the witches did not have many clues to the whereabouts of the Stealthstars, nor did they know where they had landed. They had heard about schools for Stealthstar children scattered through the world but the ravens had so far been unable to locate them. "This indicates that a higher magic is protecting these families," a witch with a rather long nose said resentfully. The oldest witch, who chaired the Dark Council, confirmed gloomily that their inability to precisely locate the Stealthstars was in keeping with the dire predictions of the high sorcerers of the Board of the Necromancers and that it signaled the coming of the fearsome Avastha warriors.

Just then, more necromancers entered through a back door and sat at the Council table. They were high dignitaries, draped in crimson robes, and the Chief Sorceress greeted them with abject reverence. They looked ghostly and provoked in Lakshman a feeling of disgust. In the ensuing conversation, he came to understand that the necromancers were in charge of spinning the web of Belzebseth around human consciousness by which many minds could then be captured. The six Dark Riders would help immensely by playing a central role in breaking down the defense barriers of the human psyche.

The necromancers seemed to be most worried about the possibility that the Glorfakir and the Sadhan could be activated once more. Lakshman's interest now became even more acute. It was confirmed that the two Avastha weapons left behind by the inhabitants of the Rock possessed properties that the necromancers much feared:

they could dissolve the web of Belzebseth and dismantle the elaborate traps that had been placed around the human mind to destroy the freedom of the Spirit. It was imperative, or so said the necromancers, that those for whom the weapons were destined, the elusive Stealthstars, should be found before they would be able to equip themselves with the powers of the magic sword and shield.

The witches concluded their Council meeting by adopting a stratagem. They decided to assume attractive human forms, to become popular trend-setters and stars within human society, and to promote lifestyles by which the earthling children would be misled in ways that would prevent them from accessing their inner powers. The witches' wicked laughter provoked a surge of anger in Lakshman and he realized that this anger revealed his presence as a hot beacon of light. At this, the witches became very agitated, casting nervous glances in his direction.

Lakshman was afraid that the witches might catch him observing them and he heard an anxious voice resounding in his head, "Retreat, retreat hastily and do not open this casket again for several days! Otherwise the witches will find you and this would be a catastrophe. Hear me, I am your friend, I am Erilie of the Sheravalian Guards, the carrier of the Casket of the White Feather."

Lakshman promptly obeyed the voice. Before closing the lid of the casket, he opened his eyes and saw that only one scroll remained. The first and second scrolls had disintegrated into a thin shiny silvery dust as soon as they had delivered their contents. They were under the spell of protective Avastha magic that made sure no one could access these messages but the one who had been so mysteriously selected to receive them.

Lakshman, his mind back in the Inn, stretched his limbs and pondered over what he had found. The last images of this eventful second scroll established the existence of the Stealthstars but did not reveal their connections, location or any reference in terms of contemporary time and space. The message of the second scroll spelled out both hope and anxiety. Hope because the Stealthstars were coming, indeed some had already arrived; anxiety because negativity was already seeking out the Stealthstar children in order to destroy them and crush the forthcoming uprising of the Avasthas in its budding stage.

The news that some of the Rock Avasthas had returned as Stealthstars in human form had lifted Lakshman's spirits but he was also confused. The Stealthstars seemed to have a plan mapped out, yet some episodes of the scroll suggested that in growing up within human society they had forgotten their powers and their true and deeper nature. He wondered: if they didn't know who they were or had no memory of their past, how could they possibly handle the weapons and recreate the Rasa vibrations? More to the point, how would he find them? How was he meant to locate and identify them?

This was important because, according to one necromancer he overheard, to have maximum impact the two weapons had to be used in complete synchronicity and harmony to emit the required vibrations.

Lakshman packed, paid his bill, and departed. It was late afternoon by the time he reached the stable in Reykjavik where he had to pay the owner somewhat more than the odds for the late return of the horse.

Back in his hotel he spent many hours of focused work recording his experiences in detail. He made three separate CDs of his account and systematically checked each in turn to ensure that it had copied correctly. Later, he would courier two of them, one to his Swiss bank account and one to his father in Mumbai, while keeping the third on his person but separate from his laptop.

The next morning, using the cell phone with the special satellite link given to him in Cairo, Lakshman spent hours in a conference call with Lakshmi and Jonathan O'Lochan. He described his meeting with the enigmatic heir of the Hllidarendi, how he had unearthed the casket, the vision of the Rock. He quoted the words of the High Lady and of the Aulyas. He explained the clues about the destination of the caskets and the content of the one that he had found and opened. He described the extraordinary nature of his experience, floating as a white feather carried by the notes of a magic flute; he related his spying on the witches. After Lakshman had described the content of the scrolls, the friends compared notes and an animated discussion followed.

Jonathan said it sounded as though Lakshman was also speaking about his own trip with the white monkey. This was correct, of course, but Jonathan could not recover memories from his deep dream in such precise terms even though the material was stuck somewhere deep in his unconscious. Jonathan's experience was now diffused into the world of feelings and sensations but he felt greatly encouraged by the tremendous progress made by his friend and felt vindicated in his strong longing to unveil the prophecy. This indeed had been the gift of the white monkey: Jonathan had overcome the depression that had gripped him in the aftermath of the assassination of the Prime Minister of Israel and the failure of his work related to the Middle East peace process: now, he felt energized and more dynamic. He dared to hope and, having listened to his friend, he was now willing to fully put this hope into the pursuit of the quest. The success of Lakshman in Iceland comforted him in his yearning to reach an inner truth that could bring peace both to his own self and to this troubled world around him. His rational mind told him this was crazy, of course, but he reasoned that rationality had not to date brought him very far. He laughed at the lingering doubts he harbored, which whispered that only fools have such hopes.

For Lakshman things were somewhat different. He had entered into an enigma that challenged his intellect, a gigantic puzzle. The challenge to find answers and uncover mysteries was what had moved him to become an archeologist in the first place. It was with his thinking mind that he was receiving the story of Triangle Rock and the further revelations from the scrolls. His brainpower was thus highly stimulated: what was the secret access to the Deep Way, how could one acquire the Gift, how could the bridge between the Inner and the Outer Worlds be rebuilt?

The very fact that they were looking for answers to such questions did in itself, in the scheme of things, indicate progress. However, they also recognized that the hidden reality was itself elusive, whether it be sensed through emotions or grasped with the intellect.

Both men had now been introduced to the prophecy: Jonathan had approached it through the aegis of the white monkey, Lakshman through the opening of the Casket of the White Feather he had so miraculously retrieved. Yet, neither owned it. They had both entered the world of the Avasthas and yet it continued to elude them. Vision of revelation in itself is convincing but it does not bring with it any movement or change. Understanding is helpful but it is not enough. The passage between the two worlds remained sealed despite the revelations brought to both Jonathan and Lakshman. The truth was that they had not concretely progressed very far and that they both admitted it was a tribute to their rigor, openness, and honesty.

Lakshmi had been keenly observing the interaction between the two friends during these exchanges. Her insights and comments were always appreciated and her priceless contribution was in bringing a fine intuitive sense to the Dagad Trikon inquiry. She began by noting that Jonathan appeared to be relying more on the blue channel of his emotional side while Lakshman followed the leads on the yellow channel of his intellectual mind. Probably, she anticipated, there would be a point where the two channels met in the central whiteness that Lakshman had so thoroughly enjoyed. This would bring balance to each, and that would be the plausible point of departure for any potential future breakthrough.

Jonathan O'Lochan pondered on how to delve deeper into the quest for Dagad Trikon. Given his experience at the State Department and his connections in Washington DC, he was well placed to follow up on their leads in the Oikos Project at the upcoming conference in Moscow.

Later in the day, he shared the great news from Iceland with Tracy, who listened enthusiastically. His initial motivation had stemmed from the sense of helplessness he had felt in the aftermath of the assassination in Jerusalem. He could not yet see a link, if indeed there was any, between the worsening of the situation in the Middle East and the Dagad Trikon prophecy. Nonetheless, if the prophecy would bring forth a clearer understanding of the modus operandi of evil in the world, the insights afforded would certainly be helpful.

Jonathan had been quick to recognize that the unraveling of the peace initiatives in the Holy Land was endangering stability throughout the entire Muslim world. Violence and rash decisions would easily wipe out the modest achievements of the peace process, which was, in any case, only timidly supported by the international community. At the same time, could the nations of the earth and their governments face the mounting challenges to environmental safety, public security, and common prosperity?

Jonathan discussed his next move with Tracy. He was now ready to explore new avenues and had obtained clearance from his Ambassador to attend the next meeting of the Steering Committee of the Oikos Project at the Foreign Ministry Headquarters in Moscow. After all, the efforts of human societies to cope with mounting challenges through Oikos were aimed at manifesting this solidarity, which, in his view, should be the cornerstone of future foreign policy. Also, these efforts were worthy episodes in the saga of the struggle between evil and good, which was at the core of the Dagad Trikon legend.

However, prospects for a positive outcome did not look bright. Many of his colleagues had taken refuge in cynicism, careerism or resignation. At this stage he could only see that the logic of destruction sped much faster than that of construction. Yet, he acknowledged, smiling to himself as the thought struck home, that hope had indeed returned.

THE OIKOS PROJECT

A black limousine from the U.S. Embassy picked up Jonathan and Tracy O'Lochan from Sheremetyevo Two International Airport. It was a chilly but sunny day in Moscow and the city had recently been brightened up to celebrate its 850th birthday. The Church of Christ the Savior had been rebuilt, the facades of Stalinist buildings freshened up, and many public monuments were newly cleaned and repainted.

"Don't be taken in by all this, the cheerful colors are in sharp contrast to the grim mood and sarcastic wit of the Muscovites," commented Colonel Eisenwood, US Air Force, who had come to receive the visitors from Cairo. Despite the fact that Moscow was draining most of the wealth of the Russian Federation, its citizens had little to celebrate. Exploited in the past by the boyars, Tsars, and the Soviet Nomenklatura, the average citizen still led a very hard life. A new breed of oligarchic business tycoon had grabbed the wealth generated by the Perestroika revolution begun under Secretary Gorbachev; seldom had so few become so rich so fast.

Jonathan had related Lakshman's incredible adventures in Iceland to his sister who earnestly expressed the hope that the archeologist would continue with his research as quickly as possible. Somehow Tracy understood the extent to which their friend was breaking new ground. As he tried to recall more details of his own vision, Jonathan felt that this investigation had landed them in a dimension that challenged the very tenets of rationality. They agreed that they could not mention Dagad Trikon because no one would believe them. There were, after all, no clear memories of Jonathan's dream, and the findings from the scrolls registered by Lakshman could not be independently verified. Of course there were the few exceptional artifacts, as well as Lakshman's and Lakshmi's records on their respective laptops, but tight secrecy was prudent particularly because Lakshman had suspected that someone had tried to break into the research project on his computer. Such fears had been confirmed by the warnings from his unusual visitor in Reykjavik.

Jonathan was delighted to find his fiancée Jenny waiting for him at the Hotel Sovjetskaya. Her father tended to be somewhat over-protective of her, and for security reasons he had been reluctant to let Jenny go to Cairo the previous year. So now, here she was, having flown in from Boston to Moscow to celebrate her birthday with Jonathan. They had lunch in the grand dining hall of the Sovjetskaya while Jenny laid out her father's plans for the wedding, which was to take place at Jenny's family home. There was to be a barouche procession followed by an evening ball in a barn specially converted for the event. It sounded fine to Jonathan, if somewhat too elaborate for his tastes. Although Jenny was excited about their upcoming wedding, she was also interested in the purpose of the Oikos meeting and asked Jonathan many questions. He answered them as well as he could but, remembering his promise to Lakshman, did not mention anything about Dagad Trikon.

In the afternoon they took a stroll down a street full of antique shops, near the Foreign Affairs Ministry where the first meeting of the Oikos Project was due to take place later that evening. As they walked, they took in the local flavors, especially the characters in the street. The return of the Romanov imperial double-headed brass eagle on the present-day military uniforms looked out of place, almost like a piece of Disney kitsch. They sympathized with the little old men in worn-out, outdated suits, with Soviet military-style haircuts, the breasts of their suit jackets covered in service and bravery medals from campaigns in the Red Army. They marveled at the pencil-thin fashion models and at the 'New Russian' millionaires. Younger people seemed better tuned in to the promises of the post-Communist era, but they all were like children forgotten by history who did not quite know how to make up for lost time. Jenny, who was zealously health-conscious, observed that nearly everyone they saw was smoking, incongruously under the gaze of the Marlboro cowboy.

Jonathan recalled the briefing from the colonel and felt happy not to be stuck, like the Russians appeared to be, in a huge question mark, waiting the dawn of a better tomorrow in place of the perpetual twilight of the Marxist harvest. A bright tomorrow had apparently been just around the corner for the last eighty years since the October Revolution, but it had never quite shown up.

Just now Jonathan was bent on having a good time, making the most of these rare moments of togetherness with his vivacious girl-friend who looked particularly attractive right now, with wayward curls emerging from under her fur hat. While Jenny made a phone call home, Jonathan bought a delightful pair of enameled Lemaire binoculars made it Paris at the time of the last Tsar, which he planned to give her at a sneak preview of a modern experimental ballet based on one of Jenny's favorite novels, Bulgakhov's *The Master and Margherita*.

Later that afternoon, in one of the secure conference rooms of the Ministry of Foreign Affairs, Professor Evgeni Ordhinikov of the Russian Academy of Sciences opened the annual meeting of the Steering Committee of the Oikos Project. The first session was devoted to a comparative analysis of apocalyptic prophecies, mainly from the Christian, Muslim, and Hindu traditions. In the second session, paleo-climatologists from the Hadley Centre for Climate Prediction and Research in the United Kingdom presented some of the models they had run on their supercomputer. They showed how greenhouse gas emissions and global warming could impact ocean circulation systems, the 'North Atlantic conveyor,' and trigger a cascade of events that ultimately would lead to dramatic and brutal climate change that would wipe out entire eco-systems. The hypothesis of the return of severe glaciations could not be excluded.

Professor Ordhinikov, in a somber mood, summarized decisively. "Incidences of natural catastrophes are steadily on the rise since the nineteen sixties. They are likely to further increase in severity and frequency as climatic and anthropogenic factors combine to destroy our eco-systems. The cost to our economies is already known to be astronomical but is kept secret. Greenhouse gas emissions must be reduced by fifty percent by twenty fifty if we are to stay below a two-degree Celsius temperature increase. If we don't, we are in big trouble. Our fate will depend on the potentially fatal ballet between energy generation and carbon release. To get their economies on a decarbonization track, politicians must take sweeping decisions. To prevent climate change, we have to change."

In this context, the Americans presented a study from the Pentagon's Office of Net Assessment, which illustrated how climate change over the next fifty years would result in a global catastrophe costing millions of lives through natural disasters and wars. Rising sea levels would engulf large cities; mega droughts, famines, and energy shortages would cause widespread rioting; conflicts induced by mass migrations were predicted to erupt across the world. The use of nuclear weapons in the context of turmoil created by climatic imbalances was not excluded. Despite all of this, the Administration had decided to shelve the study for lack of, they insisted, enough hard scientific evidence.

The cost of flooding caused by climate change in the United Kingdom alone was predicted to rise to twenty billion pounds a year by twenty fifty, a figure confirmed by the British Office for Science and Technology. How many countries could afford such an expense? After a pause, Colonel Eisenwood concluded gloomily, "Nature is striking back and our coping strategies are defective given the present condition of our political and economic systems." So dramatic were the scenarios of the report that the Committee received the presentation in stunned silence.

Tracy muttered to her neighbor, Dr. Jana Pimenieva, "The coastal marshlands of Louisiana are disappearing into the Gulf of Mexico at the rate of thirty football fields a day. It is hard to overstate this case and even harder to understand why politicians look the other way. We need a mighty effort to raise our level of preparedness and we need it sooner rather than later."

At the conclusion of the day's formal agenda, Jonathan and Tracy left the Foreign Affairs Ministry building and looked around, blinking in the bright sunshine at the crowd around them. "They don't know how nasty our common future looks," Jonathan mumbled to himself. " How can we tell people?" added Tracy, looking somewhat crestfallen. " If we told them the truth and the extent of the incompetence of our rulers in dealing with the situation, governments would be toppled and there is no one to replace them."

"Better keep people in the dark, they'll be happier. There is nothing we can do anyway. Besides, you would be surprised: people probably don't care." Tracy knew well that this sarcasm was Jonathan's way of expressing his own frustration and so she did not bother to answer. Jonathan now felt jet-lagged, helpless, and tired. His goal at this point was to forget it all and just to enjoy the weekend with Jenny.

The next morning Jenny had intended to shop in Moscow, but on a whim she decided instead to take Jonathan on a stroll around a stretch of the Sadovoe Koltso, the ring of boulevards that encircle the city. They walked past silver birch trees, so beloved by Russians, and lines of topol trees, a variety of poplar, whose seeds, known as pooshok, blew in the spring breeze like the first flakes in a snowfall. Later they took a taxi to the Muzey Vostoka to see some of the Nicholai Roerich paintings on display there. Jenny had visited Roerich's one-time home, now a museum, on the upper west side of Manhattan. Although she understood that the Vostoka only had a few examples of his work, she was curious to see exactly what the Russians had in their collection.

That afternoon the Oikos Committee traveled to a dacha in the woods near Moscow. It was a traditional wooden building with thick walls that kept it cool in summer and warm in winter, and with exposed beams that strengthened its rustic appeal. The cozy interior provided a comfortable environment that contrasted with the formal and solemn offices of the Ministry of Foreign Affairs.

Their brief was to finalize the Oikos action program for the next biennium. After four years of activities, the project had taken on a sense of common purpose but the Oikos task force was still gathering data, projecting trends and variables, and simulating scenarios. The atmosphere was more casual but still not exactly relaxed, which was understandable given the gravity of the subjects under discussion. The task force faced the huge challenge of con-vincing politicians and decision makers to take immediate and serious action. The emerging picture was ominous enough on the biophysical side of eco-system services, which were shrinking under the pressure of population growth and expanded economies. They consequently pursued their search for a unifying paradigm in the area of socio-anthropology, to build a compelling case for a change in consumption patterns.

The day was given over to the introduction of the research results. The African and Asian scientists made presentations on how traditional beliefs and customs expressed their people's belief in the existence of life after death and of parallel worlds. The Europeans and the Americans concentrated on neurology, psychiatry, and medicine. The Russians focused on parapsychology. The U.S. military establishment had conducted some special investigations and Colonel Eisenwood introduced the NASA project on ancient civilizations: this included satellite photographs of pre-Columbian landing sites in Southern and Middle America and the discovery of an underwater causeway between India and Sri Lanka. The images appeared to validate the account of the military campaign waged by the Hindu God king Rama against the demon Ravanna, which is related in the ancient scripture, the Ramayana. Similarly, underwater exploration off the coast of Gujarat in India had revealed the remnants of the ruins of the Yadava capital of the God king Krishna. The fall of the city, some six thousand years ago, had been described in another great Hindu epic, the Mahabharata. Jonathan then summarized the latest mathematical models, which suggested that the pyramids of Giza may contain messages from earlier civilizations. Participants agreed that past mythologies could point to bridges between parallel worlds and states of consciousness.

At the end of his presentation, Eisenwood reverted to a more worrying subject, a presentation of findings from the field of space sciences, the latest news from NASA concerning the threat of large meteorites colliding with Earth. The first serious possibility of a hit was expected in twenty thirty. His conclusion was chilling. "It is still too early to predict with full certainty, but depending on if and where the impact occurs, this could have consequences of Armageddon proportions. Of course, together with our NATO partners with nuclear capacity, and with Russia and China, we are studying coping strategies."

The Steering Committee was already aware of this issue, which was handled under the Eschatology File, compiling worldwide predictions made in the last four thousand years concerning the so-called 'last days.'

In the evening they gathered in plush leather armchairs around a fireplace in an atmosphere freer of stress than might otherwise have been expected. Aided by generous supplies of vodka, they reviewed some aspects of their discussions and brain-stormed freely. Evgeni Ordhinikov came back to a point he had made the previous day.

"As you know, the technology that enables us to record alterations in the state of human consciousness has made great progress over the past years. The registration of brain waves through Kirlian photography, to measure energy levels or aspects of our auras, is now very reliable. We recently had the intriguing case of a respected Russian physicist who tested a sophisticated instrument on a foreign visitor, a woman, I believe. The level of energy he registered was way beyond anything we could imagine for a normal human being. Unfortunately I do not have the details here."

"The instrument must have malfunctioned."

"Apparently not. It registered normal parameters on people tested before and after this extraordinary occurrence. The problem is, I cannot trace the scientist who controlled the experiment because... "

"Evgeni, isolated individual occurrences have limited scientific validity," Dr. Jana Pimenieva from the St. Petersburg Medical College interrupted him. "I am more attracted to replicable, collective phenomena. For instance, three years ago I sent my assistant Tatiana Voytchenko to a large gathering – over twenty thousand people gathered in a sports stadium in St. Petersburg at an event organized by some spiritual revival movement. Many participants reported specific sensations in their central nervous systems. It does not appear to be a case of collective hypnosis. It seems clear that some consciousness states mature into an expanded level of power when shared by a collectivity."

"I guess you don't mean the frenzy induced by Hitler at the Nuremberg rallies," said Dr. Anthony Vince, a psychiatrist from the University of Colorado. "This is just tapping crowd dynamics, politics by other means. It also works for rock concerts or the open-air mass of the Pope on International Youth Day."

"No," said Jana, "the symptoms and behaviors were quite different. Something much subtler happened."

"What did they feel?" asked Jonathan.

"A cool breeze on their hands, and a powerful sense of oneness."

"This sounds like Pentecost, doesn't it?" observed Professor Alyona Goldowsky, Chair of the Ethno-sociology faculty of the University of Kiev. "The *nous* or *pneuma* of the Syrian Gnostic fathers? We knew about it in the early days of Byzantium. They must have been Pentecostals on ontogenic training… "

"No," replied Jana, "Tatiana is one hundred percent certain on this point. The participants had different backgrounds and did not know what to expect. Many were not even Christians. There was a large group of Muslim Azeri from Baku. I found this intriguing enough to send her report to the Central Secretariat of Oikos. I'll get you a copy if I can find it in my file."

"It is true that we have entered a period where the incidence of strange occurrences has increased," observed Professor Derek Speighton, an ethnologist from Cambridge University in the UK. He was a congenial academician with lively eyes behind heavy spectacles, a bushy beard, and a dry sense of humor. "Since the end of the nineteen seventies, as we know it, something happened around our famous Stonehenge menhirs… some unexplainable anomaly in the growth pattern of wheat that created complex geometric figures. When seen from above, these figures are perfect in proportions and evoke huge spirals, serpents, stars or mandalas. These patterns are formed in a very short time, sometimes overnight, and the crop productivity of the wheat affected increases fivefold. These designs have also started to appear around nearby Avebury and I understand some similar phenomena have been sighted in Oregon too. The scientists investigating these phenomena are at a loss for a rational explanation. I have proposed that the U.K. Oikos team should report on this at our next session but for now please take a look at these pictures."

Jonathan examined the photos. First, he rapidly glanced over them and then studied them more carefully. He selected a few, then passed the rest to his colleagues. He showed them to Tracy, sitting next to him, and whispered in her ear, trying to conceal his excitement: "Remember the file we received from Laksh's laptop? See these star formations? Count their points! I think the numbers correspond to those of the stars Lakshman described in his vision of Dagad Trikon. I mean, the stars on the helmets of the Avastha knights carrying the caskets: stars with four, six, ten, twelve, and sixteen points. Look here, in this field, one can also see a spiral or a serpent... Maybe there is a connection." Tracy nodded and smiled benignly to divert the obvious curiosity of Charles Clairmont, of the Institut Pasteur, who was straining to catch their conversation.

The discussion then turned to near-death experiences – instances of people suffering severe accidents or advanced sickness who died, that is, whose heart stopped but then restarted after a period of time and they regained consciousness. "We have a considerable number of files on such near-death experiences," said Anthony Vince. "Usually people describe how they leave their body and then see it left behind. After a time, they feel attracted by a white, shining light, which glows at the end of a round tunnel, pretty much as represented in the famous painting by Hieronymus Bosch. The interesting thing about the light is that it is not just a visual effect. As they walk or fly – we don't quite know which yet – towards the light, they begin experiencing a growing feeling of well-being and deep happiness. Some describe a loving presence waiting for them within the light that fills them with incredible longing and expectation. They frequently don't want to come back to their earthly existence or return to their human body and indeed, a few who returned to consciousness even tried to commit suicide later on, in order to go back there... to reconnect with the white light."

"Yes," said Lama Kazu Rimpoche, who had been flown in from the monastery of Tonga in Bhutan with an interpreter. "But if they die by suicide they'll get into big trouble. In the Bardo Thoedol, our Book of the Dead, it is indicated that after death we enter the Bardo, where we are in a kind of floating state. Higher beings can circulate at will in that condition but lower beings cannot control their movements. Most people see the white light in the beginning, but then it changes. Your patients did not stay long enough in the Bardo to find out. Those who have done some evil, carrying the debt of a bad karma, cannot reach the end of this tunnel. The light of the blessed whiteness recedes and is replaced by other, more threatening colors. Black shapes also can intercept them and lead them astray."

"Well," mused Dr. Vince, "this reminds me of a couple of ghost movies we have taken note of. It seems that some in the Hollywood crowd got it right. There are movie directors who, consciously or not, have displayed and described patterns of after-death phenomena consistent with our research, even with some of the detailed results not yet made public."

"We must not forget that until the nineteenth century the belief systems of all human cultures were rooted in the conviction that other strata of consciousness existed," recalled Professor Alyona Goldowsky. "Take, for instance, the 'Jus Quiritium,' which is the foundation of Roman law. It started as a protective exorcism against interference from the souls of departed ancestors. Pleasing their spirits was and remains all-important, as we know from the burial traditions of ancient Egypt, pre-Columbian empires, and the current practices of many African tribes or of the indigenous population in Australia."

A colleague from Minsk University interrupted: "There are other interesting aspects of traditional knowledge and popular beliefs, for instance, if we look at the folk customs of Byelorussia, you'll find several pre-Christian rituals corresponding to the passing of the seasons. We find similarities with other customs we have studied in Vietnam, Laos, and Iran, rites that remind us of the practices of Hopi Indians, or the beliefs of the American writer Henry D. Thoreau. These rituals were meant to help us tap into the energy of nature itself, a bit like animist or shaman practices were trying to harness the power of the dead."

"Quite so," intervened Derek Speighton. "Tuning into the force of nature sounds much healthier to me. This probably makes the difference between forms of white and black magic. I heard recently how the practices of tantrikas in India, voodoo in Haiti or cri-cri in Benin could harness the powers of the dead in order to harm people while on the contrary; the subtle powers of nature are always life-enhancing. The common ground here is that the individual is seen as part of a living web, one element in a network whose very fabric is made of hidden, interwoven relationships. The trouble is, these subtle relationships turn out to be beyond our mental grasp and are ignored by most of present-day science. To discover theses connections or how to make use of them, we have to take off our thinking caps and somehow find other paths of consciousness to pass into parallel territories."

Charles Clairmont observed, "Of course it is a bit hard for a fellow citizen of Descartes' land to digest such statements. In France, we called all this stuff superstition at the end of the eighteenth century. At that time we thought we had grown up and had discovered that we were, after all, reasonable and rational people."

"That may well have been one of the most irrational assumptions of modern times," observed Professor Rahul Rahurikar of the All India Institute of Medical Sciences in New Delhi in a friendly but slightly ironic tone.

"To me the basic question seems to be: is there any other way of finding out other than by dying?" This was more than a rhetorical question. After a pause the Professor answered his own question. "We think so, but we have not found it yet. I suspect it has a lot to do with the neuroendocrinology of our brains. Those of us who work with drug addicts know very well how chemistry can alter the working of the brain and states of consciousness. Yoga devotees claim it can be done without chemistry, but the training required for this is simply not available. Most yoga courses today are just forms of physical exercise at the fitness club. No one really knows what happened to Siddhartha Gautama at the point when he became the Buddha, and to a number of other spiritual masters who are said to have gone through the experience of Samadhi or Satori, as the Zen masters called it in Japan.

"Is this the same experience under different names?" asked Jonathan. The professor nodded affirmatively. "We have descriptions but no how-to manuals. I am sorry to say that the vast majority of meditation groups popular in the West have been much more successful at making money than at validating their pseudo-scientific claims for consciousness improvement. Of course we have monitored some very remarkable yogis at the Institute, people who can go beyond physical pain, or stay awake for weeks without drinking, eating or excreting but no one knows how they do it, not even they themselves. Frankly, I guess that most people would rather have a good dinner and go to bed for a restful night. Modern men and women generally do not see the point of all this."

"Rahul is right," commented Professor Ordhinikov. "This is the dilemma we are facing now: we have a huge body of circumstantial evidence. These pieces of information all converge towards the same conclusion: they strongly suggest the existence of alternate or improved stages of consciousness but so far we have not found a means of accessing them. The paths we know of are exceptional – such as near-death experiences, or dangerous – such as drugs or sorcery practices that we do not quite understand, so we are making little progress. No matter how convincing these bits of evidence may seem, they cannot currently be scientifically validated."

Tracy muttered to herself: "The path? The blessed whiteness? They are looking for the Avastha passage, the gate of the Elephant. I must tell this to Lakshman. He should stay tuned."

As they moved to the dining room, Jana Pimenieva asked with a smile, "Are you sure dinner is safe?"

"What do you mean?" replied Ordhinikov.

"Listen to this folk story from the Karelian peninsula. One day, a priest from a small village, much worried for his parish of sinners, prayed to God that there should be a place where men could dump their sins. That evening the Archangel Michael appeared before him and told him that men could pour their sins into the sea and that each sin would be carried by a fish of the corresponding size. When all the fish in the sea had been poisoned, the Archangel would come back and present them with the bill. Now you may know that dioxins have contaminated the food chain in the Baltic Sea to such an extent that the Health and Nutrition Institute in Stockholm has told pregnant women not to eat fatty fish more than once a month, otherwise the neurological development of their unborn babies may be at risk. Expect the Archangel to knock at the door."

"Well, let's hope we have some other seas available, but I rather doubt it. This deserves a note for the eschatology file," said Derek Speighton, and then the group began their meal with suspicious looks at the salmon.

Professor Rahurikar pursued his reflection, "So, where do we go from here? Or, rather, why did we get into this Oikos venture?" Turning towards the U.S. Air Force colonel, the professor asked with a broad grin, "Tell us, Colonel, why on earth is the Pentagon financing research on lost civilizations, of all things?"

"I have had the opportunity to discuss this with some of you in the past," said Robert Eisenwood, clearing his throat. "We understand from Mr. O'Lochan's presentation that the pyramids in Egypt contain knowledge we know was not available to our immediate ancestors – knowledge that we don't possess ourselves, as a matter of fact. So the question is, can we rediscover it in order to help us face today's mounting challenges? I think Russia agrees with us on this."

"As was said, the Pentagon, the National Defense Agency, and the CIA have run truly complex computerized scenarios," pursued Jonathan. "They are researching security trends for the next century, which includes several biophysical and socioeconomic factors: climate change, demographics, and economics but also indicators on what we call a scale of psychological expectations. In short, in a globalized world, expectations are rising but opportunities aren't keeping pace; on the contrary, in some places they often decline because of drastic environmental degradation and rampant poverty... "

"... linked to the sub-optimal distribution of wealth in the global capitalist system!" interrupted Professor Goldowsky.

"Well, perhaps yes," replied the colonel, "the economic variables indicate a growing level of stress. In a nutshell, the probability rises for more frustration, increased social tensions, and multiple confrontations. We see fundamentalism and terrorism on the rise in the poorer, most vulnerable ecosystems, with the return of intolerance within other belief systems in the developed world. Through various scenarios we gradually reach a high likelihood for what we call 'breakdown point,' that is, the end of present-day civilization as we know it."

"What does the American government expect and hope from Oikos, exactly?" asked Clairmont.

"The government hasn't paid much attention yet," grumbled Eisenwood, "but we ourselves are happy enough we have a green light to run this project. Of course we have factored in scenarios validated by recent or plausible new technological discoveries. It would seem these models can postpone but cannot prevent break-down point. We need to open a completely different field of possibilities; we need to help people to adjust their expectations."

"In other words," added Tracy "you would not satisfy people through the supply of more goods and services but through changes in the demands for satisfaction. If Oikos gives us access to the inferred state of higher consciousness, a whole new range of options for satisfaction will be available to the human race. Satisfaction of spiritual needs could top our pyramid of needs. This, according to Oikos research, would enhance satisfaction of needs for the whole pyramid, including at relational and psychological levels."

In response to Clairmont, who was expressing his strong doubts about Tracy's hypothesis, Jonathan said, "In short, if we can access true satisfaction through states of being, not through having or possessing, the demands of our societies would shift and thus cause the destructive patterns of the economy to shift to more sustainable models. This would relieve pressures on the environment. Once upon a time, some advanced human beings experienced the states of mind we talk about. We should be able to rediscover them and this would most likely connect us with those brain patterns experienced by more evolved beings during the lost Golden Age. Historians consider these earlier periods as mythical or utopian and spurn such hypotheses but, by now, we simply have more data than they do. This is why we continue our investigations into past civilizations, with a view to discovering, if possible, how to access the level of consciousness some of their enlightened people had reached."

"Back to the future! Are we looking for the Lost Age or is the Lost Age looking for us?" asked Dr. Vince. "It seems some of its content is flowing through various messages into our collective unconscious."

"Some of this coming back is ominous and it does not come from the Golden Age," commented Francis Fieldburn, a criminologist from the FBI. "Let me go back to these black shapes, if I may. We are registering a disturbing increase in weird and ghastly crimes: serial killing, sexual fetishism, child molesting, cannibalism, and witch-craft-related murders, to name but a few. Sadistic or masochist practices are widespread and many of the offenders claim to act under some sort of compulsion or to be inhabited by an entity or entities, which compel them to practice perversion or perpetrate crimes. They say that they kill, torture or rape to satisfy the parasite entity in their consciousness. We have made thousands of in-depth psychiatric evaluations of these criminals and whilst clearly some offenders use such arguments to plead insanity in an attempt to escape punishment for their crimes, others certainly seem to be infected by some sort of 'psychic compulsion virus.' We call it PCV and have identified something quite sinister, something like a 'possession-induced crime category.' It looks like the dead have started attacking the living through penetration of their mind. This is now happening on a much bigger scale than ever before. There may be other areas of consciousness, but not everything is pretty out there. It's hell on the move."

An uneasy silence settled upon the gathering. Jonathan was about to take the floor again but he remembered his promise to Lakshman and kept quiet. He had to struggle to resist the temptation to share information on the emerging discoveries concerning the Dagad Trikon legend, although in a sense it validated much of what had been said during this Oikos workshop.

Jonathan was indeed well advised to be discreet. Nobody had noticed that for a split second the retinas in the eyes of Charles

Clairmont retracted much like those of a cat. There was an entity hiding behind those eyes, an entity that had come from Belzebseth in the nether worlds to spy on Oikos, and the phenomenon Agent Fieldburn had described was a key element of the demonic offensive. Oikos was getting close.

After a while, the chairman resumed. "The strategy for the correct way ahead would seem fairly simple: to look for heavens and to avoid hell. We clearly need a road map though, something to guide us on our way and with a clear path to the right destination. It would be regrettable to end up at the wrong place. Frankly, I am a bit embarrassed to find nothing better so far than a discourse for young monks, taken straight from a class in a monastery of the Middle Ages."

"That monastery may just as well be Orthodox, Catholic or Buddhist as in the case of our venerable abbot," said Clairmont, nodding politely at Lama Kazu Rimpoche. "But I rather think we are a bit better equipped than Thomas Aquinas or Saint Milarepa to find the answers to these probing enigmas. It is just a matter of time."

"Time? Do we have time?"

And, on that note, the meeting ended somewhat inconclusively.

Back at the Sovyetskaya Hotel the next day, Jonathan treasured Jenny's company and managed to forget the anxieties provoked by the more recent Oikos findings. They enjoyed an evening at the Bolshoi and spent two pleasant days together. The evening after she'd left for Boston, Jonathan received a phone call from Lakshman. Although they were both still gripped with disbelief and incredulity following the discovery of the Avastha casket, it seemed to them that, from the Oikos standpoint, the unveiling of the Dagad Trikon prophecy was indeed becoming a matter of urgency.

The Embassy had arranged Jonathan and Tracy's flight to St. Petersburg, where they had hoped to meet Dr. Tatiana Voytchenko.

Jonathan had been intrigued by the account of the ceremony in the sports stadium and by the fact that the report forwarded by Dr. Jana Pimenieva could not be traced in the Oikos file. Unfortunately, the young doctor was by now on a trip abroad. Jonathan and his sister spent much of their last day in Russia strolling through the magnificent city with their kind host, Dr. Jana, who spoke excellent English.

"Look, Jonathan," she said, "I think 'breaking point' is not the point. Don't you see it more like a gradual affair? I mean, getting slowly into greater turbulences. Look at the everyday news in the world. I admit I do not have an overview on what is going on, even in Russia, but the course we are taking is fraught with uncertainty. With the demise of the Soviet Union, the disappearance of this repressive bureaucratic fraud, we were full of hope for a truly new beginning for our country. Maybe we were just idealistic fools. In the meantime, the 'New Russians' have discovered again the seduction of greed, and predator capitalism is free to run rampant. The privatization process blessed by the World Bank and the International Monetary Fund has resulted in thousands of workers being thrown on to the streets, and more old people face brutal poverty. To give you one personal example, my mother, on her own, had two jobs for most of her working life and she put both her daughters through university, but her lifetime's savings were wiped out in a twenty-four-hour period. When academicians, university teachers or the professors at my Institute earn in a month what a teenage prostitute can make in half an hour at the service of the new masters, you can imagine how corruption sets in. The daily room rate of some hotels in Moscow is twice the average monthly salary."

"I know, Jana," responded Jonathan, "but things are not as good as they seem in our countries. Democracy was created on the assumption of a reasonable sharing of wealth and power but now I see a split: the aging middle classes are on the road to poverty, while the few who are already rich are climbing to dizzying new heights of wealth. Pharaoh was a pauper compared to some of our ruling crooks."

Tracy stepped into the argument. "As I see it, the problem with capitalism and its resultant materialism is that everybody tries to grab a piece of the pie for himself, regardless of consequences, with the assumption that an invisible hand will somehow fix everything. It is damned naïve."

Her brother giggled. "It isn't really naïve. They simply don't bother about what happens to others as long as they think they themselves are managing to keep on top. Evil manipulates so many people so intelligently in this satanic empire. Whether or not we can fix our problems is going to be a thoroughly watchable drama. The only trouble, is that we are in it; we are stuck in this drama. No exit."

With an affectionate gesture, he ran his fingers through his sister's hair. He raised his voice to be heard over the noise of the street and his tone was serious now,

"As the Hopi Indians knew, we all belong to circles and cycles, in both the physical and the psychological worlds. Take an example at the biological level: alteration of the nitrogen, phosphorus, sulfur, and carbon cycles with the dire consequences of acid rain, algal blooms, fish kills in rivers and coastal waters, and the destruction of eco-systems. Our scientists know all about it by now but the pollution goes on. Take another example at the psychological level: the Freudian fraud has done untold harm to human relationships with damage to our social circles, to couples, and to families. There are hundreds of such examples. But who bothers? How many more life-sustaining cycles must we break before the regular guys will notice? I bet the Grand Scheme is itself a huge cycle in which all these smaller cycles, circles, and ellipses whirl and gravitate along and around us, in a great dance, to sustain what should have been the path of our ascent."

"You are very poetic, Seagull, and you may be right. I think you described well the play of evolution but, when I think about our politicians, I doubt that poetry will carry the day," Tracy said, and she gave her brother a calming but cheery kiss on the cheek.

They continued discussing the prospects for Oikos. It had merits, no doubts. It was a limited attempt by governments and scientists to find for society a new unified ground, a good-faith effort to bring a deeper foundation to the togetherness of the entire human race. Yet, a revival of solidarity and common purpose was precisely what Thanatophor wanted to stop at any cost.

CASTING LIGHT ON THE WAYS OF DARKNESS

When Gorshkak heard the piercing shriek of the Icelandic troll in his abode deep under the city of Moscow, he understood its ominous significance. The petrified troll, itself a last vestige of a lost and split identity, had faced its contrary power. For the Sheravalian rider of the White Feather had carried the message of the opening of the central channel and this message was an important step towards man's reconstructed identity. The possibility of redemption had expressed itself in the pure light, released by the opening of the casket. Thus, the servants of Thanatophor received a clear warning that the old powers of goodness were returning to protect the Gate of the Elephant and to overcome the evil of the Great Schism.

Although Lakshman, Lakshmi, Jonathan, and Tracy had their suspicions, they were unaware of the magnitude of this cosmic battlefield. They had not yet begun to understand the extent and ramifications of the master plan of Thanatophor, nor could they fathom the ways in which the Gods planned to help them. While Jonathan and Tracy, in Russia, were learning more about how human societies were making belated attempts to face such daunting challenges, in the aftermath of his adventure in Iceland Lakshman had yet to complete the reading of the third scroll of the White Feather. Protected by Avastha magic and following the warning of the Sheravalian messenger in charge of the casket, he had interrupted his telepathic reading to avoid being detected by the witches. Meanwhile, Lakshmi was studiously conducting her research into sacred Indian temples.

It was daybreak in Reykjavik. Lakshman slowly stirred, waking from a dream, but the sight of the platinum casket on his bedside chair reminded him of his strange adventure. What he'd thought was a dream was now reality. The frontier between the worlds of myth and certainty was blurred. He felt a bit anxious, not quite knowing where he stood in this confused landscape of consciousness that oscillated between legend and reality, past and future.

In any case, he had now fulfilled his mission in Iceland. So after another day's rest, which afforded him a full recovery from his arduous task under the glacier, Lakshman took the early-morning NordStar Airlines flight to Amsterdam.

Just as he was easing himself into his seat, a familiar voice greeted him from the adjacent seat, its face hidden behind a newspaper.

"It would seem that you like Habit Rouge de Guerlain?"

Lakshman wondered who was taking such an interest in his aftershave. An elderly gentleman was peering at him over the top of his newspaper. He noted an Audemars Piguet watch adorning the wrist of his fellow passenger, who was elegantly dressed in a suit of impeccably cut Scottish tweed. The man's eyes were shining with humor and warm intelligence; his smile was urbane.

"But, you are...

"Yes, I am." The beard was gone, the eyebrows trimmed, the inquisitive eyes were hidden behind tinted glasses, yet there could be no mistake. It was the furtive person who had first introduced himself as the heir of the wizard of Hllidarendi in Reykjavik.

Lakshman grumbled, "You have told me your title but not your name: who are you?"

"Call me Sanath," said the man pleasantly. Lakshman abandoned his newspaper and was happy to have run into the strange gentleman again. Lakshman spoke effusively but in a low voice, detailing his adventures. The retrieving of the casket was a spectacular enough story on its own, but opening it had been an experience almost beyond human imagination. Sanath listened intently, unable to disguise his satisfaction.

"Remarkable, remarkable... All this goes beyond my best expectations. You were well tuned to the message and without even knowing it; you spontaneously received the first initiation as soon as you opened the casket. Congratulations, Lakshman Kharadvansin, you are truly special! Indeed, you witnessed the last days of Dagad Trikon. Feeling the energy in the spine is not easy; you cannot take it for granted. Your past quest is now being rewarded. I am immensely relieved that you recovered the scrolls even though I sense you may well have exposed yourself to some of the servants of Thanatophor. However, we shall see about that later. But first, let me answer your question about my title, as you call it.

Some of the Aulyas that you saw in this vision could live for centuries if they so wished. One of them was Rasmus, the magus of the North. He converted some of the Axioms of the Deep Way, the Avastha secret knowledge, into mathematic formulae. He then went to the Western Islands where he settled in what was to become Ireland, and there gave initiation to a few disciples. The knowledge was thus transmitted through the generations until it reached a Celtic druid who codified it anew and later founded the order of the Hllidarendi. He was a great wizard who could read into the past and into the future. He knew that when the Romans, and later Christianity, penetrated the islands of Great Britain and Ireland, the last members of the Order would be persecuted and forced to go underground. I am the last member of the Order and I come at a time when the fight against evil reaches its culminating phase."

"Not many people believe evil exists as such. If I am to understand the context of all this I wish I could figure out what you mean. Can you be a bit more specific?" asked a bewildered Lakshman.

"Certainly. Darkness, too, has its history and I have spied on the nether worlds for a very long time to find out how it had unfolded through the Four Ages. Unfortunately I had not paid adequate notice to just how little human beings would be able to understand history or to learn its lessons. Let me talk a bit about the earlier ages.

Long before men started to record history, the Avasthas had fought alongside the Gods to repel the titans, for they had challenged the leader of the Gods, who was known later as Indra in India, Zeus in Greece, and Jupiter in Rome. Invariably, the leader of the gods is depicted brandishing a thunderbolt, symbolizing that he actually controls the earth's climate. This struggle continued unabated over many centuries, first in the Indian subcontinent and then across the area stretching from Egypt to Afghanistan. The purpose of overthrowing the leader of the Gods was to destabilize both climate and society so that the Darkness would prosper in the resulting chaos.

Initially, it was the titans, perceived also as azuras or demons, who were repelled. Consequently, their followers suffered. The ancient creatures serving Thanatophor became stuck in an evolutionary cul-de-sac as half-finished freaks on the margin of consciousness, such as, for instance, the Icelandic Conosaur troll, or they found themselves exiled in the realm of bacteria, viruses or even ghosts.

In the Fourth Age and closer to modern times, these powerful but evil creatures returned from hell, escaping through well-prepared routes. They reentered the cycles of death and reincarnation. Many of them now took their birth in human guise and in this form demonstrated their ancestral links to the dark dominion of the Evil One. These links can never be severed unless one receives the seventh order of initiation from the earlier-born themselves. But the Avasthas would not, of course, bestow such a lofty gift to corrupt or lowly beings. It is a vicious circle: once trapped in the Darkness's network, you are in a spider's web and the old witchery is at work. Let me go back to the commanders of the army of dread.

Four of the most powerful titans were suspected of remaining on Earth, each of them sometimes appearing in a malevolent physical form that was as conspicuous as their previously formidable antique forms. They were poised and ready to do the bidding of Thanatophor. I found out they are known as the four Titanosaurs, the highest dignitaries in the Dark Council of Belzebseth although they rarely attended the Council's sessions. The Titanosaurs are in charge of the four horizons, North, South, East, and West. Second only to the accursed kings Hangker and Belzebseth, these chief demonic operators patiently work their malice from the four cardinal points, helping each other and being helped too by the Dark Riders. The results of their murky work can be seen in modern times.

The West, weakened by lust, the East, swept by an emerging desire for power. In the North, acquisition, exploitation, and greed rules over all. In the South, anger, jealousy, and resentment are breeding. All these poisons are mixing together in a gigantic cauldron to increase each other's potency, and are meant to rot the human consciousness and breed hate between family members, tribes, and nations. The conflict raging around Jerusalem that so preoccupies your friend Jonathan is a central case in point.

Let me give you another example. Some time ago Hangker sent Gorshkak, the Northern Titanosaur, from America to Russia to set about the ruin of that great and proud land. He had to work on the Foul Rift, which, as the ancient Avasthas knew, is the breeding of systematic divisions, tensions, and conflicts, both among and within human beings.

Consider this. Economic conditions have been created to facilitate the widening of the Foul Rift as concocted by Thanatophor. In the North, developments in recent times have been more than helpful. Technology, allied to capital, has accelerated the generation and concentration of wealth. The greed that has ensued is excellent fodder for the Shadow's progress. The new wealth extracted from the work done by human beings thus primes the Stock Exchanges, rewarding wealthy gamblers and intermediaries. This wealth is not distributed equitably in these countries and leaves working men and women increasingly impoverished. Hence resentment grows, another positive point from Thanatophor's perspective. The scheme is replicable: money easily crosses borders to repeat elsewhere a process of wealth generation that will likewise prove cruelly unbalanced.

On the whole, you may say, the restructuring and re-engineering within business results in the firing of workers in pursuit of higher profits for shareholders. As a result, insecurity increases for all workers, and fear proves to be a perfect medium for the Shadow's progress. A simple question arises, my friend: to whom shall all the goods and services be sold when the masses of consumers have lost their purchasing power? Consumers buy less when they are insecure about their jobs. And so it is that, in the case of Russia too, the dastardly purpose of Gorshkak is for wealth to breed scarcity.

In these circumstances, the Foul Rift is able to mature, grow, and eventually tear apart the fabric of society. I discovered that was the basis of the plan Thanatophor has for modern times. Within the specter of rising poverty he foresaw the coming of increasing violence for men, more and more women forced to turn to prostitution, enslavement for all, and his own return to the light of day, slowly rising to triumph, feeding on the utter dejection of the human race. Indeed, he reckoned that without a fair spread of its distribution, wealth itself was bound to dry up and the virtual reality of the stock markets would go up in a puff of smoke, wiping out all the savings of the last stock owners in a final grand collapse."

"Some get poor, some get rich, isn't it the history of the world?" observed Lakshman somewhat sententiously. "Why mention Russia specifically?"

"For the Foul Rift to take root worldwide," continued the wizard in his patient and relaxed manner, "Darkness has to operate on many fronts. Conditions in modern Russia seemed propitious. Gorshkak wanted Russian capitalism to be a monster at birth. His strength lay in his colossal ability to cajole, influence, and corrupt others. Of course, his ability to enter into peoples' minds on a mass scale was greatly enhanced by the art of sorcery, an art in which each high dignitary in the council of Belzebseth was a master.

Let me try to explain the way in which Hangker and Belzebseth planned to combine their strengths. Belzebseth breaks into the psyche of human weakness through his malice and artifice, and Hangker can then more easily use them for his purposes. In exacerbating the human appetite for selfishness and egoism, he reconstructs their personality through their ego and spreads his legions of violence through them. Needless to say the riders of doom serve both of the evil overlords.

History has recorded this," added Sanath sadly, after a pause. "Under the command of those evil overlords, Gorshkak has received great praise from the Titanosaurs for his masterful handling of a Bohemian corporal named Adolf Hitler and a former Georgian seminarian, later known as Joseph Stalin. Through them, the Darkness has enjoyed some of its best moments in the twentieth century and the necromancers thus gained further insights into the modes of penetration of the human psyche."

At this point Lakshman recalled his telephone conversation with Jonathan. By aiming to rediscover the deepest foundations for the reunion of the human tribes, the Oikos Project was trying to create a counter-trend to the Foul Rift. Yet, the role played in the world of men by the legend of the Avasthas was not clear. He probed further, "Does anyone else know about the legacy of Dagad Trikon?"

"Yes, a few human beings did but they lost the trail in the Middle Ages because of the persecutions of the Church. As far as we are concerned, other forces want to gain control of the caskets and it was unfortunate that you were somewhat unwise in your choice of where you opened the first one. Let me try to explain these otherwise unbelievable Icelandic legends as well as I can.

At the end of Earlier Earth, many of the remaining trolls were banned to Iceland, far away in the midst of the Atlantic Ocean. In opening the box at that ill-fated spot, you managed to reawaken the troll who resided in petrified stone on that small peninsula from his millennial slumber. I don't know what he could do about it, but these Conosaur trolls from the old ages are a special variety. They accumulate the forces of inertia and brutish stupor that can throw people into a comatose condition and they have their own links with the Darkness. The trolls can emit some kind of primeval shouts in coded frequencies, which travel through the earth. Creatures of magic recognize magic: I fear those who heard the warning from the peninsula troll may have realized that the first lines of the Dagad Trikon prophecy have now been deciphered on Icelandic soil."

"How do you know all that?"

"I know what I know but obviously, I don't know what I don't know, which is what worries me. I don't know what the Darkness knows, but if one raven was following you in the uplands, where they do not fly willingly, it means that they know that you were onto something."

"You know, Sanath, I have other things on my mind than walking into transcontinental riddles, volcanic eruptions, and trolls. Let me just exit from this mad story. Perhaps I'll just dump these weapons in an antique shop or into a lake, and forget all about it."

"There is no going back, my friend. If you stick with me, you may possibly come out of this with your life and a great deal more. If you don't, losing your life is not the worst thing that might happen to you."

The small plane was purring quietly, the business class cabin almost empty. Through the window Lakshman could now see below the rolling Scottish highlands through a green and blue haze. He turned towards Sanath. "I'm afraid you have some serious explaining to do now, otherwise count me out," he said nervously.

"'*The Knower*' is the one who knows that his own life is none of his damned business, said one of my friends, a distinguished British psychiatrist," replied Sanath somewhat wryly. "All right, each thing in its own good time. What I may tell you now is this: no human being before you and your cousin ever reached beyond the Kaal Ben Muzur oasis or knew about the location of the Dagad Trikon mountain system. Much of the Rock sank into the earth and you visited whatever remained above the surface. However, the high priests of the Rock left in place a stealth system that hid it from satellites, radars or other forms of geographic information systems. The same devices tampered with the flight systems of airplanes, and even no caravan could pass nearby. Those who came too close were either driven away or perished in sandstorms. You alone broke through the cloaking system, and for a good reason, which has more than something to do with you personally. The scroll would have revealed even more if you had been able to stay silent and focused.

When you set foot in what remains of the central canyon that was once the Gundaldhar Fault, you walked into something really big, something of potential importance for all of mankind... something waiting to happen. Finding the Sadhan and the Glorfakir was only the beginning. If you join me, the challenge will be hard to meet. If you don't, your life will become impossible. I was able to follow you during most of your journey to the Vatnajoekull glacier as I have more than a few camouflage tricks up my sleeve. Actually, it was me who dispensed with the raven at the Walaha Inn but even as I killed it, I saw another one flying in the direction of the cliff at Reykholar, which is the center of their spy network. This does not bode well. When the spy ravens of Reykholar fly in patrol, it indicates a prepared mission, which means serious business is afoot."

"Why have a network of spies on this rather remote island?"

"The Darkness is present in Iceland because of the intense volcanic activity that it wants to harness. Besides, they know of the drakkar, which brought the Norwegian navigators and the platinum box. The problem for Belzebseth is that the casket would self-destroy if touched by a devil and, in any case, he could never break the code of the Avasthas. Remember, stealth is the very genius of the people of the Rock. Belzebseth needed someone to find the box for him."

"How do I know that I can trust you? You... you've already used me once as bait! Or have they?"

"No, not quite. The time has come for the prophecy to be revealed. From the description of your visions, I think you discovered the box carried by a holy virgin, the Sheravalian rider with the White Feather. This is extremely fortunate for it talks about the central channel of our evolution."

"What is the meaning of the feather?"

"The feather indicates how to win in the game of life. We must learn to play with the wind like a feather. The art is to be carried like a feather, to let the breeze guide us within the perfect rhythms of the Rasa music, the perfect cosmic timing. It is the art of catching the waves, and this is why I sometimes call this 'surrender surfing.' A surfer uses the force of the wave. It takes a lot of practice, though.

Imagine a similar process to tap your inner powers: it implies action within inaction. When you access your inner powers you make things happen without moving a finger. It also implies inaction within action: while you are in full swing, you are perfectly tranquil and relaxed inside. That knowledge would be useful to the modern man for it means achievement without stress. Surfing on the waves of existence is quite an art, brought to perfection by the Deep Way."

"Right now, whilst I understand your words, I don't get their meaning so please would you explain it again one more time? If there is so much magic around the box, how was I able to open it so easily?"

"For the same reason you could access the Alwakil fields." Sanath waved the question away with a gesture of his hand. He seemed to be enjoying himself and to welcome the opportunity to explain. "I trust the Iceland casket is still with you? The remaining scroll should answer your question when you complete reading it through telepathic deciphering. When you reach this stage, don't react – try to just see instead. Try to be a witness to your own story and listen, even if it hurts. You may see five oranges. These are symbolic of the five senses but the casket may tell you more about it."

"Meanwhile, what about the content of the caskets, please?"

"Yes, let's get back to the subject. We have now retrieved the first of the ten caskets. We know of the location of two more but we have no clues as to the identities of the Stealthstars. The children need the weapons but their names were not contained within the first box. The problem, as I see it, is rather daunting: the cloaking tricks of the Rock Avasthas have turned against them. The Stealthstars probably do not know any longer who they themselves are. I am beginning to fear that, having become human, they are hardly in touch with their true selves and are consequently falling into human illusions."

"So what happens now? Please, Sanath, I don't understand this business about the Darkness, this old mythological stuff. Can you tell me how it works today?"

"The Darkness works well today because it has adorned itself with bright colors. Hence, no one recognizes it for what it truly is.

No one really knows where it is either but you have seen enough already, in deciphering the scroll, to get an idea about the genealogy of evil."

Sanath paused for a moment as the cabin attendant served refreshments. When she moved on the wizard continued in a low voice.

"Thanatophor, while keeping a separate identity, basically divided himself in two: Belzebseth haunts the blue zone and Hangker the yellow zone. These are the two provinces of the psyche, covering emotions and thoughts as you discovered from the scrolls in the casket. From these areas Thanatophor wants to invade the white corridor, the central channel of human evolution. He thinks that if he succeeds, it will be he and not the human race that will inherit the earth, the opposite of what was foreseen in the Grand Scheme of Adivatar. Together the two demon kings have created major devils, the Titanosaurs, who also incarnate on the Earth to create mischief but the most constant enemies of the human race under Thanatophor's command are the six Dark Riders. They are called riders precisely because they are constantly on the move: they ride our thoughts and emotions and they are timeless because they are never really defeated. In the period of human history known as the Middle Ages, they were defined by the poisons they spilled and we have never since given them better names than Lust, Anger, Greed, Attachment, Jealousy, and Vanity. They breed many ramifications, of course, and work in subtle permutations and combinations."

"These seem to me the fairly normal traits of the human psyche," said Lakshman, rather bemused.

"Perhaps you are right, in the sense that these seeds, emitted from the blue or the yellow zones, are easily planted in the minds of ordinary humans. They correspond to the accepted conditions of the mind when the dosage is minimal. However, we cross into the danger zone when we lose track because it is in excess that these become lethal. The Riders of Darkness become effective Deadly Sins when the seeds germinate and produce addictive or compulsive behaviors. Even the higher races feared the workings of the Dark Riders. To prevent such dangers, the Avasthas had organized themselves into six clans that were meant to block them. To do so, these lordly houses of the Avastha age were the custodians of positive, divine principles. I shall name them because this will explain the ongoing battlefield to you.

"The great House of Kalabham cultivates purity of mind and deed in order to keep the freshness of wisdom, maintain the sparkling of spontaneity, and preserve the gentle art of loving. With this bubbling of innocence, they could counter the addiction to Lust. The field of Kalabam is to master access to the present moment.

Falkiliad activates the storehouse of divine inspiration and creativity and channels it towards art or scientific thinking; it brings to a constructive purpose the energy from the yellow zone that could otherwise be available to Hangker to feed the horse of Anger. The function of the field of Falkiliad is to master the rules of action.

Elnur maintains a peaceful balance, generating harmony within and without, in the mind and in the society, securing an equitable and prosperous environment for the community to deny Greed the chance to launch its sneaky attacks. The Elnorians are dedicated to honor, fairness, and justice. The purpose of the field of Elnur is to master the rules of evolution.

Eleksim, helped by Kalabham, is devoted to bringing inner security, confidence, and trust so that love is possible without bondage. Hence, the cravings and dependencies linked to Attachment are unable to turn love into a matrix of sorrows. Teachers of the House of Eleksim impart what you today would call 'emotional intelligence,' a critical component of the knowledge of the Deep Way. The purpose of the field of this house is to master the rules of the emotions.

Anor is devoted to solidarity and to the art of sharing in order to build the togetherness of families, clans, and tribes. This oneness blocks the path of Jealousy, which is always looking for an opportunity to divide and strike. The Anorians bring the cement, the binding together of any successful and happy community. They prepare conditions for a deeper collective consciousness that can imbibe messages from the Gods. The purpose of the Anorian field is to master the rules of manifestation.

Last but not least, under the white banner of the House of Anorhad, the Avasthas pursue the truth with great strength of purpose and faith, yet in meekness and humility. The noble Anorhadans dedicate themselves to accessing the true identity, which makes Vanity or Pride superfluous. The Anorhadan masters penetrate deeply into the glory of the innermost reality. The purpose of their field is the mastery over transformation.

All the houses put together are the collective stewards of Avastha culture, each helping the other. For the duration of the Golden Age, they managed to keep the Dark Riders in check. If someone in those times found himself under the approaching shadow of one of the Riders, he would discover the nature of the foe through the fine art of introspection and would immediately correct the defect."

Lakshman scratched his chin to hide his embarrassment. He responded hesitatingly, "Well, Sanath, I think I now understand what you mean, but frankly all this sounds terribly old-fashioned. You see, today lust is okay, even cool; aggressiveness, as a derivative of anger, is taken as an asset if you are in the field of finance or business; Wall Street says greed is good and love is a bind; jealousy is a fact of life and vanity drives the fashion and advertising industries. I simply don't know what you want us to do about it."

Sanath sighed. "Thanks for the reality check," he said, "I am aware that on the face of it you are right. We touch on an important point here. Camouflage is the great art of the Devil. In the gentle days of the Avasthas, evil was ugly and goodness was beautiful. It was therefore hard for the Devil to seduce. What was once revealed through ugliness now looks pretty and seductive on the outside. Verily, only the discovery of the beauty and the bliss of the inner Self can help man today. This is what the return to the knowledge of the Deep Way can really bring."

"Sorry, Master, but this is the way we run our lives today: with sex and shouts, winners and losers, much egoism and little morality. I don't see much Darkness in all this; this is just the way people are and have always been. Somehow, as before, we will continue to manage our competing needs, our shortcomings, and our differences; frankly I don't see the problem."

"Our kinsmen in this age of modernity have lost the connection to their true Selves. Small, indeed, has become their capacity for love. When the hearts do not store up love, they are empty and the Darkness knows how to fill that emptiness with selfish whims and petty desires. It is not easy to infuse gaiety back into them. They will sway easily between good and evil."

"Okay, we are not perfect. What does it matter?"

"Look, I am trying to explain the consequences of what the Avasthas were calling the Great Schism, the divorce between the outside and the inside worlds. Again, let me repeat: outside everything looks fine; inside, things are rotting. In the ancient age, Belzebseth had not yet achieved the famed status of Prince of Seducers. Righteous men and women looked beautiful. Beauty within was reflected externally, on their faces and on their bodies. Goodness was attractive and graceful. Sly or cruel people looked ugly because their inside was revealed in their physical appearance. Crooks looked crooked. The advantage was that the Shadow could not penetrate much into the human brain because those under its sway were not terribly seductive. As you aptly point out, in modern times this has completely changed: confusion replaces clarity. Today, an evil man may look amiable; a witch can look very sexy, as you say in this world."

"Sanath?"

"Yes?"

"I know that you are not quite a man of this world but, pardon me if I say so, but it shows. You are not going to get anybody much worked up in fighting what the Church used to call the Seven Deadly Sins. Today, no one bothers about them. Talking about sins is out; committing them is in. Nobody will see the point of going to war about it; I'm not sure I do."

"In a sense, I agree with you. The Church made a mockery out of the notion of sin: it wanted to scare the sinners with notions of eternal damnation in order to exercise control over the flock. So Catholics, for example, would buy indulgences from the Pope, a source of afterlife insurance, to avoid getting into hell or to shorten the waiting period in purgatory. Martin Luther attempted to put the Church out of this business but still today, for the Catholic Church, sinning and confessing and then happily sinning again until the next confession means 'business as usual.' Yet, if making mistakes is not deadly, it is not helpful either. No sin is deadly for the compassion of the divine is greater than any sin, but a sin is harmful because it offends love and produces evil consequences. On top of this, sin weakens the immune system of the subtle body.

Moreover, Lakshman Kharadvansin, this is no ordinary fight but a battle between demons and men, or at least those amongst men who want to remain free. Men and women of good will must now build complete solidarity. You must understand the magnitude of the danger confronting the human race. Adivatar has created man through the process of evolution so that he may enjoy the fullness of being and love. To experience knowledge and love is such an overwhelmingly beautiful feeling that, when men and women really get there, they will understand. But it is to counter this possibility that

Thanatophor is using the power of hatred. Hate is a very dangerous weapon and the sport of Hangker is to use it.

Christians are supposed to follow Lord Jesus Christ but Catholics and Protestants killed each other for centuries and still do, for example, in places like Northern Ireland. Look at the Middle East: Mohammed brought the message that God is compassionate, merciful, and peace-giving, but the Wahabis teach cruelty in their madrasas. They teach how to hate infidels and to despise women. From Kashmir to Algeria, they kill. And so it goes on in this monotonous story of hate.

Look at history: the French invaded German territories under Louis XIV and then again under Napoleon. The Germans then turned nasty and consequently initiated two world wars. The Third Reich invaded the Soviet Union who in turn kept half of Europe prisoner for five decades. The Germans also persecuted the Jews. In turn, the Jews mistreat the Palestinians and thus the oppressed invented a new form of aggression through terrorism."

"It is horrible, I know, but what has this to do with the Seven Deadly Sins?"

"Everything. The Dark Riders of doom help this hate to inflate within the brain in so many ways. Yet hate can be extinguished when the principles of the great houses are upheld."

Sanath spent the rest of the flight to Schiphol Airport casting light on the ways of the Darkness, explaining to Lakshman how to recognize the traces of the Shadow.

He paraphrased himself. "The code word for Evil's master plan is 'disintegration' – disintegration of societies, of families, and, most importantly, of the individual psyche itself. Ultimately the victim of Thanatophor may fall into the pits of dread. Hell exists, you know. To achieve his dominion over the human race, Thanatophor has had to promote this disintegration of man, to widen the gap between thought and feeling, heart and mind, fact and belief. His task was and is to precipitate swings between action and reaction, to heighten tensions between husband and wife, to crystallize the split in society, breed fanaticism, and raise the fundamentalist flag of hate between faiths. All these widening gaps together form the Foul Rift: modern man with a split consciousness, easy to haunt and to possess. Part of the battleground is outside us, part is within but the battle is now nearing its climax," said Sanath in conclusion.

"This makes me think of the telephone call I just made to my friend Jonathan," said Lakshman. He told Sanath about the feedback he had received on the Oikos Project and its attempt to build new foundations for the integration of the international community.

"Of course, I wish them well, but I fear this is too little, too late," said the wizard, "if the Oikos Project looks like it will succeed, it will be stopped or sidetracked because the Shadow has infiltrated the upper echelons of power in so many of its member countries. No, we certainly need to find another solution."

THE AMSTERDAM VISION

As the plane was about to land in Amsterdam, a blonde stewardess in a tiny mini-skirt whispered in Sanath's ear, "Mr. van Jetzlar, your limousine will be at the foot of the staircase as usual."

"Thanks, my dear, and please convey my compliments to the captain," Sanath said, and the young woman retreated to the flight cabin. Sanath grumbled in Lakshman's ear, "I do not much fancy the way she dresses." He then sensed Lakshman's astonishment and graciously explained, "You see, Baldur van Jetzlar is a Dutch executive who is developing a multi-million dollar mineral water business with pure spring water from Icelandic glaciers. I find that an identity with money is quite helpful in their kind of world – as a cover, that is. However, it was a pleasure chatting with you. Here is my card – please call me tomorrow. We shall meet again. By the way, I do not like or trust that stewardess one little bit; I have a most disturbing feeling about her."

The plane landed and Baldur van Jetzlar disappeared into the dark green Bentley that was waiting at the gate. Lakshman entered Terminal F of Schipol Airport. Ten yards behind him the NordStar flight attendant progressed as hastily as her mini-skirt permitted. She was whispering into the walkie-talkie hidden in her watch. "I confirm contact, confirm contact with Jetzlar. What should we do next?"

In the central terminal of the airport a huge LCD screen flashed a message. "Ha ha ha, hee hee hee... " Lakshman stood below it, wondering what invisible power was laughing at him. He checked in, receiving his boarding card for the flight to Geneva where he had further business to conduct. While checking his appearance in the window of the duty-free delicatessen shop he noticed the reflection of the blonde stewardess who thought she was concealed behind a pillar. He did not mind the long legs as much as Sanath did, but he hated being followed so he decided to test Sanath's warnings. She saw him checking in at Gate 46 and then disappeared. Shortly before the aircraft doors were closed for takeoff, Lakshman complained of acute chest pains and he was promptly escorted off the plane with his luggage.

He checked into one of those cute little hotels that overlooked the old canal near the train station. He was fond of old Dutch cities built on the banks of the canals, which reflect the procession of clouds high above in the sky. After a good night's sleep, sitting up in bed reading his newspaper he enjoyed a breakfast of orange juice, bacon, and two fried eggs sunny side up. With the radio playing Mozart's Turkish March, he felt ready to take on the world anew. He turned on the television.

The first news item was shocking. The flight he had been meant to take had crashed into the Black Forest en route for Geneva. The smoking remains of the Boeing 737 covered five square kilometers. Lakshman was profoundly shattered as he listened to the details of the plane crash. The threat was now direct, lethal, and personal.

"I'd better call Sanath; he could be in trouble, too," he thought. "That nice wizard seems to know a lot, after all. Let me see what he has to say. In any case, I must change my plans." He called Lakshmi in Rome to warn her of the need for extreme caution. A little later, Jonathan returned his call from Cairo. He shared his friend's concerns and revealed his own bad news. Tracy had reported that a few countries, led by France, had decided to withdraw completely from the Oikos Project. They decided to meet next week in Rome to assess the situation. He finally called Sanath on the cell phone number shown on Baldur van Jetzlar's business card. Sanath answered the phone immediately but did not want to speak. He knew about the accident and, two hours later, he was in Lakshman's room.

"Yes, I know, it is most upsetting. That airhostess, Gulda, must be working for them. I should have taken you to Geneva in my private jet. I will change identity soon because they have definitely recognized me. I have been Baldur van Jetzlar for over twenty years now, and the time has come to part company with him. Do not worry about me – I have already taken precautions, but in your case, don't fly to Switzerland; it's too risky. They may have found out already your business connections there. The Darkness usually works from behind; if they came forward in this brutal manner, it means they know about your find in Iceland."

"Is there any place the negativity cannot find?"

"There is, yes, how shall I put it? Do you know the painting by Johannes Vermeer, the girl with the pearl earring?"

"Well, of course," replied Lakshman, somewhat surprised. "It's a famous Dutch masterpiece but I've never seen the painting itself."

"Come visit me in The Hague, I will take you to the Mauritzhuis museum, for the painting delivers the secret answer to your question."

"Please, for God's sake, stop speaking in riddles."

"It is for God's sake that I speak in riddles. Remember the painting? The girl turns her head. She casts a sideways glance with her mouth half-opened. The pearl shines in the sun. In a split second, Vermeer was able to catch the beauty that reveals itself when we can enter into the essence of the present moment. But who can stay in the present moment? Few can escape the train of their thoughts, ceaselessly moving between past and future. Here, between two thoughts, there is an entry point into the present that the Shadow cannot find. The Global Positioning System of Thanatophor cannot find you if you can switch off the beep signals of your thought processes."

Lakshman was startled by this surprising answer. "But I can't do that! This is terrifying. How can they follow me through my thoughts?"

"That was the danger, in deciphering the contents of the casket. Exposure! A risk you had to take. Remember you saw the witch and a demon? You moved too far into the blue or the yellow spectrums, away from the whiteness in the center. When you moved too far to the extremes, you revealed yourself to them: they saw you. And when they see, they enter. This is what happened to Esitel, thousands of years ago. But the spell cast through the ophtalir was much more powerful."

"But what should I do now?"

"Nothing, I am the last Hllidarendi, carrier of the Deep Way. I will protect you now."

Sanath took a small box and a lemon from the pocket of his cloak. He opened the box and put into it some of the red powder stored within a ring worn on his right ring finger. He made a red mark on the lemon. Then, taking the lemon in his right hand, he drew parabolic movements around Lakshman while muttering what appeared to Lakshman to be mantras. He even thought he heard what sounded like Sanskrit in the incantation. Lakshman relaxed instantly but felt a pain in the back of his head. Gradually the pain changed to a feeling of pressure and then this sensation slowly ebbed. Suddenly, he felt much lighter. The wizard seemed pleased with himself and said, "Now you'll be all right. No one can pierce the bandhan of old Sanath."

"Bandhan?"

"Ahem, yes, I forget you don't know these things. It is a defensive aura the Avastha who received training in the Deep Way can project around somebody they wish to protect. To place this invisible security shield, they harness the powers of subtle vibrations in the universe. Tell me, do you still have the casket? We had better experience the final scroll together."

The two men sat cross-legged on the carpet, close to each other. Lakshman felt much lighter after the bandhan of Sanath. Having completely forgotten his fears, he removed the casket from his luggage with great care and opened the lid. As the white glow from the remaining scroll filled the room the two men closed their eyes. Lakshman felt a sense of excitement and vibrant curiosity. There was no way to apply spin or damage control if something went wrong on this weird journey, yet the fascination of new territories to visit was overwhelming.

In the beginning he was just aware of the sounds of cars passing in front of the hotel. Then he entered a state of inner silence and complete relaxation.

He could just see himself in the central channel. Its dazzling whiteness faded and waves of light emanated from the front of his head. Their fluid shapes gained in sharpness as they enveloped him, until they formed distinct images. He was in a palace of white marble with richly ornate columns, in the manner of the Mount Abu temples he had once visited. In this moment Lakshman realized that he was himself contained within the message. This revelation was so unexpected that he felt a knot in his stomach, which transformed into a diffuse pain in his chest. The distance between him and the strange objects of his vision had disappeared. He found himself reacting emotionally to the unfolding of the telepathic message because, strangely, it was now telling him his own story, a story that came to him as remembrance of his past with each image that unfolded.

He saw himself standing in a majestic temple of white marble. The hall was filled with a noble gathering of princes and princesses, all wearing golden crowns. He had the sense that this palace was an important place, the hub of a golden universe, a congregation where important decisions were made, and a place where wishes came true. There was a huge live tortoise in front of the steps of a high throne, her carapace inlaid with dazzling rubies, sapphires, emeralds, and diamonds. As she lazily moved in circles, her jewels caught the rays of the sun that flowed through the side windows in multi-colored sparkles.

A court herald proclaimed somewhat mysteriously, "Behold the great tortoise, the symbol of what is yet to be achieved." The courtiers seemed to understand, but Lakshman was puzzled. Then the herald announced the entrance of a visitor, "The high lord Aslerach Nizam of Dagad Trikon." A tall knight entered, bearing his helmet under his right arm, and marched straight to the throne on the northern side of the great hall. Lakshman was overcome with the confusing feeling that he had seen or known him before. Though he was of proud and noble bearing, Aslerach of Anor bowed with great humility, before she who sat on the throne, a queen flanked by a tiger on the left and a lion on the right. Aslerach's words of greeting resounded in a clear and melodious voice,

"Immaculate Queen, may I greet you with the words of Shankaracharya, foremost amongst the Aulyas. Whatever action is mine may be taken as intended for Thy worship, my prattle as muttering Thy prayers; the manifold forms of my manual labor as the gestures employed in Thy worship; my loitering as going round Thee clockwise; my taking nourishment as offering oblation to Thee; my lying down as prostrating before Thee; and my attending to all other comforts as dedicating my entire self to Thee."

Lakshman's attention moved from the Nizam and was finally captured by the central figure on the throne. Her dress was white with a red and gold border. Her hair was black. Her eyes smiled. The entire court was visibly in awe of her. Courtiers, ambassadors, and generals surrounded her with deep reverence. She looked like the High Lady of the Rock he had seen in the first part of the scroll, but she was not as young as her. Yet her beauty was dazzling, so much so that Lakshman looked away from her. This brought him to a realization of his own position in the durbar, the royal court.

He was the jester. For months he had been training at home to perform simple juggling tricks with five oranges. He could remember his heartfelt desire to please the high queen as he trained. He could manage the tricks at home but whenever he thought he was ready, whenever he went to the durbar to entertain the queen, he became gauche and clumsy. Alas, this time too, when his time came to perform, he tripped over his own feet and the oranges fell to the ground. Lakshman experienced the shame, the perspiration, and the burning cheeks even as he sat in the hotel room. He was a failure, overwhelmed by a feeling of guilt and worthlessness.

Aslerach looked at him with sympathy but did not move. Some court dignitaries, fed up with his ineptitude, wanted him thrown out. He stood before the throne in abject embarrassment but the queen smiled at him with compassion and said encouragingly, "Let him try again, another time; he must have faith." An old minister, to the left of the steps leading to the throne, walked towards him and touched him gently on the left shoulder. "Come, child, you must go now."

Lakshman abruptly closed the lid of the casket. He was back in Amsterdam, in his hotel room, but still inhabited by the feelings of desolation, helplessness, and failure. He was almost in tears because his sense of personal failure was overwhelming. He could not understand how this ancient foreign object could expose something so close to him, so private. He opened his eyes. The minister was looking at him with sympathy. It was Sanath. Yes, Sanath was the minister who had touched his shoulder at the durbar.

They remained silent for a long while. Then Sanath spoke softly. "I was not quite sure how that scroll was supposed to work, but obviously its message interacts with the content of our own psyches. As far as I understand it, this is why you were given access to the Dagad Trikon scrolls. For eons you never managed to juggle those five oranges. Yet your desire to please the queen was so sincere that she maintained access. It is your sincerity that brought you to the Rock; it is your sincerity that delivered the casket to you. Now we must count on you."

"What is all this witchcraft, what is the meaning of this psychedelic movie?" Lakshman sounded angry. "What is the link between juggling with oranges and finding the scrolls?"

"More powerful and intimate than you might think, but I shall tell you another time and explain too the significance of the tortoise. However, I shall tell it with someone else's voice. Juggling with these oranges is at the core of the praxis of the Deep Way, my good friend. Don't see it as a trivial or futile exercise. For now, let us finish the reading of these scrolls."

They opened the magic casket again. Silence again settled within Lakshman's head, behind his closed eyes. First he saw the room in which he sat, then the vista around the hotel, the canal network of Amsterdam, then the outer environs of the city of Amsterdam, and eventually the trading waterways that criss-crossed the whole country and linked Holland to the sea. Now he was on the beach before the Kursaal Hotel in Scheveningen, near The Hague, facing the gray-blue sea. Crowds of people, some playing, some exercising, some walking or arguing in scattered groups, animated the vast beach. He suddenly realized the subtle nature of the nether lands, linked as they are through innumerable channels to the water principle and to the ocean. The ocean, lying higher than the land, was both its teacher and its master. One channel in the far distance rose through dark clouds from the ocean towards the sky.

Water was the bearer of justice; it could generate wealth or bring punishment. Lakshman saw a succession of talking images: the genesis of wealth manifested in a lovely apparition. A feminine, Venus-like silhouette emerged from the sea, delicately balanced on a marine shell. She slowly transformed into a princess richly adorned in pink silk, escorted by two elephants and nonchalantly holding the cornucopia of plenty. Gold coins fell   from her outstretched hands. Then, the image transformed again: the elephants disappeared into the background, the Goddess seemed to grow larger and her hair, now matted in a Chinese style, seemed to touch the clouds of the heavens. The tune of the waves was repeating rhythmically: Kuan Yuin, Kuan Yuin, and Kuan Yuin... As Lakshman stared in awe at the mighty vision of the Chinese Goddess of good fortune, she slowly diminished in size until she disappeared altogether.

In her stead, Lakshman saw the genesis of justice: a gigantic pair of scales had risen above the water. At first it looked as though it was supporting the moon on the left scale and the sun in the right scale. Then tiny black human silhouettes appeared; the scales began to oscillate according to the behavior of the people who walked on them. On the axis of the pair of scales, at equal distance from the two poles, the vertical channel he had dimly perceived a while ago had transformed into a shining white staircase. It led towards the heavens, far away, beyond the swelling, roiling clouds, mysterious yet inviting. One could glimpse living shapes and beings dwelling there in an aura of liquid blessedness. They did not seem remote or aloof but an embellished version of the crowds on the beach.

Equity was the ruling principle of the scales and the movement of distribution and the sharing of wealth held the scales in balance. Lakshman observed that the width of the staircase would open only when the left and right scales were perfectly balanced. When the width was enlarged, Lakshman felt a breeze flow down the staircase. This cool wind was bringing hope: the stairs were a way to exit from the agitation and contradictions of the crowd on the beach. The stairs symbolized the optimal future of humanity: upwards, ascending was its destiny.

As he realized this, the white stairs began to float in the air and to rotate on themselves in an ample movement, forming a huge ascending spiral, akin to a drawing by William Blake that Lakshman had once seen in London. They disappeared in a dim light, shining now from behind the foam of a cloudy sky, which seemed as liquid as that in the sea, for the sky itself now seemed to be as a second sea.

Beings, clad in white, angels or Avasthas, began descending the spiraling staircase. They were men and women, and the nobility of their bearing evoked the sight of the dwellers of Dagad Trikon as revealed in the first part of the scroll. They carried liturgical objects, perhaps the caskets themselves. Among them, he saw youngsters, boys and girls, hurrying, calling to each other to speed up their descent; Lakshman saw this as symbolically expressing the coming of the Stealthstars. But then the vision changed again.

The scroll now projected a vision of modern times. Enterprising men and women, uniformly thin and dressed in gray or black, talked incessantly into cell phones as they walked hurriedly by, gradually destabilizing the balance of the scales. With a growing acuity, Lakshman realized how modern societies, propelled by competitive greed, deny justice to their people and how, without justice, the staircase of man's higher evolution closes, out of reach for the guilty and the innocent alike. Automatically, the central staircase narrowed until it became invisible and the path of the descending Avasthas was blocked.

The last image was of Sanath, the Hllidarendi, and a majestic but almost desperate elder, standing between two swans on the ocean. He was trying to exhort the crowd on the beach before the Kursaal, unsuccessfully attempting to teach them how to open the staircase. He was shouting, trying to explain how dangerous it would be if the human race became stuck in an evolutionary cul-de-sac, or worse, regressed into barbarism. He was telling them that discretion had to take them in the right direction; that only discretion could control the mechanism of the scale and the staircases. But the ocean drowned his voice and would not allow him to be heard. As each crash of a wave deposited shells and gems on the shore, people were madly jostling each other to collect the wealth pouring out of the sea: pearls, precious stones, and rare jewels. In this agitation, the crowd on the beach completely ignored the lone wizard.

"Perhaps they no longer deserve to hear," thought Lakshman as the vision of Sanath's sadness faded away. That was the end of the scroll whose last images dissolved into the foaming waves of the ocean: only a deliciously scented dust remained in the empty box.

Still struggling with the harrowing emotions unleashed by his identification with the jester, Lakshman did not notice that it was his companion's turn to be troubled by the last message of the scroll. The wizard looked utterly despondent and was shaking his head sadly.

"The Order of the Hllidarendis sent me to show them the way. Sooner or later, the disappearance of the staircase means doom for humanity. To carry this knowledge without being able to share it – what a fate! Their fate does not allow them to hear any more. What you saw in this scroll is that the power of Adivatar has changed the sea into the Ocean of Illusion. Thus, I spoke in vain for so many years, I cannot help men, and they cannot hear me. The sea is rising, how can I protect them?

Yes, it was like that, for so many lifetimes, all this knowledge and guidance that I had in store for them. Oh, how much I wanted to give! What wonderful gifts I had for them! But I could not force it on them. They would not take it and I could not break through their ignorance. At times I thought I would suffocate with all those secrets I was meant to reveal and couldn't. I cannot give if they are not willing to receive. This has been my torture. I am a teacher of a precious lore, wandering in loneliness. These people have no intuition left, they lack common sense, and they are incapable of introspection. Merlin was right to give up. Today, Lakshman, both of us have touched our innermost pain."

They closed the lid softly and looked at each other. The wallpaper in the cozy hotel room was blue and for a while they still felt immersed in a palpitating ocean. The intensity of the shared vision had brought the older and the younger man closer together. Now, for the first time, they felt they understood each other. Despite being different from each other in so many ways, the two men had shared a genuine sense of loss as the scroll unfolded. The Amsterdam visions somehow told about the failure of man, about the failure of the individual seeker to reach inner balance, and the failure of human society at large to achieve a collective stability. The consequence of failure was the impossibility of moving on into the next phase of evolution. Modern man had apparently conquered his environment but did not know what to do with his newfound freedom. Civilization, unable to move forward, would inevitably regress.

Lakshman finally spoke. "Isn't it strange? The part I read in Iceland was more about the Avasthas. What we saw here seems to be about us. What do you make of that?"

"I guess the content of the scroll is not static," replied Sanath. "It must be reacting to people and places. In Iceland, where magic is strong, it speaks about the Avasthas. Here, where matter is strong, it speaks about material man. The Rock Avasthas wanted to help men to grow beyond matter, otherwise Thanatophor would surely ensnare them. But it was never to be an easy task.

Philosophers have known all this in theory, but unfortunately not in practice. Theory is but scaffolding around the brain, it supports the construct and shape of rational ideas. Mankind has enjoyed ideas in an aesthetic sort of way. Thoughts are like a photograph of a real thing but not the real thing itself. Knowledge in the brain is only seen. Knowledge in the heart is truly gained. It takes wisdom to love with the brain and know with the heart. Only then we may grasp the real thing itself. There is an invisible limit between the finite and the infinite. And there is an invisible door through which that limit may be crossed. 'It is the Gate of the Elephant,' said the blessed ruler of the Gundaldhar Fault. But it is not easy to find it."

"Not if juggling with oranges has anything to do with it. I feel a failure, really, this was the message of the scroll."

"No, it wasn't. Discover your mistakes, your weaknesses, then rectify them. Learning to see oneself is the first step in the knowledge of the Deep Way."

Lakshman felt sorry for the older man who seemed, in a world of fools, to be isolated from other beings by the deep well of his wisdom. He went on, "Tell me, Sanath, did you ever before meet someone who believed you and your message?"

"Rationality fossilizes living knowledge. This is why William Blake hated rationalists. He too belonged to the order of the Hllidarendi. He, too, tried to tell them, through poetry and drawings. It's all right," said Sanath, casting a glance over his shoulder as he was leaving the room. "He was a good friend of mine. I still have a few left; they are precious to me and I should be happy to share them with you. You will meet them soon, but we must part now." And with a sad farewell smile, Sanath, alias Baldur van Jetzlar, took his leave.

Lakshman was exhausted. He had seen much through Avastha magic, but this time it was a bit like taking a drug: you may fly high but when you land it feels like a bumpy crash landing and you are back to square one. Having visions could not be the solution. Also, he missed Lakshmi and her insights. Maybe she would know where to pick the thread towards the exit of the labyrinth. Little did he know that, very soon, he would have to call her with terrible news.

THE TALE
OF COUNT PHILIP

L akshmi Vani was a woman of versatile interests. She was a
successful jewelry designer who was well known among the
Mumbai jet set for her style and elegance. A trained biologist,
she also worked as a consultant to various international organiza-
tions. She now found these activities to be a safe cover for pursuing
her main interest, which was to help her cousin in the quest of Dagad
Trikon. For now, she was coordinating the Plenary Committee of
a large conference in Rome on the impact of climate change on food
security.

It had been a hot, sticky, and busy day at the Headquarters of
the Food and Agriculture Organization. Its Mussolinian halls still
exuded some faint whiffs of nostalgia from Fascism's marmoreal
dreams. She was happy that the day was over. The pleasant evening
found her sipping a fruit juice at a cocktail party on the terrace of
the Spanish embassy overlooking the Eternal City. Rome was glittering in the pink and yellow shades of an approaching dusk, its many
domes and turrets softening in the soft September warmth. The
terrace was buzzing with small talk. Nimble waiters in white gloves
served alcohol and mini-pizzas, tapas, and canapés. In a corner of the
empty grand salon, Mansour al Bemoth, a Sudanese desert chieftain
with a notably quick temper, was kneeling in prayer towards Mecca
beneath a portrait of the late Austrian emperor, Franz Joseph.

Lakshmi was briefly distracted by the confusion of imagery within such an unexpected scene but her mind soon retuned to her private worries. Two days after the crash of the flight he was supposed to have been on, Lakshman had phoned, almost in tears, to announce a new catastrophe. He'd just heard on the radio of an explosion in the affluent area of Vaassenar, at the home of a Dutch magnate, Baldur van Jetzlar, probably caused by a faulty gas connection. The unexplained malfunction had occurred during the night and the sudden collapse of the mansion, at a time when its residents were asleep, had buried them under piles of rubble. Some bodies had been recovered the following morning and that of Mr. van Jetzlar himself was said to be among them. Lakshman had been devastated by the news for he had by now formed a deep attachment to Sanath, seeing him as the only mentor who could guide him through the unfolding of the Dagad Trikon enigma.

To foil further attempts by their enemies at locating him, Lakshman had secreted himself in a mountain village high up in the Alps. He now felt safe but clueless as to what steps he should take next, but he resolved to consult with Lakshmi in Rome to help him decide. The Spanish Ambassador was entertaining his guests, speaking to them in turn in four languages, each with gracious ease. He brought an affable Monsignor over to meet Lakshmi. The Monsignor was dressed in his official regalia: scarlet hat, crimson belt, with and a golden cross that dangled on his ample stomach. "Ms. Vani, may I introduce you to His Eminence, Cardinal Sadaka."

Lakshmi tried a polite smile but it was hard for her to brush aside her dark thoughts. The Monsignor was speaking to her in Italian with a slight accent that she could not quite place. He was explaining that the columns of the magnificent baroque fountain on the Janiculo hill, at the gate of the embassy, had been taken from the ancient forum of Nerva by one of those eager builder Popes of the Borghese family. Lakshmi found it difficult to summon any interest.

She was thinking that their adversaries had been ruthless and swift, ready for the kill, having monitored the meeting of her cousin with Sanath on the NordStar airlines flight. What had really happened to her cousin's new friend and how come he had been caught off guard so easily? How would they ever meet the Stealthstars whose existence had been revealed to Lakshman by the Dagad Trikon Icelandic scrolls and what would they now do with the Sadhan and the Glorfakir weapons? She made polite excuses and walked away, trying to hide her preoccupation and her profound sadness.

Later, as she boarded the car for the Villa Madama, where the Minister of Foreign Affairs was offering a state dinner for Ministers of the Environment and a few key officials, Lakshmi found herself sitting next to the cardinal. The attention of the driver was entirely devoted to keeping pace with the police car, which was leading a high-speed motorcade. A police officer was half-hanging out of its window, gesticulating at the evening traffic to give way. The wailing sirens almost drowned out the voice of Cardinal Sadaka.

"This may seem a bit excessive but these days you cannot be too careful about security, as you well know."

"Sorry?" replied Lakshmi, feigning politeness again, while her actual train of thought was disturbed by the violent swerves of the car.

The prelate pursued his theme with obvious detachment. "Before you know it, as your friend and his mentor found out, you risk being blown up in mid-air or even in mid-sleep."

Lakshmi froze in her seat, speechless, and she wondered if the beads of perspiration on her forehead were visible to the prelate. How could this man read her thoughts? Was he friend or enemy? After a long silence, she managed to mumble, "I beg your pardon?"

The cardinal continued helpfully, "You see, Signorina, I am not quite what I appear to be in the same way that you are not solely the biologist you present yourself as. I am an old friend of the gentleman that your friend, Mr. Lakshman Kharadvansin, met in Iceland at Easter. Mr. van Jetzlar, on his return to Vaassenar, asked me to take care of you when you came to Rome. But I am worried, as you seem to be, by what happened with this plane crash and the gas explosion. I have no doubt that both the plane and the house were sabotaged. They almost got your friend but right now, I do not know whether they really killed Baldur van Jetzlar or not. If they did, it would be an irreparable catastrophe. We certainly do not want them to get you too." He added with reflective self-pity, "Now please excuse me, I did not have my siesta; I am quite tired." And ignoring Lakshmi, he immediately dozed off.

Lakshmi was too dumbfounded to react; like most people and specifically her cousin in Iceland, she was plainly uncomfortable about meeting a stranger who seemed to know a lot about her. Now the motorcade had reached the Villa Madama. The blue flashing lights of the escort cars bounced off the columns of the imposing building, one of those splendid palaces that had been built in the countryside by the Roman nobility as a place to spend cool summers away from the city's heat. She briefly noted the splendor of the park, which shielded the palatial residence from the outside. Giant pine trees looked like bloated black mushrooms against the turquoise evening sky. The Italian authorities had provided tight security, and elite troops from the Interior Ministry surrounded the palace. The guests climbed the winding staircase between cypress trees and carabinieri in gala uniforms, who stood at close attention.

While thinking about the strange behavior of this prince of the Church, Lakshmi greeted the guests as they arrived. She then walked through a number of salons before entering the brightly lit reception hall whose vaulted ceiling was exquisitely decorated with Pompeian frescoes. She almost bumped into a waiter while looking at a detail in the ceiling when a tall, elegant captain of the carabinieri saluted her briskly. "Ms. Lakshmi Vani? Please follow me at once."

A surprised Lakshmi left the elegant crowd behind and followed her guide through a terraced French garden. About two hundred yards farther on, they entered a small house hidden behind a tall baroque fountain. A bodyguard at the entrance checked her bag and she was shown into a small, cozy living room, dimly lit by small lamps and candlelight.

"She is here, Eminenza."

"Thank you, Luciano. You may leave now, but please make sure no one disturbs us."

Lakshmi blinked in surprise at Cardinal Sadaka who now seemed fully awake. Next to him, an elderly man in a large armchair was scrutinizing Lakshmi attentively. Lakshmi noted a large forehead under a silvery mane, a proud bearing, and a handsome face. He had long fingers, one of them adorned with a gold and lapis lazuli ring that bore a crown over a family crest.

"Ms. Vani, I have organized this encounter under the cover of the reception of our Foreign Minister because the Villa Madama, for the duration of this dinner event, is under full security protection against terrorist attacks. Nobody can enter the grounds of the estate and this will also keep at bay other undesirables who might be following you. Nobody will trouble us here. I also took the liberty to excuse you from the dinner on grounds of ill health and later you can leave with Luciano under military escort."

"But... Eminence, this seems very strange to me and I am not at all sure that I want to miss my dinner. What is the meaning of all this?"

"I am coming to that. But let me first introduce to you my friend Philip, Graf von Jetzlar."

"Are you a relative of Baldur van Jetzlar?" Lakshmi asked immediately. She eased herself into a vacant armchair, trying to remain calm. She looked intently at the prelate and his friend for any signs of possible hostility; however, within moments she found herself relaxing and feeling secure in the candle-lit glow of the tiny room. Her instincts told her that the pieces of the Dagad Trikon puzzle were coming together again. She was pleased to be picking up the trail Lakshman had just lost: she couldn't wait to tell him. The room was very quiet and she could hear the babbling of a nearby fountain.

Monsignor Sadaka continued, "Our knowledge of the matters your cousin is investigating with your help goes way back in history but at this stage we no longer understand what is happening. There is, of course, an imminent threat to our lives as well as a formidable danger looming over our societies. It is hard to explain, but we will tell you what we know. I will ask Philip to do the talking. I take it you understand German?" he asked, to which Lakshmi nodded.

The count began, "Ms. Vani, I am delighted to meet you. Yes, I am indeed connected to Baldur and he told us about your quest. As your cousin trusted Baldur, I hope you will also consider us friends. Kindly allow me some time, for this story cannot be rushed and I would be grateful if you can, in due course, report the full content of this discussion to your cousin Lakshman. We need to share important information with you and I will now do so in some detail."

"Please go ahead."

"The extraordinary encounter with Baldur, which changed my life, took place a long time ago. I need to take you back to the summer of nineteen forty-one, the time when Hitler's armies attacked the Soviet Union. I was then the youngest lieutenant in the Wehrmacht and commanding the first scout platoon of an armored attack division attached to the Central Army Corps. After heavy bombing, the fortress of Brest-Litovsk fell and our Panzer divisions rushed headlong towards Minsk, the capital of Byelorussia, en route to Moscow. But a Russian battalion, which, unlike the rest of the Red Army at that particular time was putting up a spirited fight, had blocked access to the main road. My orders were to find an alternative way through the forest so that a crack brigade of the SS could remove the enemy in a surprise attack from the rear.

My platoon set out one misty morning, guided by a local boy called Ivan who had been recommended to us by our military intelligence service. We were dressed in civilian clothes and driving Russian vehicles. We left the main road and by noon we had already taken a small village by surprise, shooting dead the Russian partisans who were totally unprepared for our lightning onslaught. We then drove through a more remote region on a feeder road. Ivan said we had to cross a dense forest to arrive behind Russian lines."

The cardinal interrupted, saying with a smile, "Please be patient. Philip is a storyteller. This will take some time but the night is young." The count laughed, his laughter clear and fresh, sounding almost like the laughter of a child. At the same time, there was an air of great dignity about him. "Strange, but nice people," thought Lakshmi. She was relaxing now.

Philip continued and, indeed, he was not in a hurry. He spoke slowly, as though he was sinking softly into a film of his memories.

"It was an old, mature forest of pine, oak, silver birch, spruce, black and speckled alder. After some time, the conifer taiga forest fused with a variety of wetland systems; it was as if the forest had its feet in water. We penetrated a network of peat marshes, bogs, swampy grounds, ponds, and small lakes inhabited by countless species of birds, reptiles, and amphibians. Hours went by and dusk settled. I tried to orient myself. I was stunned to see the needle of my compass swinging from left to right and back again, as if encountering a crazy magnetic field. I grew suspicious. Swamps and tall grasses surrounded this stretch of the path and we could see the trees in a half-light. Our vehicles got stuck, bogged down. I stepped out of the lead vehicle, but it was too late.

Our vehicles were sinking fast into the mud. This segment of the road was a well-concealed trap on marshy ground and the road underneath us was rapidly giving way. As my men were scrambling to reach firm ground, arrows whizzed at us from the nearby trees. It was an ambush! I grabbed my Mauser and shot twice at Ivan who was trying to flee through the high grass. The arrows were aimed with deadly precision and my men were falling one after another, like a line of fairground ducks. One or two managed to escape from the rear and disappeared into the swamps. However, we never found what their fate was, what became of them.

As for me, I realized that the only possible escape route was the one followed by Ivan. I found a path of stepping stones scattered through the bog that had been hidden by the tall grass. Followed by my driver Stefan, I finally reached firm ground under the cover of darkness. I had seen blood on the ground that proved that Ivan had been wounded. We progressed through a birch wood as fast as we could, but after some time we realized somebody or something was following us at a distance. It walked when we walked and it stopped when we stopped. From the sounds it made, it seemed to be much heavier than a man.

It was out of the question to use our flashlights or shoot at this creature because of the possible proximity of the Russian partisans who undoubtedly were still looking for us. The mist was coming in again, diffusing the moonlight and transforming the trees into ghostly shapes. Exhausted, Stefan and I decided to get some sleep and we hid in a crevice between two mossy rocks.

The next morning, a shout from Stefan woke me from a weary slumber. "Herr Lieutenant, look here!" I sat up and rubbed my eyes. A couple of yards away, standing on a mound, a huge bison stood, staring at us quietly. Its behavior was so strange that we did not even try to reach for our pistols. Shaking its mane, the animal retreated a few steps, as if inviting us to follow. A strong intuition told me that I was being invited to enter into a different dimension and indeed, that my very life itself was about to change.

We followed the bison. Without hesitating, the large animal knew how to choose the best path through the labyrinth of woods and wetlands. It waited for us when we stopped to eat some berries. Toward noon, we crossed a brook full of somnolent turtles and entered a part of the forest that had a completely different feel to it. It was full of ancient oaks interspersed with lovely ponds and grassy marshes. The ground was covered with a rich diversity of grasses, moss, and lichen. There was suddenly a strange lushness of plant diversity, flowers, royal ferns, wild tulips, and lobelia. The forest was teeming with life; we saw squirrels, bears, and deer in increasing numbers and, on top of the tallest trees, the nests of golden eagles, two of whom circled high above in the sky.

I had noted, above our heads, a peregrine falcon that seemed to escort us as if it was monitoring our progress. The sun shone brightly through the branches, lighting up the undergrowth with bright patches of green and gold."

The count shook his head. " It was all so incredibly beautiful and I can still remember the details as if it were yesterday. The place looked enchanted. Stefan and I almost forgot the horror of the war and the terror of the day before when we had lost our companions.

We now found a man-made trail, winding through sharp rocks, which led into a clearing. On the rim of the clearing were a dozen large wooden huts, almost hidden by the undergrowth, their reclining roofs camouflaged under live moss and lichens. We gazed upon the central feature of this clearing, an enormous ancestral oak. Its lower branches spread out almost horizontally, keeping other trees at bay. In the empty space thus created, we saw a group of people who seemed to be waiting for us.

On the left, three young women were attending to Ivan, who was lying wounded on bloodied moss. I found that I had shot him in the shoulder. On the right was a group of woodsmen holding sophisticated crossbows. They stared at us without sympathy. My first impression was that everybody had blond hair and was dressed in green. Gold and green, I thought, these indeed are the colors of this forest. The bison joined its mate. Her back was still covered with Ivan's blood, and both walked slowly away.

Then I saw a wooden throne under the oak. The peregrine falcon was perched on top of it. An old man with intense green eyes sat on the throne. This is how, for the first time, I met the man who would open the book of secrets: Sanath, the wizard of Hllidarendi. He looked at us without a word and waved the women away. They disappeared, taking Ivan with them.

Then, in a commanding voice, he spoke to me. 'Take off your uniform, Lieutenant von Jetzlar.' To my surprise, he knew my name and he addressed me in German. Clearly neither my pistol nor my arguments would be of any avail with all those crossbows pointed at my chest. My last hour had come. I thought of how undignified it would be for a German officer to die in his underwear in front of his own driver. I was about to die under a volley of arrows, transformed into a kind of Saint Sebastian without an artist on hand to record the scene.

The warriors were now arguing with the wizard, but he silenced them with a barely perceptible movement of his hand. The wizard looked at me again and, in my humiliating condition, the glance seemed to be all the more piercing.

"Young man, you were going to lead the SS, the men in black, with narrow foreheads and large jaws, onto these sacred grounds. You came with death and war in your hands and my crossbowmen are strongly inclined to kill you. However, that I have other plans for you. For you belong to the elders of your race who, unlike the thugs who now run your country, had large foreheads and narrow jaws. You came from before the time of this scum and I know this is not your war. First, dive into the first pond to your left and bring me the object you will find lying at the bottom."

Under close escort, I approached the pond, which was encircled by an ancient circular stone wall. Metal glistened faintly in its depths. I dived into the fresh water and retrieved a strangely shaped golden helmet from the paved bottom. I brought it back to the wizard who explained in an angry voice, 'This pond is the final grave of the first-born son of Ogotaï Khan, the general who led the Golden Horde of the Mongols through Russia. This is the place where he was killed. Despite repeated attempts in the twelfth and thirteenth centuries, the Mongol cavalry never managed to go beyond the marshes surrounding this forest. They were wiped out, having been led astray in the mists of the swamp. After them, no one ever tried again. This ancestral oak is protected by a higher magic. It allowed the Slav people to survive Asian invasions from Attila, Genghis Khan, and Tamerlane. The tree will also defeat the Teutonic brutes you are serving. Your Hitler is Tamerlane returned: he will invade the whole of Byelorussia, but he will never find this place that he is seeking. Its keeper will watch you. You may stay with us but do not try to escape. That's all for now."

Thus, we became the prisoners of the sylvan tribe. I tried to escape, of course – three times as a matter of fact. The first time the bison found me in a state of total exhaustion and brought me back. The second time I was brought back by a pack of wolves. The third time the women helped me out of a mud pit into which I had fallen and been trapped for many hours. They laughed a lot and told me that the next time their men would shoot me with their arrows and transform me into a porcupine. I decided to follow Stefan's advice; he was the careful type. I stayed with the tribe and learned from Sanath.

After two months of captivity in a wooden hut in the custody of Ivan's family, I was released and allowed to move freely among the people of the oak forest. Further homes were scattered around the trees. The summer and fall went by quietly. All the huts were covered with earth and moss to offer camouflage in daylight and protection during the winter. Stefan showed them how to improve the stone stoves during the first cold season. As we had to spend five months a year under the snow, the locals much appreciated his contribution.

Often I heard the faraway rumbling of the German Air Force, the Luftwaffe's bombers, flying towards the Eastern front. The people of the wood were now quite friendly. They knew that I was a prisoner of the marshes and they didn't worry about me. Ivan had explained to me that, in the tribe of the oak wizard, wisdom and forgiveness were the rule. This was why I came to be so trusted by the family of the man I had wounded and tried to kill.

I gradually came to see that it was the Hllidarendi who was protecting the forest, ruling over the tribe of the oak keepers, communicating with the animals and the trees. He could influence magnetic fields and interfere with the radio communications of the planes. At the core of his magic was an ability to access a central code, a primordial vibration that connected all living beings – those we could see and also some we couldn't.

Stefan eventually married a cheerful local girl, who lit up his otherwise taciturn moods. The tribesmen were no ordinary partisans. Even their faces were different from those of neighboring villagers, with finer traits, slanting eyes, and light blond hair. They seemed hardly concerned by the war raging around them: their sole focus was to deny outsiders access to the sacred oak tree. They taught Stefan and me how to move around in the mist, to fish using only our hands in the brooks, to listen to the forest, and to survive under the snow. We hunted only those specific species that were not part of the wizard ring of awakened beasts.

Winters were long indeed, and as I was young, I too eventually fell in love with a local girl, Laira, Ivan's sister. With the permission of the elders and the blessings of Sanath, one crisp day in winter I married her under the great oak. The sun shone on every icicle on the branches of the ancestral tree, we walked around a fire, pledging our trust to each other in a ritual, which, Sanath said, had been in the custody of the Hllidarendis since the time of Zarathustra in ancient Persia.

Lakshmi was growing impatient, but she realized she needed to let the old man follow the thread of memories as he reconstructed events that had taken place a long time ago. Thus, she waited for him to continue.

"From then on, my bond with the tribe grew stronger every day and Sanath began to reveal some of his secrets. For instance, he told me the source of the power of the oak tree. He told me that Evil had a dual face named Hangker and Belzebseth and explained how they acted upon human history. The invasions from Asia to Europe are a case in point. Likewise, in the Middle Ages... "

"I am sorry to interject, but you describe Sanath as if he were the same man who sought out my cousin in Reykjavik." Right now, Lakshmi was not too interested in European history and so she interrupted the Count's narration. "This is almost sixty years later. How come? Could you clarify this before going on?"

The cardinal replied, "It is indeed the same man. The Hllidarendis age much slower than normal human beings. They live for centuries and they choose the parents of their next birth. They keep some of their memory while going through the cycle of death and rebirth. You know, we all reincarnate but we do not remember. The wizards do: they often know us from our previous lives. This is why Sanath knows so much more about us than we know about him."

"What an unpleasant thought," mused Lakshmi.

Philip added, "At the end of the war, Sanath needed to return to normal society in order to fulfill his mission. Of course, he needed a fake identity and I helped him by substituting him for my elder brother, Baldur, an Air Force colonel who had been shot down and killed over Stalingrad. Thus, Sanath-Baldur slipped into Germany unnoticed, taking advantage of the confusion created by the country's surrender to the Allies. He spent many years based in our family castle on the river Rhine. He told us that the Rhine was the source of the creativity of the German nation. After ten years or so, he followed the river downstream and moved to the Netherlands.

"Count, this is certainly fascinating but I wish we could finally come to the point because I cannot spend the night reviewing World War Two, or counting the leaves in your Byelorussian forest," said Lakshmi somewhat rudely. "And, if at all possible, Eminence, please let me know how we got a cardinal of the Roman Catholic Church mixed up in this saga."

The prelate nodded approval at Philip, who continued with a broad grin. "Meet Ivan, Cardinal Sadaka, Laira's brother: my brother-in-law," he said.

"Yes, and the shoulder you shot is still hurting, now with rheumatism," grumbled the Monsignor, "but how and why I went from the oak forest to the Vatican is something you will learn later if you show a little patience. We will make things clear."

"Perhaps," sighed Philip, "perhaps, but I am old and the tale of the Hllidarendi is too heavy a burden on my shoulders. This burden has grown heavier since we no longer know whether the second Baldur is alive and well. So, listen to the teachings of Sanath, my mentor and friend, while I may still recall them."

At that moment, the three heard a disturbance and loud shouts from outside. The bodyguard and Luciano burst into the room pushing a handcuffed man who was wearing a torn tie and broken spectacles. Luciano threw a listening device and a miniature tape recorder on the table. "This spy was hiding in the granary, recording your conversation. What should we do with him?"

"This is an outrage and a scandal! I am a diplomat and protected by diplomatic immunity. Release me immediately; you have no right to detain me in this way. I shall say nothing more, nothing, let me go," said the man indignantly.

"Well, well, Mr. Al Bemoth," replied a bemused Lakshmi. "And how does this immunity bring you to this granary so strangely equipped?"

"You are meddling in serious business: this is not a meeting of the United Nations," said the cardinal to the Sudanese delegate dryly while Philip was still in shock. "Luciano, it will be treatment C."

In the twinkling of an eye the bodyguard grabbed the protesting Sudanese and forced him on to his knees. Luciano took a syringe and a small flask containing a greenish liquid from the cardinal's attaché case.

"C as in confession, my son," remarked Ivan Sadaka gleefully. "I never move without my toolbox. We, at the Vatican, in our search for truth, have developed a serum of extreme potency that will unearth the full truth that we all seek, don't we? Behold our very own high-tech witchcraft."

Luciano injected the serum into the shoulder of the unfortunate Arab diplomat whose attempts at screams were smothered by a gag. After a few minutes of quaking, the intruder calmed down; the gag and the handcuffs were removed from a dazed Mansour Al Bemoth. He sat quietly on the floor, trying to mend his broken glasses. The prelate said softly, "What are you doing here?"

"I was meant to listen to your conversation and record it."

"Why?"

"I don't know."

"Who asked you to?"

"The lady at the NordStar airline office."

"Why did she ask you to do it?"

"Because of the Brown Specter."

"Who or what is the Brown Specter?"

"I don't know."

"How did you know about the Specter? Explain, my son, explain in detail."

Al Bemoth started hesitantly. "Six months before the Rome Conference, a terrible drought and heat wave affected my small kingdom, in the western ranges of Sudan. The wells in the villages dried up. The men who were able to do so left for Khartoum but the women and children were left behind to die. Every day, my people turned to me, crying for help. I could not bear the pain of those it was my duty to protect. I went to see the most powerful of our marabous, a famous African witch doctor. He said he could not do anything because the drought was under the control of the Brown Specter." Al Bemoth started to stutter and shake, looking terrified.

"What did the marabou say about the Specter?"

Speaking falteringly, the Sudanese diplomat explained, "He said that the Brown Specter was haunting the dunes and hunting departed souls in the deep Sahara desert since the most ancient times. That he had been a mighty devil before, but he had been defeated in the early age of the Earth when he tried to assault the rock fortress of the angels, which in our legends, was the custodian of the Paradise of Allah. The marabou said only the Specter could lift the drought curse because it was he who had induced it."

Philip's face became pale. He stared at his brother-in-law. "They go back to Dagad Trikon. Oh my God." The prelate nodded with a worried look and replied, "I fear this is a mischief of Abuzinal, the southern Titanosaur, or maybe one of his forms, as he can change himself at will. Remember, Sanath warned us that he had something to do in this tale." He pursued his questioning with a commanding voice. "What did you do then?"

"I asked the marabou if he could contact the Specter and he said he would, but first I had to give him many gold coins. I had to save my people so I paid him and returned home. The next night, a moonless night, somebody knocked at my door around midnight.

The dogs howled and the children started crying in their sleep. I went out. A shape stood before me draped in a long brown cloak. I experienced sheer dread. He gave me an envelope and walked away in the darkness without a word. The next day the clouds came and it rained." The effort seemed to have exhausted the chieftain. He was sweating and had closed his eyes. "In the envelope I found a name and an address in Rome. I knew I was coming to this Conference. I knew that I had to obey because the rain had come. Even the marabou was afraid of the Brown Specter. The address was of the NordStar airlines office in Rome and the name belonged to a woman who told me not to ask any questions. She told me the only thing I had to do was to follow Ms. Vani at the Foreign Minister's party and to monitor her every move. If there was a meeting, I had to listen in and record the conversation. She even gave me the spying equipment." After giving this explanation, Al Bemoth fainted.

"Poor man, the drug is very strong," said the cardinal. "He will wake up in four hours and he will suffer from a total amnesia for the twenty-four hours preceding the injection. He may wet his pants, an unfortunate side effect we will have to correct one day. In these cases doctors usually think it's been a mild stroke. Let's go now. Philip, they only know about Sanath and the two cousins, not yet about us. Luciano, let's head for our refuge near Tarquinia. Lakshmi, do not return to your hotel; we'll settle your bill and we will retrieve your luggage tomorrow."

MEETING AT THE CASA DELLA MINERVA

Lakshmi was shaken to find out that she too had become a target. Suddenly, the threat had become very real to her. The four men and Lakshmi hurriedly left the gardener's house, avoiding the villa where the Minister's reception was winding down. As they drove away in Luciano's police car, Lakshmi asked the cardinal, "Who is this Brown Specter?"

Ivan Sadaka responded, somewhat sententiously, "In the fifth century, the Briton Aurelius Clemens Prudentius wrote a literary essay called Psychomachia. I think you could translate this as 'Soul Battle,' or 'Battle of the Psyche.' In it, he described how each of the Deadly Sins is an individual character involved in a horrific assault on the human soul. These unpleasant characters appear also as the six Dark Riders. I suppose Thanatophor had begotten them at the beginning of time. The Brown Specter is now the master of one of them: he controls Anger, the fast-galloping Rider who is the closest ally of Hangker. We may be flattered but not exactly comforted that we command such interest from the top guns of Thanatophor."

The cardinal made a few phone calls on his cell phone and arranged for Lakshmi's luggage to be moved from her hotel to the Hotel Sant Anselmo. They remained silent for the rest of the journey. Lakshmi was dropped off at the Sant Anselmo and the Alfa Romeo sped away towards the northern highway.

The next day Lakshman arrived at Fiumicino Airport and joined Lakshmi, who updated him on the recent developments. Lakshman was immensely relieved that she had picked up the trail of the legend again. As the cardinal had made arrangements for her to be excused from the Conference on health grounds, the cousins took a stroll through the old city. They made sure they were not being followed and finally sat on a terrace on the Piazza Navone to enjoy some ice cream. It was a beautiful day, with passing clouds that distributed a succession of sunshine and sudden showers. They debated at length about what they should do next.

Like the Hyperion of Hoelderlin, Lakshman felt torn between two inclinations. On the one hand, his yearning for new horizons, for change, and making things right was pushing him further into the Dagad Trikon legend. On the other, the more sensible part of him continued to insist that he drop this inquiry so fraught with uncertainty and danger and settle down perhaps, to find some quiet domestic happiness away from the dangers of a troubled world.

Once again it fell to Lakshmi to inspire him. She was persuasive, encouraging him to go ahead in the search for the lost messages from the Avasthas. She reminded him that, in fact, he now had few viable options. Besides, the lure of finding the other caskets was working subtly on him too. How could he ever forget the extraordinary sensations and the powerful insights that had been released by the casket found in Iceland?

Lakshmi's arguments were difficult to fault and so Lakshman made a couple of phone calls to associates in the family business. He freed himself from further commitments in order to investigate the path that had opened with the finding of Dagad Trikon and the Avastha weapons. He resolved that as long as he was their custodian, he would not let go and besides, there was no doubt that some obscure but hostile forces had taken an interest in them. He feared they would always know where to find him and his cousin and so the two of them agreed they would not just wait around for the next unpleasant surprise.

That afternoon, Jonathan arrived from Cairo en route to the U.S. The taxi took him to the Hotel Sant Anselmo, on the Aventino hill, where the cousins were now staying. They had decided to meet Philip von Jetzlar at a discreet location, near the French garden in the Villa Pamphili Park. The count arrived with four of Ivan's bodyguards who quickly secured the perimeter. The young men took an instant liking to the count and for his part, he was especially happy to meet Lakshman because Sanath had told him about the discoverer of the Triangle Rock and of his courage in retrieving the Casket of the White Feather.

It had rained but now the sun shone brightly. There was no news from Baldur-Sanath and Philip's anxiety was palpable. Although immensely knowledgeable themselves, both Philip and Ivan were relying on Sanath for guidance and protection. Only Sanath seemed able to oscillate freely between the two worlds, the known and the unknown, the future and the past, while remaining firmly anchored in the present. Lakshman had developed complicated feelings about the enigmatic personage in the short time he had known him. The Hllidarendi had already become a figure of mythical proportions, Sanath was an awe-inspiring wizard, and Baldur had become a friend. Lakshman already missed the facets of this relationship and so his feelings for the wizard brought him closer still to Philip.

On the way back from the Villa Pamphili, Jonathan had a long exchange with Lakshman; both of them knew that they needed additional security precautions. Jonathan decided to join the cousins the next day after paying a visit to his younger brother Joseph, who was finishing his theology doctorate at the Angelicum Pontifical Academy. Joseph had called Jonathan in Cairo to say he wanted to see him about some important business that he didn't want to discuss on the phone.

The cousins had accepted an invitation to accompany Philip to the cardinal's hideaway. The count and his wife, Laira, together with their two grandchildren, Lothar and Lorelei, usually spent their summer vacation with the cardinal at his secret residence. His Eminence was resourceful and well organized. Indeed, messing around with his team of Byelorussian bodyguards would have been a poor idea and no one had yet pierced his security cover.

Ivan had gone ahead to his country home, so Philip, Lakshmi, and Lakshman got into Philip's old Mercedes, driven by a now-jovial Stefan, who wore a dark green chauffeur's uniform; the bodyguards trailed them in a BMW 500. During the drive to the Etruscan country-side, in the vicinity of Tarquinia, the Count mentioned how much he had enjoyed his summer holidays in Italy with his family. Lakshman wondered aloud how Philip and Stefan could look so fit and young despite their advanced age. Stefan responded that the count and he had aged much slower because of having spent those remarkable years in the immediate vicinity of the sacred oak. He added, with mirth, that their Russian wives were also taking good care of them, and they chatted happily in this way for the whole trip. The absence of Sanath brought them closer and they were coming to realize that, in his absence, they had to rely on each other. On the way Stefan took several precautions to ensure they were not being followed.

Having passed Civitavecchia, they left the coastal highway and followed a country road that took them across green rolling hills, sprinkled with lovely patches of yellow flowers, between Viterbo and Tarquinia. After almost an hour they turned left abruptly under the arches of an ancient Roman aqueduct. The narrow path was hardly visible from the main road and disappeared into a pine wood. After a short while, they emerged from the small forest and abruptly, the car turned into a side road and Stefan negotiated the few last curves between curtains of bamboo that intermittently obscured their view. After a few hundred yards, they stopped before the monumental entrance to a walled estate; it was a baroque gate from the seventeenth century with an ornate wrought iron portal.

On both sides, large statues of owls topped granite columns. A Russian bodyguard recognized the car and opened the gate. They had reached the hidden retreat of Cardinal Ivan Sadaka: the Casa della Minerva. Lakshmi looked at the entrance with a dubious grin. "Owls? They are not supposed to bring good luck in my country."

Philip responded, "I know, but here the owl is the bird of Minerva, Goddess of Wisdom, which, as my fellow citizen Hegel observed, takes its flight at dusk. Between the fading light of the day and the approaching night, when we aren't sure any more of what we see and know, when certainties are no longer so, when the inquiring mind is prepared to venture into uncharted path, then new discoveries are possible."

The estate consisted of a main building and two others: a farmhouse and a primary school for gifted children. The Casa della Minerva was a fifteenth-century manor whose sturdy ocher facades were partly covered by dark green ivy and decorated with tall and elegant marble-framed Renaissance windows. The cardinal had had it restored impeccably. On three sides of the secluded property, the ancient wall shielded the estate and its wooded park. On one side, a thick curtain of bamboo ran alongside a lively brook. In this secluded space, animals from the school's farm – geese, rabbits, cows, and ponies – roamed freely to the delight of the schoolchildren. More unusually, two large eagles were perched in a pine tree, watching the horizon.

When the cars drove up to the manor house noisy and cheerful kids were playing on the grass and some of the more curious among them rushed to catch a glimpse of the visitors. The atmosphere was light and happy. A butler led the visitors into the Gothic, vaulted-ceilinged entrance hall where they deposited their luggage and were introduced to the cardinal. Ivan came out of the kitchen where he was preparing pasta in the company of a beautiful woman. He was dressed in old gardening clothes and welcomed his guests with a broad smile.

"Hello, nice to see you here. Meet my wife Alexandra. I am a cardinal, but not seriously, so you know. Sanath would not have inflicted such a predicament on me. I just became a priest under his instructions but I do not live as one and so, you may say, I really have two lives. It is enough that my fellow priests think I am one of them and kiss my golden ring. This school is possibly the most important of my activities, but no one knows about it. We showed immense trust by bringing you here, into the safe heart of our territory. Come, let us leave the children and get down to business."

Alexandra greeted their guests with natural warmth and a few kind words. Ivan left the kitchen in the hands of his wife and some Russian women and, taking Lakshman by the arm, he crossed an enfilade of vaulted salons. The visitors were shown to their chambers on the first floor and later spent a leisurely afternoon in the company of the children and the farm animals before briefing each other on recent events. Lakshman again gave a detailed account of his adventure, taking his time to relate how Lakshmi and he had initially picked up the trail of Dagad Trikon from an ancient Sanskrit manuscript in Delhi. He related his adventures from Cairo to the south of France, to Iceland and Amsterdam and he narrated in detail his reading of the scrolls found in the casket brought by the Sheravalian Guard of the White Feather. He finished by giving an account of his experiences and discussions with Sanath – his audience was captivated.

Jonathan arrived on the next day, having been driven there by the Russians. Ivan greeted him cheerfully, " I am glad, Mr. O'Lochan, that we meet at last for I hold your brother Joseph in high regard. He has been of immense help to me in my researches and he has told me a lot about you. It gives me a great feeling to know that we are all joining forces at last."

The group gathered on one of the side terraces of the manor that was adorned with elegant marble statues representing the four seasons and was shaded by a large pine tree. Philip was already there, sitting on one of the comfortable bamboo chairs, sipping tea and reading the newspapers while enjoying the cheerful freshness of a soft morning breeze. He stood up to greet Jonathan. "Ecological disasters and economic meltdown in the making, political corruption and smoke-screen solutions, bombs blowing up all over the place – this does not make for ideal breakfast reading. Why do I still read the newspapers? Are you sure you were not followed?" he asked with an engaging grin.

"I left my hotel for good, changed taxis twice, went through the subway and a department store before taking the train at the Termini station for a wrong destination. Yes, I am pretty sure it was all right," Jonathan assured him.

"One of our people also covered you," observed Ivan. "Two suspicious fellows, not Italian, followed you from the Aventino hill but you lost them in the supermarket. Well done! They looked quite upset and were shouting into their cell phones. They must have been the ones who followed the moves of Ms. Vani as they picked up your trail at the Hotel Sant Anselmo. I am glad we told you to be careful, but now you can relax. The Shadow will not harm you before you lead its goons to us. Tough luck! We foiled them yet another time. The members of Ivan's clan selected for our security team are not always tender-hearted and some of those who followed you had a very unpleasant time. In any case, this palace is under special protection," he concluded, without elaborating further.

Just then Laira, Philip's wife, accompanied by her grandchildren, Lorelei and Lothar, joined them on the terrace along with the two cousins. The Jetzlar family, plus their friends from the neighborhood, were about to celebrate the eighteenth birthday of Lorelei that evening and the Casa was a-buzz with the preparations. Multicolored garlands and lampions were already hanging in the grand salon. Laira had organized everything. She was a lively woman, six years younger than her husband, and Lorelei and Lothar were handsome teenagers. Lorelei had a regular oval face, luminous long blond hair, a delicately shaped nose, and light blue eyes. Lothar, in contrast, had short curly black hair and was tanned and athletic. They scanned the visitors with penetrating glances and courteously greeted each guest in turn before taking their leave.

The adults sat in a circle around a table laden with refreshments: home-baked bread, sun-dried tomatoes, olives, mozzarella, wild boar sausages from Sardinia, Parma ham, and juicy melons. Harpsichord music wafted through a window on the second floor. Life was as good as it gets in the Casa della Minerva. Lakshmi, whose curiosity had been whetted by the initial briefing from the count, continued the discussion, "What does Sanath know? This is what you were about to tell me in the gardener's cottage,"

"Up to a point, we can tell you up to a point," Ivan replied with more than a touch of ambiguity. "Philip spent much time with the wizard and became quite a philosopher himself. But before I start, let us hear your story."

Lakshmi gave her account of the Dagad Trikon search up to the evening in the gardener's cottage of the Villa Madama and then, with Lakshman's assent, asked Philip to continue his narration of the teachings of Sanath. At this point Philip invited his wife to share her recollections of the wizard's teachings, saying encouragingly, "Why don't you start, Laira?"

"How can I start? Ivan, will you try?"

"No, you start, Laira. I know it's difficult, but words are all we have and he taught you long ago about the Deep Way." With some shyness, Laira von Jetzlar, Ivan's sister who, as a small girl, had accompanied the wizard on many of his forays into the forest, started to recount her treasury of memories.

"The teachings of Sanath were not conveyed mainly through words. In our village, whatever was going on, the people used to sing. We sang at weddings, harvest festivals, and mostly just for pleasure. But he taught us how to sing as a way of communicating with all the living creatures. For instance, we had a song for the silver and gray-winged seagulls that flew all the way from the Braslau lakes just to hear us. I know it doesn't make sense to modern people, but it was so. Then he taught us how to speak to the birds and he showed us how to draw energy directly from the earth itself."

"How come?" asked Lakshmi, much intrigued, for as a biologist involved in ecology, she was fascinated by the possibility that the teachings of Sanath could open a deeper connection to Nature. "How is it possible to make this connection so directly?"

"Mother Earth gives what we ask for, according to our desires," answered Laira. "To materialistic people, she gives material blessings. To spiritual people, she grants spiritual blessings. But when doing so, she chooses carefully. She does not shower her finest gifts in an indiscriminate manner, nor does she reveal her spiritual self all the time or just in any place. She doesn't share her secret energy with those who do not know how to ask. There must be a place, a time, and a protocol to be properly observed. For instance, when we were still little kids, three times a year we went with the wizard to a special place, a small island covered with many different kinds of moss, shaded by strong oaks and fir trees and surrounded by a vast complex of lakes and bog mires."

"And what was so special about that place?"

"There were strange-looking rocks and in the middle of the island there was a living stone. It was a large monolith, like a polished basalt column but it had not been fashioned by man. Sanath said it came out of the Mother Earth herself, at her own will, and he called such stones Sao Iambu. Such living stones are born out of themselves and are magical. He told us if we put our hands toward the stone we would experience a cool breeze coming from it. He was quite right, we could feel it. He told us that there was another large and well-known Sao Iambu in an Arabian city, with hundred of thousands of people walking around it in worship, but that the worshippers mostly did not understand the special nature of the stone and were unable to feel the energy coming off it."

"So, the wizard told you about the Kaaba in Mecca?" Lakshmi's attention was now fully held by the story. Laira ignored her question, rapt as she was in her memories. "When we congregated around the Sao Iambu with the wizard, a miraculous bond would form between man and beast. The bears and the wild boars would sit at the edge of the bog, looking in our direction. The gray herons would be on alert; the elks and the deer would stand to attention. The wolves, lynxes, and foxes would stop hunting. Our two bison would block the path behind us. "Actually," she said with a touch of pride, "Ivan and I were able to talk with the bison."

The festival would begin like this. We would sit in a horse-shoe-shaped formation before the monolith, close our eyes, and put the palms of our hands flat on the moss. Sanath told us to be aware that we are sitting on the back of a living being, the great Goddess, who nurtured the lady of the holy desert mountain who had ruled the mountain fortress of Dagad Trikon. 'Mother Earth is our own grandmother,' he said, 'and can free us of any troubles if we learn how to pray to her.' He himself used to pray to her in an unknown language, I can only remember one word he would repeat… 'twam' or 'twamev,' or something like that. First, we would feel our heaviness going into the earth through our hands and arms. Then, surging from the earth through the trunk of our bodies we would feel a new strength, the rush of a sweet love. It was a delightful, sweet love that made us one with Mother Earth and filled with her tender protection. Then we would sing and dance."

"That's right," said the count. "Sanath would only celebrate this earth festival with the children, but eventually I was permitted to sit with them. I learned that the earth could feel us and recognize us individually. It was an extraordinary feeling, like a meeting. When we reached that state of union with the Goddess of the earth, the animals and birds would also be aware of the moment. Flocks of migratory geese and herring gulls would change their route to land on the neighboring ponds and lakes. All the species were in unison, the wood grouse next to the golden eagle, the willow ptarmigan next to the fish hawk, all in peace and all silent: it was the great mass of the Hllidarendi. It seemed to me that even the clouds knew. We stayed there in complete and blissful togetherness, each one of us experiencing the oneness of the world. We would eventually fall into a deep and restorative sleep, huddled under warm blankets and lying on the moss around the Sao Iambu. Sanath would himself stay awake all night, praying to the earth to forgive the many sins of the sons and daughters of Man."

"The swans were the birds who came closest to our little group, almost sitting amongst us when the oneness came," continued Laira, her black eyes shining. "I was just a little girl then, but I really felt the entire universe as one. If it became too cold, the sun would warm us gently; and in summer, if it were too hot, the breeze would blow to cool us down. It was an energy that bound us all, innocent love pouring out from everywhere, an invisible firework of love. We felt so united and yet so free. I asked the wizard whether it was magic. He said that it was the Ananya magic that was within the world and that men could feel before the Great Schism, before things started to fall apart."

They remained silent for a time. It was as though, for a fleeting moment, they had touched that special place and time themselves, but soon their thoughts returned. The world described by Laira was so far from the one they knew. How could this little island in the midst of the bog mires ever be recreated? Was it at all relevant for them? Lakshman felt upset that the children from the Byelorussian forest village had learned so much more from Sanath than he had ever managed to. He missed the wizard, missed everything he should and could have learned. "Did Sanath teach you other things, I mean, in relation to what we are investigating now?"

"Let me take you back to the time of the village in the forest," began Philip. "Sanath was living in a circular hut. It was the largest in the village and the closest to the sacred oak. It served as his library, study, and laboratory, and had a round fireplace at its center. The cupboards were overflowing with old manuscripts and books and this was where he taught many things to Ivan, Laira, and the other children of the clan. This is where we spent long snowy and cozy winter nights together. He took us into his confidence, telling us about the past of our race, of Dagad Trikon and the Grand Scheme of Adivatar, the Highest One we call God. He told us that in former ages, long gone by, before the accounts of history as we know it, various races occupied the earth. Things were different then and yet, in a sense, much the same as they are now. It all goes in cycles, you see, we keep going back to the future and forward towards the past."

"This doesn't make sense."

"Well, at the beginning it doesn't, but then again it does. Man is presented with a series of riddles that he must solve until he can climb to the next higher level of evolution. The movement is not linear, more like a spiral or an ascending circular movement, all of which is heading somewhere, as you shall see.

Let us start at the beginning. The purest beings, those we call divine, are not usually seen here as they reside in other worlds although they may visit the earth from time to time. They are diverse manifestations of Adivatar. I will not say much about them. They are within the Grand Scheme. They lead the Game, which is the part of the Grand Scheme that applies to this Earth."

"If so, we should have known about it," observed Jonathan.

"Of course, and so we did. When some of these highest forms come into the Game, they usually change the course of history. They can manifest the Father aspect, like the Aryan kings, Rama and Krishna in India, or the Son aspect as with the lords Siddhartha Gautama, the Buddha, or Jesus the Christ. They can come as the Mother aspect, as Lakshmi or Parvati in India, or Kuan Yin in China or as the Virgin Mary in the West. Or they can come as masters and prophets like Lao Tse or Confucius in China, Zarathustra in Iran, Socrates in Greece, Moses and Abraham for the Jews, or Mohammed, the prophet of Islam. The problem for men is that they never recognize these forms when they are alive, because the divine beings are not easy to recognize. After the messengers of Adivatar have departed this earth, people then begin to follow and worship them. But the followers eventually mess everything up and fight among themselves. This, unfortunately, is the story of all organized religions so let us leave it at that.

Long ago, once the gods retreated it was left to us. Those inside the Game were of unequal lineage. Sustaining the Grand Scheme in the beginning were the earlier born, the Avasthas, who shone with goodness and brilliance, but who were not immune from pride. The highest Avasthas became angels, Lucifer being one of them. But the highest angels and the archangels, such as Michael or Gabriel, are beyond the Avasthas. On the other hand, those powerful beings, called Titans in Greek mythology or Asuras in the Aryan world, lusted after might and power and turned to the demonic side. There were also serpent beings, those still called nagas in faraway India, who were the guardians of underground treasure cities and who could transform themselves into handsome human shapes. But with the exception of the angels, all these have now taken human form. Our race has become a big genetic whirlpool of all previously existing species, including the prototype of Jurassic animals from long ago."

The visitors were listening in rapt silence, astonished at what they heard. Philip continued, "Men and dwarfs went about their business, picking a path through their confused destiny, quarrelsome and greedy. Some angels, men, dwarfs, and nagas came under the spell of the Shadow. Lucifer fell, while some naga lords became flying reptiles, the dragons of Earlier Earth. Then there were those lower beings that had been subdued by Thanatophor, the ruler of the Shadow. They became demons, goblins, and monsters that fortunately we cannot recall."

"Are they also around?" asked Jonathan with a shrug.

"They are probably waiting for the triumph of the Shadow, then they will emerge from the nether worlds like the hordes of dread. Some of them are already here having taken human form as pornographers, child molesters, or serial killers. But the army of the Shadow is much vaster, much closer too. Some live at the margin of our world, between life and death: they are called ghosts, pretas, bhoots or golems: the living dead. The Titanosaurs, lords of creatures of abomination, worst among the rotten fruits of dark magic, have the power to lead thousands of them."

"Like the Brown Specter?"

"Yes. Sanath spoke about the northern and the southern Titanosaurs. Somehow, they help each other in achieving their goal, which is to increase the level of hate and of all feelings, attitudes, and behaviors associated with it."

"Okay, if these are the players, what is the Game?' Lakshmi, as usual, was the most matter-of-fact of them all.

Philip continued, "It's a bit like hide-and-seek but with discovery and a big prize at the end for the winners. I guess the losers will get another chance. It depends how badly they lose... It's a play between Good and Evil. This planet is center stage. The show covers many cycles of time and each one of us is in it, whether we know it or not. Most people don't, of course."

"Who is hiding and who is seeking?"

"That's the question, isn't it?" said Philip thoughtfully. "Can you answer that one, Laira?"

"I can try, Philip, but you know I am not very comfortable with words. Sanath explained it in this way. He said the lady of the Rock revealed it to him in a dream. In the beginning, Adivatar was completely alone and the universe was unformed. Because love is his nature, he did not wish to remain alone – he wanted to share his perfection, his boundless joy of existence. To share, he needs to share with someone. So that someone had to be created and hence creation began. Sharing his divine nature was the primordial act of love. Someone had to be worthy of this sharing, worthy of this gift. So evolution unfolded to bring every living creature to the level where it could recognize and enjoy the gift.

Gradually awareness grew in Adivatar's creatures, from the rock to the lichen, to the amoeba, to the animal, onwards towards man, onwards towards the twice-born and the higher beings. Adivatar was hiding, the creatures were seeking and also finding. Thus, the Grand Scheme unfolded. Adivatar started sharing and many beings delighted in his generous gift. The ancient texts spoke of a magic fluid flowing through the central nervous system of the twice-born, bringing both bliss and illumination. Adivatar, for the elected, was hiding no longer. He stood revealed and the absolute joy that the higher creatures were seeking was found in the deep well of their very being, because – and this is what Sanath wanted to share with us – divinity had hidden itself within them." As she spoke, Laira became more animated, color flushed her cheeks, and suddenly she seemed to feel the message. She had to stop, overwhelmed for an instant by the magnitude of what she was saying. And again, for an instant, they all felt it too.

"Lairouchka," intervened Ivan, with brotherly affection, "I can see that the winter afternoons you spent as a little girl with the wizard were put to full use. He revealed much of his lore to you."

As Laira signaled that she did not want to speak any further, Ivan continued. "In this ancient age under the rule of the Avasthas, many beings found their truth inside themselves. It is said that the whole of the outside world exploded in a new dimension of perfection. Nature delighted in the ecstasy. The water was living water, so bathing in the rivers brought an intense feeling of freshness, vigor, and well-being. The sun's light was a soothing, energy-giving caress, never scorching nor burning, bringing strength and creativity. Every sunset was a magnificent rhapsody of hues and colors. Sun and water carried spiritual powers and our cosmos was awakened. The animals communicated, the trees understood, the breeze was perfumed and regenerative. All food produced by Mother Earth was exquisite in taste. Human societies were self-ruled, advised by colleges of wise and benevolent seers. Settlements were scattered across the globe in rather small communities, with just sixteen beautiful metropolises. Technology was advanced and non-polluting."

"So this was the Golden Age?" asked Jonathan. "The faraway period that fellow researchers of the Oikos Project are tracing back. But how did we go wrong? How did we go from there to the present mess?"

APPLES AND ORANGES

Philip nodded at Lakshman's question and responded. "Thanatophor worked patiently, planning and scheming over many centuries. He also favored brutal events, such as conflicts and wars, in which people would lose their sense of the Law of Maat. But let me be more specific. The clouding of the consciousness happened gradually, a surreptitious sickness that developed slowly. It was a combination of ignorance and mistakes that the six Dark Riders had left behind in their wake.

We cannot rise again if we do not understand how we fell from grace in the first place. This is what I gathered through the years I spent with the wizard. During the Golden Age, at the beginning of what Sanath calls Earlier Earth, Thanatophor hid in caves, close to the magma, keeping Hangker and Belzebseth within himself at the boiling core of his own split identity. He was surrounded by the armies of his defeated minions, occasionally sending spies to the surface to find out whether and when his time might come."

"But if this cosmic house was so perfect, why was this fellow sulking in the basement?" Jonathan had always been bothered by the oldest philosophical question: why does evil exist if God is good? He had never been convinced by the explanations offered by the Genesis account of Adam, Eve, and the apple. Moreover, he could not understand the role of Satan appearing as the serpent in the Garden of Eden, luring Eve to bite that fateful apple.

"Of the origin of Thanatophor, the Hllidarendi did not speak, although I asked a number of times. But why mankind continues to decline and regress is clearer. Adivatar could reveal himself only to the earlier race of the twice born, for the brilliance of his sheer presence would have overwhelmed less-evolved humans. Twice born are those who went through the seventh step of Avastha initiation, of which I know nothing. The evolutionary process to produce a twice born takes a lot of work, so they were always few in number. The vast majority of beings remained confused. They were not sufficiently evolved to bathe in the absolute knowledge of the Deep Way; they just basked in its reflection."

Ivan added, "In a sense, this is what propels the game forward. The apple in the Garden of Eden is the symbol for the fruit of the knowledge of good and evil, which belongs to the core knowledge of the Deep Way. The Dagad Trikon prophecy, supposed to facilitate access to this knowledge, seems meant for the human race rather than the Avasthas. Only human beings can walk from darkness to light. Higher beings cannot because they are already in the light. In other words, the true return to divinity starts within the human race. This is what makes humans so precious in the Grand Scheme and so dear to Adivatar. This is also why man is the target of evil, which wants to prevent this.

There are obvious risks in this pilgrimage. Darkness contains ignorance and the Shadow carves its shape out of human ignorance. We have to be free; this is a sine qua non rule of the Game. In this freedom we make choices. When choices are made in ignorance, human beings commit mistakes. Indeed, error emerges from the combination of freedom and ignorance merged together. Thus, bred from error, evil gradually took root. The purpose of our pilgrimage on this earth is to seek that knowledge that allows us to properly exercise free choice and this explains the importance of accessing the Deep Way."

Philip nodded approvingly and continued, "Over millennia, the flow of divine auspiciousness slowly dried up. This brought about the end of the Earlier Earth whose last remnants remain buried in the Dagad Trikon Rock. Nature froze, higher beings left the earth, and human awareness regressed. History, as we know it, began."

"So, in a sense, we have to play this Game all over again?" observed Jonathan, incredulous that he was realizing the enormity of the wheel's movement. "But what's the point?" He was still thinking about learning from past mistakes and feeding it into the Oikos Project.

At this precise moment, two small boys, laughing and giggling, climbed the staircase. Their foreheads were bright and their eyes were limpid freshwater pools around large brilliant retinas. They tugged at Ivan's hands and tried to pull him away. "Come, Uncle, play with us, we need someone to be the king." The Cardinal laughed and leaned over the railing. "Look at the kids in the garden." With a couple of blankets hanging from branches and a few pillows, the children had created a palace. Three small girls with paper crowns, the princesses, sat inside; they were the prisoners. Two boys with sticks as swords were the warring knights. In the other corner of the garden, some other boys were pretending to be a train: "Uhuuu tchouk tchouk tchouk uhuuu…" they hissed.

"Basically, that's the point," said Ivan. "Take these kids as an example. When you play, you impersonate someone else, for fun. You create a sort of virtual world for entertainment, but when your game gets too sophisticated or your virtual world becomes too seductive, you may lose yourself in it. Didn't Christ say we must become like children? We should play as these children do: they are totally involved but they are quite detached too – all at the same time. They play, but a moment later they are back in reality and they forget all about the fantasy of their play. Kids can drop their games in an instant. On the whole, adults cannot most of us get lost in our games. For example, we begin to believe that we really are business-men, cardinals, and housewives. Yet all the great teachers used to say that in spiritual growth we give up the myth of involvement."

Philip said softly, "We have to walk outside of the darkness of Plato's cave, get rid of the shadows of mental opinions and rational-ity. Instead, let us have the courage to look straight into the sun of direct knowledge, the revelation of all mysteries. Those who live in illusions have the illusion to live. Those who live in reality touch the deeper dimension of existence. The Deep Way is about something that is so simple: it means getting high just on existing. People who are too brainy find it a difficult concept to grasp. But it is simply fabulous. We went into that state for a few moments, but we could not remain there."

Lakshmi looked at Philip with some astonishment and a little envy; he was so confident in what he was saying and seemed to know a lot about the Deep Way.

Ivan continued, "The Game is to get out of our games. The Game is about becoming real. The point is to come back to reality. Inside. People do not know how to turn their attention inwards. It constantly flows outside through the five gates of seeing, hearing, smelling, tasting, and touching. 'The five senses are like five oranges in the hands of a juggler,' said Sanath. When you reach an equilib-rium point you create a movement, a new sense, by which the atten-tion can turn inside. Or, if you prefer, we reach a stage where we can draw our senses inside, like a turtle retreating into its shell."

Lakshman had a flashback to the vivid imagery of the Amsterdam vision: the white marble palace of the tortoise, his painful failings before the queen, when juggling with the oranges, and Sanath's words rang in his memory: "I shall tell with someone else's voice." He realized now that the meaning of his inner vision in Amsterdam was his failure to turn his attention inside, to break through the higher order of direct knowledge. This must have been the meaning of the tortoise with the carapace bedecked with precious gems at the step of the throne. "Sanath knew about this, he knew about this moment!" he exclaimed, "I saw this with him in Amsterdam as we absorbed the content of the casket but why are these oranges appearing in the Dagad Trikon scrolls? I am rather confused."

Ivan nodded at Philip. Laira went downstairs to play with the children in the garden. The count continued, "The wizard of Hllidarendi is a true master. He sees things because the present, for him, spreads into the past and our future. Let's go back to our hiding place in the Byelorussian forest surrounded by the advancing Wehrmacht. That's where and when he gave us some answers to your question.

After the Great Schism, man lost contact with the truth. Sanath told us that the Shadow grew stronger again about ten thousand years ago. It steadily brought more creatures under its rule, working to widen the gap of the Foul Rift as men gradually lost the sense of inner balance. Hitler and Stalin, incarnated demons who were recently battling each other at the cost of millions of human dead, represent a major episode in the old war that the Shadow waged against mankind. It is what we may call the attack from the outside, that is, bad things happening to man. This is Hangker's brutal way: wars, terror, calamities, epidemics, natural catastrophes, and accidents. Now, the strategy of the Shadow for the end of this millennium is to intensify the attack from the inside, in other words, bad things happening within man. This is Belzebseth's sneaky way."

Ivan added, "When Sanath concluded that the Shadow would also ensnare man from within, he investigated what methods had been developed in the Fourth Age of man to turn the attention inwards; he wanted to match the process and to respond to the attack. He might have been sorely disappointed. We don't think he found the answer, otherwise he would have told us."

Philip continued, "You see the five oranges are the five senses that must be kept in constant equilibrium. With the senses in balance you do not fall into the extremes where the servants of Thanatophor can snatch you. If the senses flow too far outside, without any self-control, man is not equipped to counter Belzebseth's infiltrations into his own thoughts and emotions. So we find the link between the oranges and the Dagad Trikon prophecy.

Men do not have ready access to the fourth state of knowing. The Avasthas want to help them. The ancient techniques for controlling the senses followed by the old masters are all beyond the reach of modern man. Even in the old days it wasn't easy. In the past, when some men followed ascetic practice, withdrew into the desert or the Himalayas, they would still, on occasion, fall for the occasional naga girl. The balance between the senses had to be a perpetually reconstructed dynamic. Like the oranges for the juggler, the exercise took much time, perseverance, and dedication."

"Don't I just know it!" interrupted Lakshman, still feeling the shame linked with his failure to perform at the queen's durbar. He still felt shy about it and did not want to elaborate on the Amsterdam vision. Yet at that moment he understood there was a relationship between mastery over the senses and stabilizing the scales of the balance, as he had witnesses so vividly in Amsterdam. Mankind first needs to establish balance within itself in order to establish it in society. When the scales are stabilized, the stairway to heaven is revealed and the path of higher evolution opens.

However, Philip ignored the interjection and continued, with a trace of emotion in his voice. "Sanath understood that the Rock Avasthas wanted to warn mankind about the forthcoming onslaught of the Shadow. They called it the sneaky way. To counter the threat within, men must be able to go within. They must find a way to receive once more, to touch and taste the gift of Adivatar. Sanath hoped that one of the caskets would yield the secret key to the inner gate, a new method for access inwards because mortals would not even consider the old method of first balancing the senses.

In Thanatophor's plan, Belzebseth and Hangker led an effective and constant complementary onslaught. They aimed at perfect synchronicity between the inside and the outside attack to keep humans out of balance. For instance, the Shadow is fond of using various forms of inner weakness to cause outer calamities."

"Take just one famous example," intervened Ivan with some excitement in his voice. "The minstrels of the Middle Ages sang the story about Belzebseth defeating the Hllidarendi. Sanath spoke to us about the rise and fall of Camelot. At that time, Merlin the Enchanter was the Hllidarendi. After centuries of preparation, he brought Arthur to the kingship and forged the brotherhood of the Knights of the Round Table. He was thus trying to recreate the noble companionship, which had secured the millennial prosperity of the First Age of the Avasthas. But the flicker of mutual desire in the eyes of Queen Guinevere and Lancelot brought down Arthur's kingdom. Saint Thomas said, 'Corruptio optimi pessima – the corruption of the best is the worst.' Of course, today flirting is considered cute but today's standards could never have produced Camelot. Morgan, the witch, had come straight from Belzebseth's own witch clan. Together with her son Mordred, who was sent by Hangker, they foiled the scheme of the Hllidarendi. Excalibur, I believe, was a sword of the Avasthas just like the Glorfakir that Lakshman found."

"Yet an Avastha weapon by itself cannot do anything," added Philip sadly. " It is the arm that grabs the sword, which brings its power to life. Galahad remained undefeated because purity of heart was, in fact, the main protection of the fellowship of the knights. Belzebseth knew it too and this is where he struck. Camelot was doomed from the moment that Arthur's wife looked with lust at her king's best warrior. It was weakness of the attention and of the heart that brought Camelot down."

"Interesting that, in the USA, Camelot was the name given to the Kennedy clan," remarked Lakshmi. "Matrimonial fidelity was not their strong suit either, but surely, Philip, historians claim that the kingdom of Arthur is only a legend?"

"Legends are meant to tell truths that cannot be heard in a straightforward fashion," said Philip in words that reminded Lakshman of his first encounter with Sanath in Iceland. "The weakness of the queen and of the first knight is so typical of the West, isn't it? We were warned. How can the togetherness and strength of the tribe establish itself without virtue and innocence? No, the fall of Camelot is real." He added gravely, "Sanath told us last time I saw him that Arthur has been born again: he is a child now, but he may one day be king again."

"Do you mean Merlin and Sanath are the same people?"

"Not automatically. The Hllidarendi is a state achieved by the greatest wizards, those who were called the Nathas in India during the modern era. Both Merlin and Sanath had reached this state but Merlin feared the rule of men and went away, but Sanath stayed."

Jonathan could not hide his skepticism. "Let us come back to earth, a place where Sanath has now been murdered. Going back to fairy tales and children's stories is not going to help much. Where I come from, someone trying to whack you is a serious sign of disagreement. I want to know who it is who so disagrees with us. I would prefer to put the CIA on to the case of this bombing over the Black Forest rather than throwing oranges in the air."

"All right," the Count said, "I see your point, of course, but let me keep you in the air for a while because I want to mention some hidden connections. I am trying to share what I know about the tactics of the Shadow. Look at the events resulting from the current attacks, those you read about every day in the newspapers such as terrorist bombing, murders, or even what appears to be, for example, just a car crash. To the Shadow, the advantage of these events is that they provoke sudden and brutal death. In such cases, the victims are stunned by their death. They are not prepared to go; they hang around their bodies and do not depart for the appointed place where the dead go. Have you seen the movie 'Always' directed by Spielberg or the movie 'Ghost'?"

"You mean 'Ghost' with Demi Moore? Yes, I saw it. "

"The guys who made those movies did it well. That's basically the way it is when we die. We leave behind the earth and the water elements, that is, the material sheaths of our being but all the rest of us is intact, without the protection of these elements. What happens then may be sinister. Under the instructions of Thanatophor, Belzebseth, with his staff of witch doctors and necromancers, has developed as an art the sorcery of capturing the baffled souls of those who have died suddenly. Some weaker souls cannot escape; they become his ghost soldiers in the army of the living dead. He then uses them for his purpose of enslaving our race from within."

"Do we know how they do it?"

Cardinal Sadaka responded, "It is what we call black magic but it goes much deeper than this voodoo stuff that so intrigues tourists in places like Haiti. Nowadays, most people do not accept that dark forces exist. This is one of the reasons why Sanath wanted to find the Dagad Trikon scrolls. He was looking for a new method to expose their plot. For this, he needed to go way back, back to the last Avasthas. Now, please excuse me but I need to join the children in the garden to collect their drawings of plants and the flowers. I'll be back soon."

"I get the idea about how destructive forces are trying to operate," said Jonathan, "but I fail to see what the antidote to black magic is or what the cure for this state of affairs might be. I understand from what you say that we must break through to a new awareness.

This song has been sung since the sixties. Fine, so what? I have seen nothing but lost souls, hippies, yuppies, drug addicts, and spiritual charlatans. Lunatic gurus from India to South Korea have fleeced gullible seekers. I had a friend at the World Bank in Washington, D.C. who broke a dorsal vertebra hopping on a mattress. He was trying to fly because his yogi had promised him that he could levitate. It cost him and his friends a lot of money, hoping to transform themselves into a flying squad. Of course, the squad remained permanently grounded. Eminence, all this and much more nonsense took place in the New Age circus, in the name of a new awareness. How can a new awareness solve our individual problems, let alone the collective challenges of our messed-up society?"

"I asked Sanath this very question," said Philip with a reminiscent smile. "The Hllidarendi explained that there is an all-pervading energy in the cosmos, something akin to the power of Adivatar. The Rock Avasthas called it by many names, each of which corresponded to its many nuances. For example, when the Avasthas felt it collectively through their festivals of music, dance, and joy, they called it the Rasa vibrations. But normal men cannot harness or tune in to this divine energy. It is like radio or television where we need a receiver set to hear the music, or see the pictures carried through the air by radio or other waves. Without a receiver, the waves are useless to us and we cannot hear the music or see the pictures. The earlier-born harnessed the sound of the energy of Adivatar in their Rasa music. Mind you, some specific spots in nature can harness and send this sacred energy. Those who can, tune in and receive guidance and protection such as that described by Laira in the company of Sanath."

"Might ordinary human beings do this too?" asked Lakshmi, "I mean, catch the waves?"

"This is precisely the answer we may find if we can solve the Dagad Trikon enigma. 'The awareness we must now achieve,' said the Hllidarendi, 'has a new dimension.' It transforms our brain into a prism that can absorb and refract the waves. The new brain becomes a device that receives the music; we tune in, we are wired. Imagine a colorless energy of love flowing into the higher brain and refracted into multicolor manifestations: wisdom, creativity, generosity, compassion, collective consciousness, clear-sightedness, and many tremendous powers that show up when the energy flows through the prism.'"

Lakshman was impressed. "Then you get these primordial powers to take over the fight against Thanatophor. Yes, that should work but what is the mechanism for this transformation of the human brain?"

"Sanath does not tell, but he says it worked for some Rock Avasthas," replied Philip. "He says man needs to reactivate the process. This is why the Hllidarendi searched for the ten caskets for such a long time. Finally, he came to know where a few of them were. He could not open the caskets himself because the Avastha magic denied prime access to any of the higher beings that would still be walking upon this lost earth during the Fourth Age of man. Sanath needed a human being with specific qualities to do so. Understand his delight in finding you!

The casket found, we now know, was the Casket of the White Feather, the one taken to Iceland and already deciphered. Sanath called us from Amsterdam when you were there. Correct us please if we got it wrong, but the message from the sea was about our evolution. We need to reach a state of synthesis between our contradictions, something like equilibrium, a harmony, a balance before we can go higher?"

Lakshmi added, "For societies, this harmony cannot be established without social justice and the vision Laksh had in Amsterdam recalls that social justice cannot be achieved without sharing wealth. Is that right?"

"I guess so," confirmed Jonathan, "but this is hardly new stuff. It doesn't tell us how to get there."

"Patience, my friends," said the Count. "We need to reconstruct the full puzzle. The casket brought to Russia by one of the Avastha messengers was buried under the oak in the middle of the Byelorussian forest. The Avastha knight, whose helmet was topped by a cross, brought it there. He was Isaprem, sire of the House of Anorhad and worshipper of the inner light of truth. Strangely enough, he came there from China. We do not know the secrets of the Casket of the Cross but we were told it had to be handled with utmost care. The great oak is sacred and the casket can be unearthed only when the tree chooses to die. Yet it gets its strength from the casket. Sanath said, 'The tree will die at the end of the Age of Pisces, and when this time shall come, let us pray we are all prepared, for the casket can bring both death and resurrection." It should be soon. The fate of Russia hinges on it. In the meantime, the Dagad Trikon magic worked through the oak and greatly strengthened the wizard himself. This is why he settled in this remote forest, soon to be adopted and respected by its sylvan clan." Philip reclined in his rocking chair, looking thoughtful, entirely absorbed in his memories.

"I think it's time to tell you about the third casket now," said Ivan, who had just returned from the garden. Lakshman was amazed at the change in his face. He looked ten years younger, radiating peace. As if to answer an unasked question, the Cardinal noted, "As a matter of fact, these children are wonderful. Whenever I play with them I feel in heaven. I love this school; my pet project is growing, developing with each passing day."

He turned to Lakshman. "Sanath did a lot of research on locating the caskets. You unearthed the casket of the Sheravalian rider of the White Feather, which is what set things in motion. We know that the Casket of the Cross is buried under the oak of my village, but we do not know its content. Sanath found a trace of a third casket. He suspected it to be the casket carried by the Elnorian whose helmet carried a ten-point star. It is supposed to be engraved with a ten-spoke wheel and, luckily seems connected with the one you retrieved in Iceland. Sanath knew that this casket would expose some of the Darkness' most devious schemes to implement the strategy for the attack from within. He discovered that this casket was the one taken by the Avastha warrior to Mount Parnassus in Greece but that, in more recent history, it had landed in a most unlikely place, which had been infiltrated by some servants of the Darkness. Fortunately the Darkness has not found it yet." Puzzled, Jonathan asked: "Eminence, can you be more specific, please?"

"Somehow, a hermit on Mount Athos who seems to have served the Order of the Hllidarendi hid the Casket of the Green Wheel within a golden reredos, a masterpiece of Byzantine craft. At the time of the Crusades, a Venetian merchant in Constantinople bought this unique piece. It was eventually sold to a Borgia Pope in Rome and is still part of the Vatican treasury. I saw it myself. But nobody knows it contains the casket. Sanath said that we must get hold of the Casket of the Wheel at any cost as soon as Lakshman arrived in Rome. He left with me a sealed envelope that I am supposed to open before we open the casket."

Philip added, "Believe it or not, we may finally get down to business here. Let's forget Hangker for the time being, and concentrate on the moves of Belzebseth. Let us thus assume that the next onslaught on our race will be the destruction from within, probably triggered by outside challenges. That's easy to imagine because, for instance, outside stresses increase psychosomatic sicknesses, psychiatric disorders, nervous breakdowns, addictions, attention deficit disorder and so on. Let us also take Sanath's word that, to counter the threat, the response is a new awareness, an illumination of human consciousness. Then, world religions will be on the spot because the achievement of this breakthrough ought to have been their exclusive preserve, the matter they were supposed to deal with. Religions, according to Sanath, were meant to facilitate access, to carry us through the doors of perception."

Lakshmi observed, "But it seems to me that religions all over the world have somehow calcified: they've actually blocked the path, haven't they?"

Philip said with his eyes closed, "Indeed, those who would try to get through that narrow gate, over the centuries, were roughed up, exiled, defamed or ridiculed. Many guardians of the clerical dogmas went unknowingly to the side of the Darkness. One of my ancestors, the sixth Count of Jetzlar, was a friend of the Duke of Saxony, Frederik the Wise, and a follower of Martin Luther. The Hapsburg troopers seized him as soon as he left the Duke's territory; his retinue was killed and, as he refused to reveal Luther's hiding spot in the Warburg, he was tortured and burned on a pyre by the side of the road."

Ivan said, "Most priests in the different religions could not get through and they would not let anyone else go through. The path of spirituality remained closed. Men walked away from it all, ate the oranges, went to the disco, got busy, entertained themselves, and eventually filled their emptiness with the noises of modernity. When he left Russia, Sanath told me to enroll in the Catholic seminary in Katowice in Poland. There, I made friends with a young theater actor from Lithuania who became a priest and eventually climbed the full hierarchic ladder to become Pope. That helped me a great deal in entering the Vatican's hierarchy. I served him as if I were his private counselor. You will not believe what I have discovered since then."

Turning towards Jonathan and addressing him, the Cardinal said, "For three years, your brother Joseph has been helping me. I took him into my confidence and he assisted in my research. He has amassed a file that is damning for the agents of the Shadow within the Vatican: links with Nazis in South America, influence peddling,

Mafia deals, money laundering – everything documented with conclusive and undeniable proof. He thinks he can work something out with you, Jonathan, as you are one of the rising stars of the U.S. State Department. Let's see."

"Oh so, that's what it is," exclaimed Jonathan both surprised and worried. "Joseph is returning to the States with me in connection with this inquiry. He started talking to me about it but he didn't divulge any details. He wanted to collect some documents first. Listen, I am not crazy, I don't intend to pick a war with the Church."

Ivan went on. "I wouldn't blame you. I myself can't talk about these things to the Pope. With great foresight I have leaked some documents from these files to a few Italian investigative journalists but they keep bumping into high-speed cars or dying in their sleep. It's unnerving."

Lakshmi interrupted him. "Let's not get too far into this discussion now because we may spend all night on this topic. In India, we have our share of trouble with clerics of various denominations, be they Muslim preachers of hate in Kashmir or scheming Tibetan lamas whose greatest skill appears to be impressing a handful of Hollywood stars."

"Never mind, my cover mission in Rome is close to its end," said Ivan. "I was told I could not access the Avastha code because, as we grew up in the company of the Hllidarendi, we are disqualified. Sanath asked me to wait for Lakshman, which is why I approached his cousin at the Spanish ambassador's party. My men are in place. Soon Lakshman and I will retrieve the reredos from the treasury room of the Holy See and, in my private office, we will access the Casket of the Wheel." He looked up. "Oh, I see Alexandra waving from the kitchen – the pasta is ready."

As they descended the staircase leading to the kitchen, the Cardinal consoled a crying child. "Ambarich always wants to be the leader, it's my turn now!"

"Democracy in the making," intoned the Cardinal senten-tiously. "Rotate leadership to secure consensus but, believe me, these days the Darkness is having a good time with politics. Today's politicians are short-sighted, selfish, and corrupt. For a long time, they have sought the blessings of the priests to cover up their deeds. Blessings and indulgences came generously because, everywhere in the world, the deals went on between the barons of money and the princes of religion."

Jonathan knew this discourse only too well, so he interrupted the Cardinal with a change of tack. "You told me this school is your most important project. I don't get it – how come?"

"Ah, well, I'm sorry if I sounded boastful. I just like kids." His embarrassment only served to increase Jonathan's curiosity. He called a child who was passing by and asked her what her name was.

"My name is Lila," the child replied. A turning of the head, a flash from shining, intense black eyes, a giggle, and the girl was gone. They had reached the vaulted dining room and Jonathan looked through the window into the garden.

The children were gathering two by two, lining up to go to class. There was indeed something special about them. The boys were confident and handsome and the girls were gracious, so much so, thought Jonathan, surprised at his own mercenary thoughts, that each of them could have made a fortune advertising children's products. However, there was more to it than outer beauty; their grace seemed to emanate from within them. Lightness danced on their smiles, on their manners, and in their gestures. Their feet hardly seemed to touch the ground as they walked. Observing them still more attentively, Jonathan sensed a sort of natural ease, a playful spontaneity that, he suddenly felt, should be present in all children.

"Most remarkable, those eyes," he remarked. "Somehow, these kids are so alive; it is only now I realize that the eyes of so many children today already seem faded, colorless, their light taken away.

Too often modern children seem to be more like sad little adults." Jonathan was clearly fascinated. Philip looked at him and smiled.

The companions enjoyed the meal. The pasta was simply delicious: nothing whatever like spaghetti as Americans know it, thought Jonathan. He had had a long day and, after eating, he went to rest in his room on the second floor. Leaning over the railing of the window, he enjoyed the emerging freshness of dusk. Opposite, there was a large statue of the Goddess of Justice on a pedestal, holding up a pair of scales and with a blindfold over her eyes. He remembered the account of Lakshman's vision in Amsterdam. "Perhaps we need to be blind to the outside in order to turn our sight inside," he mused. "The inner sense will help to keep the scales in balance."

EPISODE THIRTEEN

LORELEI´S PARTY

In her room on the top floor of the Casa della Minerva, Lorelei was lying on her bed sobbing, her face buried in her pillow. Furry, stuffed animals, piled up alongside books on the bookshelves, looked on in sympathy. Lothar was gently massaging Lorelei's shoulder. This was the final act of a small drama, but an important one from Lorelei's perspective, which had mostly taken place during last year's summer holidays. It had sent tremors through the Jetzlar family and the grandparents had also taken it much to heart. "But Lothar, they all know about it. They'll laugh at me. I feel terrible, it was such a foolish mistake; they won't respect me anymore."

"Don't worry, sis. That guy is out of the group now and the friends arriving downstairs all support you. Come on, get up and come downstairs. They're all waiting for you. It's your birthday party, after all."

"All right Lothar, if you think so, give me half an hour and I'll try. When we came back to Italy, the memories and pain of last summer really hit me. I had fallen in love with Silvio, you know." He wiped the tears off her cheeks.

"I know, but remember what Grandpa told you: falling in love is one thing, rising in love is another, and better. Remember everything they told us. Come on, big girl, you are over this now."

211

The youngsters coming tonight were their usual group of friends in Italy – fun kids, yet straightforward and decent. She had felt safe in their midst until Silvio had appeared and she had been caught off guard. It had indeed been a drama. The tribulations of a juvenile love affair may sound banal to sophisticates in the modern world, but in a family that had tried to connect with the subtler dimension of the Deep Way, the episode of Lorelei and Silvio was a serious matter. Lorelei had fallen in love with an Italian boy whose family had a summer residence in the neighboring village. He was a handsome lad who was precociously adept at charming young girls with tender hearts and a large measure of naivety. He had met Lorelei with a few friends at the ice cream parlor under the village's main arcade and while she had been ordering pistachio and strawberry, he had made up his mind to strike. He had had no qualms nor any guilt about it, for Silvio prided himself in making such moves with expertise and style.

The handsome blond outsider from Germany with quite a touch of class was a real trophy. The first sight of the attractive girl had triggered Sylvio's hunting instincts. For someone who has a taste for the sport of seduction, there is something inherently attractive about innocence. Lorelei exuded an air of freshness, the spontaneous freshness that is hard to maintain as we grow into adulthood. She carried herself with genial ease, a natural gift that is impossible to fake. Such unspoiled vibrancy springs from the depths of the being and so is much more appealing to the discerning hunter than the availability of the easy girls on Italy's summer beaches. Beyond the intensity of his Latin temperament, what made Silvio such an effective Don Juan was a certain cuteness, an air of boyish ingenuity that allowed him to approach and ensnare unsuspecting prey. The first meeting had laid the trap.

Thereafter, they had met a couple of times and Silvio was doing well. In the turquoise tenderness of a warm Latin summer evening,

212

the boy had stolen a few kisses. It was a night for lovers and for discoveries. The young couple had hidden themselves behind the thick curtain of bamboo along the brook that marked the border of Ivan's property. A large flat stone offered a propitious abode. A few kisses were stolen some were given. The air was warm and soft and Silvio was so seductive.

Lorelei felt a bit dizzy. One thing led to another, a kiss to a caress and suddenly the girl realized she was involved in something that she had not intended. She felt uncomfortable and very vulnerable. This romance was going too far too fast, no matter what her heart was telling her. She asked him to stop, then began to defend herself when he ignored her plea. In the heat of the moment, the boy would neither listen nor give up and was now pressing her against the ground with the full weight of his body.

Lorelei was a strong, athletic girl and she managed to free herself and ran tearfully towards the Casa della Minerva. In the courtyard, she bumped into Lothar. She looked a mess, with her blouse half-unbuttoned, her hair disheveled, and tears coursing down her cheeks. There was no hiding anything from her brother. When he heard his sister's plaintive confession, he raced at top speed to the bamboo wood, ready to draw blood but Silvio was long gone.

Later, to further compound the insult, Silvio boasted to the kids in the next village of his conquest of the pretty German girl from the Casa della Minerva on a bed of soft bamboo. This was untrue, as Lorelei had fought him off in the nick of time, but it had been close enough. The whole incident had ended in a family discussion because the children and their grandparents were used to sharing all the important happenings in their lives.

There were good reasons for this. Lorelei and Lothar were orphans who had lost their parents at a tender age in a car crash; Philip and Laira had raised them ever since. Philip loved Lothar very much but he especially doted on his granddaughter. He had always felt the need to nurture the freedom of his grandchildren while at the same time bringing them up according to the teachings of Sanath. Yet, when the matter of Lorelei's heartbreak was brought to his and Laira's attention, they were alarmed. They feared that perhaps they had not been firm enough in the face of the mounting peer pressures the children had been facing at school. Both kids were good-looking and radiated a strong magnetism and in their school, picking up a boyfriend or a girlfriend was a way of life – or, rather, a way of conforming to the ruling lifestyle.

Because Lothar was able to resist the charms of the many pretty girls from the school, his schoolmates had concluded that he was probably gay. To put the rumor mill at rest, he cooked up a story of an enticing American girlfriend he had met on the Spanish island of Majorca, and this had given him some respite. His best friend, Ali, came from a traditional Arab family, the son of an ambassador in Bonn. He was the only one who understood Lothar and knew that he was just buying some peace. Lorelei too had fended off the advances of her many suitors, but with the passing of time she found it difficult not to succumb to peer pressure and be like the other girls in her class. She wanted to fit in, and being unattached at the age of eighteen did not help. Silvio had astutely offered to resolve this dilemma himself.

Lorelei had always admired her grandfather greatly and she was shocked to see how much this event had upset him. Her grandmother tried to explain that the heart cannot be flaunted or given on the cheap, otherwise it is returned in pieces. Heartbreak can mean a wounded and dried wasteland or, worse, a frozen piece of black iron. That was the alchemy of Thanatophor: to stun the human heart with emotional pain so that it dries and freezes: to sow short-lived pleasure and to harvest real sorrow.

"A young heart is a precious but delicate flower," Laira had explained. "Only when trust and security are established and sanction the uniqueness of the bond can physical love best blossom. The heart must be respected." This was a cardinal principle of the Avasthas, and the foundation of the exquisite relationship to be nurtured between man and woman. Of course all this was hopelessly old-fashioned but what is fashion compared to wisdom that has matured over countless millennia?

Shaking off his sadness, Philip told Lorelei that her virginity was a well of hidden power that had yet to reveal itself. With this power she could heal, comfort, and protect others; with this power she could crush the brain waves of Belzebseth that had already penetrated unsuspecting victims. This power was called chastity, a notion that had gone out of favor in modern times. Many of the great women of history, who had raised children, built up entire kingdoms, and for whom the white knights of yore would die knew the power of chastity. The women who made fathers, brothers, husbands, and sons proud lived by this principle. With this power, Joan of Arc had thrown the English out of the kingdom of the lily. What would be the fate of a race that forgot to respect its women? What would be the fate of such families? Only a bruised and wounded society.

Lorelei had always wanted to please her grandfather and so was ashamed about what had happened. However, her grandfather's notion of proper behavior was a little bit remote compared to the world of her friends at school. Which one of her schoolmates could understand how much she valued the esteem of her grandfather? How could they relate to his subtle teachings advocating the merits of virtue or decency? To them, this would all be off track and decidedly uncool.

Still, Lorelei had an innate understanding of the need for self-respect. Although she had a beautiful body, she never flaunted it. She always dressed modestly, willing to buck the increasingly ubiquitous fashions of the world around her. On MTV for example, female teen icons acted as if dressing skimpily, shaking and strutting in a vulgar fashion was necessary in order to sing. Lorelei's school friends had even chipped in to buy her a G-string swimsuit, a clear invitation for her to adopt what they discerned to be a more progressive dress code.

This summer she was taking a break from it all, enjoying the children who had been carefully selected by Ivan to be admitted into the Casa della Minerva School. The school helped to identify kids who had a special potential and many of Lorelei's local friends were its former pupils.

The graveled alley was filling up fast with the cars of the guests who were arriving for Lorelei's party. While Laira von Jetzlar and Alexandra Sadaka had supervised the logistics, Lothar had organized the events and the music.

Joyous shouts and greetings, laughter, and the first notes of music wafted upward invitingly from the room downstairs. Jonathan decided to go and mingle with the youngsters. The three adjacent vaulted salons were full of teenagers; some of the younger children mixed with adults. The orchestra, which had positioned itself around the large fireplace, had started playing. Jonathan walked out into the garden where Fabian, a friend of Lothar, was tending to the barbecue. The courtyard had been re-arranged; a tent erected on the left side of the entrance served as a sitting area for those who were tired of dancing and just wanted to sit down and chat.

Jonathan took the opportunity to call Tracy in Washington DC, to tell her that he was on his way back home. She, in turn, told him they were encountering unexpected difficulties in securing the necessary funding for the Oikos Project in Congress.

Lorelei made her entrance and greeted all the assembled guests. A few splashes of cold water on her red, swollen eyes and a touch of make-up hid the traces of her tears quite well. At first, she felt gauche and a little apprehensive because it was the first time she had seen some of her friends since the events of last summer; soon, however, their warm greetings and embraces reassured her. She chatted with a friendly Fabian at the fireplace and began to feel more confident. After helping with the barbecue, she went to her grandfather in the grand salon, reached for his hand, and whispered, "Grandpa, wish me well. I know they are all very gracious but I am still unsure of myself, you know, because of last year. I feel I have fallen."

Philip threw her a penetrating glance and replied in a low voice, " Sanath used to say, 'Innocence is like the sky. Whatever we do against our innocence is like a cloud hiding the sky.' The clouds hide the sky. They cannot erase it. When the clouds are dispelled, it is back, in all its splendid vastness. Yes, Lorelei, you did fall, it's true, but look at it like this: if a warrior falls from her horse on the battlefield, she is defeated only when she admits her defeat. When weakened, she must be careful about the moves of the enemy. When she is still on the ground, she must be doubly alert but she can also choose to climb back on the horse and continue the fight. And this is in your power! Climb back, and reclaim your innocence. Fight for your self, your precious self. Is that what you want to do?"

"I do. Grandpa, you are the best. I love you so much. You always know what to tell me, how to get me back in the saddle. We are so lucky to have you." She reached up and gave her grandfather a big kiss on the cheek; they stared at each other for a second with a glance of acknowledgement that said more than words. Philip continued to look in her direction as she ran off, and he thought how much he loved it when she smiled with her eyes; the girl had genuinely understood what he wanted to convey. The dance had started.

Back in the main room, Jonathan stood against a wall, absorbing the atmosphere. "This is going to be some party," he thought. There were all kinds of music; there were lights of all shapes and colors with massive loudspeakers speakers to carry the powerful music. There was a general sense of fun and shared enjoyment –

which was surprising, thought Jonathan, for no alcohol was served in Alexandra's house and people usually needed a couple of drinks to get going. Ivan was mixing with the youngsters, enjoying himself fully. Lakshman and Lakshmi were familiar with Bollywood hip-hop dancing. The orchestra played Indian bhangra and the two cousins, in the middle of the improvised dancing floor, had joined the teen-agers with much gusto.

Lakshmi emerged from the group of dancers and, taking Jonathan by the hand, led him to the dance floor. The American was a little gauche at first for he always felt clumsy on a dance floor and, having admitted it, was not keen to prove the point. He admired people who had an innate sense of rhythm, who danced with ease and grace and could easily flow in the swirling of beats and sound. But tonight the music was so compelling that it was impossible to resist the urge to join in the dance. As he loosened up and melted into the music, he found himself dancing well. Spontaneously, his movements became better synchronized with those of Lakshmi. She looked at him with a big smile, visibly enjoying the moment.

For a split second, he received the intensity of her brown velvet glance and thought he saw something else in her expression. Then he faltered, missed a few beats, and she laughed. But swiftly getting back into the music, Jonathan erased that missed step and its accom-panying missed heartbeat from his memory. After all, it was just a small misunderstanding: he was engaged to Jenny and he felt sure about his feelings for her. Indeed, nothing else in Lakshmi's behavior this evening betrayed what he might have sensed or seen in that one powerful glance from her large brown velvet eyes.

The evening proceeded joyfully, with a slow but steady build-up of energy. There was a heady mix of music, from Rock to Viennese waltzes, from current pop tunes to South American salsa. A special dance that came next was even more remarkable. They waited for the moment with anticipation; it was the first collective dance that the group of friends had planned and rehearsed for in advance. To the tune of an Indian village song, the teenagers formed two circles with the girls on the inside and the boys outside. The boys moved clockwise, in a rhythmic pattern, the girls anti-clockwise. The music brought them together and gradually their whirling movements became perfectly tuned. Then they started shouting: "Lorelei, Lorelei... "

Lorelei, the birthday girl, went to the center of the circle and started dancing. From one side of the room, Philip watched his granddaughter intently with a look that was both grave and compassionate. Laira noticed him and moved to his side. At first Lorelei was shy and hesitating but then she closed her eyes and became subsumed into the music. She moved slowly, with an element of hesitation; then suddenly she was dancing extremely well. The pulse of the music brought her a sort of fluidity that was both gracious and rhythmical. Her body was gyrating; her heels were tapping an ever-faster beat like a Kathak dancer. The floor had become as a rumbling drum. Bystanders were clapping, cheering, singing, and swaying in unison.

The rhythm accelerated.

Lorelei was now at the hub of the liquid wheel of dancing youngsters. At the center of this special group of friends, she seemed to call up beats and rhythms, drums from within the entrails of the earth itself. As the young people moved in a synchronized pattern, Jonathan and the cousins, who had gone back to the side of the room to watch the amazing scene, felt a distinct sensation in their bodies, like the imperceptible churning of pleasure, a soft shiver of energy. This was no ordinary disco, Jonathan felt; something greater was happening thanks to this extraordinary group of teenagers.

Laira was also looking at her granddaughter, now the engine of the well-oiled, spinning wheel from which energy flowed in all directions. She whispered in her husband's ear, "I feel it now, the power is back. I was afraid she would lose it, but she didn't, Philip, she still has the power, she can still do it." The count answered with a thrill in his voice. "My dear, she had indeed lost the power. As you know, the Avasthas had to protect themselves to be able to carry the Rasa power but, you are right, and this is the wonder. The power is back. It is they who have brought it back, Laira; look at all the kids together: they brought it back to Lorelei. They protect and heal each other, working together like a precision clock; it is their togetherness that is working, just as Sanath had foreseen it. It is the wheel that is working out the calling; it works as a whole, not through any of its parts alone, not even the hub: the power is becoming collective, as was the case for the Yuva platoon. Lorelei is still weaker than she was, but, with their backing, she will recover fast. This is indeed a miracle."

Laira pressed Philip's hand with a sigh of reassurance. She was confident that the damage caused by her granddaughter falling for Silvio and his charms was not permanent.

In spectacular fashion, the night was living up to and exceeding all expectations. The moment finally came when Lothar, acting as the DJ, announced that he was playing the last song of the night. The song had been a big hit in all the charts: it was called "Where is the love?" Lothar requested that everyone form a large circle; there were about fifty or sixty boys and girls, all standing with their arms around each other's shoulders. They faced each other, and, even though there wasn't much light, they saw each other clearly, for every face shone like a dancing flame; every eye dazzled and it was almost as if the dancing spirit blazed through each dark iris.

The moment was one of light. There was a sense of belonging that sprang from the boundless expanses of pure friendship. It was as if the fire of their spirits had come together. There, in that house deep in the countryside, they formed a ring of fire that burned with a love that the world outside knew not. It was such a strong love that it was almost tangible: a magical moment. They were united with such intensity that not a word was said, and in that reality the answer to the question "Where is the love?" was manifested. They knew the answer because they felt it inside, deep in their hearts. There was a warm smile on every face. Lothar looked at his sister: his plan had succeeded. She shone too and he knew that the light was back within her.

The level of energy stunned Lakshman. Lakshmi's eyes were sparkling; she had melted into the common warmth of hearts and joined Jonathan who was close to the rim of the circle, standing next to Ivan and Alexandra. He said, "Isn't it amazing, Lakshmi? They are having so much fun; I've never seen a party like this. All of a sudden, there was so much energy that seemed to come from nowhere."

"From nowhere? Are you sure? I think it came from a well within each of them and when they joined to form the wheel this well became one, a large well from where the Rasa sound beats arose. This must have something to do with Ivan's mysterious pet project, the grooming of these remarkable children."

Jonathan threw her a penetrating glance; he had not expected her to be so tuned in to what was happening around them. He struggled to find the right words as he tried to decipher the situation. "It's so... unexpected and spontaneous. We didn't see it coming, but all of a sudden, did you notice? We just arrived at another level. I don't know how these kids did it. No one is out of time, there are no drugs, no alcohol; what's the secret? I never saw anything like this. This is a hell of a party, sorry, a heaven of a party! Such compact friendship and togetherness, you can touch it, you can breathe it!"

Ivan and Alexandra were feeling so rewarded that their Casa della Minerva could host such a festival of collective joy. This was, after all, the fruit of years of patient nurturing and the very purpose for which they had acquired this estate: to provide a refuge to all these wonderful people. Laira exclaimed: "What a night! This is as close to our dancing around the Sao Iambu as I could possibly imagine! Do you remember?"

At that instant, Jonathan felt the pressure of a hand on his shoulder; it was Philip. Laira was holding Philip's other hand. His face was radiant too and he looked even younger. He said simply,

"Now."

"Now? Now what?"

"Now!" repeated Laira. "At this moment! At this time. The now is the eternal time in which we move without movement. When we enter in the present moment, we can dive into a whirlpool of energy and joy. This is what it is. It is waiting within each instant, a treasure waiting to be found. It can also happen without the kids' dancing. It can happen if we know how to call upon the magic." She looked affectionately at Philip and added, "This is the teaching of Sanath. God has given us the here and now. The next minute is a gift of the devil." Jonathan nodded, and at that moment he seemed to understand and share the feeling. It simply made sense.

Their sleep that night was deep and restorative. The next day Jonathan and Joseph parted reluctantly from their friends and flew to Washington DC.

Joseph hurried out of the terminal of Dulles International Airport accompanied by his brother Jonathan. He hugged a bulging attaché case to his chest that contained the files he had patiently amassed during three years of research within the walls of the Holy See, under the guidance of Sanath's spy, the head of the Pope's Privy Council, H.E. Ivan Cardinal Sadaka. He had packed his Dominican cassock in his luggage and was dressed in casual sportswear. Their younger brother Michael was waiting for them. They exchanged hugs and Michael drove their father's Range Rover directly to Birchwood House, the comfortable estate of this prominent Irish family in Virginia. Michael was a handsome young man, with high cheekbones, unkempt hair, and an air of intensity about him. He was a student at Georgetown University and presently worked as an intern at the State Department, as well as helping Jonathan with research for a policy paper.

As they arrived home after a pleasant flight, the two travelers immediately felt the difference between those worlds: the bland tediousness of their family's polished lifestyle contrasting with the burst of spontaneity and the raw power of joy they had just experienced in the Casa della Minerva.

Whenever Jonathan found something wonderful he wanted to share it with those dear to him, but how could he possibly describe his experience to his self-important father who spent all his time cajoling his mistress? How could he share it with his mother? She was so frustrated that she complained daily about her situation, but was not enraged enough to consider a different way of living.

Both his parents were the privileged scions of important families and took their wealth and status as a matter of fact. They each moved through life like corks dancing on the surface of the water, never able to dive into the depths. Jonathan was an affectionate son and would have loved to help his parents but had no idea how to go about it. As these thoughts scurried around in his brain, he didn't even notice that they were slowly being replaced by his deep attachment for his family, until he could think of nothing but his loved ones... he had been dragged outside the magic of the present moment that had been revealed to him during the party. His thoughts had drawn him away. Oh, how subtle was the inner divide in the brain between the plane of thoughts and the hidden plane of deeper perception.

The teachings of Sanath were indeed hard to follow.

EPISODE FOURTEEN

A STORMY FAMILY REUNION

Back home after a long absence, Joseph explained to his brothers how he had found himself under the patronage of a high-ranking prelate, Cardinal Sadaka. "The cardinal is a fascinating man and always seems to be one step ahead of the game," he said. "He is adept at arcane politics and Byzantine intrigues and yet he can forget it all in an instant and be laughing about something else the next minute with all the gaiety of a child." Joseph had become Ivan's assistant and his trusted friend.

At the prompting of the cardinal, Joseph had unveiled a network of shoddy deals and illegal transactions, directed from within the Holy See. The cardinal had no reason to believe he could bring these affairs to light within the walls of the Vatican. Indeed, he was convinced that the Pope would take no action against the culprits. He first became alarmed when an officer of the Swiss Guard, who was helping him, was shot dead along with his wife. Something else needed to be done. In the security of the barn, Jonathan examined the file: the evidence he saw before him was unarguable and overwhelming.

These documents implicated some of the highest prelates of the Catholic Church in murky financial deals and un-Christian projects such as the falsification of corporate bonds and the recent murder of a prostitute: she had catered to the comforts of an influential archbishop but had forgotten to turn off her video camera. Every case was documented with precise information about where the incriminating evidence could be found and even included samples of falsified bonds and letters signed by ecclesiastic dignitaries, as well as evidence provided by audio and videotapes. Originals of the evidence were now stored in a bank safe in Vienna. Later, when they joined the rest of the family for lunch, Jonathan and Michael were still disturbed and preoccupied by Joseph's news and unsure about how to proceed further.

Their father, Joseph Senior, greeted them cheerfully. He was a pillar of the Catholic establishment in the United States, with excellent connections in Congress and the Chicago business world, a solidly wealthy banker, with a weakness for whiskey and for his gorgeous but scheming mistress. The next day the family, including Tracy and a house guest, had dinner together to welcome Jonathan and Joseph back from Italy. They gathered in the richly decorated dining hall around a table adorned with fine silverware and crystal. The guest, an old friend of the family, Father Paul Vanguen, was director of the Faculty of Theology at Fulham University and over the years he had often spent his vacations at Birchwood. As the butler served the main course, his father asked Jonathan, "What's up in D.C?"

"I am just back from a briefing in Foggy Bottom. The whole U.S. foreign policy in the Middle East is in a shambles because of the recent events in Jerusalem. The peace process with the Palestinians is moribund. One of my bosses at the State Department, a Jew who shares my views, is worried that in the long term Israel cannot prosper without a peace that includes everyone. In the meantime, fundamentalist Muslims have gotten out of hand... "

Margaret O'Lochan was an intellectual who had become very embittered by her husband's extra-marital affair. She found solace in the counsel of her confessor and in the support she gave to number of charitable institutions. She interrupted her son. "These Orthodox

Jews, like the assassin of the Prime Minister, do not want to see the point. We were discussing this with Nancy Blumstein during bridge at Donna's last Thursday. Somehow all these people in the Middle East are so fanatical about their religion. If they are so religious, why can't they behave in a reasonable and decent manner? Christianity is not like that. It was so beautiful, I remember, when the Holy Father invited the heads of other religions for an ecumenical prayer in the Basilica of Assisi. I was in the front row and recorded it on video. We Christians are very tolerant: we even have a mosque in Rome, don't we?"

"Yes, Mom, but we've also had the IRA exploding bombs in London and we, good Christians, have been killing each other in Belfast, haven't we?" answered Jonathan.

Their father interjected. "Agh, don't start with this again: that conflict is not about religion or faith, it's about land, land that was stolen from us by the British."

Jonathan continued. "Ditto, 'our land was stolen by the Muslims' say the Jews and 'our land is being stolen by the Jews' say the Palestinians. It is land and water, it is crops and money, I agree. It was already like this at the time of the Crusades. But religion is precisely what makes reconciliation or compromise so difficult. Religion is the problem, and American diplomacy is not good at understanding religious conflicts. I think the point of Tracy's present work, Dad, is that we should first seek the common ground between religions and... "

His father interrupted, "In any case, Muslims are hopeless troublemakers, from Kosovo to Bali. It makes you sick to read the newspapers these days. Again, yesterday, Islamic fundamentalists butchered women and children, and there was a horrid massacre in Algeria. I can't believe it! Such a fanatical religion, so primitive. How can they do it? It was said on Sinai 'Thou shall not kill.' If you want a definition of sin, it is certainly to kill in the name of God."

Jonathan observed, "I agree, but things are not so simple; you need to give hope and options to millions who are without jobs or income, you need to... "

His father intervened yet again, this time with a laugh. "Muslims were always like that: they conquered half the world with their holy book in one hand and a sword in the other, and the only choice they offered was 'the book or the sword.'"

Jonathan became mischievous. "Well, Dad, congratulations, you've appeared to have offered a perfect description of the Spanish conquest of South America, except that Pizarro and Cortes were a bit smarter: they generously brought blankets infected with smallpox to wipe out the Incas and the Aztecs. Saddam himself would have loved it – bacteriological warfare."

Margaret O'Lochan could not conceal her irritation. "Don't confuse things again; that was completely different. The Christians brought civilization, education, science, and the words of the Gospel... "

"And in medieval Spain the Muslims brought civilization, mathematics, astronomy, the translations of Plato and Aristotle, and the words of the Koran – without blankets, I believe. Sorry about your faith in decent Christian behavior, Mom, but a short memory can be very convenient. Recall a few elements of European history. Last year when I visited Joseph in Italy, I went to a medieval castle near Rome. In the kitchen there was a huge fireplace. The guide cheerfully explained how the Pope at that time had a couple of cardinals roasted alive in that very fireplace because they were plotting against him. He showed us the room next door where the Pope was listening to the screams coming from the kitchen and reading his breviary. Call him a gastronome, if you like, or call him a holy man, but to me it sounded awfully barbaric. Seriously, I wanted to run out of that papal fortress," Jonathan said with a broad grin.

"Don't be ridiculous. That was an exception."

"Oh yes, Mom?" intervened Joseph Jr. "Look at France, a country that you so admire: it was called the eldest daughter of the Church but it wasn't much better. On the night of Saint Bartholomew, when the Huguenots were massacred in their sleep in Paris, the priests were shouting, 'Kill them all, God will recognize his own people.' That sounds pretty fanatical to me. Europe was full of stories of this kind for centuries: the Inquisition, the Thirty Years' War, and so on. That's why people came over here, remember, to America, to be free to believe." Joseph, a former history student, was warming to the argument and concluded almost vehemently, "What blows my mind is how conveniently everyone forgets about these things."

Joseph Jr. had shocked his parents. His mother looked at him sternly, "Are you a priest or what? Whose side are you on?" As the tension was rising between the parents and the sons, Father Vanguen threw in a conciliatory note. "It is true that Catholics did things they would not approve of today. However, we must understand the historical context; after all, we are only human. The Holy Father himself has recognized it. We must agree that the Church in the past has made mistakes, but this is understandable. It has also reformed itself... "

"Until the next mistake?" interrupted Michael.

Joseph Sr. snapped." That's enough Mike. Don't fall under the influence of your silly brothers who only want to show off their so-called erudition and make a mess of everything." Joseph kept quiet until the end of the meal, wondering how he could break the news of the files to his traditional Catholic family.

After dinner Michael, Jonathan, and Paul Vanguen went for a walk in the park on the family estate, pursuing the discussion, but Jonathan could not conceal his concerns about the sorry state of the international scene.

"The credit our country still enjoys abroad is because of the older generation of Americans, not to McDonalds, Pizza Hut or Wall Street currency speculators who earned record bonuses last Christmas for helping wreck the Southeast Asian economies. Roosevelt said, 'Poverty anywhere is a threat to prosperity everywhere.' But when we are interested in Africa today, it's just for getting at its mineral wealth and the poor can eat cake if they can find any... No, Paul, I tell you, we don't have a foreign policy any more. The generations of Americans who fought the Nazis, implemented the Marshall Plan, who created the U.N. and the Bretton Woods institutions – they had a vision of international solidarity. They were both idealistic and pragmatic. They were doers. They delivered."

Father Vanguen nodded in agreement.

Jonathan continued. "Today that generation is long gone. Our prestige is fading fast. Our foreign policy is controlled by a bunch of fundamentalist right-wingers in Congress who don't even know where Kuwait is on the world map. They think leadership is a free lunch. They only see their rights, not their responsibilities. They want to impose crazy restrictions on countries that follow necessary popu-lation-control policies."

The priest looked doubtfully at Jonathan in disbelief at this open challenge of the Church's doctrine. He protested, "The pro-life movement is a great contribution of the Church towards a moral U.S. policy. We have created a powerful trend, which must be reckoned with worldwide. The Holy Father took the lead and spoke with great courage against contraception and abortion."

Michael decided to be naughty. "Come on, Paul, I always felt it strange that priests considered themselves experts on condoms and felt they could preach to women about what to do with their bodies or how to have sex. Who gave them that authority? What do they know about raising a family in the Third World or in Harlem?"

Jonathan went on as if he hadn't heard the jibe. "The globalization of the financial markets has given such power to financial operators. Are they accountable for it? Of course not. It goes against democracy. The USA is like a Titan with big economic muscle but with an undersized brain. We are like a huge ship navigating without a radar system. We are the Titanic. I always thought spirituality should be the brain, spirituality should be the radar system!"

"But it is, Jonathan, it is."

"No, it's not!" exploded Jonathan rather more vehemently than he had intended. "Get real. D.C. is corrupt to the bone. Everybody talks about Christian values, but nobody practices them. If a politician preaches morality, it is only for political gain. Where is your Christianity? For thirty years, kids have been resorting to drugs, silly sects or fake gurus for guidance. Do they believe in Christianity for solace or guidance? Parents go to psychiatrists. The pornocrats are in the children's room, courtesy of the Internet. People who fear the clash of civilization between Islam and Christianity should relax: there is no Christianity left. Where are your Christian values? Hiding in empty churches? Did you ever ask yourself how we came to this?"

Vanguen was getting annoyed. "Come on, calm down, it's not that bad. Our churches are not empty. The Holy Father addressed a million young people gathered in Paris last summer."

"Yes, granted, grand mass entertainment. However, when he went to Holland I saw a young Dutch guy on TV with a poster saying 'Pope, step down – we want to see Christ.' But the protester was taken away by the security service. The Pope Show is not enough. It doesn't improve society."

"Come on now, the Holy Father is not alone. There are a lot of good people in the Church," interrupted Paul, visibly offended.

"Perhaps, but they never have the upper hand. I can understand Francis of Assisi being a saint but the founder of Opus Dei?"

Jonathan continued, "I'll tell you how we came to this: the churches, all of them, failed to deliver spirituality. Their message got bogged down in power politics, conformism and, in the best of cases, social works. However, the Catholic Church doesn't want competition, doesn't want anyone else to deliver when they can't. Remember what Christ said of the Pharisees? 'They block the door so nobody can enter.' Somehow, Paul, we must break through to a new awareness, we must evolve further otherwise our race will self-destroy."

"You are completely misreading the Gospels, my poor Jonathan," said Father Vanguen, looking increasingly frustrated. "Christ brought the words of life. There is nothing to evolve from there. We must go through Christ: He is the door."

"Okay, where is it, where is He, where is the door? Can you get specific – away from metaphors, parables, and sermons?"

Michael felt the discussion was going nowhere. "Please guys – don't start another of your endless arguments. Let's go and play tennis now."

As his invitation was turned down, Michael went jogging in the park. Exasperated by the sterility of their family discussions, Jonathan had forgotten that he was a diplomat who was supposed to keep quiet and out of trouble. He made his big mistake. He had so much faith in his long friendship with Paul that, in order to convince him, he went back to the house and asked Joseph to show him some of the files.

They took the priest to the barn and presented the evidence of Joseph's research into the Vatican: corruption, the Mafia, reopening the case of the possible murder of a former Pope. Fortunately they didn't mention Cardinal Sadaka. The priest studied the documents for some time and became very pale. "For God's sake, I don't believe a word of these ridiculous fabrications. Joseph, you've been completely misled. This is blasphemy. Don't go down this road, or disaster will be waiting for you and your brother."

"I wish Joseph was wrong," answered Jonathan. "But there's one thing about Joseph. He is honest and he goes straight to the point, like an arrow. What do you mean by disaster, exactly? You, such an old friend, are you threatening us?"

"No, no, of course not, but think about it. How can you forget all the good the Church has done – in art, education, and in charitable work? How can you forget Mother Teresa in Calcutta who helped those poor, miserable Indians who were totally destitute? Do you want to take away their hope, to stab all these good people in the back by spreading false rumors? Think about the consequences to yourself and your family. Jonathan, do you want to… "

This time Jonathan said, "Paul, you know, I am sad and horrified. You know I studied Greek and Latin, I served Mass for five years almost every morning and I met the Pope in private audience; I know and respect the roots of my culture. I grew up with the Church and I wanted its revival. But what can I do? Truth is what it is. You can't eternally paper over the cracks in the Church's building. If you are not prepared to face it, there is no hope for reform."

"Don't meddle with it," replied Paul sternly. "If the Church has made mistakes, it will correct them: leave it be."

"Sure, like the good Father Peter we both knew." Jonathan's tone was sarcastic. "He did not like women much, in the true Pauline tradition. He was caught two years ago near Chicago: eighteen counts of pedophilia with young boys. The Archbishopric covered it up, paid out-of court-settlements with parishioners' hard-earned money, and then moved him to San Diego where he started all over again, this time Californian style: sea, sun, and sex. Sex with minors, a minor offence? Remember? This is our Church's style of self-censorship. Such cases don't allow much room for faith in your proposition."

"Please, Jonathan, I am afraid you do not understand that I am trying to help you. Stop and listen. You know I love you and

Joseph, we have known each other for so long. When we were kids, we played together. You explained Aquinas to me. You were so gifted in philosophy. But what's happening to you both all of a sudden? What pride! What arrogance! For two thousand years the Church has confronted and defeated all kinds of enemies, empires, intellectuals or armies. It went through so many crises and always triumphed in the end." The theologian raised his voice. "Do you want any better proof than that it stands on the indestructible rock assigned to it by our Lord Jesus? And now, you two madcaps, do you think you will bring it down or what? Get real. Your bones will rot in the earth and the Church will still be here."

Joseph was shattered by the onslaught. "But, Paul, what about truth, the truth must prevail in the end, at least you should agree to that much as a theologian.

The priest was still excited. "Ah! The truth! What is the truth?"

Now it was Jonathan's turn to be taken aback. "Hey, that was Pontius Pilate's question to Christ, wasn't it? The trusted model for all bureaucrats, ecclesiastic dignitaries, and offshore bankers: "Keep your hands clean, no matter what." So you guys, you are on the side of those who wash their hands, are you?" Jonathan's voice was vibrant. "This reminds me of cousin Charles working for the Union Bank of Switzerland in Zurich. He is all for cleanliness, but don't look under the carpet, in the closets or in the numbered accounts…"
The angry priest shouted back, "Charles is entirely honorable. My poor Jonathan, you have fallen under evil influences and the only thing I can do is pray for you. Remember that I tried to warn you."

"Well, frankly, to hell with your prayers."

The priest turned to face him with icy composure. "And it'll be hell for you, I am afraid, if your pride takes you further on the path of blasphemy. You are from one of the most prominent Irish families in this country. Do you intend to betray your blood, your tradition, and your family? Do you know what you are going to lose because of your brother's mad ravings?" A long and acrimonious exchange ensued, but Joseph categorically refused to hand over the files to Paul or to his father. The priest finally burst out angrily, "You are the most deluded pair I ever had the misfortune to meet" and stormed out of the barn, without looking back at the two startled brothers, slamming the large door shut behind him as he departed. He went straight to Mr. Joseph O'Lochan Senior to tell him of his sons' intentions to denounce all the wrongdoing in the Vatican. The Shadow was rising.

The brothers were now alone in the barn. Joseph looked at his elder brother fondly; he knew that Jonathan had only entered this argument to support him. Also, Jonathan had always been a supporter of the truth. For his part, Jonathan had always had a deep respect for Joseph's honesty and straightforward nature. "To wash or not to wash one's hands... that is the question?"

When Jonathan told Tracy what had happened she became quite worried. To top it all she told her brother that the financing for the Oikos Project had been blocked in the Budget Appropriation Committee of Congress; its future was now in question.

It had been a bad day, but it would not stop there. Jonathan had to leave the family estate in a hurry to go on a mission to the Middle East. Upset by the pressure put on him by his parents, Joseph left Birchwood for Michael's flat in Georgetown. The same evening Father Paul called the secretariat of the Cardinal of Chicago, a friend of the O'Lochan family. The secretariat immediately contacted someone in the Holy See in Rome. Three days later, a special envoy from the Office of the Prefect for the Congregation of the Faith arrived at Birchwood with precise instructions, and convened a secret council of the O'Lochan family, but without the children. The meeting lasted half a day. The representative of the Holy See sought and obtained the agreement of the parents to ruin the reputation and credibility of Jonathan and Joseph, starting with the former, who, as a well-regarded diplomat, was more of a threat. It would be easy to deal with the Joseph, the younger of the two brothers, back in Rome.

Thus, the plot to neutralize the misguided brothers unfolded in Jonathan's absence. His aunt Elizabeth, his father's twin sister, was a dry, gossipy woman who loved to meddle, especially in family affairs. She was thoroughly convinced of her own self-importance and always glad to find a role for herself in any situation. She called the Deputy Secretary of State at the State Department, who was a personal friend.

"Hello, Richard, how are you? How are Jane and the children? I wanted to know – could you drop by on Friday evening at Birchwood House? By the way, I met Senator Len Helmer yesterday at the board meeting of the Cato Institute. I remembered your problem and chatted with him. He said he would try and help with your nomination to be our next ambassador to Beijing."

"Great, thanks, Betty, that is really so kind of you. This is good news; I know both of you go back a long way, and if he promises you something, there is a good chance that he will deliver. We would be delighted to drop by at Birchwood. How are things? Everything fine with you?

"Alas, Joseph and I are going through very difficult times."

"Why? What's happened?"

"It's so hard to speak about it, but, well, I know you are a friend of the family... "

"That's for sure! What's it about?"

"You know my nephew Jonathan, of course. What's happening is so sad, so sad... "

"What? A health problem? What's the matter? He is doing just great here. The Secretary intends to entrust him with a delicate mission to the Middle East. He is on the promotion list for next year and... "

Elizabeth interrupted. "Richard, I regret to have to say it, but if I were you, don't let that happen: it could become a major embarrassment for the Secretary of State. You see... please, this is confidential... Jonathan has become involved in some kind of secret sect, real bad, against the country, the Church, and everything we believe in, I'll tell you fully another time... "

"Betty, what are you telling me? Jonathan is a sensible boy. I don't understand this. What is your brother saying? Does he know about it?"

"Richard, it's so bad that Joseph, with great sorrow, has decided to disinherit Jonathan because he does not want the family wealth to end up in the bank account of this dubious sect."

"My God, then it must be true! What a shame, what a disgrace!"

"Don't talk to Jonathan because, of course, he would deny everything. He was such a bright boy. This is a tragedy. But I'll tell you more on Friday. See you at Birchwood."

While Elizabeth was doing her hatchet job with the State Department, her brother had invited Stanislaus Robkowicz, Jonathan's future father-in-law, to a round of golf. Stanislaus was in a jovial mood.

"What a beautiful day. Good idea to get out for a game of golf. So, our kids are enjoying themselves, aren't they? I understand the wedding is all set for the end of May. My wife is all excited about it and is already shopping like mad. We are planning a very large reception."

"Alas," replied Joseph O'Lochan Sr. in a somber mood, "I am most disturbed about this prospect for your daughter."
Stanislaus was shocked. "What... what do you mean? Is there any trouble?"

"It's worse than my worst nightmare. My son has gone berserk."

"Come on, Jonathan is such a fine, promising young lad. Last week I met Donald F. Campbell, our Ambassador for Disarmament Affairs. He congratulated us on Jenny's engagement. He says Jonathan is one of the most brilliant young diplomats at the State Department, highly regarded at the National Security Council and the CIA."

"Not for long, I'm afraid. Two of my sons have got involved in some kind of wacko sect that goes against all the Christian values we stand for. They are fanatical and immoral. They deny our cultural heritage. It's disgusting, really. These fools even attack the Church with all kinds of cheap, third-rate stories. They've lost control of their senses. It breaks my heart but you must tell your daughter to think twice about this marriage. I really don't want to see her suffer."

"Really? I can't believe my ears; I don't know what to say. Jonathan is your own son. They love each other, you know. This sect must be a passing fad Jonathan has got involved with. It will last only for a short while. It can't be serious."

"Well, I don't think so. I saw my lawyer yesterday and discussed with him my decision to erase Jonathan and Joseph from my will. I don't want them to inherit a penny from me, if I can help it. I am proposing to put all my estate under a separate foundation. I wanted you to know about this. Don't you think it breaks my heart?"

A stunned Stanislaus suddenly turned more businesslike. "Gee, this is serious! This is very sad and upsetting news. I need to go back home and talk to my wife. She'll be devastated, poor thing. Such a fine young man! And of course we must talk to Jenny. Playing golf doesn't seem like such a good idea any more. Please excuse me. What a pity. Curse these sects!"

A few days later, back from the Middle East, unaware of what had been happening in his family, Jonathan burst enthusiastically into Michael's flat in Georgetown. It was a comfortable penthouse studio consisting of a bedroom with a bunk bed, a kitchen-dining area, and a living room opening up onto a small terrace that offered a pleasant view of the Potomac. One wall of the living room was covered with shelves that held magazines, stereo equipment, CD racks, as well as books, a soft toy pet monkey, and a guitar. Jonathan joined his younger brother on the terrace.

"Listen, Mike, the Brookings Institution has accepted our analytical paper on the US-Asia relationship. They have accepted our argument for stronger links with China and India and our warning against the Hollywood Tibet policy. They think the paper should be published... what's the matter? You're not listening... "

The pain he was about to inflict on his elder brother devastated Michael. He said hesitatingly, "Father has changed all the locks at the house, so you can't go in anymore. He has emptied your room and put all its contents in the barn. He was so angry that he smashed your new music system. He says he never wants to see your face again. He has legally disinherited both you and Joseph. He has warned Tracy that she must break with you two or he will do the same to her. Meanwhile, I am playing the guy who doesn't know anything."

Jonathan's heart missed a beat and then he became quite livid. He sat down slowly. "But... but it's not possible... what are you saying? What have I done? I'll talk to him. Come on, this is a nightmare, but where's it coming from? Why? Why would he do such a thing? What's Mother saying?" He loved his father, of course, despite their disparate and diverging views and the obvious fact that his father had never understood his aspirations. The O'Lochan father was happy enough that his sons would take their appointed leadership roles in society, as duly expected for the scions of such a prominent family, as long as they did not bother about useless questions such as truth, the meaning of life, or worse, utopist ambitions about improving the world. Joseph Senior considered such tendencies as the mere foolishness of kids who had failed to grow up.

A quick succession of images flashed through Jonathan's mind: his childhood at Birchwood, the summer family holidays on Nantucket. But now, a chunk of his life, the whole context of his emotional surroundings, was sliding out of sight. What would his future environment be? This was hurting badly. What would he tell his fiancée? Joseph came out of the kitchen with two mugs of tea, trying to lighten the somber mood.

"Come on, have a cup of tea: it's British first aid for major crises. It works for the Irish, too. Mother discussed the situation with her confessor and says that Dad is very courageous in doing the right thing. All of them, the confessor, Auntie Elizabeth, and Paul, are telling everybody that you two are under the influence of some sect. But I know for a fact that Dad's mistress has been pushing him to do this and that the story of the sect is her idea. She wants him to cut his links with us, the bitch, to get all the money. Jenny is very upset. She tried to get in touch with you many times when you were on mission. She called me in tears from Vassar two hours ago. Her father insists that she cancel the wedding. As for Joseph, he was called back to Rome but he refused to go. He has one week to give back the files or he'll probably be excommunicated."

Jonathan stared at the wall with an empty expression on his face. "So, that's it, the wacko censors from the Middle Ages strike again. Four centuries earlier, they would have delivered us to the Dominican Inquisition and burned our feet until we confessed to having made a pact with the devil. Then, with a little luck, we could have kissed the cross from the top of the pyre. Well, this is the United States of America, not Spain. We are a couple of years away from the third millennium, and I am not going to take it."

Michael smiled proudly at his eldest brother. "I'll never let you down, Jonathan."

"Sadly enough, complete nonsense in the name of God is to be found in all religions. That was my point," the elder brother said with a sad smile. "But clearly it didn't have much impact. I am not sure either that I wanted the point illustrated so effectively within my own family."

"But there is something else. I overheard, or, more truthfully, I eavesdropped on the family council at Birchwood. Did you know that you can hear what they say in the smoking room through the chimney of the library? They spoke about friends in Chicago who could get the files back. I think it's the Mob. They also suspect Joseph of working with a highly placed mole in the Vatican and they are now investigating frantically who it could be at the Holy See. We were waiting for you to decide what should be done. The files are in a safe place."

Jonathan said, "Joseph, please call Ivan at once but not from here. Make sure you are not followed and call from a public call box. Don't use the cell phone. I won't use my office secure line any longer either. As for me, I will try to straighten this out here in DC, there's no use in talking to my Ambassador in Cairo. This Administration won't have the guts to challenge the Church; they need the Catholic vote too much. They'll try to settle this quietly. They may ask me to do the proper thing and will offer to help if I agree to resign. I know a journalist who would be willing to write about some of this, but this country is now so used to scandals, it won't help much. What we need is something much more effective, but what?"

At that moment Tracy hurtled into the small flat. She burst into tears and threw herself into Jonathan's arms. It was the turn of the brothers to wipe away a few tears. The family had been broken up. The tension had been high after that last stormy family reunion in Birchwood and the road ahead was very uncertain.

Using her special nickname for her older brother, Tracy said, "Come on, Seagull, we are with you, anytime, anywhere. Soar high and you will weather the storm. This is so unfair. You're the legal heir of Birchwood. Dad got it from his father: he has no right to take it away from you. If you want, I'll move out of Birchwood too. I'll tell Dad he's lost his marbles."

"No, no, stay, Tracy, it's better if you stay. Father is under the influence of his mistress – thirty years younger than him, pretty, ruthless, and a gifted estate hunter. Mother has retreated under the grip of her confessor and is preparing for divorce. So what's left? You and Michael should hang on there. And we need to go about our own business," he said, looking meaningfully at his sister. Tracy was the only one who knew about the Dagad Trikon inquiry and she understood that Jonathan wanted them to keep their promise to Lakshman. It had to remain a secret still, even from Joseph and Michael.

The O'Lochan children were too absorbed in their drama to notice that they were no longer alone. The eyes of Mike's soft toy monkey had suddenly become very much alive and it had momentarily offered an abode for the white monkey. He grumbled to himself, "Brave kids, but no use to pick a fight with dogmatism. I find myself squeezed between two heavy books, "*The Wealth of Nations*" by Adam Smith and "*Das Kapital*" by Karl Marx. It is not really comfortable. If we cannot bring the children of men on the right track, mankind will continue the waltz of its "*isms*"; the Evil One will go on enjoying the stupid joke of dogmatism – he prospers on it. We must speed up the process of awakening. Let us see, our good wizard need some help." The white monkey repressed a grin because fluffy toys are not supposed to smile.

At this point, Michael grinned. "Brothers and sister, I am confident it will be all right. I don't know what is going on, but last night I had a dream. It was both confused yet very real. I saw a tall warrior on a winged horse bringing a box to a cardinal. A wheel was carved on the chest of his silver armor. Jonathan was next to him, struggling to stand upright in the strong wind, and shouting, 'Open it, open it now!' Somehow, you forced him to open the box. I was the younger companion of this warrior, standing next to him. A shape came out of the box, a power in the form of a wheel, which, whirling on itself, turned into a hurricane; the gale roared like a tiger and I felt a cool wind blowing from my own hand.

Then the warrior turned and although a helmet hid most of his face, I saw that he stared at me with eyes that shone like diamonds. His rumbling voice mixed with the thunder. In fact, his voice was the thunder. I distinctly remember his words: 'It was said in Fatima and it was said by Fatima: what is two thousand years to the power that created you?' I saw flashes of lightning, I saw buildings blown away and I woke up, on the floor. I had fallen out of bed! What does it mean, Jonathan?"

Jonathan did not know. Nor could he know that on that same day the companions had left the Casa della Minerva for the Eternal City to find the answer to this very question.

EPISODE FIFTEEN

THE CASKET OF THE GREEN WHEEL

The Swiss Guard immediately recognized His Eminence Ivan, Cardinal Sadaka, as his limousine entered Vatican City for what would prove to be the last time. The Guard saluted and did not ask about the passenger dressed in a black cassock sitting next to the cardinal. The car drove off in the direction of the Santo Damaso courtyard. It was a bright and sunny day in Rome. The cardinal and the accompanying priest walked briskly through the corridors of the palace and passed the throng of tourists lined up to visit the Sistine Chapel. Feeling rather hot under his cassock, Lakshman followed the cardinal though an imposing gallery of Roman statues. They entered the vaulted rooms decorated with Raphael's frescoes that he admired for a fleeting moment as they hurried by. The two men vanished through stairs hidden behind a small door to which the cardinal had a key.

"This takes us directly to the Pope's apartments," explained Ivan. "He returns this evening from his apostolic tour of Cuba. The Pontifex Maximus met the Leader Massimo: it was a humility contest. If Cardinal Saladorda, the chief of the Vatican's police, has discovered by now that Joseph was working for me, he must first talk to the Holy Father. He can't make any move against me before talking to the Pope: I am too senior in the sacerdotal hierarchy. That leaves us a couple of hours to retrieve the casket and vanish. The events in Virginia have accelerated the process. Let's avoid the floors of the Holy Office. I gave my private secretary leave for the whole week. The Superintendent of the Vatican Treasury was informed of my desire to show the Constantinople reredos to an eminent expert of Byzantine art – you, my dear! There should be no problem."

Ivan responded affably to the deferential greeting of the few nuns who were used to seeing him in the pontifical apartments. He entered his private office and checked his secret camera. Linked to a photoelectric cell, the device automatically recorded everyone entering his office. Besides a photo of the nun who regularly cleaned his office, there was a picture of two grim-looking priests. Ivan froze and started to perspire slightly. He examined his desk drawers while speaking aloud about the beauty of Byzantine iconography. From behind his large desk, he silently gestured Lakshman to come closer to the screen and typed a message on his computer. "Office bugged. Two telecommunications specialists. Opus Dei agents. We must be fast. Let's talk art," it said.

"... and this is how," Lakshman improvised, "this Bulgarian monastery acquired the silver reliquary cross. The sacred piece was initially kept at the monastery of Saint John the Theologian in Patmos. In 1451 AD, the cross was removed from Constantinople on the orders of Constantine XI Dragases, the last emperor of Constantinople, a few years before he died defending the gate of his city against the Ottomans. It then came to Bulgaria with the arch-priest of the Greek court who'd escaped the plundering of the imperial capital. I estimate it dates from the ninth century because it shows a close affinity with the inner cross of the Plasma reliquary. It consists of two hinged sections, decorated with incised design and niello, containing a third, smaller cross in which the relic of the true cross was kept. The monks believed that the energy of the Logos of Christ went into the wood of the cross, which retained miraculous properties. At the ends of the horizontal arms are the symbols of the sun and moon and on the vertical arm a gate under the feet of Christ Pantocrator who sits in glory."

The telephone rang; the reredos was on its way. Ivan packed a few essential documents in his attaché case and cleared the conference table of its mountain of papers. He hastily opened a locked drawer and grabbed a folder of ancient Latin manuscripts that he had borrowed from the Vatican archives to show to Sanath.

A friar knocked at the door and entered, followed by four Swiss Guards carrying the reredos. They put it on the table and were instructed to come back in two hours. It was impressive, a masterpiece, its base framed with a golden-gilt revetment encrusted with precious stones. Ivan started to describe the Byzantine piece out loud in an attempt to drown the sounds Lakshman was making while extracting the casket from the base of the reredos.

Cardinal Ivan began, "Professor, you must note the main panel facing the Royal Chapel of the Basileus. Look at the perfect proportions. The archangels Michael and Gabriel clad in imperial garments are holding a circular mandorla, surrounded by cherubim and wheels, within which the Virgin and Child are represented. Two small figures of Abraham and Moses stand in adoration before them. I think we can safely attribute this beautiful work to the great Cretan painter, Michael Damascenos. Each cherub rides a red wheel, but the central one at the feet of Abraham and Moses is engraved in malachite; it shows ten naves while all other wheels have four. This is intriguing because..."

"I have it... I have it in my camera shot, what a nice angle" Lakshman had not been able to conceal his excitement at discovering the hidden casket.

This Dagad Trikon casket had a rectangular form and was smaller than the previous one he had unearthed from under the Icelandic glacier but it was much richer in design, certainly the work of a renowned master, perhaps one of the old dwarf craftsmen from a tribe allied to the Rock Avasthas. It was made of an unknown metal, had a fine green patina and incised decoration consisting of geometric patterns and floral arabesques that seemed to announce Ottoman ornamentation. Attached to the center of the lid was a medallion of cloisonné enamel, on which a small wheel made of a large emerald was outlined with thin strips of gold. This miniature jewelry was exquisitely crafted. The wheel had ten naves.

Ivan looked at it with powerful emotions; the retrieving of this Avastha masterpiece meant his liberation, the end of his long assignment as a hidden spy of the Hllidarendi within the Vatican. Carrying the casket in an attaché case, the fugitive cardinal and the archaeologist hurried through the corridors. They soon bumped into one of the two men who had been caught by the secret camera in Ivan's office. He was a member of Saladorda's Praetorian Guard, staffed with recruits from various fundamentalist subsects. He had been rushing towards the cardinal's office. His eyes were cold and hostile.

"Eminence, Cardinal Saladorda wishes to see you at once on a matter of great urgency."

"Very well, my son, tell him I shall meet him in two hours. I must celebrate mass for the Eastern European pilgrims in the Trastevere now." Waving aside the Vatican security agent with sovereign ease and a broad paternal smile, the cardinal and his companion entered the Pope's private elevator to which Ivan had the key. The frustrated cleric had obviously no power to stop a prince of the Church.

They hurried out of the pontifical palace, called Luciano on the cell phone, and arranged to meet him outside. He was waiting for them in a police car near St. Peter's Square and while making sure that they were not followed, drove off at once in the direction of the Piazza del Popolo. Looking at his watch, Ivan sighed with relief. "Exit Cardinal Sadaka. Until they heard about Joseph's file, I was above suspicion. But from now on I am a fugitive. They may put a contract on my head. I shall leave Italy for some time to foil the Mafia. I will arrange my disappearance in a private jet accident over Malta next week. It's already been lined up with my team: Alexandra's idea. I'll set a false trail, which will sidetrack them for quite a while. Philip has a chalet in a remote corner of the Tyrol. May be I'll use it to hide in for a while."

"I've hardly had time to meet you and you're going to disappear already? The same with Baldur van Jetzlar. What's next? Do they know about your Etruscan hideout?"

"No, they never suspected me before. I am a close friend of the Pope, remember? Luciano, please park the car in this street. I have with me the sealed envelope left by Sanath. I must open it now."

With an impatient gesture he tore open the envelope. Inside there was a page, hastily handwritten by Sanath. Lakshman read the note over Ivan's shoulder.

"Congratulations, friends! Karudas, prince of the eagles and mightiest amongst the cherubim, protected the flight of all Avastha warriors that mounted the winged horses. But he took special care of the Casket of the Wheel. It is in his honor that Rome took the eagle as the totem for its imperial power. It is the eagle that led the Roman legions.

You must hurry now. The casket you retrieved can have a most powerful impact. Avastha magic interacts with those it touches. It can be dangerous if you open it in Rome.

The casket contains a key moment of the Dagad Trikon prophecy. There is only one place in the world where this specific scroll will release its full message. Go to the place where Ivan was ordained a bishop. There, look at the frescoes painted by Pinturicchio. Read the inscription and you will find the destination. But you must open the casket at nighttime and at the exact spot, I repeat, the exact spot! Farewell friends, I shall see you soon."

"He's alive! He's alive!" Lakshman shouted joyously.

"With Sanath, you never quite know what it means," said Ivan cautiously. "This paper is not dated. He may have written this before the accident at his home in Holland. In any case it was written so that only I could make sense of it, as not many people would remember where precisely I was ordained a bishop. Luciano, *ti prego*, take us to the Chiesa di Santa Maria del Popolo."

During the drive, Ivan and Lakshman changed clothes in the car. With sunglasses, cameras, and casual wear, they now looked like the thousands of standard-issue tourists who crowd the streets of Rome in the pleasant days of early fall. Half an hour later the two men were pacing up and down inside the Church of St. Mary of the People, carefully scrutinizing the numerous paintings that richly decorated its walls and ceilings.

"Look here!" said Lakshman excitedly. He pointed to the elegant figure of a woman in a yellow and green Renaissance dress. Her right hand was raised in a gesture of protection; her left hand rested on an inscription: *"La Sibilla Delphica."* Behind her, a purple scroll hung from a tree. They could read: *INVISIBILE VERBUM PALPABITUR* in yellow roman script; mythical creature – chimeras, griffins, and unicorns – surrounded the escutcheon containing the painting.

"The Pithy prophetess at Delphi," muttered Ivan, dumbfounded. "Delphi in Greece. The *'ombrilos gaies,'* the navel of the earth where the Pithy, the greatest prophetess of antiquity rendered her oracles."

"What do you make of the other inscription?" asked Lakshman, intrigued by the ambiguous message. "Translated, it means 'the invisible word will be examined by the feel'; surely this refers to the Word, the Logos at the opening of John's Gospel, but how does it relate to the scrolls?"

As he scrutinized the rest of the vault, Ivan was too absorbed to answer. They checked the other frescoes one more time. None could be construed as indicating a place or pointing to a clear and specific geographical destination. The two companions did not hesitate for long. Delphi seemed to be the location assigned to them by the hand-written note from the wizard. They drove back to the Casa della Minerva where Alexandra and Lakshmi were waiting anxiously for them, eager to know that they had retrieved the casket and that they were safe. On the way there, Lakshman had asked:

"What are these ancient manuscripts you carry in your attaché case?

"The records of the Holy Inquisition on the Trial and Questioning of Renaud of Cormorant, renegade crusader and heretical templar knight. Under torture, Renaud spoke of the Dagad Trikon prophecy, linking it to the sayings of his mentor John of Jerusalem. It implied the end of the Church and of Christianity as they knew it. However, Renaud mysteriously escaped from the prison of the Albi Cathedral in the south of France where he was incarcerated and thus his testimony is incomplete. This was a closely kept piece of evidence stored in the top-secret archive room. I was really looking forward to showing it to Sanath," he added with a deep sigh.

Late that night, Ivan sorted out his files, got rid of some documents, and packed his archive of CDs and some clothes in a single suitcase. He bade farewell to the beautiful Alexandra, who would be looking after the school, and left instructions with his trusty Russian team. Ivan suspected that the Cosa Nostra, on being contacted by Saladorda, would send its hounds on the scent of the renegade prelate with so much inside information on the wrongdoing within the Holy See. They had to organize the accident in Malta to foil the Mafia but they also planned to strike back at the bunch of thugs who had engineered the destruction of the house of Baldur in Vassenaar, near The Hague. Ivan's boys could be ruthless when required and some contingency plans were also prepared to neutralize, if need be, the henchmen of Saladorda.

They bade farewell to Philip and Laira von Jetzlar and, skillfully disguised and equipped with new passports, credit cards, and cell phones, Ivan, Lakshman, and Lakshmi drove to Fiumicino Airport. To their immense relief, the mysterious metal of the casket did not set off the alarms when it went through the metal detector during at the security check. They flew to Athens where they rented a small Toyota and, with Lakshman driving, they immediately set off for Mount Parnassus in the Eastern Mountains of Beotia. They were in a buoyant mood, full of expectations. Ivan asked Lakshman, "What do you know about Delphi?"

"It was the center of ancient Greece, with oracles, games, wars, politics, and crimes. The great temple of Apollo was built around the eighth century BC in the place where the God who represented the solar principle had killed the great serpent python. I guess you would call the python one of the former naga kings. It was the place where the treasuries of many cities were stored. The Romans – I mean Sylla, Nero, and Constantine – finally ruined Delphi and looted the sanctuary, probably the richest of its kind in the ancient world."

Ivan interrupted, "It is interesting, because Sanath has described the overlord of this casket to be Karudas, the prince of the eagles, and eagles are the traditional enemies of the serpents, you know, but I think there may be some other connection."

"Do you have something in mind?"

"Some of the ancient lore of Dagad Trikon contained songs about the Gods who came, at times, from the Himavat Mountains to visit the desert fortress. Prominent among them was the God of Magnificence, the leader of the Grand Scheme whose color was emerald and blue. In the ancient testament of the Jewish faith, the Prophet Ezekiel is said to have seen him on his throne in a vision of glory. Heavenly beings like Karudas moved about him, standing on wheels of energy. The emerald deity is the Lord of Evolution and the Master of the Grand Scheme. When He, the Supreme One, traveled through the air, it was Prince Karudas himself in the form of an eagle who carried him. So, if Sanath mentions Karudas in connection with this casket, maybe the casket could lead us to Karudas, and I wonder where Karudas might lead us? Perhaps to the place of his God." Ivan stopped talking, lost in the enormity of his supposition. Lakshmi brought him back to the present.

"What is the name of this God?" she asked.

"Who knows the ancient names today? He had one thousand names and one thousand shapes but, in his blue form, he was called The Sower, because all seeds of growth, change, and transformation were sprouted in his body. In the past, emperors, kings, and rulers followed Karudas in worshipping him under various names. They worshipped The Sower as he was the maker of history, the one who brought fortune or misfortune. The wise rulers understood that change was unavoidable but they wished for changes in their states to be propitious and for ensuing events to be auspicious. Kings drew their authority from his name. Of this worship, nothing is left of course. Today, Garuda is just the name of an Indonesian airline. Only the outer symbol of the vehicle of the God remains, like an empty carriage left on the banks of history, a shell whose content is lost."

"I see what you mean," intervened Lakshman. "The Roman eagle has become the universal symbol for the imperium, for the might of the state. It flew from Rome to Constantinople and from there to Moscow. The eagle of the Hohenzollern is on the wall of the German parliament. On the armorial bearings of the Romanovs and of the Hapsburgs, the eagle eventually became bicephalous, with two heads looking for troublemakers on the left and right sides, I guess. He landed on the coat of arms of so many modern states, from Poland to Mexico. Think too about the seal of the President of the United States of America."

"Perhaps the casket has something to do with the rise and fall of empires," said Ivan with a sense of gleeful expectation as the winding road began its ascent of the increasingly rugged slopes on the southwestern side of Mount Parnassus.

"Well, gentlemen," said Lakshmi from the back seat, scribbling with her pen on a notepad, "I'm looking at my notes; let me see what we have and whether I've got it right. The Casket of the White Feather speaks of our collective and individual evolution. In both cases it seems we need to reach a precise point of equilibrium, which unlocks the access to the staircase. In other words, it opens the possibility for further ascent. At collective level, these are the scales that Lakshman saw in Amsterdam, which have to do with fairness, equity in wealth distribution, and with just societies – agreed? At an individual level it has to do with a certain mastery over the senses, knowing how to turn the senses and the attention inwards, inside. This is expressed by the symbol of the tortoise. The juggling number with the oranges is about mastery over oneself, right, Laksh?"

Her cousin nodded. "Yes, I believe Sanath once quoted the High Lady of the Rock as saying: 'Don't react, just see.' I've begun to realize that we can see only if we are in the central channel. Otherwise we react and lose control, which is the case when we are afraid or angry, jealous or frustrated, or in any of these moods linked to the Dark Riders. If we go too far to the extremes, away from the whiteness of the central channel of balance, we move deep into the dark blue or yellow areas of consciousness, past and future, emotions and thoughts. This is where, in extreme cases, the Shadow can see us and entrap or catch us."

"But this whole business about the Darkness is not very clear to me, if I may say so. There are six Dark Riders, six houses of Avasthas. It should be pretty clear that they must be sworn enemies. Let's move now to the other casket of which we know practically nothing. It's buried under an oak tree in Russia, which thus became sacred, but the Casket of the Cross can't be retrieved until the oak dies. It came from the Rock through China, brought to Russia by the sire of Anorhad carrying the cross on his helmet. It protected Russia and all of Europe from external invasion. It gave energy to the Hllidarendi and to the whole forest. But what else, Uncle?" said Lakshmi, addressing Ivan by the affectionate expression of respect used for male elders back home in India. "What else do you know?"

"Sanath once said that the casket under the oak cannot be opened before most of the other caskets have been found; that is why the oak is still alive, telling us to leave the casket alone. The wizard said the Casket of the Cross is a kind of locking mechanism for the whole system. Opening it could be truly wonderful – or truly terrible. So, as long as we do not know how to go about it, we'd better keep it where it is. In the meantime, it acts and it protects."

"Well, that doesn't take us very far!" replied Lakshmi. "So, what about this one we are carrying to Delphi? The wheel is the Buddhist symbol for dharma, the rule of righteousness, and by the way, it's also on the Indian flag. Sanath's reference to the Lord Karudas may also point to the deity they call The Sower, the master of the Grand Scheme. The Casket of the Wheel could have something to do with societies, empires, and wealth, the way we move through history. Pretty big stuff. It sounds to me that it's connected to the first casket. Without reaching a point of equilibrium on the central channel, the one you saw in white, Laksh, we cannot play our role in the Grand Scheme. Elementary, my dear Watson."

"Sherlockolmina," Lakshman replied, using a nickname for his investigative cousin, "I see progress here, but nothing I hadn't figured out already."

"All right, but did you figure this out: why were you specifically told to go to the Church of Santa Maria del Popolo? Why were you so attracted to the script *'invisibile verbum palpabitur'*? Do you think Sanath did it by chance? He could have just said, 'Go to Delphi in Greece.' I think he did it for a purpose. See, it is written *'palpabitur,'* that is, the invisible word, the Word of God, is something that must be felt and touched, not something that must be believed.

Ivan, you and Laira felt the energy from the Sao Iambu when you were kids. Children at the school at Casa della Minerva told me they felt the special wind sometimes – for instance, the last time Sanath visited. Actually, I am almost sure I felt it when we danced at the party. What is this wind? In the Christian tradition it is the 'Pneuma,' the Holy Breath spoken about by the Gnostic fathers, the wind of Pentecost."

"Wow, sister, this time, I admit, I am impressed. The connections you've established here are most promising. It reminds me of something Jonathan told me about that Oikos meeting in Moscow: he related an event in St. Petersburg where the wind was mentioned, I believe. I must ask him again. But how all this relates to our quest, I don't know."

"My friends, you make a good team," added Ivan. "Let us not forget one point, however. All this business of bringing history back into balance has something to do with each one of us individually, no matter how small and unimportant we think we are. The space where balance can be achieved is within us. It is the window from where we can enter into the present moment. The ancient hedonists said 'carpe diem,' 'seize the day,' and enjoy it: they meant that we should forget about tomorrow, but surely there is more to it than that. We must not only seize the day but also seize the present moment for it opens a passage to live spirituality. This is the way I see it after discussing these matters with Philip." He half-turned to address Lakshmi on the back seat as the car climbed the hills of the Beotian mountain range.

"The pressure of modern life and related stress has an impact on us. We are more and more absorbed in thoughts and immersed in emotions, all of which have spun a cocoon around us. We are thus cut off from reality. If the people of our modern age walk in the street and pass by a flower, they will not see that this flower has a message of love just for them. Most of us spend our days behind a firewall of thoughts. The love that is there for us in this creation simply cannot reach us any longer. We must blast a path through this wall for we cannot see the love if we are not at peace."

Lakshmi observed, "You are right, Uncle. It is peace we need; it is peace we want – peace within our minds, peace within our borders, and peace between our nations. Hopefully, the Casket of the Wheel can teach us something about peace." They had reached the last village before Delphi and slowed down behind a cart pulled by a donkey. Suddenly, they became more aware of the immediate environment, an olive merchant in a roadside shop, elderly men on the terrace of the coffee shop, a girl with a bright scarf who was giggling with a friend. "Slowing down is sometimes helpful," thought Lakshman, "to see better."

The friends reached the archaeological site at Delphi towards the end of the afternoon. As they checked into the Hotel Hellas, the receptionist asked them, "Are you part of the group that is meeting under the big tent? People are coming here from all over the world."

Indeed, they had noticed a throng of young people with backpacks and sleeping bags strolling down to a large tent. In the excitement of reaching their destination, they had not paid much attention to them, glad that their own presence was thus much less conspicuous. Ivan and the cousins asked a guide to show them the exact spot where the Pithy had delivered the oracles. He took them into the fenced-off archaeological site, through the maze of staircases and ionic columns until they reached an unusual rock, slightly above the road. Lakshmi look at it closely,

"Strange, very strange. Look at this rock. It is certainly a natural formation. Yet I can distinctly see the shape of a standing elephant, like a statue oriented towards the right. It reminds me of the way we represent the elephant God, Lord Ganesha in India. See these two small cracks with the grass growing in it? They look like the eyes. And the trunk goes off towards the left. See the ears, and the big belly? You can almost see the navel. Look, Uncle, can you see? It's an elephant."

"You're right. It looks like a solitary sentry, some kind of gate-keeper. I can't make out what it means. The shape appears after some time. I see it clearly now, without a doubt. It is amazing; I wonder whether everybody notices it?"

"I rather doubt it," said Lakshman, sharing in the excitement. "So, this is the sacred ground of Delphi, the exact place where the Pithy prophetess stood. Ivan, could this really be the Gate of the Elephant, the one mentioned in the Icelandic scrolls? If so, it could be the passage between the outside and the inner world!"

"I'm not sure, but I suspect things are not so simple; the sayings of the Avasthas always have more than one meaning. We shall see. We'll come back with the casket tonight."

They gave a generous tip to the guide so that he would leave the door to the archeological site open. They just wanted to sleep in the ruins, they said, a tourist's whim… As a peaceful dusk painted Mount Parnassus with various hues of gold, pink, and ocher, they tried to get some rest in their rooms but it was difficult because of their growing excitement: the sight of the elephant-shaped rock, bizarre as it may have been, seemed a good omen, a welcoming sign.

Around midnight the companions left the hotel. Sounds of music, songs, and applause were coming from the tent in the field below the hotel, so nobody paid much attention to them. The full moon caressed the three silhouettes walking towards the rock of the Pithy. When they reached it, Ivan and the cousins sat in its shade, protected from the milky moonlight by the body of the rock elephant. They wore light but warm clothes whose dark coloring provided good camouflage at night. With trepidation, Lakshman took the casket and placed it between Ivan, Lakshmi, and himself. They were amazed to see that, at this very spot, the emerald carrying the golden wheel with the ten naves glowed with a faint green shine. The two men looked at each other, fully aware that a new chapter of their adventure was about to begin. With a deep sigh, Lakshman put his hand on the lid of the casket. It opened easily.

Lakshman couldn't remember what took place immediately after that, only that he was overcome by a feeling of dizziness. The first event that the ex-cardinal and the two cousins could recall later was the appearance of two huge beasts. A lion and a tiger, looking almost white in the pale moonlight, approached silently from behind a nearby ruin. It seemed to the visitors of the sacred rock that they witnessed them approaching as if seeing through one eye, or through a porthole in their forehead. Scared by the sight of the majestic beasts, the friends huddled up against the Pithy rock, as if wanting to disappear into it. And lo and behold, this is exactly what happened! They vanished into the rock of the Pithy.

EPISODE SIXTEEN

WHERE THE STARS HAVE YET TO SHINE

I n Washington D.C. the days were now pleasantly cooler after a hot and sticky summer. But the O'Lochan children hardly noticed the improvement in the weather because the past week had been a tough one by any standards and the turmoil in the family had deeply affected them all. Jonathan had valued his relationship with his father and mother despite its ups and downs and he found it hard to be suddenly and completely cut off from them. He and Joseph had moved into Michael's small studio in Georgetown where Jonathan had been sleeping on the couch, Joseph in a sleeping bag on the living room floor.

Jonathan was struggling too in his relationship with Jenny. His affairs with women since his teenage years had been often exotic, sometimes romantic, and always great fun but he now felt the need to settle down. Jenny and he had been quite attached to each other. He really wanted to make the relationship work and did not wish to lose her, especially in the context of this stupid family breakup, which had made him feel overly vulnerable. Despite the fact that Jenny's father had now withdrawn his support for the marriage, Jonathan and Jenny were still seeing each other, but Jenny herself had changed. She was more aloof, less affectionate, and did not provide him with the support he badly needed at this difficult time.

They were squeezed into the small penthouse apartment where at least their proximity was comforting. Inspired by Jonathan's lead, gradually and with brave humor, they tried to keep each other in good spirits. As the children of a well-off family, they were not used to worrying about making ends meet and the prospect of being entirely on their own in such circumstances was decidedly unpleasant. Of the three brothers, it was Jonathan who had been the worst affected by recent events. Aware of his role as elder brother, he felt duty-bound to comfort his brothers and sister. It was he who mostly endeavored to keep their spirits up when they found themselves feeling low; he helped his brothers to fight their fears and their rampant feelings of insecurity.

Michael, for his part, had not been sleeping well. He had been waking up every morning exhausted by disturbing dreams. The younger brother could only recall his first dream, in which he had clearly seen the Avastha knight of the Green Wheel. In view of the family schism, and with Joseph now closely involved because of his links with Ivan, Jonathan had called Lakshman just before his departure for Greece. He obtained his and Lakshmi's consent to telling Joseph and Michael everything they knew about Dagad Trikon.

After briefing Joseph and Michael, they discussed the matter for many hours. Swinging between incredulity and curiosity, Michael was both fascinated and disoriented by the story. He felt his life was getting too complicated too fast. Joseph, for his part, saw the saga in the light of his own research at the Vatican and his sense that the times were changing rapidly. He was now looking for a job. His own future was most uncertain, yet under the circumstances leaving the priesthood was a huge relief.

The next morning found Jonathan waiting for Tracy at the coffee lounge in the grand atrium of the World Bank Headquarters in Washington. An Oikos expert panel meeting was about to begin. The atrium was white, spacious, and well lit by the morning sun that flooded through the glass ceiling fifteen floors above his head. It contained a waterfall and its noise was soothing in this beehive that hummed with planning, banking, and the smug certainty of those convinced that they were in charge of doing the best for the world.

Jonathan once again reviewed the events of this harrowing and fateful week. As soon as he had heard about his father's plot to discredit him, he had gone to the State Department. Ambassador Campbell had been as supportive as possible. The ambassador liked Jonathan and appreciated his work and he did not believe the rumors that had begun to circulate. However, Senator Helmer, Chairman of the influential Appropriation Committee, had called the Secretary of State and now there was no way that Jonathan could ever be listed for promotion. In fact, his career prospects were most uncertain. The O'Lochan clan was powerful, and as it had turned against one of its own, there was little the ambassador could do to protect Jonathan. As Jonathan had guessed, he proposed to give the young diplomat a one-year unpaid sabbatical leave, with immediate effect, in the hope that things would calm down over time, as they often do. Jonathan would remain a U.S. delegate to the Oikos Project.

Jonathan accepted the proposal, even seeing a potential silver lining in it. Perhaps all of this was pointing to a new direction: the possibility, inspired by his dream with the white monkey, for a better understanding of himself and his purpose in life. If so, this could bring him what he had always sought, which was a response to his deepest curiosity, this accursed curiosity that his father could never understand. Any step towards a revelation of the meaning of his life would be welcome. Achieving this would be satisfaction enough for him even if money and status were not included in the package. His trip into the unconscious on the tail of the white monkey had left him with a deep longing to reconnect with a lost dimension of existence in which life could be fully enjoyed. He had been deeply impressed by Count Philip's account of Sanath's teachings in Rome and welcomed the opportunity to dedicate himself more fully to helping Lakshman. Jonathan had the feeling that what the wizard was talking about would completely vindicate the efforts of the Oikos Project. He vaguely sensed that some thread could show him the way. Not everything in his life needed to become a calamity and indeed this new path, forced on him by circumstances, could open up the life he most wanted to pursue, instead of one that followed the dictates and needs of the State Department.

He had decided therefore to spend more time on the Dagad Trikon quest, a prospect that had been greeted with enthusiasm by the cousins in Rome who, for their part, had always been nervous at the potential consequences of the links with the U.S. security agencies that he had secured.

Tracy arrived. Her auburn hair was slightly disheveled and her cheeks were red. She was late, having spent more time than she had intended on Capitol Hill. They kissed briefly; he teased her for being late. They enjoyed doing things together, and it was evident that a special bond of fondness existed between the eldest brother and his only sister. They hurried up to the large conference room on the executive floor of the President of the Bank. A team of top scientists representing the international nature conservation community had been gathered by the Bank to review prospects for the Oikos Project. They brought to this exercise all the latest strands of knowledge in the natural sciences. Rolf Walton, chief scientist of the Bank and Director of the Prospective Studies Department, chaired the meeting. He was a friend of Tracy and had called for a scientific assessment of ecosystems, which could be helpful in mustering the financial support of governments who were prepared to invest in the environment.

The O'Lochans found their respective places at the table and sank into plush beige armchairs, readying themselves for delibera-tions punctuated by Power Point presentations that would last the whole day. The scientists, naturally, were totally absorbed in the subject. Like most specialists, they enjoyed meetings among peers, who understood each other's importance. They reviewed status tables, debated system analyses, modules, modeling, and scenarios; they discussed thresholds, irreversible changes, regime shifts, loss of ecosystem services and limits to the ecosystems' carrying capacities. They glossed over the level of uncertainties and the usefulness of qualifying them. They even reached a consensus.

The prospects for the first century of the third millennium of the Christian era, according to all available trends and indicators, pointed to a rise in average temperatures, higher sea levels because of melting polar ice caps, and more extreme weather events. Societies would hardly be able to cope in the present context of population growth and the resulting increased demand for food and water. "More of the same," whispered Jonathan to his sister in a disgruntled tone. Somehow the dry dissection of threshold breakdown scenarios that endangered the well-being of millions of people seemed surreal when contrasted with the carefree, business-as-usual, and we've-seen-it-all-before attitude of the public out there in the sunny streets of DC.

John Baker, Head of the Department of Life Sciences at the University of the West Indies in Trinidad and Tobago, spoke of the plight of many small island states, which were encountering increasing problems with tidal floods and who could not survive a further rise in the sea level. Viktor Seydlitz, Chief of the Climate System Research Department of the Potsdam Institute for Climate Impact near Berlin, confirmed the gloomy scenarios introduced in Moscow as temperatures were projected to rise up to 5.8 degrees Celsius by the end of the twenty-first century. The consequences of climate change would break national budgets as countries tried to cope with rising sea levels. On the other hand, in the high mountains of Europe, heat waves and poor snowfall were causing the melting of ancient ice fields and the loosening of the permafrost that holds the rock surfaces together; some mountains were already starting to crumble.

Mountain climbing had been prohibited in some places because climbers were at severe risk of being killed by falling rocks and ice. At the same time, irregular precipitation in the Alps would see a succession of extreme weather events in Europe such as droughts, landslides, and flash floods. Droughts were certain to contribute to widespread forest fires. The condition of marine ecosystems, with disappearing coral reefs, oxygen depletion, and loss of fish species, was hardly more encouraging.

Prospects for poor, developing countries were simply frightening, according to Rajesh Kumar, Coordinator for Environmental Economics at the World Resources Institute in Washington D.C. Marten van Wuren, from Wageningen University in the Netherlands, added that the risks of extinction were on the increase for many species that were already vulnerable and the high costs of biodiversity loss would further impoverish societies.

The scientists were required to make their point as an advisory service to policy-makers and to avoid being prescriptive. However, from the position of the government representatives and the account contained in Walton's somber conclusions, it was quite clear that the scientists were unable to catch the attention of the policy makers. Politicians were following the public mood and reflected the lack of interest in doing anything concrete that would have a financial cost for consumers and taxpayers. To make matters worse, reforms in land management that were needed to protect the fertility of the soil were endangered by the failure of the negotiations, in the framework of the World Trade Organization, to deliver a fair deal to developing countries for their agricultural produce. At the same time liberalization and delocalization, promoted by the rich countries, allowed corporations to bypass needed social and environmental adjustments.

Jonathan shook his head, overwhelmed by skepticism. The scientists were discussing such matters with a laudable sense of detachment, absorbed in the seriousness of their methods and approaches. They discharged their function of being the eyes and the ears of mankind through competent but dry assessments. "They may see, they may hear," thought Jonathan, "but they cannot do anything. Mankind's response to the challenge is way too slow."

As they were leaving the conference room, he said to Tracy with a sarcastic grin, "Venice's gondoliers are being forced by ever-higher tides to remove the gracious wrought-iron stern mounting of their gondolas in order to squeeze under the city's bridges. At the same time, the city of Las Vegas is budgeting thirty million dollars in subsidies to suburban homeowners to persuade them to rip up the grass around their houses and to replace it with 'desert landscaping' because they no longer have enough water to water grass! That's the way we adapt to climate change. Look, honey, what we discussed today is but a small fraction of the spectrum of issues covered by Oikos; these environmental aspects only cover one side of natural science: the loss of resilience of ecosystems. And look at the magnitude of the challenge."

"Oikos cannot cope with this any longer; it doesn't get enough support," Tracy responded to her brother in a similarly despondent tone. "I'd better look for a new job like you guys. Seagull, if you can see some way out of this mess, please let me know; from the discussions I heard yesterday on the Hill, it seems to me that we are going nowhere. I feel we are letting the Oikos Project down. Without the U.S. playing its part in this, the whole thing will simply collapse. Perhaps the Russians will continue on their own because of their interest in parapsychology, but the results, if any, will have a limited impact. The French have already opted out and this stupid Clairmont fellow has contacted some influential academics here telling them it is all nonsense. Why on earth is he doing that?"

"Look, Tracy," said Jonathan, as they were walking down H Street at the end of the meeting, "it's simply hopeless. I don't think the difficulties you are having in Congress to raise money for the next cycle of Oikos activities are a surprise. Remember what we heard about Sanath's teachings: the Darkness is also at work. Politicians just want to look good and this means, in this case, to look in the other direction. Take, for example, this ecosystem business: we know the threat, we even know what to do, but the politicians and the bureaucrats will simply not do it, of course, because it has a cost. I fear they'll try to look as though they are doing something, make sure nothing happens, and just pass on a much worse situation to the next generation. Are they capable of acting for the common good? They will be tempted to react to their own corporate interests, the pressure groups, and their re-election agenda. Democracy can't function in the long term if our rulers are more interested in allocating their budgets to please some voters and big business rather than addressing longer-term survival issues. The right kind of leadership is missing. How can we make it happen?"

"I don't know," responded his sister. "I think Lakshman is right. If we can't find a breakthrough at a different level, we may possibly find ourselves in a range of apocalyptic scenarios that are being mapped out at present by the scientific community. I wish I could meet that wizard. I called Laksh yesterday; he is on his way to Greece. It is really great they now have that casket; just imagine, right in the middle of the Vatican. I'm glad Joseph cooled down about the files too. He should ask Ivan what to do about them. God knows what may come out of it. Still, I don't know how come Mike dreamed about it."

At that point Tracy's cell phone interrupted them. It was Professor Rahul Rahurikar, the head of the Indian National Oikos Committee, calling unexpectedly from New York, where he was attending a world medical congress on alternative medicine. Tracy had mentioned the interests and credentials of her brother to him, as well as his temporary availability. Dr. Rahurikar, who had already met Jonathan in Moscow, expressed a wish to meet him again. The professor wanted him to be a senior research fellow on a project he was launching in the U.S. Indeed, as the Indian representative on the Steering Committee of Oikos, he had a small budget for research activities.

What was more intriguing was that the professor was now asking whether the younger brother, Michael, could also join. Tracy suggested that her brothers should go with her to New York the next day. She thought Dr. Rahurikar was probably looking for a student in the U.S. to work as an intern in the context of that research. Jonathan, who was looking for a temporary job away from the U.S. administration, thought the offer was one not to be missed. They decided to drive to New York. Flying the three of them there would have been quicker but considerably more expensive.

On the next day, the weather during the five-hour drive was somber and gray, with intermittent showers reducing road visibility. Michael had a good collection of CDs in the old Jaguar that his Dad had given him a couple of years ago. The music kept everybody cheerful and they finally reached Riverdale in the Bronx in the early afternoon. Their destination was the house of Adam Leary, a friend and publisher of Dr. Rahurikar, who had published the research papers of the professor in the U.S. where they could have more influence. Adam and his wife Lioudmila were gracious and jovial hosts, and they introduced the three young visitors to Rahul Rahurikar and an old friend of his. Nobody noticed that, on seeing Michael, this latter gentleman's face was briefly moved by a powerful wave of emotion. Tea was served.

The group discussed Dr. Rahurikar's proposal and why he had summoned them to New York right away. It was most interesting: still committed to Oikos, the Indian government had asked Rahurikar to make a comprehensive survey of U.S. sects, consciousness movements, ayurvedic therapy groups, and yoga practices that

269

had sprung up from Indian culture or religions in some way. The purpose was to survey practices, trends, and results, and to identify what worked with a view to identify benchmarks for best practices and to establish a 'code of good conduct.' The review would thus also expose many of with the abusive practices, sexual exploitation of disciples or financial frauds that were increasingly damaging the image of India abroad. Jonathan would be the coordinator of the survey, providing the authority and the impartiality of a foreigner. He was to be supported by a number of Indian officers located in the various consular offices. Mike could also help in the research with a temporary job contract.

However, it was obvious that Michael was not really listening. On seeing Dr. Rahurikar's friend, he had become quite pale and felt a sudden sensation in his chest. During the ensuing conversation, he could not take his eyes off the gentleman. After a while, he interrupted the conversation and asked the unknown gentleman, "Excuse me, but did we meet somewhere? I don't think so, but I have a feeling I know you." The gentleman looked at him intently and replied with a trace of affection and sadness in the voice. "If we had known each other, wouldn't you remember?" The answer was a bit unexpected.

Tracy intervened, protective of her younger brother "Mike is somewhat stressed out at the moment. He is preparing for exams, plus we've had a tough time in the family recently, and he hasn't been sleeping well. He talks in his sleep, but we can't understand what he's saying!"

"Of course, I understand," said the friend of the publisher thoughtfully. "It is quite natural. I believe Adam is inviting you to stay the night, as it would be too far to return to D.C. today. Perhaps, Michael, you'd like to go to your room and rest, while Rahul and Adam finish their business here. I could take Tracy and Jonathan for a short walk to Wave Hill: it's a beautiful estate above the Hudson

River and it's just around the corner. Charles Darwin, Thomas Huxley, Mark Twain, Arturo Toscanini and Theodore Roosevelt all stayed there at various times."

Michael answered, "Well, thanks, that's very nice of you and your wife, Adam. That's a really good idea. I feel quite exhausted, I don't know why. Perhaps Tracy's right: I need some rest."

Lioudmila took Michael upstairs to show him to his room while Jonathan and Tracy left the house too, right behind the professor's friend. The day was warm and the sun was now peeping through the clouds. The park was graded and contoured; rare trees and shrubs adorned the broad lawns, and secluded gardens blended harmoniously with the natural beauty of the Hudson River highlands. Enjoying the splendid view of the dark basalt cliff on the other side of the Hudson, they passed under the shade of the huge beeches and walked through the winter garden where carnations showed their generous pink and white blossoms.

They sat on a bench, under the pergola of the monocot gardens, protected from indiscreet eyes or ears by wall shrubs. Holly, yew, cotoneaster, pyracantha, and boxwood added magnificent and varying textures. Above their heads, large leaves with fine, downy chocolate undersides offered glimmers of reflected light from the glossy upper surfaces. They remained silent for a while, basking in the soft warmth of the returned afternoon sun. Then Tracy said aloud, "Well, maybe we should have left Mike at home… "

"Not at all. He is actually the main reason for this invitation to the Bronx."

"I beg your pardon?" Tracy thought she hadn't understood properly, but Jonathan felt a shiver in his spine and experienced a sudden rush of adrenaline; he was like a feline in a state of maximum alert: not scared, just intensely focused on the first dawning of an intuition, a revelation that was about to come. He asked slowly, "Sorry, but I didn't catch your name."

The unknown gentleman sighed. A long silence followed, then his expression seemed to change. He became grander and more imposing. He responded pleasantly with a soft voice, "Well, you can call me Sanath."

Tracy and Jonathan looked at the elderly gentleman with stunned surprise. There could be no doubt because Sanath's expression had changed enough now to reveal the profound wisdom and majesty of the heir of the order of the Hllidarendi. They stared at him with a sense of fulfilled longing and a surge of expectations – at last, they had run into the master they had believed was dead, the wizard who knew so much about the Dagad Trikon prophecy. No one could recall how long this moment lasted, but it must have lasted a while because passers-by turned to stare at the strange trio who looked petrified in time.

Then Sanath continued, urbanely, "Tracy, Jonathan, please sit down. Rahul knows a bit about me, not as much as you do, though, but he is one of my most reliable friends in Asia. He brought me here and arranged this meeting with you at my prompting. I shall explain you where we stand now in the rising of the tide."

Tracy and her brother were still dumbstruck by this latest twist of fate. They could not quite believe their luck, that they were actually facing the mysterious mentor of Lakshman who had apparently died, vanished without leaving a trace. The wizard explained, "You see, after what happened to the plane that was to take our friend Lakshman from Schiphol Airport to Geneva, I understood that we had entered a new phase of hostility and I took certain precautions. I was very sorry that it was impossible for me to save some members of my household who died in the explosion at my house in Vassenaar. Also, I most sincerely regret having caused such anguish to my friends who feared I was dead. I had to conduct some dangerous investigations indeed, and I shall not speak of them now. But, for this errand, it was simply better to completely disappear. I have learned much in the meantime and now the time has come for me to return. And I had to come to you, for you are companions in this quest."

"Sanath, oh my God, I can't believe it! We've heard so much about you. Yes, you correspond to Lakshman's description. Count von Jetzlar also told me about some of your teachings at Ivan's residence, the Casa della Minerva. They will be so happy when they will know you are back. This is incredible! You have come to us at a good time, just when we need it most. We seem to be stuck and we really need your advice." Jonathan continued, suddenly remembering what Sanath had said. "But why do you say the meeting took place because of Mike?"

"Because it is so. I brought you here so that we might talk, for you need to understand many things kept hidden until now. You have to promise me that you will not say anything to Mike for the time being, otherwise, in ignorance, you may spoil everything."

"We promise, Sanath," said Tracy. "But what's wrong? Is there a problem with Mike? It seems that troubles are raining down on us from all sides at the moment. Jonathan told me yesterday that he felt like a wet dog in the rain."

Sanath replied with a smile, "Perhaps he feels that way, but the fact is that there is always an umbrella moving about just above his head. He just doesn't see it. The protection of the High Lady of the Rock is on all of you, otherwise the Darkness would have snatched you already." Jonathan smiled. Although he didn't quite understand the meaning of these words, he felt a sense of security, a feeling of warmth in his heart. He felt it through the powerful presence of the wizard, yet the sense of being protected seemed to come from the heavens. For a brief moment he recalled the sensation that he had experienced before the cave of the Gundaldhar Fault when the white monkey had brought his awareness to witness the Lady of the Rock. That same security had pervaded his deep unconscious state. Curiously, he felt like a lost child who was about to find his mother. He asked, still smiling broadly, "What about Mike, Master Sanath?"

"Lakshman, Philip, Laira, and the good Ivan have told you much about the Dagad Trikon legend, but the prophecy is moving as we go along and it is difficult even for me to catch up with what has happened. I was intrigued and concerned that the blessed vision of the Casket of the White Feather in Iceland and Amsterdam did not say anything much about the Stealthstars. So, I had the hunch that if Lakshman were to help me to find the Stealthstars, it may not be for him to look into the casket but for me to look into him and his surroundings. I could not find anything until he started speaking to me about you. The wind, the cool breeze, spoke to me and I felt I had to follow this lead. I went to Washington to see the members of your family. I often see without being seen, you know. And then I felt both great joy and great sorrow."

Tracy interrupted the wizard: the love of a sister for a brother is a powerful thing and at that moment she was not at all concerned about the Dagad Trikon story – she was solely concerned about Mike. "Why, what is it? What is the matter with Mike? Could he be, do you mean, is he… "

"Yes, he is. He is a Stealthstar. And yet he isn't. This is what I need to tell you now and this is also what you should keep secret for the time being. Now listen carefully: imagine an airborne assault by a parachute regiment. To simplify things, let me tell you that you have two kinds of landings when an assault is launched. In the first category there are the unlucky parachutists, who land in swamps, ponds or get caught in the branches of trees. It is difficult for them to adjust to their ground situation and to become operational. The second category, the lucky ones, land on firm ground. They can gather themselves up rapidly and, given a little time to regroup and recognize their environment, they are ready to function and fight."

"So?" Jonathan was a bit bemused by the military analogy and found it quite strange coming from the wizard's mouth.

"So, this is the condition of the Stealthstars. The second wave, the lucky ones, has come into this world in optimal conditions. This means they have landed mostly in harmonious families, where the parents love each other and where there are no great levels of stress. A nest of emotional well-being is a must for the Avasthas: it nurtures their ancestral qualities. With the help of the angels and of the divine wind, we have been able to collect a number of them. That is why, with the agreement of the parents, we began the school to the north of Rome that is directed by Alexandra and Ivan." Jonathan remembered the cardinal's pet project, the fire of joy in the eye of the small girl Lila, and how all the kids looked so positively adorable.

Sanath continued, "But the problem is that most of those of the second wave that we could find have come only very recently. Like lion cubs and puppies, they are still extremely vulnerable. We do not know if and when they will remember their powers, and they need more time to grow. In the meantime, the witches of Belzebseth are looking for them. If the negativity finds them before they have recovered their might, they are lost – I mean, lost to the purpose for which the Stealthstars were sent. And I can give you an example of such specific dangers they face, even if it is in an apparently benign form."

But Tracy interrupted the wizard at this point. "Please, sir, what about Mike?"

"Yes, sure, I am coming to it. Please hear my story. I offer it in all honesty even though it is a tale that gives me no comfort. Mike is an ancient personality. He walked on this earth in the days of Dagad Trikon. At that time he was a gem among the faithful who served the High Lady of the Rock. He was also a warrior of considerable might. But today, when I saw him after eons and eons, he looked to me to be a shadow of his old self. The poor fellow, he was struggling to recognize me but he could not. He belongs to the first category of parachutists, the elite battalion that took the greatest risks. You know your own family, the conditions of your parents, their materialism, and the narrowness of their religious faith. On top of this, he has made all the usual mistakes of a young man of his generation. Nobody was there to guide or protect him, or explain why he was damaging himself. Avasthas cannot afford to make mistakes because, unlike regular human beings, they have so much more to lose. I mean, they can lose the subtle powers that made them different in the age of the splendor of the earlier born."

"It's easy to lose something if you don't even know you ever had it," observed Jonathan.

"That is exactly the point: they do not know themselves! In this world, these powers are within them, certainly, but still hidden. The trouble is that Mike was part of an elite battalion that landed some time ago to prepare everything. So I eagerly awaited this group because they were the best. Yet, I couldn't find them. Mike is the first one I have encountered."

"So, shouldn't you be happy?" asked Tracy rather anxiously.

"A contact has now been established with the Stealthstars of the first wave and thanks to your link with Lakshman, I finally found Mike. It fills me with great compassion, yet with great sorrow also. It is hard to explain. Mike is like a Rolls Royce, but he is like a third-hand Rolls Royce: much of the engine and the body have been damaged and the owner does not know whether he can use it any longer. It looks as though the first wave of Stealthstars has been lost; they can't meet the high expectations we had for them. They don't reconnect to the Deep Way. This is a tragedy. Something has gone wrong, as if they landed in a spider's web. Thanatophor very much feared their coming and he certainly prepared his traps. Maybe because of this, or for other reasons, Mike cannot connect with his true nature. His consciousness and his Self are not yet one. And this is the source of my grave concern. Because, if the returned Avasthas cannot connect, who can?"

Tracy remembered *A Bridge Too Far*, an old movie about World War II, in which a party of British parachutists, looking to destroy a bridge, land in a trap prepared by the enemy and are devastated by hostile fire. She felt the sadness of the fate of the fallen Avasthas penetrating her heart. She shrugged, "But, master, why don't you tell him, why don't you help him and then he will recognize you, for you also come from the ancient days of the bygone age, when goodness ruled the earth, don't you, and in these days, Mike knew you, didn't he?"

"Michael knew me but in another world, not this one. And when he is in this world here, his world as a human being, he doesn't remember anything. Telling him anything at the wrong time would be of no use, it would be like trying to force open the narrow gate to the inner world. His conscious mind would not relate to what I would reveal with external words. It has to come from inside, his inside. He has to discover it himself. Otherwise we would just create a sort of schizophrenia. He would be split between the belief of what he was and what he knows he is now, unable to reconcile the two. Unfortunately, the solution does not lie in belief, only in experience. And for this type of recognition, the only experience that works is that brought by the Deep Way. Furthermore, being told who he was at this stage could also depress him because, just now, the reality of his past is so much greater than his present. So, this must be kept a secret from him for the time being."

"But why then did you tell us?"

"So that you could understand him better and protect him perhaps, if you can understand the purity that flowed in the veins of an Avastha of yore. Help him to avoid behavior that would take him beneath his level. As I said, things are moving fast now, faster than I can comprehend. He has yet to play a role, although I don't know which one. Since when has he been having these 'disturbing dreams,' as you called them?"

Tracy answered, "It was a couple of nights ago, but he says it seemed much more real than any dream: he could really feel things in his body, but he cannot recall what happened or where he was at the point when he woke up." She described how Michael had a vision of the opening of the Casket of the Wheel. Sanath looked absorbed in a deep meditation that they did not wish to disturb. When he emerged from it, he simply muttered, "So this is a way as well, but it is very dangerous and it is not the Deep Way." He closed his eyes and was silent again.

After some time, Jonathan asked another question. "Sanath, when my sister interrupted you, you were going to give us an example of how the returning Stealthstars had been foiled or tricked."

"Oh yes," responded the wizard as if coming out of a long dream, "do you remember the party in the Casa della Minerva?"

"Of course I do. Lakshman told me that what he experienced felt like Rasa energy and I thought I understood it. It was amazing: such fierce joy, such roaring power, and all synchronized in perfect oneness. It was truly special; I was in another world."

Sanath smiled approvingly. "And this is the world to come, dear Jonathan, our world, a world where spirituality is not the obscure pet project of frustrated nuns, sad monks or fanatic mullahs. A world where spirituality is what it is, organic, living, life itself, the receiving of the Gift! You had a touch of the joy of the Stealthstars at the hideaway of our good friend Ivan. In seeing the children playing at the school near Tarquinia, you had a sense of the mettle of the Avasthas who came in the second wave. Many of the kids who came to the party were also Stealthstars whom we identified years ago as being from that second wave, the category of those who did not have a difficult landing. Yet we discovered that as they grew they also walked into traps. Their immune system was not fully activated.

"Now, remember how the last dance started?"

"It was the girl, wasn't it?"

"Lorelei is a Stealthstar like Mike, but she lost the ways of the earlier born, despite the fact she was born into a family that protected her. The Darkness is really on the look out for them. However, Lorelei alone could not have triggered the rise of the Rasa through her dancing, although this is a power she had achieved in her past. It worked out because her own magic was restored, carried, and amplified by the power of the togetherness of the Stealthstars, another secret of the Deep Way: so she still has the Rasa power in her, despite her fall. This is why we should try to protect them and keep faith in them, even if they fall into some of the pitfalls prepared for them by Belzebseth."

Jonathan remembered, in that moment of loveliness, how beautifully the girl had danced: she was slender and shy, yet carried the decisive beauty of some hidden power in the graciousness in her movements. He interjected, "Her fall? I don't understand? She is the granddaughter of Philip and Laira and surely she could not have landed in a better family."

"That is what we thought too. But we learned that, unfortunately, even the safe landing of the Stealthstars is not a guarantee of success. They also need to learn how to move out of their defense perimeters. Her school friends had adversely affected Lorelei. Stealthstars are very sensitive. Young Avasthas need the comfort of friendship; they seek love and do not easily bear loneliness. When they are still young and before their defense system is fully operational, people can take advantage of this. If a teenage girl, in the springtime of her life, offers her tender heart to a boy of a lesser level who takes her body as a prize in return, much is lost for that girl. This is even more so if you are an earlier born. I know that today cheap relationships are a way of life for many youngsters of your world, but this is only because they do not know what they lose.

They have never heard about the treasure of their subtle energies. Any behavior that brings a lack of self-respect constricts the possible access to the inner world: the blessings fade, self-esteem is low, confidence is lost. As I already said, I now fear that in this modern world something went wrong with the return of the Avasthas and this is of great concern because they were our hope."

"Surely, Sanath, this was all planned; surely the Avasthas must have foreseen these difficulties."

"They are more stealth than stars now," said the wizard sadly. "Indeed, their own cloaking tricks have played upon them so well that they don't access their store of energy. If they cannot connect consciously with the Deep Way, we are all lost. And of course, the Darkness is closing in on them. As Belzebseth does not know exactly where to find them, he haunts the places where he thinks the youngsters may turn up. He wants to enter into their minds if given a chance: schools, pubs, discos, clubs, and so on. The witches of his council have become trendsetters on some TV channels. I fear for the kids.

Her brother, Lothar by the way, is one of the most solid second-wave Stealthstars we have; I think he has the Angkura gift, the germinating power, although it is not manifested yet. He took his sister out of it; he opened her eyes. She knew she had stooped below her level and became despondent. Guilt is a useless feeling. Then, with the love of her family, she partly recovered. She was too great to be completely brought down, so you witnessed the power of the dance. It shows that the power of the earlier born can somehow be restored. It seems to work through the bond of their togetherness. I know there is still hope, but hope is not enough for they can't maneuver the power and I, the last Hllidarendi, simply do not know how to reawaken or activate the Deep Way in them. Their condition is weakened by the onslaught of Darkness into the surrounding modernity."

One of the gardeners had come to tell them it was now closing time so they got up and walked towards the exit. In a manner completely unexpected, even to himself, Jonathan asked, "Sanath, do you know about a white monkey?"

It was Sanath's turn to look dumbfounded. "Why do you ask this question?"

"I don't know. When I heard Lakshman's account of his reading of the scrolls in Iceland, I recalled a very vivid dream I had in Cairo. The day after the assassination of the Prime Minister of Israel, I went on a fantastic journey in my sleep. Lakshman and I may have seen the same scene from different entry points. Now that I come to think about it, I may even have seen Mike in it, but I am not sure. It's quite foggy. The clearest image I keep in my memory is of a white monkey. He looked cute at first, and then formidable. But he changed all the time, the sequences were fragmented, and I forgot everything else."

"The white monkey came to you? I never knew about this. These are glad tidings indeed, light in a dark hour! Jonathan, you don't know what a relief you bring to my soul. If he came to you, the white monkey must have foreseen our plight and this is enough for me!"

"Who is this white monkey?" asked Tracy.

"The very mastermind of stealth. He may yet regroup the Stealthstars," exclaimed Sanath joyfully. "He may take any form he pleases, gigantic or as small as an atom. He is the master of mystic powers and none can withstand him. The white monkey is one of the traveling disguises of Lord Hanuman, the Magnificent, the messenger of the Emerald God. He also has been entrusted with patrolling the yellow area of consciousness pertaining to action, thought, and to shaping the future. The Christians recognize him as Gabriel, one of the great archangels. To humans he is more hidden than revealed, yet he constantly helps them in ways unknown to them. You are blessed indeed, Jonathan O'Lochan, to have seen him.

"Why should a dream matter that much?" Tracy was obviously slow to understand the elation of Sanath. The wizard continued, " The impact of Lord Hanuman is wide ranging. As Jonathan received his visit, it is quite possible that many others did, in the sense that they received hunches, dreams, and intuitions to bring them on to the path of the quest, to come closer to a better mastery of their life. I am certain, in fact, that thousands of other people have benefited in some way from the silent coaching that is always associated with his manifestation. This is indeed a good day! I've received the first good news in a long time and I am going to check on this. Now, let's return to Adam's house. They must be waiting for us and dinner must be ready."

Jonathan asked hesitantly, "Sanath, I remember the recollection of Philip and Laira and how much they benefited from your teachings in Russia. Could we perhaps spend some time together tonight to share in your knowledge of things past and things yet to come? And won't you spend more time with Michael and try to give him some guidance too?"

Sanath hesitated for a brief moment and answered, "I would love to but tonight, I am traveling and, yes, I will meet Michael." This sounded like a straight enough answer but it turned out that it wasn't, because when Sanath returned to Adam's house, he skipped dinner, went straight into his room, and did not come out until the next morning. "I thought your friend was traveling tonight," grumbled Jonathan at the dinner table, addressing Rahul Rahurikar, who had finished drafting a new contract with his publisher.

"Well, with Sanath, you never quite know," was the predictable answer from the doctor. Tracy looked at her younger brother, trying to hide the confused mixture of feelings that had been stirred up by the revelations of the wizard: admiration, sadness, affection, and protectiveness. Mike was still tired and retired for an early night. Despite the fact that it was three o'clock in the morning in Greece,

Jonathan tried to call Lakshman on his cell phone. It was switched off and indeed, at this very moment his friend was in no position to answer the phone.

THE NAVEL OF THE WORLD

The mighty shape of Mount Parnassus, the lights of Delphi, and the view of its archaeological site bathed in moonlight had disappeared. Ivan, Lakshman, and Lakshmi felt the depth of the rock within their own body as they pushed into the rock of the Pithy to escape the approach of the two large felines. It was not a disagreeable sensation, just a bit gelatinous. The darkness was almost total but they found that they could move with ease. The cousins could guess the shape of Ivan, who, following a crack within the center of the rock, had moved ahead of them. He was penetrating deeper into the ground, spiraling downwards with increasing speed. The crack widened and the feeling of viscosity they experienced while walking through the stone disappeared.

Lakshman realized that they had now emerged out of the rock and were progressing along an open cavity. He was not aware of walking; rather, he was moving by means of propulsion emanating from his willpower, but he found himself too baffled to even wonder what was going on. The cave opened onto a grotto, which was bathed in a bluish light. Ivan turned towards Lakshman. His lips were moving, but somehow no sound emanated from them; Lakshman could understand him without any difficulty.

"See, we are not alone," said Ivan who was so intensely involved in the turn of events that he did not pause to question their strange circumstances. They could see two small silhouettes standing in the middle of the grotto. Drawing nearer, they could discern the features of two teenagers. They had white or blond hair and were dressed in white tunics; they looked both distant and friendly.

"Greetings," said the taller boy. "My name is Aliskhan and this is my friend Lidholon of Anor. You were expected."

"So, I've found you at last," exclaimed Lakshman, as he looked at the two Avasthas from the Yuva platoon, possibly present here as the Stealthstars to whom he might deliver the Glorfakir and the Sadhan.

"Not really," replied the teenager, somewhat sadly. Again, no sounds were uttered. "You were meant to find us in your world. But we never met there and our paths may never cross. You have now transgressed into the unknown, through the threshold of the other world into which human beings can only venture at great peril. This is the area that is traveled by dead souls as they join their appointed places. But you should not fear because Avastha magic will protect you. Also, you are not dead. Your physical bodies are now in deep sleep at the foot of the Pithy rock. You are facing us in your subtle body, without your physical sheath. It is you, everything you are, mind, soul, emotions, your full awareness, but without the physical body. You are still wearing its appearance though, because your physical body was nothing but the graphic expression of the subtle being inside."

"Oh, this is it," said Lakshmi, who had finally started to focus on her disincarnated condition. "The Tibetan lamas used to call this state the 'Bardo.' I'm glad not to be dead. Has the casket sent us on some kind of astral trip, or what?"

Aliskhan said, laughing, "Yes, but... a very earthly one, because we are going to fly not to the stars but through Mother Earth. We asked permission from her guardians. The navel of the world is under Mount Parnassus: it is a hub of underground channels of access to all the continents."

"Flying through the earth? What's our destination, where are you taking us?"

"We are going to escort you to the Council of the Daskalians. You are expected."

"The Council of the Daskalians," Ivan cried out in anguish, "but we are not ready. How can we appear and face them? These, these are the Masters. You're making a mistake, please let us go back."

"What do you mean?" asked Lakshmi, surprised by her friend's reaction – she had never seen him lose his poise before.

Lidholon spoke. "The Circle of the Aulyas, the seers, and, later, the Order of the Hllidarendis, the college of the greatest wizards, receive their guidance from the Council of the Daskalians. The Daskalians are the masters of knowledge: they are immortal beings, the elders of all the intelligent races who have ever visited the planet. To them, Adivatar entrusted the task of assisting evolution towards the catharsis of history, the great transformation. Why are you afraid?" he asked mildly.

Ivan replied, "They are clear-sighted; they can see everything in you, even the smallest speck of dirt. We are going to discover what it means to feel as naked as a worm."

"They are not the judges of the Last Judgment, you know," Lidholon said kindly, trying to sound helpful. "That moment approaches but is still hidden from us all."

"Enough, now," Aliskhan interrupted firmly. "We must go. Please follow us and do exactly like us. If you lose us, if you stray from our path, you will never return to your physical body. I warn you, that means death."

Aliskhan and Lidholon, followed by the young woman and the two men and unimpeded by their physical bodies, moved through the wall of the grotto. As they penetrated it, Lakshman found it needed some effort to speed through solid matter. It was a bit like churning cheese within his limbs. Gradually the running became easier, more like churning milk perhaps. And when the running felt completely free and liberating, Lakshman realized that they had left solid matter and entered a huge cathedral-like cave. The Avastha boys had increased their speed. Suddenly the whole party took off, like airplanes, cruising a few centimeters above the ground: they were flying!

They realized that it was so simple because they actually propelled themselves by a concentration of attention and willpower. Lakshmi was the last in line of the small flying squad and the sensation was exhilarating. She started moving up and down, swaying from the path traced by the Avasthas and slaloming between the stalagmites. She could accelerate and brake at will. It was like playing with a remote control toy, being both the player and the toy.

After frisking about for a while, it seemed that her freedom to move was gradually being hampered. Beyond her will, an unknown force began to pull her in a given direction. In the dim gray light she saw a depression in the ground that could have been the crater of a small volcano from which a yellow glow emanated. Although much intrigued, Lakshmi tried to resist the pull. She slowed down and, on reaching the edge, she used a boulder to block her movement and hid behind it. To her surprise, she found that this worked. She sighed with relief but continued to feel rather anxious. Peeping from behind the boulder, she saw a strange scene. Forty feet below, the remains of an ancient temple occupied the bottom of the small crater. Its massive stones and geometric features evoked pre-Columbian architecture more than the Hellenic world they had just left. The glow came from an impressive stack of precious objects spilled carelessly all over the center of the ruin: piles of gold, ornamental cups and plates, crowns, bracelets, armor, and ornate weapons decorated with precious stones and jewels.

Straining her focus to better see these exquisitely crafted objects, Lakshmi saw the occupiers of this desolate treasury chamber: dozens of serpents swarming in all directions. They came in and out from the inner walls of the crater, through richly embellished gates and windows. Light was coming out of these apertures as if the mound in the middle of the crater represented the pinnacle of a buried city. Even more surprisingly, some of them were only half serpents: the lower part of the body was the tail of the serpent, while the upper part of the body was that of a man or woman. Their faces were beautiful but ominous. Their heads, chests, and wrists were richly decorated with gold ornaments. As if unnerved by Lakshmi's proximity, some of them became agitated, darting their magnetic eyes towards the edge of the crater. Lakshmi was terrified as the pull increased and she felt as if the boulder could not help support her much longer. She thought she was about to move through it as she had done through the Pithy rock. She increasingly felt herself unable to withstand the pull. Horrified, she realized this was the peril described in the Tibetan Bardo: floating souls, depending on their inner condition, would be pulled or sucked by diverse forces and projected in the corresponding compartments of the nether worlds.

Just then, she felt a tingling on her shoulder: it was the hand of Lidholon. The pressure brought instant release; the pull stopped. She felt hidden and secure again. He whispered in her ear, "The nagas are very sensitive. They cannot see you yet, but they can sense your presence. As soon as you left our flight path you lost most of the cloak of Avastha stealth. Soon they will discover you. Please, I pray, do not leave us again. It is very dangerous. The last thing you want is to be captured here."

"Who are they?"

"Some of the souls of those who loved gold too much. I know it sounds a little old-fashioned to your ears. These people were addicted to acquisition, trapped by greed, and masters of wealth. But

they did not share it. Do you see what I mean? This frenzy of acquisition is the curse of your western world and it degrades the surface
of our planet. Now – whatever 'now' means outside your human
time – these souls captured in the shapes of snakes are stuck here,
in everlasting boredom, with no possibility to move away from the
surroundings of the crater, to evolve or escape. There are thousand
of places like this in the underworld. Some are beautiful, many are
much more terrible. Dante Alighieri, the Hllidarendi who blessed the
land of Italy, visited a few of them. But, like you, he had a guide."

"You mean that Hell exists?"

"Of course. Dante had special protection and could return.
Most humans who ventured here never returned. A man can take an
astral trip but basically he has no control. If he is captured by a more
powerful entity, he risks being stuck in the world of shadows and, of
course, at this point, the physical body that is left behind dies. These
nagas, for example, are much more powerful than your present astral
condition."

Since the arrival of Lakshmi, more snakes were emerging from
their underground city into the vast cave, pouring out of all the
crevices, rifts, chinks, and cracks in the crater. The larger ones were
hissing furiously, turning their heads towards the main door. After
some time, a huge python emerged and moved ahead up the slope.
They all began to crawl towards the top of the crater.

Lidholon said, "That is one of the ancient serpents, of the
largest kind, one of those who was killed by the lord Karudas in
Earlier Earth. We are in trouble. Enough talk, let us leave quickly!"

As swiftly as possible, Lidholon and Lakshmi sped away.
Lidholon seemed to be working hard to make a getaway, but by
following the Rock Avastha, Lakshmi could again gather speed
without any obstruction.

It took the heir of Anor and Lakshmi a little time of high-speed
flight to join the rest of the group, which was anxiously waiting on

the shores of an underground river. Lidholon explained what had happened. Aliskhan looked distinctly annoyed.

"Do you think you are on a roller coaster in a Luna Park?" he said. "There are ways and tricks to avoid the pitfalls of this place, but I do not have time to teach you. It would take long time for your mind to absorb them: it does not have enough focus power yet. You must keep with us at any cost, otherwise we will lose you."

They continued their journey, following the river. After some time, it disappeared in a siphon and the Avasthas entered the river. They started swimming, with Aliskhan leading. The pace accelerated and the small group was now flying in the water. The sensation was delicious, like a thorough, refreshing shower. The earth and the water around felt soothing and friendly. The river washed away the heavy feeling that had burdened Lakshmi since discovering the city of the nagas.

Onwards they went, through water, earth, and emptiness. At times, the humans had glimpses of various shapes of the nether world, some benign, some fearful, but they kept their curiosity in check. They did not want to repeat Lakshmi's experience with the nagas and carefully kept in the trail of the Rock Avasthas. They were somewhat reassured by the fact that these creatures did not react to their passing. The Avastha camouflage was effective. After some time, their sight blurred, their awareness became confused, and they were only conscious of the tremendous speed of their flight within the earth. Aliskhan was following his own road map through underground caves, rivers, and water reservoirs. Whenever necessary, he pierced through solid ground but it slowed their progress. He avoided pools of petroleum and naphtha, layers of minerals, coal seams, and pits of molten lava. It was impossible to tell how long the trip in the Bardo dimension lasted. Finally, they emerged from an inner lake into another gigantic cave: the sight was awesome. A soft orange light glowed from the cave's luminescent ceiling. On three sides the bottom and the ceiling were dramatically decked with large stalactites and stalagmites, some of which joined to form giant columns that looked like the pillars of a formidable underground temple. Some of the pillars emerged from the lake. As the companions looked more attentively, they saw that the pillars carried spiral staircases leading to hanging structures that served as lookout posts. High above the surface of the lake, hanging bridges made of lianas linked them together. The largest posts seemed equipped like battle stations from where platoons of archers could reach most of the surface of the lake with their arrows. The companions wondered where they had landed. They rapidly reached the shore of the lake, next to the remnants of a ruined harbor. Everywhere, they could see traces of fierce fighting and they were most intrigued by their surroundings. They were soon to find the answers to their unspoken questions.

The astral travelers had reached the farthest side of the cave, where the lakeside was bordered by a flat, empty space. Behind it, they saw what looked like a large opening of a tunnel in the wall of the cave. They followed a dilapidated road, which led to it, passing between two large boulders that carried remnants of embattlements. Leaving the cave, they progressed through a warren of underground galleries, chambers, and tunnels about two miles long, all adorned with stalactites and stalagmites formed over the past two million years. Aided by the dim orange light from the ceiling, they could see unknown signs carved in the walls, a few high statues of helmeted warriors, and the ruins of some fortified guard posts. The road ended in a second large cave that also looked like the interior of a cathedral, immense, soaring, and sublime. Its vast floor was scattered with large stones. The glow from the vaulted ceiling was stronger than in the first cave that contained the lake and it was brighter here too, with a rich golden hue that magnified the spectacular rock formations.

And then, as they emerged from the shadowy light of the last chamber, they saw it. Pressed against the opposite wall of the cave, they marveled at a structure that had not been carved by Mother Earth. The shape of an impressive construction appeared more distinctly.

Here, rising from the floor of the cave, the underground fortress residence of the Rock Avasthas was revealed before their eyes. They stood – or rather, floated – in awe at the magnificence of the subterranean palace.

A broad flight of steps led up to the lofty façade of the citadel, which emerged between fortified walls; it was topped by a series of battlements. Four high circular towers flanked the central building. They saw distinctly the colors of the house of Elnur painted on large moldings on the two inner towers: green with a wheel of gold in its midst. This was, surprisingly, the symbol on the casket they had just salvaged from the Vatican.

Two gigantic, four-armed statues of the ancient deities worshipped by the Avasthas flanked the grand entrance portal. The statue on the left had long matted hair and carried a trident; the other, on the right side of the entrance, wore a crown and carried a discus and a mace. Above them, the high wall at the center of the complex was pierced by seven double-lancet windows joined by a cornice in relief. In the upper part, there was a small loggia between large sculptures of a griffin and a unicorn, set beneath an elegant marble rose window depicting a ten-petal flower surrounded by Avastha symbols. Still higher, a large vaulted terrace topped a larger loggia, which was artistically defined by twelve arches supported by slender twin columns interwoven to form an elegant entablature.

They paused before the entrance of the citadel and Lidholon whispered to his companions, "I shall explain to you where we have arrived. This is the underground Avastha fortress of Elnelok. When the power of the Avasthas of yore was on the wane, they retreated underground to escape Thanatophor. The last Nizam left on this earth, from the house of Elnur, led them here. The Elnurian Avasthas loved the sea but, in deference to the remaining Avasthas, they agreed to live together underground with their brethren from the house of Kalabham. Most of the members of the other great Avastha houses of Falkiliad, Eleksim, Anor, and Anorhad had followed my father Haslerach of Anor when he departed for the stars in the cylinders of fire. The remaining Rock Avasthas built this underground fortress to protect their clan from the inhabitants of the nether worlds. But the nagas considered themselves the sole owners of the underworld and came from far away through the underground galleries to claim lordship and to repel us. They emerged from the lake by the thousands and a great battle ensued.

Two huge pythons led the nagas. They could smash stone columns in their mighty coils and crawl as fast as a galloping horse. They were from the ancient race, older than the python killed by Apollo in Delphi. The Avastha warriors had long lost their original strength and they reeled under the onslaught. They lost the harbor and the galleries around the lake. The nagas took over the access corridor linking the lake to the fortress, which is the path we just followed. Most of our warriors perished from venomous bites, others were strangled or crushed by the pythons. Before the entrance gate of the underground castle, Olophon of Elnur, Lord of Elnelok, took his last stand with his two sisters fighting by his side. He was a formidable warrior and he burned with the fire of despair. Never did the naga lords meet such a fierce foe and the serpents could not pass through.

Nonetheless, in those days, able-bodied warriors were few in numbers. Elnelok was filled with elderly Avasthas who were maintaining the culture and manners of their world through their meditation but they would not carry weapons in such a battle. There were also women, clad in armor, fighting by their men, and a small number of children. The banner carriers of Kalbham and Elnur had retreated behind the gate with a small party of the Nizam's guard. Olophon could see that the hour of doom was coming.

At the moment of greatest peril, the ancient eagles, called by the meditation of the elders, took human form to fight the serpents. These offspring of Karudas could not continue to carry the body of a bird under the earth, but they could still subdue the snakes with their dazzling brilliance and their piercing eyes. The nagas were defeated by the men-eagles and by the remaining Elnorian swordsmen. The Lord of Elnur wisely chose to spare them; he recalled that his lineage had maintained friendly relations with the great serpents of the sea and he concluded a peace treaty with the nagas. So now you understand why the late Avasthas revered Prince Karudas, lord of the eagle folk. He remained for them an angelic figure, both terrible and benevolent, the symbol of the ancient power of goodness. Come now, we must proceed."

They followed Aliskhan who had waited patiently while Lidholon was speaking. The small party passed the monumental entrance of the underground citadel through a carved archway. The massive door still carried traces of the ancient battle, corroded in some parts by snake venom. They followed a spectacular climbing corridor, decorated on both sides with fanciful bas-reliefs representing winged animals: bulls, horses, lions, eagles, griffins, phoenixes, and even winged centaurs. The vault of the corridor was equally luminescent. Lateral corridors opened, framed by giant arcades through which, in the golden orange haze, they could see palaces perched on the mountainous side of the huge cave and the delicately carved ogive-arched windows of lordly cliff houses. Lanes and tunnels openings, connected with gracious bridges and staircases, linked hanging terraces with richly decorated columns that offered a stupendous view of the giant cathedral cave. Like in the days of yore of the Dagad Trikon Rock, these terraces had been the centers of the social life of the gentle Avasthas.

The palace city was silent and seemed deserted but they had the disagreeable impression that they were being watched. Yet the place was not hostile. Lakshman thought he recognized Avastha symbols glowing in the penumbra, under a gallery of small arches. The corridor ended at the foot of a majestic staircase. The luminescence dimmed as they climbed the long staircase, which passed through various layers of chambers and smaller caves that contained the ruins of Avastha dwellings. The ascent lasted for some time until, finally, they passed through a singular horseshoe-shaped gateway guarded by two large stone felines. Lakshman felt uneasily that they looked almost alive and very much like the ones who had pushed them into the Pithy rock in the first place. Finally and quite suddenly, emerging from a short, narrow, and dark tunnel, the companions saw a magnificent moonlit night above their heads. They had emerged from their long journey in the underworld and were back on the earth's surface.

The companions stopped and stood still under the sky, feeling greatly relieved. How good it was to be back on the ground. The night was clear, the air was pleasant and warm, warmer than in Delphi: a funny feeling, thought Lakshman, for someone without a body. After a short while, he could see his surroundings better. High cliffs surrounded the open area; it had a familiar feeling.

"Welcome to the central canyon of the Dagad Trikon Rock," said Aliskhan gravely. "Please follow me."

They crossed a large sandy empty space that was surrounded by high walls of rocky mountains, Emerging from the shade of the nearest cliff, a party of ten hooded sentinels walked briskly towards them. The moon briefly revealed armor glittering under the coats. At their head, a tall Avastha barred their path. Aliskhan greeted him. "Hail to Philthalas, the Elnur of the sea, Captain of the Fleet that once was, father of Olophon and lord of Elnelok." Philthalas greeted them courteously. Aliskhan the Swift and Lidholon of Anor responded to his greeting with due respect. In the milky light, Lakshman saw a ten-nave wheel engraved on the breastplate of the Lord of Elnur.

"This may be the rider on the winged horse who brought the casket to Greece, thousands of years ago; how old is he? I have no way of knowing whether he is alive somewhere, floating like us between two worlds, or whether he is a ghost." Philtalas was surrounded by a group of hooded attendants who had escorted him there. They were his followers, warriors from the house of Elnur who tried to protect mankind from the evil ghosts that Belzebseth had scattered in different locations of the Bardo. Lidholon turned at this moment, whispering, "The escort is comprised of some of the Stealthstars you are looking for, but you are not allowed to see their faces while meeting in the twilight world."

Philthalas escorted them without uttering another word. High above them, they heard the flapping of the wings of a very large bird. For an instant, its enormous shape hid the disk of the moon. The companions didn't feel too reassured. Moving about without a body is not unlike the feeling of walking naked: it carries a distinct sense of vulnerability. The companions instinctively kept close to Aliskhan and Lidholon. They were relieved to reach the mountain flank and saw a slightly circular facade, topped by a dome half-emerging from the cliff, shaped somewhat like the Pantheon in Rome. A large statue in the likeness of a sitting dog had been carved in the central portal, forming an arched entrance through the front legs of the animal. The lord of Elnur paused. "This is the dog Anubis that was also worshipped in ancient Egypt. The dog represents loyalty and devotion to his master, the qualities of a disciple. It is fitting that the dog frames the entrance to the hall of the one who is verily the primordial master. Be prepared to enter the Chamber of Maat. This is where the code of the immanent and absolute righteousness is kept. Maat is the universal law that binds all beings. Let wisdom and humility protect us before Diyakoson, judge and Herald of the Chamber of Maat."

The weapons of the four Avastha guards at the arched entrance gate shone like silver in the moonlight. They saluted Philthalas of Elnur with great deference and allowed the group into the sacred temple, which no human had ever visited before.

The party following Philtalas of Elnur entered in the anteroom that opened into a wide ceremonial hall. The solemn and austere interior was built to a circular plan with a roof supported by large ogival arches resting on ten half-columns, and concluded with a great square apse lit by three large gates that emitted a green light. The circular wall was lined with ten richly decorated but empty high thrones. Behind each throne, symbols were inscribed on the wall. Lakshmi recognized some of them: the table of the law of Moses, the yin yang of Tao, the star of David, the seal of the Sikh religion, the moon of the prophet Mohammed. She looked ahead and on the opposite wall, the three doors facing the entrance filled her with an eerie feeling.

The central one was higher but narrower than the other two. It was flanked on both sides by two great statues of Prince Karudas. He was portrayed as a mighty eagle, carrying a disk above his head. This came close, thought Lakshman, to the statues of the Egyptian God Horus carrying the disk of Aton, the sun god of Pharaoh Akhenaton's heresy. Was it he who was circling like a bird of prey above the entrance of the temple?

On top of the three doors, the companions noticed a large balcony, beautifully carved with the coils of a giant snake, with his thousand-headed hood hanging over another throne on the balcony. However, in the ambivalent light of the temple, it was hard to say whether the snake was just a sculpture or whether he was alive, motionless, and perhaps ready to strike at intruders. Philtalas whispered without further explanation: "Do not look at this balcony lest you awaken Ananta Quetzalcoatl, the dragon feather of the morning star." The higher throne could not be seen from the floor of the temple but it also emitted a different light, perhaps more vibrant and energy giving.

In the center of the hall they saw a large, round table surrounded by benches. In the middle of the table there was a basin whose diameter was three yards and a half – it contained a most extraordinary fluid.

They peered in fascination at this liquid substance. It looked like water made of wide silky patches, intertwined with large turquoise, indigo blue, and emerald filaments, which gently floated in the air, twisted around each other, and pulsed with an inward light. This was unlike anything a human eye had seen before. Respectfully and in awe, the group stood next to the benches and waited.

THE ASSEMBLY OF THE DASKALIANS

After a short time, a man dressed in an ample cloak, emerged from the central door that was hewn into the side of the temple. He walked briskly towards the table. The party of Avasthas greeted him ceremoniously. Much to their surprise, Ivan and Lakshman instantly recognized him as Sanath. They noted how the turquoise and green reflections of the water danced on his face. He looked cheerful. As Ivan bowed in utter relief and gratitude, Lakshman exclaimed, "Sanath, you're alive!"

"Am I?" the wizard of Hllidarendi smiled. "Remember, we are not quite in your world here." His face immediately became serious again. With the reappearance of Sanath, the diffuse and dreamy connotations attached to the underground journey dissipated; the scene became clearer. Sanath's words were uttered and perceived with crystal clarity, with an exceptional acuteness that contrasted sharply with the more emotional moods previously experienced in the Bardo.

The three visitors seemed now to be in yet another dimension. Sanath turned to Lakshmi and greeted her warmly. "Welcome, daughter of the ancient land that was once called Bharatma. It is well that you assist and protect the guardian of the Glorfakir sword. Men are not always as lucid as they think they are and often need the intuition of a woman to bring them to their senses." Lakshmi's heart leapt with pleasure at the warmth of the welcome extended to her by the great wizard. She joined her hands and bowed in a traditional Indian namaste greeting. "So, my assumption was correct – Bharatma is India. That is why we picked up the trail of Dagad Trikon in those old Sanskrit manuscripts," she thought with some excitement. After this salutation, the Hllidarendi whispered hurriedly.

"The Casket of the Wheel that you opened in Delphi has also brought me here. Congratulations, companions, I am most pleased that you successfully completed the journey through our Mother Earth. In the need of the hour, you came under the protection of the Avasthas, for this mode of crossing borders between the worlds is unauthorized. I am glad you could resist the various pulls you were subjected to in the Bardo. I must say I was worried about you, because mortals are not used to traveling in this fashion. Out-of-body experiences are usually fatal. In the Bardo, creatures easily fall prey to the nets of Belzebseth.

Humans have not yet evolved enough to appear in the flesh at such a sacred and hidden place. Be careful: you are in a delicate condition; try to avoid being swayed by thoughts or emotions for they can drag you away and you can be removed from the sacred chamber."

Sanath continued in an affectionate tone, "Friends, let me explain where we are. This is the Chamber of Maat that serves as the circular hall for the Assembly of the Daskalians. There are few such halls in this world. This one was the sacred temple of Dagad Trikon that only the initiated could enter in the olden days, a place to invite one of the forms of Adivatar when it pleased Him to manifest as The Sower, the Master of the Grand Scheme. It was also meant for some occasions when the Daskalian lords came here to consult with the divine Lady of the Rock."

Lakshmi interrupted abruptly, "Shri Sanath, who are the Daskalians?"

"The Daskalians are the forms of the Ancestral Teacher. They awaken the self-mastery principle in their followers. They have always been the guides of the human race. Basically, the Daskalians are the original discoverers of the precious qualities each of you have within you. They exist to help you to find them with your own internal knowledge. They help make you knowledgeable about your own treasures. Before receiving this knowledge men and women live in duality: they may be wishy-washy or cocksure, doubtful, anxious, spineless or forceful. Their eyes cannot see because their minds are constantly in the process of reacting to all they witness. They don't know how to guide themselves and are thus never satisfied.

The Daskalians want to bring us to the shores of inner knowledge where we discover the Deep Way. Without this practical inner navigational system, humans, on the whole, do not know how to face or correct themselves; instead, they prefer to blame others and so cannot solve their own problems. The Daskalians have appeared in human history, taking ten forms of the principle of mastery to uphold the Wheel of the Law. Seen from above, this crypt looks like a wheel with ten spokes. It is not visible to human eyes. This is why Lakshman, who visited this very canyon some time ago did not find it."

In a flash, Lakshman recalled his flight through the Libyan Desert and landing in the mountain complex of the Triangle Rock. Then another memory surfaced suddenly within his consciousness, which revived a scene of one of his former travels in Bhutan. He saw the golden effigy of the Wheel of the Law, flanked by two deer that the Penlop, the abbot of the Dzong or monastery of Tsonga had presented him during his visit to the monastery.

The venerable monk had told him that this symbol represented the teaching of the Buddha of course, but that he would come closer to its meaning during another trip, a most significant journey. The old man had predicted with a broad grin, "But this will be a different kind of travel." Lakshman had forgotten his remark but now wondered how far his destiny had already been traced by powers greater than himself. He whispered to Sanath, and his voice was audible only to the wizard. "I feel, and perhaps I fear, that my fate has already been decided for me."

Sanath responded gravely. "Fate is what happens to you. Destiny is what you do with what happens to you. The destiny of an enlightened being is to invite the master of the Grand Scheme to take charge of fate. Then fate becomes providence. You lose an illusion of control but achieve connection with that power. Thus, you lose control but you gain mastery; you lose illusions but you gain reality. That's all. That's it."

Lakshman kept silent, absorbing these words. He felt an intuition from deep within, feeling liberated somehow by the words of the wizard.

Sanath went on, "The Daskalians are all powerful, yet their impact has been limited because Adivatar did not want them to interfere with human freedom. Basically they taught why morality is good for us. Men, in crossing the border between freedom and license, have lost the benefits of these ancient teachings. Hence modern people are increasingly lost in a thick fog of confusion, in the web of a virtual world they consider to be the real one. We must learn to navigate a passage between the paths of the Daskalians and those of men and to transmit the knowledge mankind needs to grasp in order to survive. This is why you are here, neither men nor Avasthas, but shadows of a dream wandering in the night."

"*Schias onar, nuktiplanytos,*" mused Lakshman in the ancient Greek tongue as he translated the last words of the wizard. Sanath had used the very words of the poet Pindarus that had been echoing bizarrely in his memory. Sanath continued, "This evening the Daskalians will manifest in the hall at the appointed moment corresponding to an exact zodiac configuration. They will use the creative power of speech. That which will be uttered will become true, to an extent, as it also depends on the absorptive capacity of those who listen to their message. Through their utterances, and the reception of these utterances in your awareness, the Daskalians will open a crack of understanding in the dullness of the human mind. Through this crack, the masters will sow the seeds of the higher knowledge needed to repel the Darkness in the collective unconscious of mankind."

"I still do not get it. What is the purpose of our presence here?" asked Lakshman incredulously.

"To witness. All you have to do in this sacred chamber is to store these messages as the ambassadors of the human race. You will channel them into the pool of consciousness from where others will extract inspiration. It would have been even more powerful, no doubt, if you could have been here in your own bodies, but of course this was not possible. Remember: it is not enough for knowledge to stay in the brain because it must work out in the heart. The heart has to imbibe what the brain knows. It works with the Avasthas but it's another matter with humans. Perhaps only humans with large hearts have a chance to receive Samyak, the integrated knowledge. Such is in the nature of this experiment."

At that moment, the cupola was filled by the noise of a mighty wind and an intense emerald green light shone from the basin in the center of the table, temporarily blinding everybody present. The companions felt the wind blowing through them. It was a blissful, cleansing sensation, similar to the one Lakshman had enjoyed in Iceland when he had opened the first casket. When he reopened his eyes, he saw the likeness of ten holographic figures sitting on thrones. All the members of the party around the central table gathered around Sanath and Philthalas of Elnur, and bowed to them with complete reverence. The silence became so intense that Lakshman felt he could hear the flutter of the wind.

After some time, the Hllidarendi turned towards the companions. "Behold the successive forms of the Daskalian incarnations that represent the primordial master. Before you can hear the Daskalians you must go through the ceremony of purification. Follow me." He took the three visitors to one of the Daskalians. They approached hesitatingly and, when they were only a few feet away from the impressive figure of an elder with a long beard, a fire sprang into life at his feet, burning with bright orange flames. The fascinating dance of the tongues of fire absorbed the friends, causing them to forget everything else around them. They felt as if the fire was communicating a playful light quality, as of youth itself. Its impact gradually burned away all their weariness, anxieties, and doubts. Did the process last seconds, minutes or hours? They didn't know but they felt that they had been washed clean of the stains of adult life. They felt fresh and thoroughly cleansed, as innocent as newborn babies. They had become the children and heirs of the creation, the friends of the fire.

Sanath spoke again, standing behind them. "Welcome to Atashkah, the place of the fire worship. Welcome to Navroz, the twenty-first of March, which is the regeneration of spring for this creation. Praise be to Zarathustra, the master of purification worshipped in Persia, the herald of the spring of the second birth and a guide to a succession of great empires." Lakshmi stared at the Daskalian who was looking at them with great kindness and compassion. The soothing quality of purification by fire was emanating from his very glance. "Yes," they thought as one mind, "this is really the primordial guide of Persia, this is Zarathustra." They felt both awed and elated and prostrated themselves before Zarathustra, devoid of all doubts and fears.

Then the central door opened and a living being with the appearance of an angel came forth. It was Dikayoson, the Herald of the Chamber of Maat. Followed by Philthalas, first Lord of Elnur, and his party of Avasthas, Dikayoson chanted a melodious psalmody:

"Salutation to the ancient Lord, the ancient dawning light. Salutation to Him, who can see the Supreme Goal; Salutation to the One, who is possessed of mercy and compassion; Salutation to the One, who blazes with light; Salutation to Him, the origin of meditation, who is beyond the three modes of existence and who takes us across the duality of yin and yang; Salutation to Him, who is simple, pure, clean, and undecorated; Salutation to the One who bears and supports that which is essential for existence; Salutation to Him, who paced the Agora giving meaning, purpose, and devotion; Salutation to the Knower of the field, who carries the authority of truth; Salutation to Him, who is in constant enlightened motion."

Sanath and the three companions had again joined the group of attendants near the central basin. The wizard turned towards Ivan.

"Ivan, your devotion to the truth is your strength. Nachiketa, take him to the King." A young man came out of the small group that surrounded Sanath and took Ivan Sadaka to the royal figure sitting second from the left of the main entrance. His bearing was both majestic and amiable.

"You may ask a single question," the King told Ivan. This was an unexpected turn of events. At this moment, Ivan forgot everything he wanted to ask or needed to know about the Dagad Trikon saga since his childhood in the Byelorussian forest. Lakshmi heard him ask, *"Ko aham?"* whose meaning flashed in Lakshmi's brain as "Who am I?"

The king answered, *"Tat twam asi:* you are That."

"What is 'That'?"

"Seeker of truth, it is your destiny to find it out."

Ivan's awareness in his dreamlike state processed the answers to the question at high speed. "Am I my body? Obviously not, because my body is a coat I left behind at the foot of the Pythic rock. It is now sleeping, thousand of miles away in Delphi. However, I must also be something else other than my mind, for sometimes it is moody, sometimes sorry, and sometimes happy. I am not my attention either, because it is unsteady. My intellect is busy analyzing. Who am I when I am fast asleep? Who am I?" Following this process of elimination, Ivan concluded he had indeed to be *'That'* which was the support of these various states, *'That'* which remains unaffected despite so many changes and which is the foundation for all the various functions of his mind.

The royal Daskalian had followed the train of his thought. He answered, "Ivan, you are the immortal Spirit but you don't know it yet. When the Lady of Grace shall bring your heart to your brain, all things will stand revealed. Through the elimination of virtual identifications you will achieve your real identity. You should meditate and become one with it." Nachiketa smiled approvingly. Ivan went back to his seat. Sanath said gravely, "Thus spoke Janaka, the King," and then muttered to Lakshman, "In front of us, next to Zarathustra, you can see Lao Tse standing under the yin yang symbol: go and kneel before him."

As Lakshman reverently approached the wise man he saw the circular disk above his head rotating. The yin was emitting a yellow light and the yang a blue light that curiously recalled the experience of his first vision in Iceland. But the strangest thing was that he could feel a similar glow emitting from his own brain: the right hemisphere of the brain was the blue side, the left hemisphere the yellow one. He could hear within the voice of Lao Tse.

"The beginning of the Universe can be considered as its Mother. Find the Mother and you will find the children accordingly. Verily, the sun follows the moon, man seeks woman, whatever rises must go down, and whatever is born must die. Everything ends in its opposite under the eternal law of contradictions. There is no escape from the labyrinth of actions and reactions but the way of Tao. Do not put your trust in duality. The swings from one extreme to another are becoming too violent now. Yin and yang, bipolarity will disintegrate man, his brain and his cities. Find the hidden door to the middle path. The path is straight and steady but the one meant to be found is coiled up on itself."

Lakshman recalled the spiral staircase, the vision seen in his hotel room in Amsterdam.

The spiral was expressing the reconciliation of the contradictions, in an ascending dialectic movement. "Hegel and Marx, they both saw this," he thought in a flash. "History progresses through the law of contradictions." Whatever the way of Tao, the messages of the Avastha scrolls told the same thing. But the blue and yellow shades of light in his brain were now oscillating like the scales of the balance. He became lost in the movement and slightly dizzy. He found that he could not steady his attention. He felt a pressure in his forehead. Any further insight eluded him; he did not find the passage.

From the escort of Philtalas, an Avastha familiar with the Muslim faith came forward and walked to the Daskalian who was sitting under the symbol of a half moon. He bowed before him. The Daskalian said, in a thundering voice:

"The tribes of the desert lived in poverty and asked for wealth. Oil and wealth was meant as a blessing to them but instead it turned into a curse. They ran after a mirage. Ask for the true blessings. The path shall open to those who honestly seek the truth. My true followers are those who believe in the power of love and not in the power of hatred. But many of those who claim to be my followers have carved out their own religion, out of their appetite for power and to suit their own petty plans. From sunrise to sunset, the day of reckoning shall be known. When that day comes, no one shall deny its coming. When people will neglect prayer and squander the divinity, sell religion to win the lower world, legalize untruth and practice usury, accept bribes and construct huge edifices, and consider the letting of blood insignificant; when women will behave as harlots, family ties will be broken and passions will rule over the hearts, when the debauched and the ignoble will become the rulers, the princes degenerate and the ministers oppressors, the twelfth Imam will return."

The word "Imam" resounded in Lakshman's memory. Was it not contained in the mysterious words spelled to reveal the new name of the High Lady of the Rock? Might it have been Imam Maitreya? Maitreya, he remembered, was the name of the returning Buddha. Buddha had taught about the cycle of the Wheel of Law, the dharmasakrapavastana. He was now standing in the hall of the Wheel of Law, the symbol of the casket. It all slowly fitted together and made sense.

Lakshman figured out that the Casket of the Wheel did not contain any scrolls but brought higher revelations through the mouth of the Daskalians themselves. This was indeed high and potent magic and Lakshman hoped he would not lose a word of what was being revealed. But the master of the Arab tribes continued, "In those days the sacred books will be decorated, the mosques disguised, the minarets extended. Criminals will be praised, the liar will be considered truthful and the traitor trustworthy. They will cover the hearts of the wolves with lambskins. Women will behave as men and men as women. They shall boast and claim their birth-given rights to practice abominations.

The twelfth Imam, the Mahdi will re-establish holiness and all the religions, abandoned and disfigured, to their original purity. He will do as I did, cleansing that which is before him. He will reject those who defiled the name of Islam. He will expose the blind rituals and monstrous ignorance of those who kill in the name of Allah. Didn't they kill my own grandchildren, the beloved of my daughter Fatima?

He will come. Al Muntazar, the awaited One, and his faithful are the friends of truth. They are those who gathered around the messengers in each age. They will join the ranks of the Mahdi and spread the power of love through the corners of the earth. They will develop their powers in such a manner that, without there being a messenger between the Mahdi and themselves, they will see him and hear him without him having left the place where he is. The Mahdi will write his instructions on the palms of their hands, and their hands shall speak."

The second Daskalian from the left addressed the speaker. "O Mohammed al Mutawakkil, you speak well. Those who claim to be your followers are fighting those who claim to be mine around our beloved city, Jerusalem, which has fallen into the hands of the arrogant and the stupid. Their war is not ours. Little do they know that You and I are One and that, in their ignorance, they are trying to tear apart the very fabric of our eternal being. They have brought dishonor to our teachings. How can we protect those peculiar disciples of ours who breed hatred and falsehood in our very names? Hate is the way of the Dark Enemy, not the way of the Daskalians. My followers have sucked the creative power of the Star of David and therefore they excelled in all disciplines. But their pride swelled up and they forgot there is in this cosmos a power beyond them that is working out the domain of action. When I took them out of Egypt, manna fell from the heavens. But it was not their doing. It was their lot to eat, not to make it rain. Our way is the Deep Way. Yes, Mohammed, we believe in the power of love, not in the power of hatred. Let us now invite the Shekhina, the holy presence of the Parampara. The burning bush of tongues of flames that burned on Mount Sinai shall now be rekindled."

"Thus spoke Moses, the Daskalian from the Sinai Mountain." Sanath bowed before the holographic shapes of Mohammed and Moses and whispered to the cousins who were bowing by his side. "The Daskalian master is actually one single personality, but he takes different shapes at successive moments of history. Watch now because the calling of the burning bush is taking place. It is the Gift of the Goddess but you cannot take it with you because you are not really here, you are only a ghost in the Bardo."

The translucent water had risen above the basin and was now floating a few feet above the heads of the congregation, shimmering softly like a tapestry of living energy, splashing pools of liquid light across the walls of the dome. In the greater glow Lakshman could see that the symbols were made of the same living water. Sanath was whispering to them, "See, Confucius is sitting next to Lao Tse. And there is Nanak, the master of the Sikhs. Abraham is the one sitting under the Star of David, just before Moses, and see, there is the Baba of Shirdi. And see... " But the attention of the companions became drawn to an amazing sight. Appearing from nowhere, as if springing from the very skulls of the ten Daskalians, multi-colored tongues of flames grew and danced on the heads of the ten masters. A thought flashed in the mind of the ex-cardinal: "My God, this is Pentecost, the calling of the Holy Ghost."

Their fire was gentle and emitted coolness, not heat. At the same time, as if someone was peeling away the layers of an onion that was their very skulls, the human visitors in this world of wonders felt their usual layers of consciousness falling away: they were in a majestic awareness of the power of the inner reality, the reality that had been severed from man at the time of the Great Schism. This was truly a unique sensation of wholesomeness.

Everything was crystal clear and as it was meant to be. They felt reassured and confident: everything was going to work out. The power of Adivatar dancing in the tongues of fire, which had chosen to manifest in the crypt of the Daskalians this night, was benevolence itself.

"This is the calling of the burning bush. You are fortunate indeed to have witnessed it. And now the mighty ones shall awaken the power of the Basin of Vaikuntha. Be silent, just watch." Lakshman heard the whisper of Sanath resounding in his head. The power in the room was almost too much to bear. Looking at Ivan, who also seemed overwhelmed, Lakshman worried that they would not manage to remember the messages of all the ten masters. Lakshmi, on the other hand, seemed absorbed in a quiet rapture, fully enjoying the spectacular oneness of the moment.

"The cocoon, that damned cocoon woven by my thinking is sticking to me, too much rubbish in my brain, I can't make it... " Lakshman muttered to himself. Why couldn't he just let go and melt into the moment like Lakshmi? He fought the wave of self-doubt and had to strain himself to the maximum, mustering all his attention to hear the next Daskalian talking in a thundering voice:

"I am a citizen of Athens and I told the elders of that city about the secret of my daemon, my inspiration. I paced the agora for many years, but they would not listen. The magistrates accused me of corrupting the youth and ordered me to drink poison. Alcibiades, my dear pupil, led Athens to its doom and the Athenian army to abject slavery in the silver mines of Syracuse.

I, Socrates, am the guide of Occident. But instead of seeking inner self-knowledge, the European tribes built a strange creed on the Seven Hills of Rome and camouflaged the true nature of my message in the jargon of my disciples – Plato, Aristotle, Aquinas, and Martin Luther. I simply taught them: *Know thyself.* Today the children of the West don't know that they are the Spirit. They have no access to the power stored within their brains. The doctors of learning closed the gate of the quest. A college of dumb clerks produced blind beliefs to erase my heritage. Over the centuries they lost faith in the search for the Gate of the Elephant. Yes, they closed the path of introspection.

The powers in the West opposed self-knowledge. They became drunken with the blood of all those they persecuted for seeking the inner path. Indeed their priests feared self-inquiry. So my disciples have run away from reality. Today few still have the courage to ask questions. They have lost self-respect and respect for the teachings of the elders. They turned away from the temple of their soul and put their pride in their machines. They conquered the world and painted a canvas of folly on this earth that She will not tolerate much longer. Are they lost for good? O Master of the Grand Scheme, please kindly answer their prayers. The Aulyas are silent, the Hllidarendis have failed, and the Daskalians themselves are invoking Thee."

Sanath whispered: "Look at the Basin in the center of the Chamber of Maat and see now what no human eyes saw before. You shall now be blessed with a glimpse of Vaikuntha, the water universe of the Emerald King. It is a world of godhead, even beyond the heavens."

From the throne over the balcony and through the three doors, the glowing shades of green lights seemed to gain in brilliance and intensity. These mixed with the colors of the liquid substance that was slowly emitting from the central Basin. It seemed to float in the air, interfusing with the mist. Heavenly music filled the bluish mist that was now spreading in the hall of the Daskalians. It sounded as if the beat of tambourines and the crystalline notes of a cithara accompanied angelic voices reciting a psalmody. The music was vibrating with intensity. The message was beseeching, enveloping, compelling. Lakshmi's composure was fully attentive, as if absorbing the dew and the notes of music with the pores of her skin. The filaments of water had become very thin, almost to the point of evaporation and the companions did not know whether they were breathing light, air or water. Immersed in the refreshing mist, they were plunged into an all-encompassing water world, which was not of this planet.

The water from the Basin of Vaikuntha was washing all over them, imparting a wonderful sense of well-being. They found themselves in a new, fluid, and musical universe. The living water of dancing hues of blues, emerald, and turquoise tones had filled the temple up to the dome and the holographic manifestation of the ten Daskalians had now disappeared. They heard the words of the Lord Philthalas telepathically. "Hail to the ocean of reality. It shall dissolve the ocean of illusion that has been woven as a prison around the human race, just like that woven by spiders. Let us all be the children of that sea. That sea is the master of my house, the master of all races; that is the sea the Elnorians worship. Let the humans hear." Indeed this was the water of life whose protocol had been entrusted to the sires of the House of Elnur.

They were in the middle of a huge space, bathing within an inherent green freshness, an empty void whose sole point of reference gradually became evident.

Indeed, at that moment, a vision whose glory almost made them weep blessed the companions. They saw the miniature likeness of a reclining God on the spot where the stone basin had stood before. He was resting on the coils of the serpent that had been depicted on the balcony of the crypt. The royal cobra had raised its manifold hoods and exuded total watchfulness. It was alive and the message that came through to them was that the scene was totally real. The God resting on the coils of the huge cobra was asleep. The words of the hymns in Handel's *Messiah* erupted in Lakshman's head: "King of kings, Lord of lords… " The hues of the skin of this God were like emeralds. For the grace of his bearing and the profound majesty of his face there was no name, no adequate description.

Philthalas of Elnur kneeled before the apparition and all followed suit. The serpent was completely motionless, except for almost imperceptible reptilian movements, which provided maximum comfort for the repose of the Emerald God. Sitting on the rim of the coils of the cobra, a Goddess was watching the sleeping Lord and softly pressing his feet. She was the one Lakshman had seen coming out of the sea in the Amsterdam vision. The atmosphere was completely peaceful and pervaded by bliss and holiness. And then the vision gradually faded, leaving the companions gasping and in a state of amazement.

After a time that was outside of time, Philtalas whispered, "The Lord is still asleep. Even the Daskalians cannot wake him up. Or perhaps they don't want to and this age shall pass away without its purpose being fulfilled. I do not know, but I fear this possible outcome. He who rests on the great cobra has now been sleeping for times that are so long, even within the measurement of the heavens."

"Perhaps he is meant to," observed Ivan.

The Lord of Elnur replied, "When his sleep lasts for so long, mankind on earth loses the knowledge of the *Book of Maryadas* that is kept in the Chamber of Maat. This book teaches the movement of the wheel of the law through the rules of proper behavior. It contains the guidelines of the Game. We must know how to play the game of life if we are to win in the Grand Scheme. Its chapters were deposited in the human collective consciousness by the work of the Daskalians or the messages from the Lord Hanuman, the one the Chinese called the White Monkey. But only the blessings of the Emerald King enable men to absorb and remember the rules. If he does not wake up we are probably doomed, for the Scheme will go astray."

Sanath added tensely: "If the Master of the Grand Scheme does not manifest again, the evolution will slip into the lateral channels, the evolutionary dead-ends, away from the whiteness of the great future that was envisaged for us. The human race shall be out of the reach of the Parampara and could risk facing utter destruction. How to raise him from his mystic slumber? Would to God that the Goddess help us in this."

Lakshman was watching and listening intently. After all, had he not been appointed to solve the Dagad Trikon riddles? He was trying to understand the location of the scene and its meaning. He strained his mental faculties as hard as he could. "Has this a relationship with the Casket of the White Feather? It looks like I am now within the sort of liquid heavens I had a glimpse of, on top of the spiraling scale in my vision in Amsterdam. But is this a geographic place in the universe or just a new spot I have discovered in my field of consciousness? This enjoyable state, this condition of elation, has something to do with the chemistry of my brain: dopamine, I guess. Maybe all this is within my brain, just pictures of my memories, emotions, and thoughts. The picture of the sleeping lord and his universe of magic waters is definitely a scene that has been recorded in mythology. Maybe I'm just computing my knowledge of past readings, cultures, and symbols. Perhaps all this will just turn out to be a symbolic projection, but who are all these people? Come on, I must make some sense out of this. Maybe... "

The train of thought unfolded, pulling Lakshman out of the quiet witness state in which he had been able to watch the Assembly of the Daskalians. At first he didn't notice that the spin of mental activities was rapidly removing him from the center of the Wheel Temple. By the time he became aware of what was happening, it was too late. The spin of his thoughts had precipitated his astral body into a whirling movement that was carrying him away. He just caught the sorry glance of Aliskhan who was looking at him. Aliskhan understood that Lakshman was being removed from the Hall of the Daskalians by the untimely reactivation of his thought processes.

Lakshman tried to return to the Chamber of Maat, like a man who has enjoyed a wonderful dream and does not want to wake up, but to no avail. He tried to climb back through the corridors of time, keeping his eyes closed but when he opened them he was back in Delphi, crouched in his sleeping bag at the foot of the Pithy Rock, covered by the night's dew.

Morning had broken. The sun was rising on Mount Parnassus. As he sat in his sleeping bag he realized that there must have been a

317

mighty storm during the night because everything around him was still wet, the grass was soaked, and there were large pools of water on the path. Miraculously, their bodies and the Rock of the Pithy had not received a drop of rain.

He was now wide awake, back in his physical body and in his world. Lakshman looked around, dazed. The astral trip had lasted a full night. Lakshman had lost the condition of the all-enveloping sphere of fluid harmony and he mourned that loss. Clearly, he had walked between the inner and the outer world, but in a manner that was probably highly dangerous. It had not secured him access. It dawned upon him that, extraordinary as his trip might have been, it did not reveal the passage between the two worlds. Thus, what seemed to be the main object of his quest had not been fulfilled. But the lesson was not lost on him. He had just been carried there by the magic of the Casket of the Wheel, but at least he knew now that parallel worlds existed. He also realized more clearly than before that his ability to penetrate the inner world largely depended on his capacity to establish an inner silence in his mind, and only that inner silence gave entrance into 'now,' the hidden dimensions of the present moment.

Eventually, Lakshman gathered himself together, stood up, and stretched. He examined the rock of the Pithy where they had penetrated it – it was solid. Then he looked at the Casket of the Wheel, lying open on the floor at the foot of the rock – it was empty. He was absorbed in the memories of the night's visions. He had seen untold marvels. The images and the words were quite clear, imprinted in his mind by an experience that felt much more real than a mere dream. This had been a huge jump into an alien condition, a deep but thoroughly bewildering experience.

He decided that writing an account of what had happened would be a protection of sorts, an attempt at making sense of this incredible journey in the other worlds. He grabbed his laptop from his backpack, started it up, and began typing feverishly: the fearful appearance of the tiger, the fear of getting lost in the Bardo, the protection given during flight by the young men from the Yuva platoon. He described the underground castle of Elnelok, the emerging to the surface of the earth in the middle of the Dagad Trikon fortress, the return of Sanath, the solemn appearance of the Daskalians. He recorded their words to mankind and the floating bliss that had filled the Hall when the translucent water from another universe had been released suddenly through the Basin of Vaikuntha. Only when he had finished did he notice the slight sound of snoring coming from Ivan's sleeping bag. Lakshman bent over the body of his friend. It was quite rigid and the breathing was extremely slow. Lakshman worried that this was an abnormal condition but then he understood: Ivan was still 'there,' thousands of miles away, in the other dimension of the Daskalian Temple. Waking him up could have unwanted consequences, he decided. He bent over Lakshmi. She was also fast asleep, smiling, immersed in another world that was perhaps only the thickness of a nerve away from his present state of conscious mind.

"God knows what they are seeing now!" A frustrated Lakshman wondered how much he was missing. He had had to pay the price for not being able to keep his thoughts in check. "Rats, I am too much of a rationalist to play this game well... God knows where else this journey will take me: India, Egypt, Iceland, Holland, Italy, Greece – now the bodiless Bardo and the water world; what will happen next?"

The ecstatic smile on Lakshmi's face was a bit unnerving and Lakshman decided that there was nothing to do but wait. He found he was very hungry. The first rays of sunshine were now beaming into the archeological site of Delphi. Warming himself up, he grabbed black olives, feta cheese, bread, and a flask of hot coffee out of his backpack to celebrate his return into earthly reality. It was so good to have a body. He saw a small mouse, half-hidden between two stones, looking at him hesitatingly. He threw some crumbs of bread to the grateful mouse. After all, food was the beginning of all seeking for something worthwhile.

IN AND OUT OF THE
BASIN OF VAIKUNTHA

L akshmi had not noticed that Lakshman had been removed
from the Hall of the Daskalians by the reactivation of his
thought processes. She was completely lost in the vision of
the Basin of Vaikuntha. The companions were no longer together;
indeed, Ivan had not noticed this either. For some strange reason, he
had been distracted by images from the past of his country Russia.

He realized that as long as nine thousand years ago a culture
had flourished throughout the Ukraine that valued and struggled
for individual knowledge of the Self. It knew about a serpentine
secret power of redemption, but much later, Christian missionaries
had wiped out the last remnants of this heritage. He then saw the
Mongol and Teutonic invasions, the exploitation of the moujiks by
the boyars, of the serfs by the Tsarist regime, and of the entire people
by the Soviet Nomenklatura and then, by the billionaires who had
hijacked virtually the whole Russian economy following the collapse
of communism. Russia, where the Casket of the Cross was buried,
appeared to him to be waiting for a resurrection, a renaissance of
some kind.

Sanath, distraught at the departure of Lakshman, placed his
hand on Ivan's forehead, repeating slowly. "Don't think. Everything
will be fine. You have already come such a long way. Ivan, stay with
us, don't go just now. In this place, be silently aware; do not let

yourself be bombarded by thoughts, no matter how interesting or noble. Do not react, do not feel identified with your land or anything else; stay in the present, be at peace with yourself. Don't think, just don't think. Thoughts are sometimes useful in the world of men, but never here. Arise and behold the Emerald King, Lord of immeasurable greatness."

The hand, the tone, and the urging of Sanath were reassuring. As the heir of Hllidarendi was speaking to retain Ivan in the Chamber of Maat, the world of Vaikuntha emitted by the magic basin was slowly changing under a new force. The trembling filaments of blue, emerald green, and turquoise waters floating from the basin of Vaikuntha had now pushed back the walls of the temple. To Ivan it seemed as though the Basin had opened a passage to another all-encompassing universe, whose end could not be seen, a fluid wholesomeness whose substance was composed of an expanding firmament mixed with living waters. Now, the sleeping Lord, the Goddess, and the great cobra began increasing in size. Ivan Sadaka was captivated by the vision of the sleeping Lord and by his own intense desire that the Lord would awaken and right the wrongs of the world.

He wanted to approach the Emerald God, and a gentle nudge from Sanath seemed to respond to his secret prayer: he went closer to the couch and knelt on the waters with hands folded and head bowed. Ivan did not dare to look anymore because Ananta Quetzalcoatl, the king cobra, now seemed gigantic and fully alive. His monumental hood raised above the reclining God contained myriads of heads and thousands of eyes, which were peering in all directions. This was not a creature any human would wish to upset.

Ivan became aware of a diffuse message slowly rising up within him. It was as if he was bringing the clamors and supplications of all mankind to the formidable occupant of this couch. He heard the prayers of those who seek justice, equality, and peace, and the groans of those who lived in abject poverty. He felt the terror of innocents caught in the cruel grip of conflict and war. He heard the cries of the old and the sick, the sobbing of children abandoned by their fathers, of betrayed husbands and wives. He felt the grief of abandoned lovers. The tumult of so much pain from bruised relationships, caused by men and women who no longer knew how to give each other strength and comfort, was now rising. This was the consequence of losing the *Book of Maryadas.*

All those who wanted to win at the game of life and ended up losing had joined in the lamentation. All the sufferings of humanity were rising up in him, like the roiling dark clouds of a gathering tempest, accompanied by the rumbling of the ancient prayer he used to say in Greek during Mass: *Kyrie eleison, Kyrie eleison,* Lord, have mercy; Lord, have mercy.

He raised his head again, unable to contain such turmoil. At that very moment it seemed as though the storm and the coursing pains were instantly removed from him. His beseeching gaze lost itself again in the Emerald God reclining in mystical slumber on this intimidating serpent. He felt soothed and appeased. A newfound beauty shone within him as if he had absorbed the reflection of what he had contemplated. That serene beauty was so deeply moving that his entire being felt comforted.

The relationship with the reclining God was universal and personal, extremely distant and so very near. It spoke to him of some memory buried within his soul, of an eternal and sacred reality. As the noises in his head died away, all that remained was the contemplation of this wonder of wonders. Nothing was desired.

How many humans who pray to God in a time of anguish really believe they will see Him one day? Ivan, of course, had read the Old Testament and now he was amazed to watch a divine being whose appearance matched the description made by the prophet Ezekiel. Had the Jewish prophet also crossed the boundaries between the worlds?

The splendor of the vision had penetrated him to wash his soul and yet, at some point, Ivan lowered his gaze because he did not feel pure enough to stare further. Perhaps it was his long training as a priest, because, once again, the words of a Latin prayer came to him. "*Domine non sum dignus, ut intres sub tectum meum, sed tantum dic verbum and sanabitur anima mea.*" "Lord I am not worthy that You come under my roof but only say a word and my soul shall be cured." These were reminiscent of the words with which the Roman centurion had addressed the Lord Christ as He was about to enter into his house to cure a sick servant. However, the assumption that the heavens understood Latin was not substantiated on that special occasion.

Perhaps it would have been better to leave Latin and other things human to the world of men. The centurion had simply expressed a vibrant faith but the priests who had repeated his joyous greeting over the ages had marred it with a creeping sense of guilt. Ivan had been Sanath's spy within the Catholic clergy but was never in his heart truly a priest, yet he had spent so much time in churches that he had imbibed a few drops of the strange poison of guilt. The church was staying on message, telling man he was a sinner. In the past this strategy had been useful for filling up the church pews. Innocent confidence is the best condition to contemplate things divine. Ivan felt his own anguish as he realized that this insidious guilt kept him away from it. Thus, the vision of the Lord on his couch faded away in the movement of the floating waters of Vaikuntha. At this point, Ivan felt a powerful presence behind him and he turned around.

It wasn't Sanath or the Elnorian lord but the angelic figure of Dikayoson, the herald of the Chamber of Maat. Dikayoson was an impressive and austere personality. As the benevolent guardian of the teachings of the Daskalians that he would eventually consign to the Book of Maryadas, the herald had become more somber as the centuries had rolled by. Indeed, under his stern watch, mankind had shown itself to be increasingly oblivious to the rules and mechanisms of the Grand Scheme. This trend had greatly saddened the angel for he knew that, in the movement of the Wheel of the Law, there is a price to be paid for mistakes and sins.

The herald said in a low voice, "It is a great miracle, Ivan Sadaka, that you and your companions came here, for your race has never before been allowed into the Chamber of Maat. No human shall again reach this sacred temple in the way you did. Your journey through the navel of the earth was deemed necessary to counter the sinister rise of the Shadow, which now covers Mother Earth. Today no God, no Avastha nor any man can break this grip of iron. Yet it shall be broken, for the Emerald God does not leave unanswered the prayers of true seekers.

Scion of the Russian forest, you have beheld the Master of the Grand Scheme, the One the Hindus have named the supreme Vishnu. In the form of the Sower, he projects the shapes of things to come, the seeds of becoming and regeneration. He is the sole maker of the fortune and misfortune of kings, races, and nations. The Emerald King is not rising from his couch, but have faith. Though the Lord is sleeping, he has absorbed your prayer. You asked nothing for yourself but pleaded instead on behalf of your fellow human beings. This is commendable. Alas, most of the sufferings of mankind are self-inflicted because the Evil One, whose name shall not be uttered in this holy temple, has penetrated the minds of men. He made them believe he does not exist. Nevertheless, the Wheel of the Law continues to spin; its motion is irrevocable. What was sown shall now be reaped. The time of the great harvest is coming. Have faith and go back to your own world now."

The ethereal form of Dikayoson withdrew and Ivan found himself once more back in the Hall of the Daskalians. But he was alone now. The light from the Basin of Vaikuntha had gone. The Daskalians, Sanath, Philtalas of Elnur, and his party of Avasthas were nowhere to be seen. Nor could he see Lakshmi. Would he be left alone in this cold and lonely place? He suddenly realized that his fear of loneliness was probably the worst of his hidden fears. What was he to do, where was the exit? Aliskhan had also gone, and without a guide, Ivan could never find his way back to the origin of his strange journey.

He stared into the growing darkness with a sense of rising terror but at that moment he saw a small dot of light zigzagging towards him. As it approached, it turned out to be a white baby monkey. This sight brought tremendous relief to Ivan, the more so because when they were chatting together at the Casa della Minerva, Jonathan had spoken about his experience with Hanuman in Cairo. The monkey came close, paused, and took a good look at the former cardinal. It jumped on his shoulder and whispered, "It is very simple: call a friend, call your friend." Ivan immediately began shouting as loud as he could, "Lakshman, Lakshman!"

Thousands of miles and a few universes away from the Chamber of Maat, Lakshman, sitting within the ancient site of Delphi, had quite a shock, dropped his cheese sandwich, and spilled half his coffee. Ivan, still in his sleeping bag, his eyes now wide open, was shouting his name.

In the meantime, Lidholon of Anor held Lakshmi's hand as she saw Ivan Sadaka removed from the Hall of the Daskalians. He did not want Lakshmi to suffer the same fate but there was no danger of that: Lakshmi's eyes were riveted on the graceful figure of the Goddess attending the Emerald King. She was adorned with nine ornaments of gold and jewels. Lakshmi felt joy in her heart as she noted that the richly decorated and enveloping pink robe was, in fact, a sari, the national dress of her country that she herself preferred to wear when she was in India. Focusing on the sari might have been an odd response or a child-like reaction; however, being like a child at this juncture was very much to the point. The Goddess looked at

Lakshmi with beautiful fish-like eyes for which the seers had given her the name of Sulochana. Her glance was magnetic and soothing. Lakshmi felt an irresistible pull; she was attracted to the sari, whose folds seemed now to open, to expand, and to float in the Vaikuntha water.

She found herself, in a rustling chamber of pink silk, entirely enveloped by the sari. She had shrunk to the size of a newborn baby and had abandoned herself to this nest of delight filled with a heavenly fragrance, enjoying the cradle of precious comfort that felt like the core of a rose or a lotus. Memories of pains, worries, desires or yearnings vanished. The Chamber of Maat and the whole Wheel Temple around it had just disappeared. There were no 'do's and don'ts' in this blessed abode.

She was immersed in a splendid peace, sheltered by the shivering walls of softness. She experienced sheer pleasure and the total fulfillment of her whole being. The sari was wrapping her in a cocoon of overwhelming love. The certainty that this room was just for her, that she was the one to be nestled and loved, that this shower of tenderness was really meant for her, was quite wonderful.

She heard the Goddess whispering her name: "Lakshmi, my child, did you believe this world had no mother? Did you believe I would not find you again? Rest softly now in the lap of your Mother." Lakshmi felt exhilarated that the gracious deity who was nursing her knew her name, that she accepted her so intimately. It gave such meaning to her existence, to her destiny. The threads of her confused yearnings were finally revealing the true tapestry of her hidden being. She stayed in the warmth of this palpitating embrace for what seemed a long time. Then recognition dawned upon her.

She was within the intrauterine Eden, the condition of complete satisfaction that a baby enjoys in its mother's womb before the moment of birth. Yes, indeed, it is the mother who bestows this gift, this sense of complete reassurance, protection, and security. It was a paradox: Lakshmi had completely surrendered, yet she was completely in control. In this depth of being there were no reactions of the mind. Perception occurred through contemplation. She was in a state of connection, a timeless phase of coincidence where she was one with the power who created her. The simple act of being itself was enough to steadily increase the condition of its own depth.

Lakshmi had shown more staying power than her companions; nevertheless, she was not equipped with the powers that the earlier born had acquired through the Deep Way. Thus, unlikely as it may seem, a first reaction occurred from nowhere, despite the tranquil placidity of the shell of silk. It was perhaps a reaction to her history of seeking and it came in the form of a little thought: how? How could this state become known in the world out there? Could she share it? When would she feel this immersion of the heart in the ease of this total union again? How could one re-enter one's mother's womb?

This was the question Nicodemus had asked the Nazarene master. It cannot be done. Was there another way to feel the cosmic oneness of the blessed Ananya state? Maybe the Gift to be bestowed was that of new birth, a birth in which we would not be thrown into the world of differences, antagonisms, and separations. Could we enjoy a birth of consciousness to return to unity? Yet who could grant such a rebirth? Was this The Gift?

Poor Lakshmi – like the other companions, she had begun to think: an all-too-human habit. Babies in the womb do not think. The serenity of the restful shelter was disturbed. The folds of the sari opened and she was released from the silky nest of love. She found herself facing the Goddess, who spoke to her in a mild voice, "Dear daughter who bears my name, didn't you know? It is love that carries all the universes. It is love that carries you all."

Lakshmi listened with immense gratitude, yet her attention

was no longer undivided. Like Lakshman who earlier confronted in the Chamber of Maat his own hyperactive cerebral activity that, at times, harbored doubts, or like Ivan, who suddenly found the useless guilt that the Church had planted in him, Lakshmi suddenly had to face her own weakness: for her, it was the specter of fear.

This was very surprising for friends and foes knew her for her bravery. But perhaps bravery is about facing fear, which means that fear is a prerequisite. Emerging from deep within her chest, she felt the surge of an unsettling emotion. Worse than missing paradise altogether is to be thrown out of it. She was no longer in the chamber of silky serenity and she experienced an overwhelming sense of loss. This was the tragic paradox of appearing as a human being before the deities: humans are not inwardly prepared for this. Her grief welled up within her and, silently, she started crying. She still saw the Goddess through her tears but her appearance had changed.

The pink hues had gone. The Goddess from the Vaikuntha was wearing a gray or blue dress, with a shawl draped over her head. The tenderness in her expression was still there and her compassion was palpable. It was the same personality. Lakshmi felt a surge of adoration as she saw what Bernard de Clairvault had seen at the center of the mystical rose of paradise, also described by Dante Alighieri in *The Divine Comedy*. The Lady of Grace was sitting in the midst of a large congregation made up of saints, prophets, or living flames. Or was it just the light of Vaikuntha through the crystal and diamonds droplets of her own flowing tears?

Slowly, as she was removed from the vision, she heard the voice of the Goddess fading in the distance. "Men will have to recognize that which is sacred in womanhood. They shall recognize it or they shall ignore the Gift." At first, nobody noticed that the reclining God opened his eyes just then. Lakshmi sobbed because she did not want to leave; "Ma, ma... ," she cried.

Lakshman and Ivan turned around. Lakshman exclaimed, "She is coming back at last... at last," and rushed to his cousin. He bent over Lakshmi's body and took her hand. She was still wrapped in her sleeping bag under the rock of the Pithy in Delphi. It was such a relief to have her back. Her cheeks were humid, but it wasn't the dew. The little mouse looked at the scene with a great sense of delight, full as he was with the cheese from Lakshman's half-finished sandwich. "Everything worked out perfectly well," thought the mouse. "The elephant is a great master, but I knew that already. He always manages everything. I even got the cheese." She scurried three times around the elephant-shaped rock of the Pithy in a clockwise ritual of homage and disappeared between the fallen columns of the old temple.

Lakshman gave a heartfelt hug of welcome to the young woman and said, "Oh Lakshmi, at last you've returned. It's almost noon. We didn't really know what to do. We didn't know whether it would be harmful to wake you up, so we just waited. The guardian of the site wanted to call an ambulance. I had to bribe him again, and I had to tell some tourists that you are sleeping because you were drunk last night. But what happened? Your face is bathed in tears."

Lakshmi sat up slowly, rubbed her eyes, yawned, and looked around herself. She responded to her dear cousin with a faint smile. "Laksh, I was drunk, you know."

"I don't know about that. But I know you were sobbing and saying '*Ma, ma.*' I remember that's the name Atha Glaukopis reported to the Circle of the Aulyas: the great priestess of Atlantis said she had heard the Lady of the Rock say it was her secret name. Please tell us everything."

But Lakshmi buried her head in Lakshman's shoulder and started crying again softly. He rocked her like a baby and heard her whispering, "Oh Laksh, it was so, so beautiful. I was completely drunk, drunk with love, that love which made the world. Laksh, let me go back there."

"But we can't, honey, we can't. Ivan and I were discussing this just as you woke up. These trips are not authorized to humans. It was the magic of the Avasthas in the Casket of the Green Wheel that sent us there, most probably combined with the magic of this elephant rock, the sacred rock worshipped by the ancient Greeks. That's how we got there, traveling through the navel of the world. If you inspect the rock now you'll see it is again solid stone. We've tried already. This passage, in a way, cannot be the real Gate of the Elephant we were looking for because we wanted an access that would be open to everybody. No, honey, there is no going back, at least not by this route."

He paused briefly. "As a matter of fact, not by any route we know."

Lakshmi shook her head and got up without saying anything further. She gave Ivan a long hug just as a party of tourists approached, curiosity on their faces as they took in the trio of friends. The peace of Vaikuntha that had still been lingering in them had not yet fully receded. The trio packed up their belongings and walked towards the exit of the archeological park. As they returned to their hotel, a throng of backpackers was leaving in buses and the site regained the calm it enjoyed off-season. After lunch the three companions retired to their rooms for a much-needed nap, then got together again towards the end of the afternoon.

They took coffee on the terrace of the hotel while enjoying the magnificent view. Mellow light lit the top of hills rolling down to the Isthmus of Corinth far away on the horizon. They shared the overwhelming feelings that were released in the Basin of Vaikuntha. The friends discussed and animatedly compared their respective experiences in the Hall of the Daskalians. Ivan felt he was nearing the end of the long journey of discovery that he had started as a small Russian boy with Sanath as his mentor. He shared his perception:

"This rock of Pithy must be a sacred stone, like the Sao Iambu on an island in our forest where we celebrated the great liturgy of Mother Earth with all the animals. It sent us into a world where we saw and heard much: the underworld of the last Avasthas, the temple in Dagad Trikon containing the Chamber of Maat, the appearance of the Daskalians and their messages. Yet the most powerful and extraordinary feeling we seem to have shared in various shades and levels of intensity is this cosmic oneness. This is what Sanath had been able to make us discover within nature itself, back then in Russia. It means, I guess, that nature itself carries spiritual powers. I understand now why our ancestors considered Mother Earth a living deity, for she carries some of that pure divinity that was concentrated in the Basin of Vaikuntha. God knows where we'll end up if we continue to disturb it as we presently are. So it seems that this feeling of unity, this Ananya state where all separations are abolished, is immanent – everywhere – surrounding us, present in us, present in the trees, present in this and other worlds, and yet we cannot feel it."

"And yet we can, although I don't know how or why," interrupted Lakshmi. "Ivan, do you remember Lorelei's party at your house? The kids touched it although I am certain they would not know how they did it. The birthday girl, the music, the beat, all of us dancing closer to each other, and that cathartic moment where all of us felt the essence, the juice of the Rasa. It was a powerful energy coursing through each and every one of us. Do you remember? It was different, in a sense, but also the same. It is as if we still have some unconscious access to the world of the Gods."

Ivan continued, " If I understand correctly, the Dagad Trikon caskets are to reveal how we can get back to the original state of oneness. In so doing we can escape the alarming onslaught of Hangker and Belzebseth on our modern civilization. I have seen the

Glory of the Lord, I am a changed man, and yet I am not. We have seen wonders, I agree, but what can we do with that vision? No one will believe us. They will rush to the Sao Iambu of the Pithy and they'll discover nothing, even if they dig underground looking for a passage. This experience has been extraordinary but the question is: what can we do with it?"

Lakshmi began to reflect on her moment in the cocoon of bliss. "When Vaikuntha started to manifest, we were in a water world. When the Goddess took me as a baby into the folds of her sari, I was still in a water world. Is this the water of life mentioned by John the Evangelist in his *Book of Revelations*?"

She did not really expect an answer and continued as if talking to herself: "I experienced love as the feeling of a living energy that understands and fulfills all wishes. In that condition, I surrendered to this higher power, and this surrender was just a further expansion of love into freedom and joy. This love was like lubricating oil, so gentle. It was a world of fluid wonders, intimate and dear. It occurs to me now that I heard about this state before: they call it the drinking of the cup of ecstasy. The old Indian scriptures describe how the Gods and the Titans churned the ocean of milk to obtain the drink of ecstasy. Laksh, do you recall our trip to Cambodia with the American archaeological team? I explained the scene described by the statues at the main entrance of the temple of Angkor Vat to you. The Titans, the Asuras, having churned the ocean of milk, fought the Gods to receive the drink called soma or amrit." She became progressively more excited as the intuition came to her.

No one noticed the white monkey watching them. He was sitting on the balustrade and grinning appreciatively at the progress of the young woman. It was, in fact, quite normal that they could not see him since he was in his subtle form, invisible to them now that they had regained their body of flesh. Lakshmi spoke hurriedly.

"In Western mythology, the Knights of the Round Table have to accomplish a noble errand. Parcival looks for the Grail and Sir Galahad finds it. The Grail is a goblet, a cup containing the blood of Christ."

"Yes, sure," interrupted Ivan, somewhat surprised. "But what has this to do with your nest in the sari of the Goddess?"

"Everything. Christ came for the entire world, not just for the Christians. When he offered his blood on the cross, he was, I am sure, giving us a powerful symbol. He wanted us to find something more. He did say after his resurrection that the Holy Spirit would reveal all things. What was to be revealed? The Knights of the Round Table focused on the cup because his blood came from the heavens. This is, I believe, the myth of the Holy Grail: it was for us an invitation to seek this blessed state I just felt. It is a state in which my spiritual being was as if dissolved into my physical body; no difference between the two any more. The cup, I reckon, contained this liquid of blessedness, known as ambrosia to Christians, the drink of immortality. Ambrosia, the elixir of joy, the mystical blood of Christ. Gods, Titans, and humans have sought it, have fought for it. Don't you see? Can you see it? Ambrosia, amrit: it is the same," Lakshmi finished, almost out of breath.

The ex-cardinal and the archeologist looked at her in silence, incapable or unwilling to add anything. The vision of the young woman was both compelling and fantastic. Lakshmi was quite excited now and went on, following the thread of her inspiration prompted by the invisible proximity of the white monkey.

"The identical account is recorded in two completely different traditions, in Britain and Cambodia: who would think of a relationship between Camelot and Angkor Vat? If I speak about these old tales now, it is because I feel they refer to this liquid universe, which was carrying this beatitude. We were swimming within this cup of bliss.

Surely old scriptures were speaking about this elevated state of consciousness. If so, the Holy Grail is the Gift and it has something to do with a mother, with woman or womanhood. We all touched it, my friends, even you, Laksh, although you left rather early, if I may say so. Then we lost it again because we had not purified ourselves sufficiently to appear before the deities. Sir Galahad found the Grail because he was said to be the purest among the knights, a worshipper of the Virgin Mary. I feel the divine drink was revealed to me as a newborn, or rather, a non-born baby, in the lap of a divine mother. I can't become a baby again or go back to that state, can I? So, what did she want to show me? She spoke about that which is sacred in womanhood; what did she mean? For a short while She granted me a drink of soma, I am sure of this for I was in perfect joy, swimming in an enveloping bliss; oh my God, she gave me the taste of the Grail, ambrosia, the water of life or whatever one calls it."

Lakshmi was panting now, her inner eye still following the trail of the legends she had woven together with Dagad Trikon and with their own lives in light of their amazing experience in the basin of Vaikuntha.

Normally, Lakshman, who often teased his cousin, would have expressed his doubts about what Lakshmi had said. But now silence was the only appropriate response. They had faced too much awesome majesty to speak lightly now about any aspect of their quest. After some time, Ivan spoke:

"If you are right, we have touched on the most ancient secret of true Christianity. But the only thing we know for a fact is that Christianity did not gain access to the Grail, so its people sought fulfillment elsewhere. Come on, friends, we had such powerful emotions and sensations although, amazingly, we did not even have our own physical bodies. Really, after this unbelievable journey, I sense the Promised Land is a place within our minds."

"You probably mean a place in our brains, as fortunately we managed to regain access to our bodies," observed Lakshman.

Ivan added: "How to get there? This is what we need to find out. Whether mankind is progressing on this path is very much a matter of doubt. For the time being we are not connecting to this higher dimension. Maybe this why the Lord remains in a state of sleep. In my view, the Casket of the Wheel has just thrown us into another dimension so that we would find out that such worlds exist. But we do not know where or how and we cannot return there. What we saw was simply awesome but I do not see what we can do with it at a practical level. I can't fathom how we can derail the plans of Thanatophor or change the world with it."

They were silent for a while and they looked down into the valley far below, now enveloped in the growing darkness of dusk, as if the answer to their question might surge from the mystery of twilight. The white monkey on the balustrade shook his head approvingly; the humans were staring in his direction but without seeing him. The friends of Sanath were getting near but not quite near enough. He jumped from the balustrade and happily ambled away into the shadows. He was always pleased whenever a gifted human was able to receive the intuitions he sent.

A blessing does not come alone. Lakshman's cell phone rang; it was Philip in a state of elation, bringing the great news of the return of Sanath. The wizard had called him from Adam's house in New York. The small party broke out in loud cheers, feeling the sweet taste of victory. It is one thing to meet someone in the Bardo and another one to know that this person still exists in the flesh. Each companion took the phone in turn to tell him what he or she had felt, heard, and seen. Jonathan told them about their exchanges with the wizard in Riverdale.

Night had fallen in Delphi but the three pilgrims back from the world of Vaikuntha did not even notice it. They continued to talk endlessly about their astonishing adventure. The companions were full of hope and energy, having been rewarded by a most extraordinary happening. Lakshman was still curious about what his dear cousin had experienced. They sat together staring at the setting sun. She put her hand on her cousin's shoulder and whispered slowly:

"Listen to my litany of love. It is love that just is, love without a beloved, love without anybody to love in particular. I was not even aware that I loved the Goddess. I was in that love and I was simply in love. How to talk about it? It is very difficult because it is so simple. It is a feeling inside. I was this oneness in the profundity of myself, at the core of my being, I was a deep sea bubbling with inner delight. Do you know we can be that, Laksh?" she said raising her voice and looking straight into his eyes. "Really, otherwise I could not have felt it. I was wrapped in the feeling of a silent and eternal caress. We all look for love, don't we? But we do not know that we are love; I mean, if we can reach this level of inner depth we shall discover the complete paradise. To be able to reach the essence of our essence, this must be the gift. And the great mother is the giver. No gift is greater than the giver. So just think how great that mother can be."

She paused before she completed her thought. "The state I felt when she kept me in her fold was itself the source, the teacher, and the master of all masters. I knew that all the Daskalians we had seen in the Chamber of Maat were only the expressions of this guiding power. In their care for mankind, in transmitting their knowledge, like your friend Sanath, the Daskalians just manifest this love." Lakshmi stared at the first twinkling stars and, with a last tear in her eyes, she burst into laughter.

"Just imagine what a world it is going to be when we all have this feeling inside... There will be no compulsion to attract the attention of others, no need to seduce, no craving for recognition. Loneliness and pain will be gone. No feeling any longer like the ugly duckling swimming among the swans. No jealousies, no stress, no demands because the supply of what we so ardently seek is deep within. What a play it would be if we could all share this pure state.

Oh Laksh, I have tasted heaven!"

Lakshman was happy to see his dear cousin so elated but curiously, her enthusiasm reopened an old wound in him. He shook his head sadly and, for the first time in a long, long time, he put his deeply buried feelings into words:

"Lakshmi, I never knew my real parents. As I was an orphan, in a school perched on a remote hill in Dharamsala, I was alone between the jungle below and the snow-capped Himalayas on the horizon above. The other kids would not let me play football with them. I was the odd kid out, for no one knew my origins." He sighed deeply and went on: "One day they bullied me and I fell on a sharp stone. My leg was covered with blood. The mistress came and scolded me, as usual, without even listening to my pleas. It was so unfair. I ran downhill into the jungle; I was in a tearful rage, I was furious with God. I felt crushed by injustice. Heaven for me was just clouds above my head. I strained all my will power so that the clouds would form the shape of the face of my mother but I did not succeed."

Lakshman's words carried so much emotional intensity that Lakshmi felt tears come to her eyes. He concluded: "Of course my life changed when your uncle adopted me but I still look into the clouds sometimes. We have gone into the Vaikuntha basin, a great blessing, no doubt, but now we are out of it again. I wish I had felt the grace of the Goddess. Maybe I would have felt my mother's presence."

Lakshmi threw her arms around her cousin and gave him a hug: "Oh Laksh, I am convinced this was not for me only. One individual alone cannot contain this love – it must be shared. It is in its nature that it must flow and spread. It was a promise to you too, a signal for the human race, we are all going to feel the ambrosia of this magic love. It is for the whole world."
She paused for a while.

"Yet I do not know how."

EPISODE TWENTY

THE SECRETS
OF JETZENSTEIN CASTLE

I n the years following the momentous trip to Delphi, little
progress was made in the Dagad Trikon inquiry. The cousins
went back to India, consulted with hermits and sages, and
visited specific temples that local folks considered to be particularly
sacred. Lakshmi thought she came close to a breakthrough when she
realized that many temples in the state of Maharashtra were built
around sacred stones, often in the likeness of the child elephant god
Ganesha. Brahmin priests told her that these rocky manifestations
called *'Swayambus'* had emerged from the earth long, long ago. She
recalled Philip's tale and had an uncanny suspicion that they were
similar to the Sao Iambu, the stone of power that had been at the
center of Sanath's festival in the Byelorussian forest. The cousins
became even more interested when they realized that all these stones
were an orange ocher hue, a color that seemed significant given what
the High Lady of the Rock had said.

She was reported to have said that when the white elephant
turned the color of the Gundaldhar Fault, the Gate of the Elephant
would be found. The color of the Fault was an orange ocher. Ignoring
the misgivings of the local Brahmins who wanted an ever-larger tip at
each subsequent visit, they searched these temples and their environs
intensively, hoping to find some secret chamber or passage that would
reveal the meaning of the prophecy.

One of the temples to the south of Mumbai, called Ganapatiphule, opened directly on to a beach overlooking the Indian Ocean at the foot of a sacred hill. When they reached there for the first time, the setting sun was falling on the statue of the Lord Ganesha, illuminating it in a splendid ocher tone. Walking around the hill, Lakshmi felt light-hearted and happy: she became quite optimistic. She sat on the beach next to her cousin who was lying on the white sand, gazing at the sunset. Here and there, foreign pilgrims, belonging to a large group hosted in the nearby bungalows of the Maharashtra Tourism Development Corporation, were also enjoying the sunset, some playing guitars and singing, some meditating or just sitting together and chatting relaxedly. Some stood in line on the beach, their feet caressed by the dying waves, delicate silhouettes in the pink mist of the late hour. The scene was a bit eerie: they were reciting prayers with their hands outstretched as if to receive energy from the air itself.

"That is odd," Lakshman observed, "I thought I just heard some of them saying '*Allahu Akbar*,' but they don't look like Muslims to me. They seem to be a mix of all races and nationalities." Lakshman remembered a quote by the poet Rabindranath Tagore in which he had foreseen how seekers of truth from all over the whole world would gather on the shores of India for the worship of the Mother. Lakshman had always assumed that Tagore had just been a great poet, India's first Nobel laureate in Literature, but given these circumstances he found himself wondering if there wasn't more to the poet, that perhaps Tagore had also been a prophet and a seer. In a friendly gesture, Lakshmi playfully brushed flecks of sand from Lakshman's hair. The cousins felt a pleasant peace descending upon them, a sensation that suggested that perhaps in the recent past they had made some progress on the inner quest. Or perhaps the words of the Daskalians were at last reaching man through the unconscious.

This friendly group of strangers also seemed to be treading the path of some worthy search, another path maybe, but hopefully leading to the same destination. They chatted for a while with a couple of young Australians who were in India to study classical Indian music. They explained to the cousins that they had found a prominent yoga master and it was much easier to meditate during such collective spiritual festivals.

However, these happy moments were not followed by any results. Their search of the Ganapatiphule temple and of the neighboring hill unfortunately proved fruitless and they returned to Mumbai. As time passed by without further progress, they became somewhat puzzled as to the direction they would have to follow to forge ahead.

Of course the cousins had been comforted by the intensely beautiful nature of the reality they had uncovered during their extraordinary journey from Delphi. The plain certitude and comfort that flowed from their vision of the Daskalians, the Emerald God, and his Goddess were truly empowering. Lakshman was convinced that these experiences had something to do with a fine chemical balance in his brain but he wisely refrained from probing any substance to re-create the sensations of elation he had experienced during this vision. The problem, as the cousins came to see it, was that they were unable to go back there and it was not possible to live off memories alone. As time went by they became increasingly perplexed. How to proceed further?

In the United States this period was especially tough on the O'Lochan children. Despite the strictures of the church he so fully claimed to follow, their father divorced their mother and married his mistress. At her prompting, he disinherited his three other children who had consistently sided with Jonathan. Jonathan tried to re-organize his life despite the hardship created by the feud within his family. His relationship with Jenny was not going smoothly either.

Assisted by Joseph, he had worked on the Oikos Project part-time as a consultant for its U.S. Secretariat and part-time on the survey conducted by Professor Rahurikar. Michael went back to school in Washington D.C. to finish his Master's degree. Then his girlfriend had decided she'd had enough and had left him. He had tried, probably unwisely, to share his interest in the Avastha saga with her. She was a regular, fun-loving American girl and it became increasingly obvious to her that his world and interests were just too weird.

Ivan meanwhile had had some interesting experiences. His Russian team had apprehended some of the mercenaries who had engineered the attacks against Lakshman and Sanath in the Netherlands. They were interrogated with much civility thanks to Ivan's infamous confession serum, which proved its efficiency once more. The Russians collected useful tidbits of information: the masters of the Darkness were now advanced in their plans. They soon intended to make a decisive strike in order to wipe out the last possibilities of an Avastha revival. Ominously enough, this seemed to target Sanath and his friends. That was all that could be gathered from the thugs, who were clearly not privy to the most secret plans of the dark overlords.

The Jetzlars spent the two following summers back in Germany. Sanath had again vanished on one of his missions and no one knew precisely where he was, but he resurfaced in South America in March and there was great excitement amongst the companions when it transpired that they were being summoned to a gathering in early May at the fortress of Jetzenstein, the ancestral home of the Jetzlars on a high cliff above the river Rhine. Sanath let them know that the moment had come to turn the tide against the forces of evil and asked that everyone be present for this was to be a time for revelations. Lakshmi could not miss an opportunity to meet the wizard in the flesh and Lakshman was yearning to see him again.

The cousins had a comfortable midnight flight from New Delhi and Stefan picked them up early in the morning at Frankfurt airport. They drove through wine country after Wiesbaden and took the road by the banks of the middle Rhine valley leading from Mainz to Koblenz.

The Rhine sets out on its proud journey from a remote mountain lake in the lonely Graubünden massif in Switzerland and, after traveling over eight hundred miles, it ends up in the open skies of the delta where its many branches flow into the North Sea between Rotterdam and the Hook of Holland. In the most spectacular segment of its journey, between Mainz and Koblenz, the river navigates its way through deep gorges and steep cliffs crowned by lofty castles; this was where they were headed.

As they penetrated deeper into this picturesque landscape they understood why many writers reveled in the ruggedness of this narrow valley. The car passed the customs fortress of the electorate palatinate, Pfalzgrafenstein, sited rakishly like a ship on the crag Falkenau in the middle of the Rhine. At this point Lakshman asked, "Forgive me, Stefan, but I would rather ask you this question than Philip, as I really don't mean to be disrespectful. I am intrigued by the fact that Sanath took Jetzenstein as his headquarters for many years; was there a special reason? After all, one may wonder, why in Germany?"

Stefan, who had initially appeared rather taciturn, was happy to respond. Suddenly, he was in a talkative mood. "It's perfectly all right. There are at least three answers. Firstly, the bonds forged during our captivity in Russia evolved into a real friendship and the wizard shared many secrets with the count. They became very close. For many years the master took on the identity of Count Baldur Joachim, Philip's elder brother, who had died on the Russian front during the war. Then, as you'll see, the castle, perched on a basalt rock on top of a six-hundred-yard-high cliff above the Rhine, is an optimal location for security reasons. You can see for miles from there. Thirdly, the wizard says that, before modern times, Germany was a country of poets, musicians, and philosophers and that many idealistic people could have manifested the Angkura power, the germinating power for change. As a matter of fact, I believe he said that some Avasthas incarnated during the Middle Ages in Germany and in Provence in the south of France to create a holy empire once again. They wanted to revive and restore the courtly art of love. He added sadly, "They all failed because there were so very few in number and the Church condemned them as heretics and wiped them out."

"This is intriguing," said Lakshmi, mildly surprised. "So you say the Avasthas tried to return once before in Germany? I would have thought it was always an unlikely place."

"I understand your surprise because, after Goethe died, the Darkness cast its shadow on Germany through Prussian militarism and, eventually, Hitler. The count says that Hitler, with his worship of raw strength and his contempt for compassion, is the closest thing that Hangker achieved, short of himself, in taking human form. The Nazis placed the Buchenwald concentration camp not far from Weimar, which had been Goethe and Schiller's center for the renewal of our culture. It was typical of their plot to pollute our entire country with their satanic vision. Although Germany was deeply wounded, the wizard did not accept defeat and he wanted to find out whether the flame of ancient values could be rekindled. He was happy to settle on the banks of the Rhine for yet another reason: he claimed that the river had hidden powers and could heal the country. It was lucky for the Jetzlars that the wizard took the identity of the eldest Jetzlar, Baldur. Indeed, at the end of the war, Count Philip was completely ruined: the castle was dilapidated and without the financial help of the new Baldur, they would have lost everything."

They had now reached the most famously dangerous curve in the river as it circles around the Lorelei rock. The river narrows to one third of its normal width and as all ships' masters on the Rhine will agree, it is still perilous because of the rocks, shallows, and unexpected rapids, all of which require the best navigational skills. In olden days many boatmen lost their vessels and their lives too at this place; they were reputed to flounder and die as their heads were turned by the enchanting song of an alluring maid, who all the while kept combing her blond hair with a golden comb. This section of the river had been altered in modern times to make it more safely navigable. As their car passed by the Lorelei rock, Stefan began singing the Ballad of the Lorelei by Heinrich Heine. Lakshmi translated, as he sang: "I know not why I am so sad; I cannot get out of my head a fairy tale of olden times."

"Hey," interrupted Lakshman playfully, "An old tale with a sad story? That does sound like Dagad Trikon, doesn't it? I find it sad after all that the Avasthas disbanded long ago, never to be seen again."

Stefan said, "The Lorelei is of course just a legend but the tale of the wizard is very much alive. Remember, after the city of Mainz, we passed through the small borough of Bingen? That is where Hildegard von Bingen founded the convent where she died in 1179 AD. She was a trail-blazing authority on mysticism and healing; the wizard said she knew about the Angkura power and the Lady of the Triangle Rock but the Darkness went after her too. So, maybe, your Dagad Trikon is a legend like the Lorelei but a different sort of legend, one that is still at work."

Some time after passing the Lorelei, Stefan turned into a private road, alongside a tributary flowing into the Rhine. He announced, "This is the entrance to the old estate of Jetzenstein but much of the original land has been sold. This small tower here is an observatory for birds of prey; we had some eagles nesting in our forest that used to fly up to the wizard's window in the morning."

They had now penetrated an idyllic natural reserve, practically unspoiled; the narrow road followed the marshy riverside meadows where cormorants, goosanders, and some endangered species had found safety and sustenance.

Stefan was happy to converse with the guests and to serve as a guide. He was well informed on many topics and knew much about the history of Jetzenstein. "Towards the end of the seventeenth century, when the marauding armies of Louis XIV of France invaded the Rhine valley, most castles were unable to withstand the onslaught and were set ablaze. Jetzenstein alone was unconquered, high up on its rocky promontory." Stefan added, quoting Philip again, "After Louis XIV, it was Napoleon who invaded us. The locals naturally resented the annexation of the Rhineland by the French. In this, the French paved the way for Prussian militarism to take over Germany in the nineteenth century. Count Philip commented that this is a favorite trick of Hangker, the devil who plays with human politics: one aggression breeds another. It is a self-sustaining business of death.

The French aggressed the Germans; the Germans replied in kind and, getting the taste of it, in turn aggressed the rest of Europe and the Jews. The Jews repress the Palestinians, the Palestinians bomb their way into despair, and so a new brand of terrorism is born, now hiding under the green banner of the Prophet."

"Yes, I know, the story goes on: ask Jonathan about the silly chain of violence – he knows all about it," grumbled Lakshman dismissively.

"At the end of World War II," continued Stefan, "Count Philip preserved his home by offering it for a time as a headquarters for the Allies. But perched as it was way above communication routes, it did not suit their rapidly advancing armies for long. He had, by that point, lost his whole family and was practically ruined. He sold most of the paintings and ancient furniture, as well as some land, but then the wizard helped him. He gave him advice and money to turn the main building into a hotel."

The road climbed around a hillside, rising high above the Rhine valley. They crossed the small village of Gundelfels perched on a shoulder of the mountain and returned the waves of children playing by the roadside. The castle revealed itself after a final curve. Dominating a protruding rock above the junction of the Rhine and one of its small confluents, the grand silhouette of Jetzenstein looked impressive to the visitors. They admired the polygonal outer wall with its battlemented parapets, turrets, and medieval towers facing the hillside.

Its tower was almost a hundred feet high and had four stories above the dungeon, decorative corner turrets, and a tent roof that dominated the complex. One of the oldest fortresses on the river, Jetzenstein had originally been built as an imperial castle for exercising customs rights. It was a fine example of a structure celebrated by Rhine romanticism, with its combination of medieval fortifications and late restorations in neo-Gothic style. The outer walls of the keep and large sections of the defensive walls had survived the centuries almost unscathed. Above, the enormous outer curtain wall reared up with three round angle towers. The car had to cross the drawbridge and pass under the portcullis of the archway. Then the venerable Mercedes passed through a gate tower that gave access to the inner castle, behind the second castle moat.

The visitors discovered the residential building, recently converted into a hotel. Its white and ocher façade was typical of the Rhenan late-Gothic period. Three rows of elegant ogival windows opened on the main courtyard. The car maneuvered to avoid a bus parked to disgorge a fresh supply of Japanese tourists in front of the hotel. Stefan stopped in front of the family's living quarters, which were in the oldest part of the castle. It was a separate building to the left of the courtyard, adjacent to a small medieval circular tower, which also contained Sanath's library. Philip had baptized the tower 'Falkenlust,' the pleasure of the falcon. Indeed, when Sanath-Baldur had settled in Jetzenstein, a few falcons, whose species had been believed to be extinct, had returned to nest in its crenel.

Warm greetings were exchanged and the cousins spent a few days with the Jetzlars and Ivan before the anticipated arrival from America of Sanath with Tracy, Joseph, and Michael of the O'Lochan family. Jonathan was intending to join them two days later. Lakshman and Lakshmi felt completely at home with the Jetzlars, who were glad to welcome them and eager to entertain their visitors. Lorelei and Lakshmi, giggling together, disappeared with two steaming cups of tea for a quiet, undisturbed chat.

In the late afternoon, Lothar took the visitors to the hotel. The building contained sumptuously appointed interiors and had been tastefully renovated, thanks to financial help from Sanath. The guest rooms were situated on the upper floors of the residential section, above the floors containing the reception hall, the lounges, and the castle chapel, which was spanned by a star-like vault and now converted into a dining room. The hotel helped support the upkeep of the property and regularly welcomed large numbers of Asian visitors. One of the main curiosities of the castle was located in the hotel building, and was very popular with clients from the Far East. It was a porcelain cabinet, lit by glittering chandeliers, containing a precious collection of Chinese and Japanese porcelain pieces that the Dutch East India Company had shipped to Holland during the first half of the seventeenth century. Sanath Baldur had bought them at auction during his stay there and Lothar was always happy to show the collection to the visitors.

In the center of the wall facing the entrance to the porcelain cabinet, visitors could admire an unusually large statue of the Bodhisattva Guanyin in the Dehua style, in pure white porcelain with a transparent glaze. Guanyin was represented as the great Goddess with a mighty aureole created by a myriad of fine arms and hands. She was seated on a rocky base at the foot of which could be seen two writhing dragons. Her eyes were closed and her face wore the hint of a smile. She was clad in a long, loose garment; her headdress consisted of a veil that flowed down behind her neck. In her first left hand she carried her attribute, the jar containing the water of life. She was accompanied by the boy Sudhana who was in pursuit of truth and whom Guanyin had blessed on his way to enlightenment. Lakshman gazed at the statue and muttered, "The garment, the dress, even the expression… it reminds me of the vision of the High Lady of the Rock, yet it is somewhat different. This is most intriguing."

Lothar explained, "Sanath said he bought only objects that carried special vibrations, and therefore these objects have some sort of relationship with the Deep Way. They emit a subtle coefficient of meaning and beauty. The master says he has poured his magic into some of them. A few people have reported that after coming into this room they have been healed of various ailments."

"What is this?" interrupted Lakshman, gesturing at a spiral staircase at the end of the hall that led to a small door that opened into the vaulted ceiling.

"The most significant objects are not on display. He keeps them in his 'Schatzkammer,' the treasury room up there." Lothar replied. "He calls it the chamber of truth but no one is allowed to enter."

"Do you know what is in the room?" asked Lakshmi.

"Not really." Lothar looked hesitantly at his sister who nodded affirmatively, as if to encourage him to speak. "But we overheard once a conversation between Sanath and Grandfather. The chamber contains something mysterious that he called the talisman of Osiris. It is an object, or a formula, we do not know exactly, that is composed of three and a half sequences or elements. It contains a tremendous power, nothing less than the secret of resurrection, that is, how to raise a man from the dead."

"Look at the spirals of the staircase itself," interrupted Lakshmi, who had scrutinized the staircase attentively. "Again three and a half coils like the canyon of the Gundaldhar fault. This is bringing us back to Dagad Trikon. What does this three and a half unit means?" Lothar didn't know but Lakshman said:

"In the rituals of freemasonry, the chamber of knowledge is to be accessed on top of a spiral staircase. They must have been on the trail of the secret kept by the Avasthas. Is there anything else in the forbidden chamber?"

"Probably, but we do not know what," responded Lothar. "I asked Sanath why we could not know the content of the Schatzkammer and he said that the objects in themselves do not deliver their secrets. Their messages can only be accessed by the living knowledge of experience. However, Grandfather told me once that the room contains a rare incunabula manuscript of the Book of Prophecy of the knight John of Jerusalem. This prophecy is supposed to have a relationship with the talisman of Osiris. It contains secret symbols and handwritings by another templar who brought back the book from the Holy Land. We have another clean and more recent copy in the library."

"What is so special about this book?" inquired Lakshman again, "and do we know who the knight is who brought it back?"

"The book unveils a prophecy for the third century of the Christian era, but according to Sanath the interest of this original copy stems from the scribbling of the knight who brought it back. His name was Renaud."

"Renaud, did you say Renaud?"

"Yes, why, what's the matter?"

"Well, I came by sheer chance across the name of Renaud de Cormorant in connection with the legend of Dagad Trikon. Why didn't Sanath tell me?" wondered Lakshman with some frustration in his voice.

"Grandfather says that asking why about Sanath's doings or teachings is a perfect waste of time. We must grab what comes our way, when we can, at the right time and in the right spot."

"All right, all right," grumbled Lakshman. "I trust we have no choice anyway. Let us see then – what do we have here?"

In each corner of the room stood a monumental dragon vase from the collection of Augustus the Strong, King of Poland and Elector of Saxony, painted in shades of dark blue. Each broad rim had a combination of peonies and stylized dragons, scrolls, and roundels of flowers. The symbol of the yin and the yang of Taoism was painted in the center. On the sides of the rooms one could admire translucent porcelain from the early Fang period, lively and delicate in its consistency.

Japanese wares decorated in the Imari style with an underglaze of blue and adorned with overlaid gold produced a splendid effect through the dense decor. Double-gourded Chinese blue and white porcelain vases from the Kangxi period alternated with bulbous, coral-toned, iron-red glazed jars relieved by white scrollwork. Lothar explained their decoration. "The three-and-a-half-coiled dragon releases peony scrolls symbolizing beauty and prosperity and the heart-shaped ruyi heads, literally 'consistent with wishes,' are considered bringers of happiness."

Lakshmi pointed to the only object that was not from the Far East. It was a late Bronze Age ceramic vase used for rituals connected with the Mother Goddess discovered in Bulgaria. It also carried the representation of a spiral. She commented dreamily: "Whatever this symbol means, it seems linked to the Goddess."

They promised themselves to ask Sanath about the secrets of Jetzenstein castle and to plead that access to the treasury room would be necessary for them to progress in their search. They then left the main building and went on with their exploration of the fortress and its surroundings. On the side of the castle overlooking the Rhine, a terraced garden with a fountain at its center had been built abutting a nine-feet-thick outer wall. The wine casks were stored under its vaults. The wizard personally disapproved of wine, indeed, of alcohol in all its forms, but the vineyards were the other source of income for the estate apart from the hotel revenues, and Sanath had failed to convince Philip on this point. At the end of the garden, a loggia on the tip of the cliff provided a breathtaking view of the up – and downstream courses of the Rhine. A pergola with red climbing roses surrounded the loggia.

In early May, Stefan met Sanath with Joseph, Tracy, and Michael O'Lochan who had arrived from Washington at Frankfurt Airport and drove them back to Schloss Jetzenstein in the old Mercedes. The car stopped in front of the entrance staircase of the Jetzlar residence and Stefan showed the guests into the pillared hall. A jubilant Philip had come to the entrance hall to welcome his guests, accompanied by his grandchildren, the cousins, and his trusty friend, Ivan. This reunion was a moment of great joy and merriment, for Sanath had stayed at Jetzenstein for some years before moving to the Netherlands. The Jetzlars and the companions of the Delphi adventure had waited for this reunion with tremendous expectations, having endured the fears linked to the wizard's long disappearance.

There was so much to talk about and the group bubbled with merry excitement. Laira was in the kitchen supervising the final touches to the meal. Alexandra, Ivan's wife, was the only one missing, as she had to stay behind to run the school in the Casa della Minerva. Philip and Ivan were of course overjoyed to see Sanath again and rushed towards him to exchange a warm embrace. Joseph then gave a big hug to Ivan, his former tutor. What happened then was unexpected.

The cousins were momentarily distracted by the figure of Michael. They looked extremely puzzled, as if seeing someone they had not expected. Michael himself stared at Lorelei and Lothar, stuttered a greeting of sorts. As the grandchildren flashed bright and welcoming smiles to him, he turned pale, as if experiencing a drop in blood pressure; he swayed for a moment and then fainted into Joseph's arms. This created a small commotion; Lorelei rushed to help and Lothar went to call Laira. Sanath freed himself gently from the embrace of his friends and said, "It is so good to be back home. I have put some magic in these walls that they may protect us. Don't worry about Mike. It's nothing; just bring fresh water." Taking Lakshmi, Ivan and Sanath aside, Lakshman said simply in his calm voice: "Michael looks strangely like one of the boys we saw in the Bardo."

In a soft whisper Sanath told the cousins, "This was not the plan, but it has happened. Keep quiet about your thoughts and we will explain everything in due course."

Lothar and Joseph carried Michael to the sofa in the study. Lorelei, helped by Laira, splashed his face with cold water. He slowly regained consciousness, opened his eyes, and saw Lorelei staring at him inquisitively. He smiled faintly and looked around him, saying, "I'm sorry; it must be the jet lag." His gaze went from Lorelei to Lothar and back to Lorelei. They could not say a word, nor could they explain the feeling of *déjà vu* they were experiencing.

Lothar and Laira reassured Michael that he would be fine because the castle was a stronghold in more senses than one; in the past Sanath had made it the headquarters of his fight against Thanatophor. Ivan entered the room and helped Michael to stand up. "Welcome to Jetzenstein, Michael O'Lochan, you've had a long journey. Master Sanath suggests we all have lunch now and then take a rest. Tomorrow evening the wizard will hold the council of the Hllidarendi, which will last three days, and he has asked us all to be in attendance."

Good company makes for pleasant times. Philip and his guests spent lunchtime and most of the afternoon narrating their recent experiences. The next day the weather was overcast, with intermittent showers keeping the guests inside, and a grayish haze surrounded the fortress. Some chatted, others rested or went for a short walk in the mist, but everyone looked forward to the evening when they would be all together again. Mike and the Jetzlar grandchildren soon became inseparable.

The party gathered after dinner in the Rittersaal, the hall of the knights, which was the largest room of the private apartments that had been rearranged on the advice of the wizard. A corridor with hunting trophies led to a small staircase that opened onto a richly appointed rectangular room that housed some of the choicest treasures of the castle. This is where Sanath the Hllidarendi would hold his council.

"Our wizard has packed this room with his magic," whispered Lorelei to Mike. "I feel quite intimidated whenever I come here. It is as if one is never alone, even when nobody else is in the room. It is not a threatening feeling though, just very strange."

Next morning, the loggia with the stunning view found Sanath relaxing over a cup of tea with Philip and Laira when Lakshman and Lakshmi approached them. Lakshman asked Sanath point blank:

"Master, forgive me for asking but, given the fact that we are all companions in this quest, can you tell us what is kept behind the closed door on the top of the spiral staircase?"

Philip and Laira looked puzzled. This direct approach also greatly embarrassed the Jetzlar children; they feared they had said too much already and that Grandfather would scold them. Sanath looked at all of them pensively and finally answered, with a trace of hesitation in his voice:

"If I would speak about what is stored behind that door, it still would not reveal itself to you. So what is the point of speaking? Some Gnostics gave a name to the secret of resurrection; they called it the talisman of Osiris. But the name is not the thing."

The cousins looked at each other and paused; perhaps there was another way to phrase their question. Lakshmi tried her best:

"Sanath sahib, what would it take for these things to reveal themselves?"

Sometimes the trick is in the asking. To everybody's surprise, Sanath gave a fairly long answer. Yet, as one might have predicted, it was not terribly clear or specific.

"You see, for the mystery to reveal itself, for the power to flow, the seven seals must be broken. This is not an easy task. On top of it, alas, the evil Riders of Thanatophor keep a tight watch and attempt to make sure it cannot happen. Each one of them has the mission to guard one specific seal and to keep it tight. There is one seal that is beyond the sight of the Riders: the last one, the seventh seal. Yet it cannot break as long as the other seals are not broken."

"Seven seals, like in the Book of the Apocalypse, seven seals that must be broken to enter in the kingdom of heaven," muttered Lakshmi.

"That's right." Sanath nodded with a smile at the insightful young woman. "And as I do not have the power to break the seals, we shall no longer speculate on this subject."

The faces of the cousins betrayed their disappointment. The wizard added as an afterthought, "The Deep Way cannot be communicated in words – I am sorry." His tone was almost apologetic: "It can only be communicated by experience. Then the truth shall be known and the Gift shall be shared." At that moment, Lakshman recalled his experience in deciphering the content of the Casket of the White Feather. He burst out to Sanath, "When I opened the casket in Iceland, I felt at one point like a magic flute, a flute with seven holes, and that the music was flowing through me. Does it mean the seven seals were broken then and so the music could flow?" At his friend's insistence, Sanath completed his thought.

"Mozart could have told you. The flute was magic. As you imply yourself, it was not real." Sanath smiled again, "If you could feel this condition in your normal state, you would know that the seals are broken for good. Otherwise you are in an imaginary world. Remember, true knowledge is in the world of reality. And now I will leave you because you are too good at asking questions and you could easily lose yourselves in my words."

Sanath stood up to signal the end of the exchange. The cousins were pleased because they felt that they had learned a good deal more. They spent the rest of the afternoon exploring the fortress and its surroundings. They visited the bibliotheca and discovered the unique herb garden in the inner bailey where there were numerous plants described in medieval herb books. They rode on horseback through the woods and vineyards of the estate. The castle was surrounded on two sides by forested hillsides that offered numerous trekking paths. During these happy moments, the cousins and the Jetzlars exchanged their experiences since the discovery of Dagad Trikon. The cousins were surprised by the quick grasp and maturity of Philip's grandchildren and spent the next day mostly chatting indoors. The weather had markedly worsened; the sky was overcast and it filtered a parsimonious gray light. The weather forecast predicted a few days of showers and thunderstorms.

EPISODE 21

GATHERING STORM

While the cousins explored the fortress above the Rhine, one of the companions of the Dagad Trikon quest was feeling lonely and left out. Ashen-faced, Jonathan was walking back from the Ristorante Piccolo on 30th Street in Georgetown, the fashionable suburb of Washington, D.C. The evening light of the federal capital glowed above his head, reverberating on the foggy mattress of haze that hung over the Potomac River. But Jonathan O'Lochan was not paying attention to his surroundings. His heart and mind were laboring, trying to shake off the pain.

"Good riddance to bad rubbish!" he breathed angrily to himself. He let out a deep sigh. That evening, he had made one last-ditch effort to retrieve his relationship with Jenny. Tonight had proved to be his last meal and his last conversation with her. She had insisted that he break all contacts with Sanath, Ivan, and Joseph and he simply would not accept the diktat. What enraged him was the realization that Jenny knew he wouldn't, and that she had used this ploy to finally dump him. He had tried to salvage their relationship, even after the Robkowicz family had canceled the wedding. The feeling of loss associated with parting from Jenny swept through him. "Better now than later," he thought sadly, trying to repel visions of her smile and the enticing memories of their togetherness that were bursting across his mind. He had always felt that Jenny was too much under the influence of her father. He reflected on how they had become increasingly estranged up until the final moment of their break-up. This was a particularly painful twist in the story of his being ostracized, which had been ongoing since his parents had disowned him. The State Department had refused to take him back, despite the repeated pleas by the Head of the Middle East Desk, who knew that the departure of his best talent would cripple the department. Jonathan had watched with dismay and some disgust how people who had claimed to be friends and even relatives now avoided him at parties, pretended not to see him in the street, or greeted him perfunctorily before making excuses and hastily walking away. The mill of rumor and defamation had taken on a life of its own, spinning stories that became magnified by gossip. He was power-less against this onslaught because he could not fight claims that were made behind his back on charges too absurd to address. Aunt Elisabeth and her network had done a good job too, without real-izing that the ultimate winner was the married mistress who would now inherit the lion's share of his father's fortune.

Jonathan had always been a good son, loyal and affectionate, and he felt that his parents' reaction to Joseph's disclosure had been completely unfair. He was angry, despondent, and could not forgive his family.

He shook his head as he climbed the entrance stairs to Mike's apartment. "I guess Joseph and Ivan did not realize that their efforts would be futile. Those who matter in society are not usually inter-ested in uncovering corruption. If this is the sort of family I come from, I'd rather walk away from it sooner than later. Yet, what nonsense! That bitch who could not care less about the Church has brilliantly manipulated Dad; I must give her credit for that. He looks like an old fool showing off his young blonde bombshell to his golf buddies. Mum is now divorced and can cry with her confessor, who will no doubt try to extract a few more dollars from her for his pet projects. The new bride in the meantime has taken over Birchwood and installed her manicure studio in my bedroom. Never mind." He was glaring at the tips of his shoes blankly, still trying to cope with his new situation.

It was bewildering that such nasty turn of events could have developed just because the two brothers simply wanted to live a life true to their beliefs. Nevertheless, Jonathan felt it was time to put the whole thing behind them and somehow start a new life. But how? In the world of Washington D.C.'s over-achievers that had been his turf until recently, he now looked like a loser and it was hard for him not to agree with that opinion. He had lost his income, allowance, connections, and job – and for what? Sure, the encounter with Sanath and the search for the prophecy were fascinating, but it was far from clear how the search would unfold.

He walked restlessly around the small penthouse and felt depressed. His life did not look too good at the moment: no solid job prospects, a gorgeous fiancée gone, and most of his relatives giving him the cold shoulder. Feeling like a nobody in the capital city where so recently he was well on his way to becoming a somebody was not exactly pleasant. He had felt entitled to nurture high ambitions; after all, he was talented, capable, and hard-working.

Then his mood swung. His deeper intelligence whispered to him: being somebody is not the point – try to become yourself. His fall from social grace, he acknowledged, had brought with it a dose of humility that he almost enjoyed. His vanity had been punctured and he saw some advantage in this. He had started to see the world differently and felt freer. In a sense he was now out of the rat race.

On top of it all his brothers and sister provided much true comfort. They were involved with him in a story that would have seemed absurd to any rational mind but that continued to captivate him.

They had just left for Germany with Sanath and he missed them already. He stopped walking and stared at the bookshelf. The little monkey squeezed between two books looked friendly and he patted him on the head. It reminded him of his vision in Cairo and for a while he forgot the churning of painful emotions in his heart. The search for the prophecy they were carrying together was certainly the main pursuit of his life at present. He would soon be joining his brothers and sister, happy to have found a cheap ticket to Frankfurt.

Jonathan was to travel very soon, but before leaving he had to finalize his report for Dr. Rahurikar so he planned an encounter he had wanted to make for a long time. A couple of days ago in New York he had discussed with Dr. Rahurikar the draft of the survey he was about to finish for the Oikos Project. At that time Rahul Rahurikar had given him the address of Tatiana Voytchenko, Dr. Jana Pimenieva's assistant at the St. Petersburg Medical College. He had tried in vain to contact her during his visit to St. Petersburg in 1996. Given his recent findings that had exposed the fallacy of many yoga practices, mostly exported from India, he was once again intrigued by Dr. Pimenieva's presentation before the International Oikos Steering Committee. Tatiana was the source of the story and she had emigrated to the U.S. and had got married. Thus, Jonathan had tried to contact her and was directed by her husband to call again.

It was time to try again. Little time was left if he was to finish his report before flying to Frankfurt to catch up on the last day of the council of the Hllidarendi. Trying to put his dismal mood behind him, Jonathan dialed the number given to him by Rahul. This time, Tatiana Wollenburg (as she was now known) picked up the phone. Jonathan briefly introduced himself, then said a few words about the survey he was directing and the purpose of his call. Tatiana's voice was agreeable and welcoming, with a slight Russian accent.

She said she lived close to the Saint Charles campus of the Johns Hopkins University in Baltimore where her husband was finishing his PhD program. Going to Baltimore from Georgetown was not a long drive and Jonathan wanted to take advantage of this coincidence. Fortunately she agreed to meet him later that very afternoon. Jonathan drove up to Baltimore. He always enjoyed the smell of the old red leather seats in Mike's Jaguar, a subtle fragrance that no longer exists in modern cars. He put on a Bob Dylan CD, then changed his mind. Dylan sang, *"It is not dark yet but it is getting there"* and he did not need the reminder. All his prospects seemed dark enough; he was already depressed and did not need any additional help from the music. He reached the campus at around four o'clock, parked, and easily found Tatiana's apartment on Charles Avenue, in front of the Eisenhower Library. Tatiana opened the door.

She was a young woman in her thirties, with an agreeable round face and curly hair, and she was discreetly but visibly pregnant. She led Jonathan into the sunny white living room with stylish Danish furniture and offered him a cup of tea. The CD player was playing the Hungarian rhapsodies from Lizst. A cat came purring and rubbed its back against his leg, a sign, Tatiana said, that the visitor was fully accepted. Jonathan scooped the cat up, then eased himself into an armchair. He spoke in general terms of the Oikos Project and recalled his contacts with Dr. Pimeniev. He asked her whether she could remember the program of a revival spiritual movement that had taken place in the early nineties in the sports stadium in St. Petersburg. As he came to the object of his visit, he could see a sudden surge of interest in Tatiana. She gave him a startled look and responded instantly:

"Of course I do, I shall never forget it. Dr. Jana, who was working like you on the Oikos Project, wanted me to cover the event. It is strange that you visit me on this subject because I was never able to satisfy my own curiosity even though the experience was a very special moment in my life." Jonathan repressed a surge of silent excitement. Maybe he was getting somewhere after all, which would be an enormous relief. He continued gently:

"I understand that a woman led the program. What did this lady look like?" The cat jumped down from Jonathan's lap as if the questioning was getting indiscreet.

"She was not tall, fair, and as far as I could see from a great distance, quite beautiful. She had long black hair and was wearing a white dress. On the whole she seemed cheerful, although her tone changed many times during her speech, but I could not really see her expressions because the stadium was huge. I was far away from the stage and in those days such places were not equipped with large screens."

"Why did you choose to make a written report to Oikos? Only significant or unusual events would normally qualify to be forwarded to the Steering Committee, right?"

"Sure, I'll try to explain although it is not so easy to put it into words. To start with, her speech was plain and straightforward. She spoke about family values, morality, how righteousness protects societies. She stressed the need for us to develop spiritually and get in touch with our own spirit. I did not find these things particularly new but what baffled me was the audience."

"What do you mean?"

"I know Russian sports stadiums. These are not quiet places. In the beginning, there was a brawl behind me between a couple of drunks. There was no security service. Yet, I came to realize, some time into her speech, that there was now total silence. This was truly amazing in such a huge stadium. She seemed to have an incredible magnetism.

She did not have an authoritative presence in terms of asserting herself, as politicians usually do. Her style was simple, her manner loving and yet, from the beginning to the end, she commanded complete attention and respect. I turned to see what happened to the drunkards that had been so noisy in the beginning; they were fast asleep like babies. I simply do not know how she did it. She spoke for almost one hour. This was remarkable enough, but what was to come was even more noteworthy."

"Now you make me really curious. What happened exactly?" asked Jonathan eagerly. He had by now investigated many weird New Age movements in his survey and generally had a good sense of what was going on. Since the beginning, he had turned a skeptical eye on Tatiana, trying to assess her credibility. In this case, visibly, he had to admit that she didn't belong to a group that followed or promoted this lady or any revival movement. Her testimony seemed detached, honest, and factual.

"The lady stood up. We were asked to close our eyes and open our hands towards her, in the posture of the apostles that you can still see on old Ukrainian icons. She told us various things that I cannot quite remember to guide us, all together, in a meditative state. I then heard a noise, like the sound of the wind and I realized that she was blowing into the microphone. Now comes the interesting part. She directed an exercise, the details of which I cannot quite recall. We put our hands on various parts of our bodies. At the end we raised both our hands towards the sky. I distinctly remember that, at that moment, I started feeling the wind on my own hands. At the same time, I felt an enveloping sense of well-being, lightness in the head, and an incredible serenity. I felt myself fully, how should I say? I was empowered from within, it is really hard to describe. I looked around me; some of my neighbors seemed equally puzzled, but they looked very relaxed. At the end of the program, there was some music and singing, and then the lady left. Many of the visitors remained in the stadium because they did not feel like leaving; the gaiety that was in the air at this point was truly astonishing."

Jonathan kept watching for any indication that the story could be a bit phony, then he asked, guilelessly:

"Couldn't it just be some 'feel good' impression, coming from an optimistic atmosphere and good music?"

Tatiana answered, "That thought occurred to me too, as I could not quite believe what I had felt. I discussed it with the people around me and conducted interviews. Many people had experienced, in various ways and with different levels of intensity, the sensation of the incoming wind, the sort of consciousness empowerment I had felt myself. Many felt much lighter, I mean physically, as if a burden had been taken off.

I tried, at Dr. Jana's request, to contact the organizers of the meeting in order to know more, but they seemed poorly organized: their telephone had been disconnected and I never received an answer to any of my letters. It was clear that we were not dealing with any established organization. It all looked a bit mysterious but I could not really investigate because I was too busy with my job and so I gave up."

"Clearly, these people, whoever they were, were not pros at proselytizing," Jonathan observed pensively. "If people who look for them cannot find them it looks like they are not keen to be found. I wonder why?

"I don't know, I got the impression that they were just poorly organized. In short, to me, this event looked like it materialized from nowhere and then evaporated again, living only in the amazed memory of those who attended it. I went to some yoga classes afterwards at which the trainer pretended to follow up on the event, but it did not bring me anything. I consigned all this to Dr. Pimenieva in my report that was forwarded to the Oikos Project."

"Now tell me please, why did you say you would never forget this encounter?"

She smiled coyly. "You see, I didn't hear anything about this mysterious lady again but still today, if I feel downcast or face a problem, I try to remember that special moment, those sensations, and my heart becomes more joyous and lighter. It lifts me up. It still does. It is as if I have taken something with me from this program, something good and helpful, something that even now, I am able to access when need be. This is why I told you in the beginning that I would never forget this experience."

Jonathan looked at Tatiana with more than a trace of envy and observed with a slightly down-hearted smile: "Well, these days, I could do with some heart lifting of my own." They chatted for a while. Jonathan intuitively trusted Tatiana; she was friendly and open, and she was not trying to sell him something. She wasn't anxious to persuade him to her point of view. She had gone through an extraordinary and beautiful experience but she did not know much more. She asked him to let her know if he discovered something. He thanked her and gave her his phone number and e-mail address in case she found out something more.

Driving back to Washington, he tried to assess the significance of the young woman's account. He was relieved not to have traveled in vain; the story was definitely worth looking into. He would enter a new category 'for further investigation' in his survey. Up to this point the findings of the study he needed now to finalize before flying to Germany were not very encouraging. They denied solid empirical results to most alternative consciousness movements, yoga groups, and New Age sects. On the contrary, the absence of objective results, once the placebo effect was discounted, invalidated much of their claims.

His year-long research was telling the story of a feel-good generation, of daring explorers who probably had more courage than wisdom. Unfortunately, they did not have much of a navigational system in their travels through the New Age landscape, although they were always happy to step on the gas pedal to discover new frontiers. Post-war baby boomers, brave yet foolish, had gone headlong into all sorts of ventures. The craze had faded by now, they had aged, and most of them were just trying to make ends meet like everybody else. Many had described their earlier seeking adventures as some sort of youthful treasure-hunting game that did not have much significance. Yet, if Tatiana was right, not everything that was esoteric was fake. This interpretation was confirmed by other Oikos findings outside of this survey. An intriguing thought came to him: there were, perhaps other paths to the Grail than the one ordained for the Avasthas.

He arrived in Georgetown after dusk, ate some junk food purchased at the local grocery store, and, after a shower, settled on the terrace with the Post. The night was hot and muggy, weighing on him like an oppressive sponge; he did not feel like reading, depressed once again by the break-up with Jenny. Somehow everything felt empty and he threw the newspaper to the ground, falling back into a mood of utter helplessness.

He began hallucinating: seeing Jenny, her face, her body, and he felt sorry for himself. He deserved better than this. Tears came to his eyes. How come a heart could feel so much pain for having been in love? Was she gone for good? Would he ever be able to love again? Wasn't it safer just to entertain oneself with a partner, picking lovers here and there? Why not go back to older habits and just select opportunities for gratification in the playboy style still favored by many of his friends? His mind wandered back and forth around the seeming hopelessness of his condition. Maybe Jenny had never loved him, or, rather, she had loved bits of him, his appearance, the charming seducer, the dashing diplomat, his congenial nature or his ability to have fun. She had grabbed bits of him for her own consumption and entertainment. Yes, that must have been the case.

If she had loved him for what he really was, she would not have been so easily swayed. But how dumb he had been to be so attached to a girl who was trendy, yes, sexy, no doubt, but so superficial. He had tried to be brave in the presence of his brothers and sister but now that he was alone, there was no escape from his grief and loneliness. For a long time he remained rooted in an armchair, not knowing what to do with himself.

He felt like such a fool and, finally, to escape this oppressive, cruel night, he considered getting drunk by emptying the bottle of Black Bushmills that Mike had whisked away from Dad's bar. Suddenly, he noticed a movement in the obscurity of the night. He thought he saw two black shapes on the nearby rooftop. As he looked more intently, he spotted two large motionless ravens staring at him with somber wickedness. His first thought was that there aren't many ravens in D.C. at this time of the year. They should have flown north long ago but he interrupted himself with a sudden insight: it was as if the palpable malevolence of the birds was flowing into him. These two sinister sentinels had directly projected into him the gloom and doom of his dejected mood. He made a move to wave them away but, at this point, the ravens took flight and attacked him.

In a sinister reenactment of The Birds, the two ravens flew straight at him. With piercing shrieks and furious flapping of wings, they exhibited strength beyond that of normal birds. One aimed at his left breast and attacked with beak and claws; the other aimed at his head and eyes. Jonathan fell to the ground, retreating under the table and burying his head in his folded arms to protect his eyes. This was insane. He was thinking furiously: these are not normal birds but ominous creatures, under the spell of the Shadow that Sanath and Philip were talking about. He tried to kick at the birds here and there, as best he could. They croaked and shrieked, making bizarre and frightful sounds that simply did not belong in this world.

He took that as a sign that he was under attack from the enemies of Dagad Trikon.

He screamed. It was a scary moment. As he muttered a prayer for help, he suddenly heard the sound of the flapping of even larger wings. Looking through his arms, he saw in complete disbelief an American bald eagle falling on the ravens and chasing them away. Of course this was crazy: bald eagles are almost extinct and they do not fly in or around Georgetown. The three birds disappeared in the night as fast as they had come.

For several minutes he sat on the floor of the terrace, panting, trying to regain his breath and his composure. Then he burst into loud laughter: he knew the magic was back; the unbearable weight, the pain in his heart was gone. He was back into the Dagad Trikon legend. He felt a tremendous surge of adrenaline. The whole struggle had not taken more than a minute yet gone was the memory of Jenny, the pangs of the break-up, his worries and concerns about job and family. The pain in his heart had gone, substituted by the physical ache of heavy scratches. He felt almost exhilarated now, sensing that he was under some higher protection, no longer lost and isolated as he had felt a few minutes ago. Staring at the sky that glowed with the scintillating lights of the American capital, he very much felt part of the story. He was connected to a greater whole and to the power that had sent the eagle. A few raven feathers on the terrace were the only traces of the astounding skirmish. He started to walk back into the apartment, thinking to himself, "I'm fine really, especially when I keep my attention on the big picture. Love that can be lost cannot be the love I seek." The mental image he had of himself as a heart-broken loser who had been dumped by his girlfriend quietly disappeared.

It was ten o'clock. Little did he know that this timing was precise and that his fight with the ravens was taking place exactly at the same time as a great battle was unfolding at Jetzenstein castle, above the river Rhine, thousands of miles away. Only on the next day would he read in the news that extensive flooding, mudslides, and forest fires had occurred all over the five continents on that fateful night, taking many lives. This was indeed the hour Thanatophor wanted to claim as his, the moment of the final blow that would wipe out the last remnant of Avastha powers from Earth.

The overlord of the dark hosts could not spy on the Gods; his creatures had no access to the deliberations taking place in the heavens but he had spread his networks on Earth far and wide and his penetration of the human race had been slow, sure, and steady. He had not wanted to leave anything to chance and had decided to destroy once and for all the lonely master of the Hllidarendi Order and his few followers. He knew well that the old man, who had been his foe for thousands of years, was still capable of much mischief but by now Thanatophor was well informed about Sanath's every move. He had carefully stirred the brew of his hate in his furnaces and was now going to pour it on the world. The boiling cauldron was full. Too long he had waited for his hour, for this moment to strike.

Oblivious of the looming danger and of all these cosmic turbulences, Jonathan walked into the bathroom and disinfected his wounds, which included a big scratch on his chest and another on his left thigh. But he was laughing now, completely energized by the realization that the power of goodness was omnipotent, ever-protective, and watchful. It was just a matter of connecting. He still had no clue how the connection occurred. Could the Deep Way act on him even without his own knowledge? It seemed like it. He shook his head. How easily he had lost courage and faith, yet, obviously, he had been forgiven. He felt a surge of gratitude and offered the spontaneous prayer:" My God, you are so generous, we live off the abundance of your forgiveness. Please bear with us, please help us."

Back in the living room, he worked for most of the night to complete the report he intended to mail the next day to Dr. Rahurikar.

369

This would leave him time to settle his affairs before boarding the plane at Dulles. He still had to pick up from his bank vault the special consignment Sanath had asked him to bring to Jetzenstein castle. Thinking about it, he grinned broadly: this should be most exciting! During this time, far away in Germany the companions in Jetzenstein were not yet aware that events were inexorably precipitating a gathering storm. Only Sanath, ever-inscrutable, knew well that the moment of reckoning was coming. He had prepared himself for this moment for thousands of years, yet his heart was heavy with a sadness that he could not share with anyone.

Phillip's guests admired the vaulted high ceiling of the Rittersaal decorated with medieval paintings representing mythological animals, angels, planets, and stars. The hall was brightly lit by chandeliers and had four large ogival windows on the left side of the building overlooking the cliff above the Rhine valley. In the center of the hall, a statue of a knight dating from 1504 AD, the late-Gothic period, stood on a pillar facing the entrance. It was a masterpiece by Tilman Riemenschneider, the master sculptor of Wuerzburg. Its bearing was remarkable: the knight stood with his head slightly inclined towards the left, his long curly hair falling on the collar of his armor. He was pressing the hilt of a drawn sword against his chest. The long face and the hands were delicately chiseled to produce an effect of resolute gravity, and his entire countenance projected a graceful dignity that was almost melancholic. The first time Sanath had seen the statue in a corner of the old chapel, he had marveled at it, seeing in it the portrait of an Avastha. He commented that this image was verily in the likeness of Olophon of Elnur, the defender of Elnelok, and that other statues of Riemenschneider were a description of the Avasthas as they reached the end of their age. He had asked that the statue be moved to the hall.

Two suits of armor flanked the large medieval fireplace opposite the entrance. The fireplace was large enough to roast a whole ox. On its mantelpiece, a molding presented the armorial bearings of the Jetzlars. The motto that the family had adopted at the time of the Reformation was engraved in the stone under the blazon: *"Du bist mein Erlöser; Ich bin Dein."* Joseph translated for his brother: "It means: 'You are my liberator, I am yours.' This was the prayer Martin Luther used to mutter to Jesus in his cell before appearing before Emperor Charles V von Hapsburg at the Diet of Worms, where the inquisition could easily have sent him to the pyre.

On the left side of the hall, between the ogival windows, two panoplies of weapons hung on the wall, displaying a multiplicity of daggers, swords, maces, bludgeons, spikes, spears, and halberds. A small shield occupied the center of the left display. In the center of the right display there was a strange weapon, a small discus that looked like a miniature sun with sixteen sharp tips.

In the middle of the right side wall of the hall, visitors could admire an admirable ornamental painting on wood paneling that dated from the late Middle Ages. Lothar explained to the visitors:

"This masterwork is called the gothic triptych of the dove, a unique piece from the early years of the fifteenth century. It represents the Virgin Mary in glory, with the white dove of the Holy Spirit above her head. See the importance given to the dove, emitting golden rays of light that influence all the colors and shades of the triptych. On her left, the splendid knight in shining dark blue armor is the Archangel Michael; he thrusts a spear into a dragon writhing at his feet; on her right the Archangel Gabriel carries a golden lily in his hand; he greets the holy Virgin Mary in the posture of a messenger. Sanath brought it here. He says this is the most sacred reliquary in the castle and he does not allow anyone to touch it." The visitors admired the magnum opus: the characters rendered by the artists seemed animated by an inner life.

On the wall above the entrance, a large Flemish tapestry from the sixteenth century was hanging, showing the discovery of the new continents of Africa and America. The various green and blue hues of its background contained representations of exotic flora, and provided the setting for the purple and golden scenes of extraordinary animals and indigenous tribes presenting offerings.

Lakshman was struck by the fact that the coats of arms hanging high on both sides of the hall, above the displays of antique weaponry and on both sides of the gothic triptych, did not really represent familiar heraldic figures. There were four on the left and two on the right side of the long walls. Then it dawned on him that they were bearing the colors of the banners of the six great houses of the Avasthas.

From left to right, Kalabham was represented by an orange field on which Lakshman was surprised to see a dark ocher swastika. This seemed to be a highly politically incorrect symbol in post-war Germany, notwithstanding the fact that the swastika was indeed an ancient Aryan symbol that dated back many thousands of years and one he had seen all over Asia, in Indian temples as well as the Mosque of Samarkand in Uzbekistan. The banner of Falkiliad bore the Star of David on a field of gold. He had already seen the arms of Elnur representing the Wheel of the Law on a green field painted on the tower of Elnelok. The red banner of Eleksim was perhaps the closest to a heraldic sign, showing a golden lion standing proudly, as in the crest of England. An unusual sign represented the House of Anor: a star-shaped discus with sixteen points on a field of azure. Anorhad was not represented by a cross, as Lakshman would have expected, but by a lily on a white field, the heraldic symbol for purity. An unusual detail caught Lakshman's attention: the left petal of the lily was blue, the right one was golden while the central petal, shooting upwards, was white and almost blended into the white background. Lothar had followed his glance and approached him.

"Yes, Uncle, this is the tricolor lily of Anorhad; I never understood the colors before but Grandfather told us about your vision in Iceland. Maybe you can explain it to me?"

"I am not sure, Lothar. It seems to me that this colored heraldic lily symbolizes some rite of passage."

"You are right, Lakshman," said the wizard, who had arrived in the hall and overheard the last part of the conversation. "It is a strange habit of human beings that they codify messages that are most important for their survival in symbols, and then hurriedly forget all about their meanings. The tricolor lily of Anorhad contains a message. The central petal of the lily, squeezed by the lateral blue and yellow petals, breaks through and emerges higher. It is white and symbolizes the space for the central corridor of our higher evolution. The dynamic of the lily of Anorhad is about pushing through the barriers of thoughts and emotions that constantly capture our attention, and breaking through into the higher consciousness of the Deep Way. Come, friends, please take a seat and let us start our meeting."

The weather had been moody, the mist had suddenly cleared and, for a brief moment, the moon illuminated the night outside, with some black clouds looking like grotesque mythical animals with bright silver manes. Who could suspect that, from the core of these clouds, some of the flying spies of Thanatophor were keeping a close watch on the mighty fortress?

The company sat around an old rectangular table in front of the fireplace. Sanath faced the room, with his back to the fireplace. On the table there were three empty plates lined up in front of him; Ivan and two of his trusted lieutenants surrounded Sanath. The Jetzlars, the O'Lochans, and the cousins were facing them. Mike, Lorelei, and Lothar sat together at one end of the table.

Sanath opened the meeting with a reference to the adventures of Ivan and the cousins in Delphi: "The fact that you were allowed passage through the rock of the Pithy only indicates the gravity of the situation as the scheme of the Avasthas seems to falter. This underground journey was truly exceptional. Normally, the passage you found in Delphi with the opening of the Casket of the Wheel is not authorized to humans. Frankly, I was worried sick as you traveled through the Bardo."

The cousins reported on their own perceptions of this experience and on their long search in India. Lakshmi narrated her powerful encounter with the Goddess and concluded, "I now know what I am seeking but I do not know how to get to it. It really is just a state of being. That's all there is to it." She looked thoughtful now and addressed the wizard. "I cannot possibly describe the love I felt when I was under the protection of the Goddess in the Vaikuntha Basin. The state slowly vanished, however, and by the time I had left Greece it was gone.

Master, I had entered this search for unveiling the legend of Dagad Trikon on the basis of my association with my archaeologist cousin, moved perhaps by cultural interest and curiosity. I end up seeking something within myself, a state of being, seeking it intensely – indeed, knowing now how blissful that state may be. However, how to get back or, rather, get within? I don't know; I feel I am left high and dry. Avastha lore does not seem to help any longer when it comes to my state of mind and my daily life. This is now the dilemma as I see it, a sort of Tantalus torture: I am hungry for the meal I have tasted, but it is out of my reach. Respected master, can this really be the end result of this entire quest?"

She ended her plea with a shiver of frustration in her voice. Sanath simply nodded in her direction, as if inviting her to be patient. He did not respond right away, asking instead for the views of participants.

Tracy gave a summary of the progress and difficulties of the Oikos Project for the assembly. She spoke of its activity in these terms: "Unfortunately, the early findings of my brother's most recent survey conducted for Professor Rahurikar show that the path of spirituality is confused. Most New Age movements and sects relating to meditation or yoga have turned into health and wellness businesses without much in the way of demonstrable or verifiable results. They have borrowed or refreshed practices from Native Americans or Asian traditions but without much success as yet."

"It's a bit depressing," added Joseph. "Many people who start such pursuits are well-meaning, and this reminds me of the early Church. But soon the Dark Riders catch up with them; the results of Jonathan's survey indicate that many followers of gurus have gone astray because of power struggles, jealousies, sex, and money. Cases of physical or psychiatric troubles have been registered. Many end up looking very much like the world they pretended to reform. They say one thing and do another. This is confirmed by the data Jonathan has compiled for Professor Rahurikar. Yet, from all this research into alternative spirituality, we find a message very similar to the canons of the established religions: man has not yet reached the full potential of his consciousness but he can if he chooses to."

Tracy offered, "Of course, globalization admits us into a world of shared and diverse intellectual, cultural, and spiritual traditions and values. These bear witness to the inherent unity and beauty of the human family. The Oikos objective is that, as human beings, we should benefit materially and spiritually by making an effort to understand this world and by becoming part of it."

"That is, of course, worthy and laudable," commented Sanath. "However, the Darkness is on the move to ensure that this will not happen. Hangker breeds conflicts in the fields of economics and politics. Belzebseth attacks the psyche. These PCVs (the so-called 'psychic compulsion viruses') identified by the FBI represent the vanguard of their armies. They work through the six Riders to bring humans to the appropriate level of decay where they can be possessed. The risk of possession was a fact known to your ancestors but ignored or ridiculed by modern man." Sanath then turned to Ivan. "Now we are going to get an update on the plans of our enemy, for this is one of the reasons I have called you as the members of my council. Please, Ivan, tell us what your team found."

The weather had deteriorated markedly and Ivan had to raise his voice to be heard above the noise of the heavy downpour of rain on the roof. He explained that a team of thugs on contract had shadowed Baldur van Bosnar, perpetrated the bombing of the plane and the house in Holland, and they were in contact with a second team hired to spy on the cousins in Rome. His people had caught some and injected them with the truth serum. More interestingly, one of them was an assistant of Gorshkak, the northern Titanosaur, perhaps himself a demon but without enough power to resist Ivan's trained Russian squadron and the serum of truth.

"The progress of the Shadow, its inroad into modernity, is sadly familiar to all of you. They have infiltrated and compromised the Oikos Project and major world centers of power, including, of course, my former turf in the Vatican. They have derailed New Age movements. It is quite clear that the Darkness is bent on crushing any sort of Avastha revival. They believe they have managed to mislead a number of the Stealthstars although they were not sure that they could identify them. The forces of Darkness, as a matter of fact, are quite buoyant. They have indications that the return of the Avasthas has misfired and these arch-enemies of theirs would no longer present a serious threat to the rising hegemony of Thanatophor."

The shrieks of an eagle could be now heard through the sudden storm that raged over the Rhine valley. Lightning struck nearby and the crash of ensuing thunder was deafening. There was a commotion amongst the falcons nesting on the Falkenlust tower. The company felt uneasy. Tracy told herself, "The failed landing of the Stealthstars, this was what the wizard was telling us in Riverdale when he spoke about Mike."

Ivan continued, "The smug confidence of this henchman under interrogation was perhaps the most worrying information I uncovered. Now comes the crux of the matter. They seem to fear one last thing: the Hllidarendi and his magic and, as I speak, they have taken unprecedented measures to counter Sanath." Ivan turned to his friend with great concern. "This fiend pretended that Belzebseth and Hangker were themselves on the move to destroy you and it could happen at any time. I must turn to the heir of the Hllidarendi and ask him what must be done now."

Outside, the storm had escalated to a new level of ferocity; the wind was blowing in gusts and a window opened suddenly, allowing rain to pour in. The companions looked at each other with a growing sense of unease and Lothar rushed to close the window. In the next flash of lightning, a startled Lothar saw an unusually large eagle and a flock of falcons circling around the castle. Was this an omen? All eyes turned to Sanath.

Sanath looked fierce and the glow of his face was now awesome. He roared in a loud and terrible voice, "I have gathered you here, all my companions for this fateful encounter. Hear, companion birds of prey and children of Karudas! Hear, my companions, seekers of lost lore and children of man! Verily, I have summoned both these devils to dine with me tonight at Jetzenstein Castle." In so saying, he stood up, grabbed two of the plates on the table before him and, rising before the stunned audience, threw them to the ground near the entrance door to the hall. They broke into many fragments and splinters, releasing brief flashes of greenish light.

EPISODE 22

THE NIGHT OF THE BATTLE

The audience was now completely captivated by the actions of the wizard and shocked by the dramatic smashing of the plates. "I know more than men about the Grand Scheme but much of it remains cloaked, unfathomable, and too great to comprehend, even for the Hllidarendi. Recently I came to realize that the Avasthas lost most of their powers in the first few months after taking their human birth. Thereafter many were themselves lost. They grew up to be normal humans adults, but as you know, 'adult' in this world has become a dirty word, as in 'adult' movies. How could they preserve the vibrancy of their freshness in such a world, that lovable spontaneity that made them a constant delight in their previous lives? Today it is hard to even imagine the warmth and harmony that was enjoyed by Avastha families in the cliff dwellings of the Gundaldhar fault or in the lovely city of Shambalpur. Yet, take heart: failure is a good opportunity to learn; perhaps something even deeper and better is in store for us. I have faith that this will be the case.

Despite all this, as I walk in the streets of the cities or the narrow lanes of remote villages of the five continents, my heart sometimes leaps with joy because I still meet small children who have not lost the light in their eyes. The Avasthas are still arriving."

"But what becomes of the grown-up returned Avasthas? What about the Stealthstars?" asked Lakshmi, with the merest trace of anxiety in her voice.

"I traced some of them but mostly I was unable to locate their specific identities. Many developed into artists or craftsmen; some shied away from society. Some were rebels, others, strange as it may seem, became champion tennis players, successful ballerinas or even top lawyers trying to beat society at its own game, but it was the wrong game for them. Hard to believe, isn't it? They lost themselves in these pursuits just like ordinary humans. Yet one thread bound them all: they remained seekers of truth. Irrespective of the walk of life they had chosen, none of them could quite make sense of what life was about."

"In this respect, I qualify all right," grumbled Michael to himself.

Sanath continued. "Many became cynical, like fallen angels who didn't know from where they had fallen or why. Surrounded by the cleverly constructed traps of Belzebseth and his witches, they discarded the values of the higher civilization they had come from but remained haunted by a hidden feeling of existential unease. The pain of the dishonor was hard to bear. A process of self-destruction started for some of them who'd tried but failed to regain their lost grace. They looked for a world of blissful harmony through hedonistic pursuits. They looked for a shortcut to the heavens by taking a deeper plunge towards hell, often ending in substance abuse or addictions, the ultimate loss of freedom. To help those children we could reach, we started a couple of schools. You saw the one in the Casa della Minerva with Ivan, but obviously this was a very small-scale response."

"You explained some of this in Riverdale, Master," said Tracy, "but where do we stand now?"

"After my recent trip to the ante-room of the nether world, I realized that I had to completely change my plans. My expectations that the Avasthas can turn the tide were wrong. Something much bigger is needed. My friends, we have to prepare for confrontation, a great showdown, to settle the matter once and for all."

"You mean with Thanatophor?" Count Philip sounded incredulous and, perhaps for the first time, apprehensive. "You never gave us any indication that you would even contemplate such a radical option."

Sanath answered gravely, "Thanatophor never shows up himself – I mean, the gauntlet was thrown down by the demon kings, Hangker and Belzebseth, who are his operative forms."

These words were met by a petrified silence. Lothar looked again at the strange discus weapon on the wall: was it emitting some sort of soft white light? He was not sure.

Sanath continued. "I left indications that would direct the Darkness to Jetzenstein. We must catch them here. One of these signs is the symbol of the three-and-a-half coil of the High Lady of the Rock, a motif that is to be found on all the jars and vases I have collected and now display in the porcelain cabinet. Recently, some spies of Hangker heard about these and came here in the guise of tourists. They have been watching the castle for the past few months and they know we are here. They reported back to their infernal masters. The great demons are on their way and will be here soon. Trust me: there is a higher magic than that of the Dark One." Sanath spoke matter-of-factly, as if unaware of the enormity of what he was saying.

They looked at each other in stunned surprise. Lorelei repressed a furious anger and a desire to run to the medieval panoply and grab a weapon for herself. But common sense prevailed, and she quickly realized that, at this point, it would be of no practical use.

"Sanath, this is madness! Who are we to face them? Indeed, how can we fight?" Joseph almost yelled, expressing the feelings of all those present in the Rittersaal. They had thought that the castle was there to keep the demons out, not to invite them in. Lothar moved decisively closer to the display of medieval weapons on the wall. The wizard was well aware of their distress but the die had been cast. There was no way back and he now projected a sense of steely determination.

"I shall tell you precisely who you are now, how to face them, and why there is no need to fight. The time is short. Hear again about the world of the Avasthas, your world, my noble friends, who cannot begin to suspect your own greatness."

Wind and rain again were battering the windows of the hall of the knights. Lakshman shook his head, reacting like the others, with disbelief. He had come to trust the wizard and was not prepared to face the brutal fact that the master was, all of a sudden, deliberately putting them in harm's way. Lakshmi meanwhile studied the walls of the hall and the chimney, searching for a potential escape route, a secret passage somewhere. Lorelei, Lothar, and Mike looked at each other again searchingly and wondered whether they were also involved in the prophecy. Sanath went on in a hurried voice that was unusual for him, as if he was pressed for time.

"At night Mike travels in the Bardo, in his former Avastha self, fighting the creatures of the shadow as a warrior of yore, but during the day he is a human again, without any memory of it. He cannot reconcile these two personalities; it is dangerous to be astride two worlds and this is why Michael is often exhausted and troubled when he wakes up. He also experiences a loss of blood pressure when the two worlds collide as, for instance, when he met the cousins and Ivan this morning in this living world – people he had previously met in the Bardo. Duality must cease, for the path forward is the one towards unity. Know that you are most dear to the power that created you and that you walked the earth in the days of Dagad Trikon. You are... "

The wizard was interrupted by an outside noise in the corridor and his eyes hardened. The door burst open and a Russian bodyguard came hurtling through. Moaning faintly, he spat blood, stumbled a few steps, and collapsed onto the floor. A dagger protruded from between his shoulder blades. Four Japanese men dressed in black combat dress, armed with knives and Uzi machine guns, followed. They must have gained access to the castle with the latest group of tourists. They gestured to Sanath's party to remain motionless, stayed close to the door, and pointed their weapons at the members of the wizard's council.

Ivan discreetly manipulated his cell phone behind his back and sent an alarm signal to the rest of his Russian squadron. Sanath remained standing, looking resolute, his calm air of authority providing a silent reassurance to his companions. The youngsters were tense and pale, bewildered by the brutal intrusion. And yet what was to come would be infinitely more disturbing.

An approaching commotion attracted their attention. They heard a thumping sound from the corridor, as if a heavy creature were approaching. The Japanese intruders reverentially lined up along the wall and looked over their shoulders at the entrance door. Two figures slowly entered the room.

A short man emerged first, with a face that resembled a devil's skull and emitted a muted yellowish glow. He was wearing a flat iron crown. His light blue eyes were terrifying, projecting a formidable and thoroughly hostile willpower that pierced Sanath's friends with its intense hatred. The man was the personification of sheer concentrated might that froze those captured in the frightful beam of his glance.

The other darker shape that followed him was taller, dressed in somber purple and enveloped in a black mantle. Under the hood, the expression on his face seemed to be constantly changing, yet his eyes exuded such a constant sense of malignant malice that every heart was filled with renewed fear. Both shapes combined to form a unified field of evil and their chilling presence created a feeling of abject terror. The members of the council of Sanath were staring in utter disbelief at the two demon kings, overlords of the dark hosts, the right and the left hand of Thanatophor. For a short while the storm outside receded and in the frozen silence of the hall the companions could faintly hear the horses neighing furiously in the nearby stables.

A living nightmare was enveloping Sanath and his companions. A numbing sense of unreality came upon them and blurred their awareness. They no longer knew what world they were in. For Ivan, Lakshman, and Lakshmi it was the reverse experience of their visit to Vaikuntha. There they had moved outside their bodies, from their world towards the heavens of the Emerald King, but now hell had entered their world and was about to rob them of their bodies. That visit to the heavens was empowering, but this visit from hell was emptying them of their very substance.

As Hangker took another step forward, a violent feeling of nausea seized everyone in the room. Laira swooned and Ivan's lieutenants started vomiting. Sanath looked grim but remained impassive, concentrating on the scene, the tips of his long white fingers softly rubbing the surface of the table as it to maintain contact with matter that issued from Mother Earth. Even the faces of the four Japanese intruders indicated sheer terror at what they were witnessing. Slowly the two demons progressed a few steps. The glowing splinters of the two broken plates on the ground before them, near the statue of Olophon, began to emit a dazzling light. The devils stopped.

A sudden rush of howling wind and rain battered the roof and the windows of the hall. Hangker, for it was he who had twisted their livers with nausea, looked at the splinters spread before him on the ground. He smiled hideously, then burst into laughter. "Old fool, you invited us for dinner and these are our plates, I see." As he spoke, the splinters moved towards each other and regrouped to form three small discuses with sharp edges. Hangker laughed again, " Do you really think that your tired tricks are a match for Belzebseth, the king necromancer and myself, Hangker, the supreme commander of the legions of doom?"

He obviously did not expect an answer to this question and he received none. His eyes slowly scrutinized each member of the wizard's council and a menacing grin appeared on his face. "To find you all together here is truly gratifying. So this is the endgame, right?"

Staring at Michael O'Lochan, he continued, "How pitiful is your appearance, Aliskhan the Swift, you, the pride of Anor who used to terrorize my troops thousands of years ago. You wander in the world of the Bardo at night and in the world of men during the day, not even connecting these two states, a shadow of your former self. Where did you hide your cousin Lidholon? We intend to catch him too. And you, Esitel," he said surprisingly, turning to Lorelei von Jetzlar. "It is in vain that you pine for this boy as you did in those wretched days when you were so arrogant and equipped with your accursed powers. My lord Belzebseth will now ensnare you for good, and not only through the power of the ophtalir. This little viscount brother of yours will not prevent him from doing what he pleases with you," he added, throwing a disdainful glance at Lothar. Then, mockingly, he said, "Hanomkar, drummer of Dagad Trikon, look at you. You were once able to induce the Rasa energy waves to play this damned music, which would throw up walls of whirling sand and bury my lizard-borne troops. You were a mere boy and yet my generals feared you. You will now learn to fear them. I shall throw whatever is left of you as food to my dogs."

Belzebseth, the necromancer king, glided a step forward. The companions shivered, their exposed hands and faces bitten by a sudden icy draft that carried the frost of death. The light in the hall dimmed and turned grey. The long, pale, and oddly twisted face of the sorcerer king expressed a grim satisfaction. He looked like a weird medieval gargoyle.

Belzebseth's soft and silky voice was like the velvet hissing of a viper. A cloud of deadly pestilence oozed from his mouth. He fixed his penetrating glare on the women, as if sizing them up:

"It is so pleasant at last to seize the prey that escaped me so long ago. You are mine, Esitel, you and your sister, the captain of the Sheravalian Guard, the proud Erilie, who is today as clueless as the rest of you. I shall extract from your tormented memory all I need to know in order to capture the dame of the Gundaldhar Fault. I shall squeeze every drop of your essence out of your body and you shall worship me until the rapturous moment of your slaughter shall come." Lorelei was quivering, every limb of her body aching, a frightful pain coursing through her. Her heart sank, there was nowhere to go, no place to hide, and it felt as though there was no floor under her feet. She was falling into a dreadful emptiness, sinking deeper into a forbidden hole at the bottom of which the clutches of Belzebseth were awaiting her. She stared helplessly at her formidable foe, sobbing softly.

Lakshmi's sensations and feelings were hardly more pleasant. Her body felt numb and a sense of helplessness and despair was upon her. Her left eye throbbed, her mouth twitched, and she thought she was going to scream but no sound came out of her mouth. Part of her brain was feverishly trying to figure out how to meet the challenge of the demons. Turning towards her as if sensing her terror, the necromancer king continued:

"Erilie, first maid of Eleksim that my troops once so feared, how pathetic you look tonight. You, who once guided the panthers with the power of your will and crushed matter with your angry glance, look at you now: defenseless and abandoned to my whims. I know you do not recall anything of your past splendor but, daughter of the high Lord Ichwaril of Eleksim, I shall pour such pain and humiliation into your limbs and soul that every nook and cranny of your awareness will be laid bare before me, my minions, and my witches."

Lakshman's forehead was covered in cold sweat. His whole body was shivering. He just could not bear to listen to these threats against his cousin. He took a deep breath and, trying to shake off the sense of numb terror that had fallen upon him, he moved a step in the direction of the medieval weapons, reaching out to grab a sword. As he did so, with a single gesture of his hand, Belzebseth paralyzed him. His face now livid, Lakshman gasped with excruciating pain.

Both demons laughed. Belzebseth seemed utterly delighted with himself and addressed Lakshman spitefully: "So here you are too, Etakir, commander of the Yuva platoon and best amongst the Avastha archers. Move a finger if you can! This is not the way it was supposed to be, is it? You are no match for us. Wretched Stealthstars," he added as he turned towards the companions. "Don't you understand? This is our age, our time. We have grown and you have diminished. You are weakened beyond recognition and we must congratulate ourselves for this. The decline of your houses and the doom of the Avasthas are now complete. When we eliminate you, we will wipe out the sorry remnants of this silly quest for divinity that the Avasthas so wanted to pass on to the human race. Your ancient powers could not survive your arrival in this world of men. Don't you see it? Mankind is ours." At that moment, the discus in the center of the panoply of weaponry began glowing lightly. It was a signal sent to them and Lorelei, Lothar, and Michael noticed it without knowing its meaning. Sanath had not yet explained to them that the discus was the favorite weapon of the Emerald King when, long ago, in the form of the Sower, he would visit planet Earth and rid her of the likes of demons such as these.

Curiously, given the mood of panic that had overtaken those in the hall, the companions of Sanath now seemed to recompose themselves. Even while being taunted by the fearful monsters, they felt a previously unrecognized strength rising in their veins and sinews. Suddenly, having absorbed the news of their past identity, they looked serious and angry with the emergence of a collective will to fight to the death, if need be. Although they felt strangely calm inside, they wondered, "How could Sanath lead us into this trap? It's not possible, he must have a plan... " However, the wizard remained as motionless as a statue.

Michael and Lothar, who were standing close to the panoply of weapons, quickly calculated the time needed to grab them. The two demon kings had turned their backs to the entrance and the large overhanging tapestry and were now standing in front of their four guards, who therefore could not easily aim their guns at them. Maybe now they should take their chance?

Belzebseth hissed: "We had carefully prepared this ambush for you. Everything has worked under our control, even the foolish attempts of the old Sand Keeper," he added, turning menacingly towards Sanath.

"For we have even recognized you, Wizard of Dagad Trikon, despite your countless disguises. I do not know by what folly you allowed yourself to be caught and this is a mistake you shall not survive."

Sanath remained motionless, moving not even an eyelash. He looked strained and said in a tired voice:

"Well, I'll soon find out, won't I?"

His passivity was puzzling to his friends and provocative to his foes. Lakshmi and Lorelei felt their worst innermost fears come flooding back. Joseph had seized his sister's hand and was holding it tightly.

Hangker thundered, "I am Hangker, who sees all and thinks his way through every obstacle. I am the one who rides the tempest of action and blows the gales of hatred. I shape the future. And this is Belzebseth who fills all corridors of the past and twists emotions. He commands terror and the army of the dead who shall return to the living. Even if you should become as small as a grain of sand, you cannot pass between us, Sand Keeper. We block the way and mankind shall not rise. How will you escape?"

"Now!" answered Sanath icily. They could hardly hear his voice over the hammering of rain drops and hail stones over the roof of the hall. Hangker shouted:

"What?"

"Now and then, to be more precise," said the wizard more loudly. His voice had taken on a steely quality: "God has given us the here and now. The next moment is a gift of the devil. You are 'then' Belzebseth, haunting us in the past. You aren't yet Hangker projecting yourself in the future. Between past and future, emotion and thought, there is the ground of the people of God, the Vilamba, and the place that you cannot find. Only I am, here in the present, where Adivatar rules. I surrender to the Ruler."

Sanath who had been as motionless as stone since the interruption of the demons, suddenly walked towards them across the hall and bowed deeply to something or someone he was seeing beyond the shapes of the demon kings.

For a brief moment the demons did not understand: was their arch foe bowing before them? This was a move that neither had foreseen.

In that moment called the present, the presence of the higher power of Adivatar was called by the incomparable faith and surrender of Sanath of the highlands, the Sand Keeper and guardian of the Dagad Trikon legend.

In a twist of fate that challenges human understanding, the power of the Deep Way manifested itself to rescue the small band of Avasthas in a manner it often does – unexpectedly. Behind the two demon kings, the tapestry hanging over the entrance oscillated.

Among the figures of exotic and fabulous animals such as unicorns, griffins, lions, and giraffes, there was a monkey. His eyes came alive, he became animated, and, in a light and gracious leap, he dropped down from the tapestry. The demons did not notice him at first for he had landed silently behind them.

Tracy, peeping from behind Joseph's elbow, saw the monkey and could not suppress a gasp of surprise. She recalled the white monkey who had been Jonathan's guide in Cairo. This monkey, who was none other than Hanuman the Great, elegantly danced his way through the legs of Hangker and ran swiftly towards the large ornamental triptych standing against the wall on the left of Sanath and his council. By now, the baffled demons had caught a glimpse of him. Hanuman jumped up and into the triptych and disappeared into the figure of the Archangel Gabriel who was painted on the right of the crowned image of the Holy Virgin Mary.

The posture of the demons had changed: their boastful stance had vanished; first mystified, than resolute, they now completely ignored Sanath and his group. Hangker opened his mouth and exhaled putrid fire. Belzebseth drew a dagger from under his mantle, which emitted a black stream of energy. The eyes of all – demons, wizard, ex-Avasthas, and humans – were fixed on the retable.

Gabriel's eyes came to life and he blinked benignly at Sanath's party. His shape extracted itself from the triptych with a movement of immense power and continued to grow in size. The air around him, his aura, began vibrating slightly as if an electric current was surging through it. The Archangel stepped down from the painting, surrounded by a blinding glow and grown now in size to that of a tall human. He began emitting a steady flow of golden light and his hair was the color of honey twisted into living flames. With a last reassuring glance at the befuddled assembly in the hall, he advanced two steps towards the other end of the retable. With his right hand, he touched the left hand of the image of the Archangel

Michael, captain of the heavenly hosts, which was clasped around a spear.

It was now Michael's turn to come to life. He, who is the protector of mankind in the blue area of the collective subconscious, opened his eyes, which burned as if made of a cool diamond fire. Frowning terribly, he too stepped down from the triptych, and standing to the left of Gabriel with his dark blue armor glittering in proud splendor, he turned to face the demons. The glory of the captain of the army of angels was great indeed for all to see. His stare was imperious, commanding. Humans and ex-Avasthas watched the scene in complete awe but only the former Avasthas heard the words that were exchanged, while their companions heard only a terrifying silence. No one moved.

Slowly Hangker and Belzebseth regained their bearing and hissed in their non-human language. "Ah, that's what it is," said Hangker finally.

"It's a long time since I've seen you, Gabriel. I never thought the old Sand Keeper could come up with such a gigantic trick! Curse him and his magic."

The Archangel responded coldly:

"I bring news, as is my custom, and this time it is of your doom." Coming close to the statue of Olophon of Elnur in the midst of the room, Gabriel seized the sword of the statue. At this point, Sanath kneeled before the tremendous figures of the Archangels and his party hastily followed suit.

His face lit by an inner fire, Michael eyed Belzebseth scornfully. Neither living men nor creatures in the Bardo ever withstood such a fierce stare. His eyes had turned yellow, exactly like those of a tiger. Belzebseth returned a venomous glance at the leader of the celestial angels. His eyes were glinting under his hood and his breathing became louder until it sounded like the hissing of the serpent army around Elnelok.

"Bhairava," he breathed, evoking the name of the demon slayer worshipped in the remote valleys of the Himalayas, "the last time I saw you was in Nepal, defending the passage to Kailash and the gates of the Himavat mountains. If you stand here in person in the form of Michael, this can only mean mankind's last line of defense."

Hazy spectral shapes in the likeness of greatly downsized pterodactyls took flight from under the folds of his mantle, casting black shadows across the hall. Bolts of fire erupted from the edge of Michael's armor and consumed them almost instantly. A sound like a tiger's growl came from the mouth of the Archangel. Both Archangels had assumed terrible and towering forms and only then did the onlookers noticed the large palpitating wings unfolding on their backs, adding strength to the wind that now approached gale force. Sanath's companions grabbed the heavy oak table to resist its pull.

However, the full force of the wind was directed at the demons. As the Archangels slowly lifted in the air, the two demons were inexorably pushed through the windows by the fierce vibratory assault of the two Archangels. In a gush, the gale broke the windowpanes into a thousand glass splinters. The Archangels pursued them through the ogival window and out into the night. At this moment the two plates thrown by Sanath and the discus in the middle of the weapons lifted and whirled slowly, then like small flying saucers they followed the path of the Archangels, leaving behind a trail of light.

An enraged clash ensued. Archangels and the demon kings fought in mid-air above the Rhine valley, now bathed in pure moonlight as if the sky had been washed clean by the storm.

This reversal of fortune was as sudden as it was absolute. Sanath's companions discerned that the curse, which had so filled them with nightmarish gloom, had been lifted. They felt again hale and hearty, regenerated by a protective enchantment. All traces of their inner anguish were removed. They rushed forward and pressed against the embrasure of the four windows, hardly managing to breathe at the sight of this titanic battle. Speechless, they watched in the moonlight the epic confrontation between the Archangels and the arch-demons high in the sky.

A flock of eagles circled the fighting shapes to keep at bay the foul creatures of the night summoned by Belzebseth in this desperate hour of his direst need. The three small flying discuses were blazing through the black clouds, searching and burning the ghosts hiding there.

Archangels and demons wrangled in midair and the fight sometimes looked like a brawl, sometimes like a ballet. The movements of the combatants were swift; lights flashed and criss-crossed from the weapons of the demons and the Archangels. It soon became clear that Gabriel and Michael had the upper hand. The spectators heard piercing shrieks, followed by screams of pain that became muffled and then died away. Gradually, the four shapes diminished in size and finally vanished, as if shifting into another, invisible dimension. The rain started again.

The angels of the Archangel Michael in heaven were not the only ones to witness this brief yet titanic struggle. On this fated night, the spirit of Ananta Quetzalcoatl, the great cobra of antiquity worshipped by the Hindus and the Aztecs, arose. He, who serves as a couch for the Emerald God, came into the river to watch the encounter. The Rhine looked now like a giant silver dragon joyously glittering with a newfound strength as it celebrated this moment of great triumph. The spirit of the cosmic cobra rejuvenated the ancient river and cleansed from it the memory of all the crimes it had witnessed when the Darkness had seized Germany and Hangker had possessed the demented mind of Hitler. That night the great river finally washed the ghosts of the last Nazis from its banks. Its rising waters engulfed the corpses of the four human henchmen of the demon kings. Their bodies were washed away to the shores of the ocean.

Most men do not know that some rivers have a spiritual co-efficient. Some are deeply cleansing of the soul, as the worshippers of the river Ganga from Rishikesh to Varanasi well know; some bring subtle blessings, and the Rhine could bestow the gift of creativity to those sensitive enough to receive it. On that night the soul of this battered land felt the promises of Angkura, the germinating power, the seed of renewal and enlightenment yet to be bestowed by the Deep Way.

The small party gathered again in the Rittersaal of Jetzenstein, now a cool and breezy environment. They had felt drained and exhausted, but suddenly, from the depth of their amazement a new energy flowed in their veins and sinews. They felt almost dizzy with elation; the companions looked at each other in disbelief.

Some cried in nervous relief, some hugged others, and tears mixed with drops of rain on their cheeks. So many emotions were released. Laira and Ivan, helped by the other Russians guards who had just entered the room, hurried to the aid of their comrade who had been seriously wounded.

Lakshman and Lakshmi were looking at each other with affection, pride, and tears of blessedness, as did Etakir and Erilie thousands of years ago. They had heard from the demons the truth of their ancient identity. They could not remember those faraway past lives nor confirm this announcement in any way. Yet what felt true to them was this renewed awareness of the bond of brotherly and sisterly love between Etakir and Erilie that had been established in the Avastha mountain fortress. They had indeed pledged the powerful protection of the brother-sister relationship to each other through the bond of the rakhi, the sacred thread they had exchanged while still youngsters in the bygone days of Dagad Trikon.

Mike, Lorelei, and Lothar were standing in a triangle, holding each other's hands. They glowed with love and energy, feeling completely washed and purified in the aftermath of the whirlwind that had surrounded the brief apparition of the two magnificent Archangels. They could not speak, they could only laugh. Sanath was sitting in his chair again, head bent, his eyes closed, a beatific smile on his lips. Philip and the O'Lochans were staring in disbelief at the triptych; in the lateral ogival windows only a golden background could be seen in the empty space that had been filled by the painted representations of Gabriel and Michael. The place in the tapestry previously occupied by the monkey was also empty.

This was mighty magic indeed. The potency of the Hllidarendi had been nothing but his extraordinary ability to connect with and call for the powers from above.

The Mother of God, in the center of the triptych seemed now to have the expression Leonardo da Vinci had depicted in his rendering of the eternal feminine. It was the jocund half-smile, as if to say, "Children, why were you worrying?"

Joseph knelt before the triptych and prayed with tears coursing down his cheeks: "O Mother of immaculate countenance, how often did I pray to you, asking you to send me a sign, to show me the way, to protect and take me where I must go? Tonight, you released your Archangels for the sake of saving the entire human race and for us all gathered here to find again the path of oneness. Tonight I know you are the giver of boons, the maker of miracles, the queen that Dante, Goethe, and the seers worshipped in paradise as the savior of mankind."

Sanath arose slowly and addressed them. "The holy hosts rejoice, the air is fresh, I feel the joy of the river over which the moon pours her milky softness. Birds have taken flight to all continents to carry the news of a great liberation. This is the Deep Way: you are not your appearance nor your status, you are not what others perceive nor what you believe about yourselves; you are not what you think, not even what you feel. You are neither Avasthas nor humans: you are the very spark of divinity inside. I know your thoughts and your emotions have taken you away from the deeper world within. You can re-establish whatever you have lost. Everything is still within you. Let the power of the Elephant be awakened within you again. Be like a child. It is not the master mind that shall inherit the world but the master heart. But let us talk no longer now; let us go back to our rooms and pray in gratitude, enjoying in silence the magic of this awesome night."

The moon shone again and although daybreak was not yet near, the darkness had receded. Lakshman looked at his watch; it was three o'clock in the morning. A chill was now in the air, but filled with the aura of sacredness left by the Archangels. There were vibrations in the air, as if filaments of fire left by Gabriel's hair were still floating around. No questions were asked, thoughts did not arise; minds were still, quiet, and rested in a state of worship, enjoying just that: the bliss of the unique moment.

Later, in their rooms, Lakshman recalled the energy he had experienced while opening the casket in Iceland and the miraculous water of the Vaikuntha. Philip, Laira, and Ivan remembered the unique atmosphere of holiness at the Sao Iambu festival of the Hllidarendi in the forest of Byelorussia. Lakshmi realized that her condition was analogous to but deeper than the wonderful state she had experienced during Lorelei's party at the Casa della Minerva and close to the extraordinary sensations she'd enjoyed when she was enveloped in the Goddess' sari in the Vaikuntha. Yes, the fluid power of blessedness was still circulating within through the manifestation of the two glorious Archangels: the inner world was still alive, here and now.

On the next morning everyone awoke very late after a deep and dreamless sleep. They all had the same impression: that what had happened the previous night had been a dream. As they entered the garden, they found that the storm had swept the castle grounds, which now looked wonderfully refreshed and purified. Sanath was nowhere to be seen. The O'Lochans returned to the hall of the knights. Curtains covered the apertures of the broken windows. The blood on the entrance floor had been cleaned away. All traces of the fight between demons and Archangels had vanished. Tracy pointed again to the triptych as if to confirm their experience of the night: on the two sides of the retable, the paintings of Michael and Gabriel had indeed disappeared for good. The sword of the statue made by Riemenschneider was also missing. The monkey in the tapestry was also nowhere to be seen.

Lorelei, Lothar, and Michael now felt as one, like a unit that was distinctly apart from the rest of their peers. In fact, they understood that their experiences of the past night had irrevocably separated them from the rest of humanity because no normal person would ever believe what they had seen and experienced.

The cities and villages in the neighborhood of the fortress were struggling with the consequences of the sudden tide of the Rhine and abuzz with fantastic rumors. Many sensible and dependable Germans, who are not prone to indulging in mystic or magical nonsense, reported having seen lights and heard strange sounds high above the river. Television crews came from Cologne and Frankfurt to investigate the UFO stories.

One or two journalists approached the castle but were firmly turned away. Indeed, the day was a busy one for the hotel. The manager reported to the police the disappearance of four Japanese tourists who had not paid for their stay. The dragon vases in the porcelain cabinet had been broken, and insurance formalities had to be completed. Fortunately, the condition of the wounded bodyguard, who had been whisked away into the family quarters, had stabilized and was now improving, thanks to the medicinal plants of the castle garden and the healing powers of Sanath and Laira.

The Jetzlar guests, still feeling full of an unusual energy, took advantage of a beautiful afternoon to enjoy themselves outdoors.

A splendidly bright light bathed the Rhine valley, visibly in cele-bration mood. The nature reserve at the entrance of the estate had been flooded too. The youngsters helped the locals to assist the wildlife that had been left stranded by the high waters.

Everyone now impatiently anticipated the second evening session of the council. As a purple dusk enveloped the castle, they gathered again in the hall of the knights, except for Laira who stayed in the kitchen to supervise the preparation of a late dinner, and the Russian bodyguards who were still reinforcing the defense perimeter of the fortress. More eagles and falcons had arrived as if in support, perched on the Falkenlust tower and the chimney of the castle.

Sanath was already sitting at the head of the council table, waiting for them. For the first time they saw him wearing a precious chain made of platinum, gold, and silver that had been stored in the secret treasury room. They admired seven gem-studded flowers with different numbers of petals and mysterious engravings on each. It was the chain of the Grand Master of the Order of the Hllidarendi. He looked happy and accepted the congratulations with relaxed ease and good humor. Expressions of glee and amazement were forthcom-ing from all sides for the trap he had prepared for the two demons.

Finally Joseph said, with his face shining, "Very well, master; you have definitely proved to us that other dimensions or universes can erupt in our daily reality. Yet, these were completely miraculous occurrences and we don't quite understand the implications. I wonder what it all means in terms of our investigations of the prophecy. We understood that the whole of the Dagad Trikon legend was geared to prepare the return of the Avasthas. It seems that we are in a different situation now, and if so, which one?"

Sanath's expression became more serious. "You are absolutely right, Joseph. Since yesterday, things have changed drastically. We have, in a sense, now evolved outside of the frame of the Dagad Trikon prophecy. The ancient seers had not foreseen this. It was not meant to happen. The Archangels took over to protect us from sheer destruction because the landing of the Avasthas had been compromised. Yet such intervention can only be a one-time occurrence… to balance the score, as it were.

You see, in the Grand Scheme, Gods and Archangels cannot normally intervene directly on this world's scene for it is all left to the freedom of men to pick their own path between good and evil, right and wrong. However, as the arch-demons had not shown the same restraint and constantly interfered in human affairs, the divine forces needed to intervene to restore balance to the Grand Scheme. I only drew their attention to the need of the hour. The core of my magic is to pass messages to the powers above. Whenever I succeed, the rest follows, shall we say, quite naturally and efficiently. But there is much I cannot see or know."

"If I may, I would like to ask you a question," intervened Lakshman rather more sharply than he had intended. "You seemed to know about my past lives in Amsterdam. In the vision granted by the Casket of the White Feather, I saw you in the white marble temple of the tortoise when I was juggling with those oranges before the queen. How is it possible that this demon mocked me as a former Avastha? Sanath, when we watched the content of the scrolls together in Amsterdam, how come you didn't warn me about being an Avastha?" Lakshman had been disturbed the whole afternoon by these inconsistencies.

"Because I didn't know, Lakshman. Only human beings could retrieve the caskets; the scrolls of Dagad Trikon were destined for the human race and you are the one who was to discover the casket in Iceland. I, of course, deduced that you were therefore completely human. I too heard that the demon greeted you as Etakir. I believe now that he was right but it implies that you saw in these visions your own story in the days of the Rock and traces of your own ancestry without recognizing it as yours.

Clearly you have become fully human. Unlike me, and unlike Aliskhan who can faintly exist in the Bardo, you no longer connect with Avastha powers; it is too far in your past. Together we saw one of your more recent past lives in the temple of the tortoise, showing Etakir struggling to regain the mastery of his senses in order to find the Gate. I realize as I talk to you now that the first landing of those Stealthstars I was looking for did not take place recently. Their arrival probably covered a few centuries, during which time they sank deeper, if I may put it like this, into the human condition. The depth of the darkness of this age has been too dense for them and for me alike. I simply failed to grasp this."

"Can you tell us where all this leads us in terms of our quest and our lives?" asked Lakshmi, as if resenting the weirdness of their situation. Sanath put his face into his hands for a brief moment, as if it would hurt them too much to hear the response; he then ran his fingers over his beard before saying thoughtfully:

"It means that I failed. It means that, for all practical purposes there cannot be an Avastha revival. From now on, it is up to human beings and their aptitude to access the Deep Way. The task of repelling evil had been originally entrusted to the Stealthstars as the returned earlier born, who in theory were equipped with higher aptitudes. Alas, they had a knack for running into all sorts of trouble. Thanatophor saw to it that they would fail. I must admit he succeeded. It now falls, for better or worse, entirely on weaker human shoulders. This is a huge challenge indeed, but there are some indications that it can be met."

At this point Joseph interrupted and almost immediately regretted the unintended tone of sarcasm that crept into his words. "Yes, please, enlighten us. I talked about it today with Lakshman and Lakshmi. We heard those demons greet some of us as former Avasthas. The whole notion sounds alien to me, yet it is also strangely familiar. I certainly do not have the aptitudes of a more evolved being but I can sense the aspirations to this dimension in me. So what are we, Sanath? Are we dangling in the air like yo-yos or stranded parachutists? Are we hanging between a Grand Scheme and a Great Schism, between spirit and matter? Are we just humans, all too human, or are we fallen Avasthas?"

"It does not really matter any longer, Joseph. You must now understand only one thing: Avasthas are the past, humanity is the present. Please remember that it is only in the present that the passage to the inner world can be secured. Even if human beings can achieve this, they are unlikely to regain the other powers of the former Avasthas such as telepathic insight, control over matter or communication with animals, but they will have conquered the greatest power: the right to cross the Gate of the Elephant."

"Then they would discover the Deep Way... " whispered Lakshman, awestruck.

"... and possibly receive the Gift," added Lakshmi hopefully, before he could finish his sentence.

"This would perhaps mean that mankind itself would finally bring an end to the Great Schism... " observed Joseph, surprised at his own conclusion.

"It would mean the Holy Grail revealed and redemption time!" concluded Ivan.

Sanath opened his mouth to respond but Laira, who came running into the room, interrupted them. "Sanath, Sanath, I have just received a message from the village back home: the oak, our great oak is dying!"

All turned towards the wizard, not quite knowing what to make of this news for the great oak was certainly the oldest tree in Europe and custodian of the casket carried by the Avastha lord with the emblem of the cross.

"So, we can access the Casket of the Cross now? It's good news, isn't it?" Lakshmi asked. Then she repeated the question more slowly and in a whisper, "Isn't it?" as she had noticed that Sanath had become quite pale.

The wizard gasped as if no air could reach his lungs. He looked all of a sudden like a shattered old man, a shadow of his normal self. They had never seen him before in such a condition. How could this be, after the defeat of the demons, after the jubilation that followed last night's fight? This was undeniably a complete contrast. The wizard muttered: "Oh no, not this, not now!"

DELIBERATIONS
IN THE HEAVENS

A nyone who loves mountains knows that they have been worshipped the world over for bringing us closer to the gods. On a clear day at the break of dawn, the sun lights up the glittering whiteness of the peaks and slowly descends in a majestic celebration of light to awaken the lower valleys. The awesome masses of ascending walls and towering domes, sprinkled with powdery snow, return its radiance. The glaciers glitter in the blue sky, in celebration of the higher clarity of the world above.

Nevertheless, mountains can also be inscrutable and shrouded in secrecy. They can hide, within thick haze, sudden gloom and whirling snowstorms. The trekker, surrounded by the opacity of a penetrating fog, may feel as if he is nearing the gates of a disconcerting and enchanted world. Like prodigious ghosts, peaks emerge briefly from passing cloud and surging mist. When it dissipates, the magnificence of the surroundings is once more revealed. Fresh brooks of pure water cascade downhill; alpine flowers offer a dazzling diversity among the chaotic array of boulders left by the latest glaciations. Larches and firs stretch towards the high slopes in a stubborn ascending march. Flower-carpeted meadows and rocks, ablaze with color, offer a glimpse of paradise and of nature's inventiveness.

Gods are reported to visit mountaintops such as Uluru in Australia, Fujiyama in Japan, Ararat in Turkey, Olympus in Greece,

Matterhorn in Switzerland, and Kailash in the western ridge of the Himalayas. The latter is reputed to be the seat of the assembly of the Gods. There, pilgrims coming from the south cross the Gurla pass and while descending the Tibetan plateau see two lakes – the Rakshas Tal, lake of the demons, and the Mansarovar, the lake of the mind. The first is often agitated while the second is ever placid, as if to indicate that serenity and peace of mind are the gates to the mountain of the Gods, the key to salvation for the pilgrim.

At the time of the battle at Jetzenstein, pilgrims to Mount Kailash noted with concern an astonishing, unusual turbulence on Rakshas Tal. To well-informed ascetics it heralded a dangerous recrudescence of demonic activity. However, to their bewilderment, all of a sudden the restlessness of Rakshas Tal ceased. They gathered on the shores of Mansarovar Lake to better interpret these signs on the day after the two demons were cast into hell. The sages reverentially gazed at the sacred mountain and in the morning sunrise beheld the formidable pyramid of Kailash, which bears the likeness of a ladder on its southern face. This ladder is believed by some to be a ladder to the heavens. Gradually, the top of the sacred mountain became surrounded by extraordinary cloud formations, which announced to the awe-struck sages and seers the convening of an extraordinary heavenly meeting. However, the human eye was unable to see the flying vehicles of the celestial beings as they converged on Kailash.

For this is where Gods and Goddesses gather on momentous occasions to ponder on the world's affairs. While they do so in other dimensions such as in the Vaikuntha, at times they also gather in their own dimension, at sites that coincide with specific geographic locations on the secret spiritual map of Mother Earth.

Thus, on the day following the epic battle with the two demons kings, the Archangels Gabriel and Michael reported to such a meeting convened on the top of Mount Kailash. It had brought together the thirty Gods in charge of the core cosmic functions, as well as divinities who sustain other aspects of life and evolution. The fearsome captain of the angelic hosts, the Archangel Michael, spoke in a tongue that was close to the Sanskrit language but not one that humans would understand. He ended his account before the heavenly assembly with these words:

"We pursued them in a fierce battle up to the very jaws of hell. As they opened to swallow them, Belzebseth turned and taunted me with vile sarcasm: 'You may think you have won, Michael, but beware, from each drop of our blood will rise a demon in our likeness; we have spread ourselves far and wide by now and you cannot reach us without killing those whom you try to protect.' These were his words. O denizens of the celestial regions, you have now heard everything that pertains to the scions of doom and we have verily reported the entire matter to you."

"I know this trick of the demons," responded a dark-bodied Goddess.

"By an evil spell, whenever a drop of blood of such a demon touches the ground, a new devil in his likeness springs forth from this spilled drop. In the ancient days, as I killed them, I would sup their blood before it reached the ground."

Gods and Goddesses expressed their appreciation for the great feat of the two archangels. Celestial bards and damsels sang the praises of their exploits. Thereafter, their deliberations in the heavens concerned the new situation.

One God summarized the situation thus: "In the emergency of the hour, Sanath the Hllidarendi threw himself in harm's way and at the mercy of heaven's gate; we were compelled by his great faith to send the Archangels to rescue him and his companions. This is an episode in the Grand Scheme that shall no doubt be remembered by the celestial minstrels. Yet if the legions of doom have been shattered, they have not been dispelled."

"This is correct, " said the God of Death grimly. " Countless times these wretched fellows have been cast into hell where my attendants keep them under careful watch. But they always manage to escape. They prepare their escape routes through the minds of the men and women they have soiled. When their influence is on the rise, they are called back to Earth by the darkened human psyches. Thus, they disappear from hell, and before we know it, they are again on Mother Earth. Nowadays it is no longer enough to kill them because, in the manner of viruses, they manage to find humans to be their hosts. Therefore, the dilemma before us today is this: shall we destroy the hosts in order to destroy them?"

At this point, Gaia, Goddess of the Earth, took the floor before the august assembly. "We have seen yet another proud deed accomplished by the great Archangels, and in so doing they gave me some respite. I am deeply grateful to them and to all of you. However, we all know that even with Belzebseth and Hangker back in hell, Thanatophor is still active. The seeds of his arch-demons have flown everywhere and found fertile soil. The Dark Riders continue to reap their harvest of doom within the human mind. I fear that the human race has given up its ancient striving for decency, kindness, integrity, and righteousness. I am afraid that the teachings imparted through the many manifestations of the primordial Daskalian over so many centuries have been lost."

The entire assembly was fully aware of the gravity of the moment, because whenever Gaia made such a plea, momentous events took place on Planet Earth. "Everything I did was for their comfort: my course in the celestial emptiness, the inclination of my axis, the rhythm and speed of my revolutions. I pushed mountains up to their appointed heights. Forests, rivers, and lakes provided humans with beauty and bounty. The sea nourished them. Each flower I produced was a song of fragrant beauty. But their rulers do not respect anything any more. Under the thick veil of ignorance woven by Thanatophor and the witches, they have become arrogant, violent, and greedy. Selfishness and vanity have become their virtues. In lust they chase love away. They do not understand that they are no longer like animals who kill without sinning; they forget they are under the Wheel of the Law. Dikayoson, the herald of the Chamber of Maat, has prepared the incriminating prosecution file. I am again buried under such a heap of sins that I cannot bear it any longer. My body has started to shiver and I do not know for how much longer I can continue to support the burden of this human race."

One of the Gods observed gloomily, "They have forgotten us. What more can we do?"

Next, the leader of the Gods who holds the thunderbolt and controls the climate rose from his golden seat. Men have given him various names such as Indra, Zeus or Jupiter. His appearance was noble and his bearing majestic. He addressed the heavenly congregation in these words. "Denizens of Amravati, city of the Gods, we have gathered on top of this sacred mountain in Goddess Gaia's hour of need to answer this question. We are duty bound to come to the rescue of Gaia. It seems that man has taken upon himself the task of destroying his own race as well as millions of species on the planet. The pollution of the earth is continuing on a grand scale: the very balance of the climate has been altered. However, if I just slightly change my stance, modify the marine currents, or raise the temperature further, it may cause a return to the glacial age for one hemisphere and widespread drought for the other. Shall we do so?"

The God of Fire stepped forward, "The Stealthstars of the House of Falkiliad were supposed to again ignite the auspicious fire of creativity and worship. Alas, this has proved impossible. They have been unable to rekindle the sacred flame because humans no longer worship the Gods but rather the fruits of their own actions. They have become lost in their selfish pursuits. Their scientists have created a civilization of machines. Consequently this race has now stored my wrath within their thermonuclear devices. This technology could fall into the hands of the new accursed breed they call terrorists. It could be unleashed by the lowest of them, at any time or place. But, of my own volition, I can also rise at Gaia's bidding. I am ready: some large areas of magma are building up close to the crust of the earth. Should I erupt through a volcanic island in the sea, that island will explode – and you know what happened last time when we destroyed Atlantis. Fire and water wrought such havoc that few remained to remember it."

"This is so," said the God of the Sea. "And I can rise as a huge tidal wave that would wash over coastal areas and penetrate inland for many miles, thus changing the face of the earth as I did at the time of the last great deluge when the humans fled to Mount Ararat for salvation. The Stealthstars of the House of Elnur no longer have access to the water of life and thus their capacity to imbibe the Deep Way has been hampered. How can they survive in the long run? Like their cousins from the other houses, they have become fully human by now. I see no help coming from that quarter."

"Likewise, the Stealthstars of the House of Eleksim cannot connect with their ancestral qualities and they no longer clearly perceive the sacred breeze on their hands," added the God of the Wind. "The very air they breathe has been corrupted. Fear has entered their hearts. They were supposed to reawaken the gentle arts of giving, sharing, and loving so that they would be prepared to receive the Gift. Alas, the scions of Eleksim have been led astray by the cultures into which they took their births. If it is so decided, I can, of course, escort the God of Death and I shall once more walk along his path in the fierce shape of whirling hurricanes. But is this really what we wish? What course shall we take?"

A large creature with the head of a proud white bull with the name of Nandi came forward. "As you know, my master, the great lord Shiva, is the holder of the moon. Should he take the moon away from the earth it would disturb its axis, and you know what this means. He can also cast the stars of the heavens down to earth with one movement of his Trishul. As I speak to you, the earth is on the flight path of a large meteorite. It is still very far away but it is coming. My master has yet to decide whether or not there should be an impact. If this collision takes place in the sea, it will wipe out the neighboring continents. If it takes place on land, the clouds of dust will block the rays of the sun for many years." He turned towards the Sun God adding, "You are lord of light, the father of life on Planet Earth; without you all shall perish. If your radiant face is withdrawn, it shall mean a mass extinction event. Most living species shall vanish. This world we cherished, nurtured, and protected would disappear. Gaia would have to wait for countless millennia for life to emerge from the dust covering her surface."

A long and profound silence settled in. All hearts were heavy. Gods and Goddesses were torn between the need to come to the rescue of Gaia and the prospect of terrible destruction. All their benevolent work of patiently assisting the Emerald King to bring evolution to its present stage would come to nothing.

It was the turn of a three-headed God to stand up. He was the original epistemic Daskalian who had sent himself to incarnate as the primordial teacher to instruct mankind in many forms, in many places, and at many times. In the Chamber of Maat the companions had witnessed the assembly of the personalities representing his successive incarnations. He addressed the assembly thus:

"When I came as Confucius, I was called the master of ten thousand generations. I taught them about the virtue of service, the beauty of serenity, good families, just government, and peaceful nations. As my faithful Dikayoson will tell you, humans have lost the sense of morality that was their shield and their protection. What did they retain from my teachings? What indeed did they retain? I have been stabbed as Zarathustra and forced to drink poison as

Socrates. In the beginning of this twentieth century, I begged for my food as the Nath of Shirdi, just to see false prophets come after me to claim my name and my followers. Oh yes, believe me, citizens of the heavens, I know about the city of man.

Nonetheless, I say let us take heart because in the Grand Scheme even evil finds its appointed niche of usefulness. Such is the mastery of the play. Without facing some crises and challenges, mankind cannot rise. It is in coming to terms with the difficulties of their existence that men and women finally face up to the dark forces. Then, they gradually rise in their understanding and they purify their emotions. Even in this Iron Age some people are still willing and desirous to ascend. We should not give up on them at this crucial hour. Many who were tainted by the Dark Riders sincerely wish they could regain the lost paradise of innocence. My wish is still that we should grant it to them."

"Of course, the words of the primordial master are true." The handsome God who now took the floor was both regal and graceful in his bearing. His beauty was such that a human being could not so much as look at him, and the few who were blessed by recognizing him over the millennia cried in ecstasy. At times his skin was a shiny light blue shade, or, depending on his mood, he would assume the hue of deep lavender. He, the Lord Krishna, manifesting the form of the Emerald King known as the Sower, now wore a peacock feather in his hair. He continued:

"We want to help human beings, but will they let us help them? You heard the words of the leader of the Gods. The balance of nature on earth has become precarious and Indra may not succeed in maintaining it. You heard the words of the God of Death: he understands the plan of Thanatophor well. What shall we do? As you know, the cardinal rule of the Grand Scheme is that we cannot transgress human freedom, and I, the Sower who leads this play, shall abide by the rule I created.

I did not mind the attempts of the Avasthas to return to earth to save Gaia from evil through their higher powers. Nonetheless, it is hard for any race to succeed outside the boundaries of its own time, and this age is the age of man. This is why the Avasthas gradually became human and we should not deplore this. It is not through higher powers that man will rise, but through the exercise of his right to choose. Freedom is the greatest power of human beings. It also becomes their greatest bane as they transgress the border between freedom and license. We must all seek guidance from the master of this mountain, who holds the drum of destiny in one hand and bestows either blissful existence or destruction. He alone can advise us." The Gods and Goddesses knew that the Sower was the operator of the Grand Scheme and they all heeded him. There was nothing to add and the Gods and Goddesses fell silent.

At this moment a commotion occurred. The Gods and Goddesses rose to their feet as the Master of Mount Kailash suddenly materialized in his form as the great Shiva on the tiger hide. The bull Nandi stepped forward to officiate as Chief of Protocol for the ceremony. His voice was deep and melodious and he recited an auspicious greeting, looking with adulation to his master, while chanting:

"Adoration to him who sits on the tiger skin, who wears matted hair, and who is the preceptor of all; Hail to the imperishable soul of the cosmos and of all existence; Obeisance to the ocean of compassion; Obeisance to him who is the field of forgiveness; Obeisance to the Lord who occupies the lotus of the heart; Obeisance to the Lord of the nectar; Obeisance to the well-wisher of the universe; Obeisance to the abode of most excellent happiness; Obeisance to the three-eyed one; Obeisance to the owner of the trident; Obeisance to him of terrible exploits, the fierce destroyer; May He, the origin of the Self, be merciful to all beings."

As a snowstorm whirled around them, the Immortals expressed their dilemma and respectfully sought guidance. Goddess Uma, the consort of the Lord with the matted hair, approached him and said softly, "My Lord, human beings pine because of their loneliness. They are vulnerable to the ploy of their enemy because they do not know how to love. Looking for love they throw themselves into despair, deeper into the web of illusions where the six Dark Riders catch them. Would you, my gracious Lord, bless them that they may encounter true love?"

"O daughter of the King of the mountains, true love belongs to the truth of their innermost being. By discovering their own truth and the glory inside they will also know true love. They must enter into the Deep Way to savor the fullness of love. Otherwise, they will continue to taste the bitter flavors of attachment and dependency, possessiveness and jealousy or suffer from love that is not mutual. Nevertheless, yes, I shall bless them that they may reach this state they have sought for ages."

The Lord of Kailash then addressed the assembly. "Verily, the horse of the day of fate is neighing and this time will itself be trampled under the hooves of red fury. For the white rider is coming and carries with him the eleven destructive powers that are the burning light of our combined wrath. We must bring solace to Gaia and to all of you, the Immortals. This is a moment when the future is unknown and when mankind, in its pride, stumbles on the border of the abyss. Humans will have to face themselves, face their doom at this hour, which is late indeed. All the same, it is so typical of the demons' foolish style that they constantly overestimate their own smartness. By penetrating the human brain, they thought they would surely defeat the Gods who cannot do the same. Little do they realize that divinity itself was long ago buried deep within human beings. But there is even more. My dear, please explain our secret to this august assembly."

"O Lord, you are existence and the giver of life. It is you who are the source of the flow of joy that is called Shivananda Lahari.

You contain the ocean of love and compassion. And when this ocean flowed from you, I arose. Nine times I manifested on this earth to fight the demons and to save my children from the effects of negativity, protecting them like a tigress protects her cubs. Nine cycles of time, as nine months in the womb, I kept them under my protection for them to mature. I saved them in the past for this day, the day of revelation, so that they might enter a new realm of God's magic and drink the cup of nectar. I am the beginning of this world and its mother and a mother wants the best for her offspring. If you know the mother, accordingly, you will know the children."

At that moment powerful lights illuminated the clouds around Kailash and thunder echoed against the wall of the sacred mountain in a deep and musical rumbling. The wind blew the snow around the mountaintop in sweeping waves and fashioned whirling patterns of angelic shapes. Each snowflake that fell on the divine assembly contained in its crystal geometric shapes that corresponded to the axioms of the Law of Maat. The divine assembly was transfixed in this moment of reckoning.

The primeval Goddess continued. "O Immortals, I am the power of existence, the mother of this universe. The five elements came from my own being. I took many forms and expressed many powers but I am beyond all of them, for I am the one who is the generator of power, the complete integrated form from whence all of you received your energy. I am verily the one who supports you all. In freedom, I allowed the children of Adam and Eve to grow and to rise in their quest. Assisted by the Emerald King and the Daskalian master I provided them with guidance and instructors who came time and again to tell them about the Law of Maat and the teachings of divine love.

Humans do not know how hard they have struggled through all their many lifetimes to evolve to the point where they can now receive the Gift. They do not know that they contain within themselves the wheels of energy that stores the powers of the Gods Nor do they know that this was all planned long before they walked on the earth, so that on the day of blessings, the offering and acceptance of the Gift would come together in the new-found unity of God and creature. But, today they are lost, dragged down, tempted, and dominated by negative forces. Nobody can meditate or feel good inside. They can neither neutralize their bad habits nor find out what is wrong with them and hence they regress.

However, a mother's love is a tremendous power, so alert and so kind. It artfully teaches children so that they naturally absorb knowledge. This is what the Deep Way is going to reveal to man: the spontaneous absorption of the union with the divine realm. My action is intricate, balanced, and efficient. Through the power of penetration, I know how devils work in human minds. Their identity is captured in their ego; they cannot grow to see the point of view of others, thus creating quarrels, divisions, and conflicts. But there is a way out.

I am not a purposeless personality. I did not nurture this world to hand it over to the creatures of evil. I took steps to make sure that the plots of the demons would not foil the heroic journey of mankind toward the deeper truth. Divinity was deposited within human beings, yes, my Lord, this is true, and the mystic seers, the greatest saints, and a few scholars know this truth.

Yet, what very few know is that the talisman of resurrection, the triggering mechanism for this divinity to manifest has also been hidden in man. This is the gift of the mother. The time has come. After the age of the barbarians, gentleness shall return. Redemption shall bring to fruition the quest for the Tree of the Knowledge of Good and Evil that our daughter Eve began. Indeed, this is why the High Lady of the Rock has concealed the nesting place of her own sacred triangle within each man and woman, well beyond the reach of Thanatophor.

Unknowingly, the sons and daughters of Adam and Eve carry within themselves the Angkura power, the seeds of the world's full renewal. This mighty seed will awaken the wheels of illumination that the great houses of the Avasthas were serving in the days long gone by. These subtle centers are still dormant within them, delicately placed along the spine, waiting to manifest God's magic. It is in the midst of great tribulations and at the darkest hour, as the white rider is mounting his fateful horse, that the beacon of divine light shall be lit. In the past, humans had to put their trust in the divine power. Now, by my love and by the force of my willpower, they shall experience it for themselves."

The Sower and the Immortals smiled in grateful contentment as they heard these words of benediction. This was a moment of jubilation. They bowed to the Mother of the universe, having instantly absorbed the full meaning of her words with awe and wonder. Exquisitely scented flowers fell as if from nowhere on the heavenly assembly, mixed with snowflakes of multifarious geometric shapes that shone with myriads of lights. It was indeed a tremendous announcement that was made on the day of this heavenly assembly on Mount Kailash. This is how the Immortals came to know that the Gift for which Gods and demons had fought so hard in the ancient world would also be available to the human beings of the modern times, lost as they may be, and that, verily, unknown to all, a prepared device had already been hidden within them to this effect.

THE TRICOLOR LILY
OF ANORHAD

The deities on Mount Kailash were carefully weighing the issues on the scales of fate, which were oscillating between redemption and destruction. At that very moment, the wizard's Council had gathered for a second time in the hall of the knights at Jetzenstein castle. They were in a state of alarm for they had not expected the Hllidarendi to react so dramatically to the news of the demise of the sacred oak in Byelorussia. After all, Sanath had remained impassive when confronting the most fearsome demons and he always seemed poised and in total control. Laira, Ivan, and Philip were also deeply moved by the news, which was an understandable reaction. After all, they had first met and then grown up under the great oak, and its magic bound them to the wizard. It had protected them in knotting the threads of their common destiny. Laira helped Sanath to an armchair. He asked, "Is it dying or is it dead? How much time do we have?"

"I asked the same question: as you know, our folks no longer live in the forest. I've asked them to send someone to check again. I am not sure but we may have one season left, perhaps two."

They stood around him waiting for the wizard to say something. He finally spoke with anguish in his voice, "The killing of the demons gave us a great respite but it is not enough to save this age, for Hangker and Belzebseth have almost completed their sinister work. I knew that this moment was imminent, yet I always feared its arrival because very few of the caskets have been found, nor have we located the Gate of the Elephant – and now the sacred oak is dying. Oh my Lord, it is too early. It is too soon. We are not ready. What shall we do? What will happen? My Lord, have mercy."

A silence settled on the group and somehow its depth was regenerative, even healing. Lakshmi, often the bravest and certainly always curious, was the first to break the silence. "Master, who is the Lord you are calling on? Has the Emerald King awakened? Did he call Prince Karudas and is he coming?"

Sanath looked at the young woman and said gravely, "Child, don't you see? The symbol of the cross speaks of He who came to die on it. You must first die in order to resurrect. Christ died for all of us, two thousand years ago, to open the Gate. But did they understand him, those who now use his name? And now the great oak is dying too. Do you understand? Death shall come now before this age resurrects. Resurrection comes after death. The death of the great oak will signal that he may manifest again, he may return, He himself, who died on the cross and resurrected, he may return. How can we open the casket if we are not ready?" Sanath put his head in his hands. Only Laira, Ivan, and Philip seemed to share the wizard's emotions. Lakshman and Joseph kept silent, watching attentively. Lakshmi ventured once more, "Surely, Master, it should be a wonderful thing if he returns? He is among the greatest ones, the very Son of Adivatar."

"Precisely," replied Sanath, who did not seem disturbed by Lakshmi's questions. "And we should be ready for such a return. Only then could we rejoice. Can we receive a king in a street where sewage is flowing? For this much is certain: he is coming as a king. No cross this time, no, no, no. This is why the eternal Daskalians mandated the Aulyas to spread the Deep Way, but they have failed. This is why the Order of the Hllidarendi was created to pass on the secret of pure knowledge. Yet, we could not. We should be ready.

The protocol of this universe is also the protocol of his light. If he comes in his own light, all impurities will be burned. The sire of Anorhad brought the Casket of the Cross to Russia. Among the Avasthas only the Anorhadans could approach his light, for they were meek and humble as only the greatest lords must be. For he is the sacred one and his hour is of untold might. Humility will then be our only safety, our only protection. Ivan, please, tell them."

Ivan left the room and went to the splendid circular baroque library in the Falkenlust tower of the castle. He returned with a version of the Bible, which was a revision of the King James Version published in 1611 AD, based on the consonantal Hebrew and Aramaic texts and a review of the Greek manuscripts of the early Christian era. He searched for a while, then cleared his throat and read.

"Lecture of the *Book of Revelation* to John 19.11: Then I saw heaven opened, and behold, a white horse. He who sat upon it is called Faithful and True, and in righteousness, he judges and makes war. His eyes are like a flame of fire, and on his head are many diadems; and he has a name inscribed which no one knows but himself. He is clad in a robe dipped in blood, and the name by which he is called is The Word of God. And the armies of heaven, arrayed in white linen, white and pure, followed him on white horses. From his mouth issues a sharp sword with which to smite the nations, and he will rule them with a rod of iron; he will tread the wine press of the fury of the wrath of God the Almighty. On his robe and on his thigh he has a name inscribed, King of kings and Lord of lords."

Ivan stopped reading. What they had just heard was quite unexpected. Sanath responded to their baffled glances and unspoken questions, "This is the Apocalypse of John, himself an Aulya. He fled to Patmos when Peter and Paul took over the Church. It is all symbolic language, of course, and no one fully knows what to make of it. The basileus of Byzantium and the emperor of the Holy Empire in Germany dwelt on it, as do the televangelists of today. They all attempted their own interpretations. Fundamentalist Christian sects proselytize and convert to meet the deadline but it will not make a difference. He will recognize as his people only those who cross the Gate."

"What about the non-Christians?" asked Lakshmi, concerned.

"They wait like the Christians do. What you heard is the Christian version of a universal story. The Hindus wait for the Lord Kalki mounted on a white horse; the Buddhists wait for Maitreya to liberate them; the Jews still await the Messiah; the Muslims wait for the Mahdi, the twelfth Imam. It is one thing to wait, another thing to be prepared."

"I don't know about a white rider, but if this is an allegory for destruction, the scenarios are ready." This time it was Tracy's turn to intervene. Her knowledge of the state of the Oikos Project made her painfully aware that the state of preparedness of societies to any major change was definitely not what it should be.

"I remember an interview I heard once on the BBC with Professor James Lovelock. He said we are now at war with the earth itself; thus, we are Gaia's target now. He said the earth functions as a single organism, which maintains the conditions necessary for its survival. Our planet attempts to restore its equilibrium. It has been upset by the destruction of natural habitats. Functioning eco-systems, he says, are necessary for planetary climate and chemistry. In attempting to restore its balance, Gaia may wipe out human civilization as we know it. If, as Master Sanath seems to suggest, the white rider is master of nature's processes, this symbolic text may announce options for disasters that the Oikos Project is familiar with. Please, Sanath, does it mean the professor is right? I mean, are doomed?"

Sanath composed himself. His countenance changed. He closed his eyes and whispered slowly, "No, not quite, not yet. I do not know the path or the hour of the rider of the Apocalypse. Yet, there is one way, there is still hope." He turned towards Ivan. "Please, my dear Ivan, read again about the woman clothed with the sun." Ivan turned a few pages, found the passage, and began reading again.

"*The Book of Revelation* 1 2.1: And a great portent appeared in heaven, a woman clothed with the sun, with the moon under her feet, and on her head a crown of twelve stars; she was with child and she cried out in her pangs of birth, in anguish for delivery. And another portent appeared in heaven; behold, a great red dragon, with seven heads and ten horns, and seven diadems upon his heads. His tail swept down a third of the stars of heaven, and cast them to the earth. And the dragon stood before the woman who was about to bear a child, that he might devour her child when she brought it forth; she brought forth a male child, one who is to rule all the nations with a rod of iron, but her child was caught up to God and to his throne and the woman fled into the wilderness, where she had a place prepared by God."

Lakshmi felt a surge of adrenaline. The secret at the core of the Dagad Trikon legend was embedded in the sacred nature of femininity. It is about archetypal womanhood, pointing to the High Lady of the Rock. The secret. She did not know how to express these intuitions and mumbled suddenly, "Again the woman, the Goddess, the birth? This is it." She turned to Sanath. "Respected Master, I saw... I felt something in the Basin of Vaikuntha; I was born again. My experience within the sari of the Goddess must have something to do with this. But it was not like this. It was just love. All enveloping love."

"Whose birth it is anyway?" asked Joseph. As a former priest, he was very familiar with these texts but he had never quite grasped their full meaning. A confidant of Ivan, he had spent the days in Jetzenstein catching up with him on the Delphi adventure and the aftermath of the opening of the Casket of the Wheel.

"It is not the birth of a man. It is the birth of a race." Sanath went on, "I must now explain everything to you, well, almost everything that I know. But it will take some time. First things first. Avasthas were always fresh and young and yet so sublime and dignified. This is because the principle of innocence, upheld by the house of Kalabham, was awakened in all of them. This power of innocence permeates everything. It is meant to blossom further through the activation of the Deep Way. The Deep Way reveals a secret spot at the root of the body, a psychosomatic center connected to the elephant God. It is invisible to science and medicine for it is part of a subtler body hidden within the physical body. As the eternal child, the elephant God is the one who gives permission to walk through the gate. Purity emitted from this center is the fragrance within the flower, the honey that attracts the bees. It is the essence of creation and gives a spontaneous sense of morality.

This subtle center acts as a magnet, connected to Mother Earth, which prevents the attention from oscillating this way and that way and thence, into the nets of the witches. The magnet keeps the attention adjusted constantly to point towards the inner Spirit, the reflection of Adivatar inside, which is of the nature of the nectar."

"So, finally, is this the secret knowledge?" asked Joseph. "The knowledge of these mysterious inner centers that some Knights of the Temple are reported to have brought back from Asia when they returned from the Crusades? This is why they were brutally tortured and burned on the pyre by the church and the king of France who wanted their secrets." Sanath nodded and continued.

"Precisely," he said. "Some knights exposed to contacts with Asia had indeed heard about it, but their knowledge was limited. This is not a reality that can be attained on a physical level. Lakshman and Lakshmi realized that the rock in Delphi, the navel of the universe through which you found the road to Vaikuntha, was not the real gate – although certainly the passage in the rock of the Sybille prophetess you borrowed to reach the Chamber of Maat is also under the control of the elephant God. Likewise, the temples they visited in India emitted the Sao Iambu vibrations, but again, they did not provide the hidden access. I need to talk to you about this now. The Blessed Lady of the Gundaldhar Fault left a clue before leaving – do you remember what she said, Lakshman Kharadvansin?"

"Yes, I noted it down in Iceland. She said we needed to find the Gate of the Elephant to find again the passage between the inner and the outer worlds that was lost at the time of the Great Schism, many thousands of years ago."

"That's the same question Erilie asked the High Lady before she vanished. Perhaps that's why I already tried to follow this lead," intervened Lakshmi. "Master, are you really going to reveal where it is? We have an elephant God in India, you know. We call him Lord Ganesha. As you say, we visited most of his temples in Maharashtra where he is most worshipped, but couldn't find any such secret gate or passage."

"The God you mention gave his life in the defense of his mother's doorstep. The God I talk about gave his life on Golgotha in obedience to his father. Both represent the same principle of the primordial son who sacrifices himself so that all may resurrect. We must search in this direction."

Joseph interrupted. "Excuse me, sir, but we have heard similar stuff in our churches and temples for centuries and it didn't make much difference, if we believe what we see around us and the sorry state the world is in today. At the same time we have known since the Middle Ages about the enemies of the soul. I read treatises in Latin on the subject. The real question is how to overcome these enemies, how to resurrect. I mean, not in theory, not by giving sermons about it, but in reality, the reality of our mind, flesh, and blood. I became a priest because I wanted to find the answer and I quit the priesthood because I still wanted to find the answer. So please, Master, lead us to the door and help us to cross it. No more theory, and with all due respect to this Avastha stuff, no more visions. Please, Master, lead us to this door, all of us, as we are, here and now. And, I have a last question I must ask: I understand the six Dark Riders are the deadly sins – lust, anger, greed, attachment, jealousy, and vanity – but in the Western tradition we always speak of seven deadly sins. Where is the seventh Dark Rider and why can't we see him?"

Joseph's intervention was unexpected and abrupt but these were issues that had been bothering him for a very long time. Tracy was worried that he might have sounded disrespectful, but Sanath smiled and replied, "Joseph you are a true seeker. It was said 'Ask and it shall be given.' I can try to lead your understanding close to this door. That will be a first, useful step. I cannot lead you to the door itself, nor can I make or help you cross it. Listen now to the tale of the Hllidarendi. I did not intend to reveal these things. It was for you to discover. But the death of the sacred oak is changing the timing of the Dagad Trikon quest. I now have to rush.

The Gate of the Elephant consists of two portals.

The first is under the control of the elephant God himself and the second is under the control of the Christ. There is a narrow bridge between the portals, a passage within the blessed flute that Lakshman experienced in the Casket of the White Feather. This passage can only be crossed on horseback. A human being can only cross that bridge and reach the blessed Gate to the inner world if his horse is white. That horse, Joseph, is your own mind.

The second portal is constituted by the center of a cross, which is a spot within our brain. This center regulates the passage between the channels of the blue and yellow areas covering the two hemispheres of our brain as we develop into adults.

The role of the Dark Riders is to catch up with the horse before it reaches the gate and turn its coat a darker shade, so that should its rider finally cross the passage and find the gate, access will be denied. There is no use finding the gate if you cannot cross through it."

"Are we now able to pass the gate, I mean, after the defeat of the demons, shouldn't we be able to?" asked Lothar.

"Not yet. Last night's victory was a necessary condition but it's not, in itself, sufficient. The Archangels defeated the archdemons and threw them back into hell but the devils have sown their multiple seeds across the entire human race. Thus, in some perverse way, their power is still multiplying even as they have been cast into the jail of the infernos where they belong. The cavalry of Thanatophor knows its job very well and is as yet undefeated."

"Why don't the great angels stop them?" was Michael's question.

"Because they ride in our brains, they ride the minds of human beings. To destroy them would mean destroying the human race. See how they operate – their foul work is going on as I speak. Belzebseth favors lust in the blue area, Hangker works through anger in the yellow area. Both join into greed, which itself is some kind of combination of lust and anger: it claims satisfaction for oneself and destruction for others that get in their way. Now we must understand how the Riders operate and this will also answer your question about the seventh Rider.

The seventh Dark Rider is invisible because he is everywhere; he permeates all the other sins: in a single word, he is Pride, the preferred sin of Thanatophor.

In pride, the human being looks after himself for his own ends. Pride brings a ravenous appetite for power, the ultimate temptation. Pride is within lust, when it is but a predatory claim for pleasure to bring instant gratification. It is within anger, which fuels aggression and swells into hate. Pride is within greed and attachment, which again aims at selfish possessiveness. It is within jealousy, which denies the achievements of others, and pride blossoms in the idiocy of vanity.

Pride is the seventh Rider: egocentric contentment. It denies oneness with the whole, which is the very purpose of the Deep Way. Pride wants to create its own arbitrary and parallel world, the world of the ego. The seventh Rider, like the six others, rides against true love."

In a few words, Sanath had simplified and finally revealed the modus operandi of the Darkness. The assembly remained silent while the words of the wizard sank in. After a while, Michael broke the silence and his words, born of his concern for his fellow human beings, sounded somewhat like a confrontation, a surprising challenge from the mouth of the youngest brother.

"Master, please tell us your own thoughts about this plight, for these sins are, to a degree, in each one of us and I wonder what hope is left when I hear you speaking like this."

Sanath responded with genuine compassion. "To err is human, to forgive is divine. Of course, these traits are within human beings. This is normal, it belongs to their condition. We all have weaknesses but it is best to be aware of them. Good human beings contain in their minds the poison of the Riders in very small doses; it then works like homeopathy as their immune system combats the poison. The horse is beige perhaps, almost white. Most humans struggle with enemies in one way or another, but either way they get on with their lives. A man or a woman with self-respect keeps them under some sort of control. The horses are gray perhaps, not yet dark. It is when addiction sets in that the horses turn black. Then Darkness is unchallenged and tries to introduce those psychic compulsion viruses, the PCV entities. The Darkness attacks the average man when the Dark Riders manage to create compulsive brain patterns. Evil breeds through compulsion and addiction, destroying the innate freedom of the Spirit. Belzebeth's work is mostly to cast a tight web of dependency.

Hangker is mostly interested in dictators, false prophets and corrupt rulers whose potential for inflicting collective damage and pain is greater. With the murder of Prime Minister Rabin, for example, he launched a grand plot of crisis, blood, and fire fused with a strong alloy: religious conflicts, economic exploitation, the politics of oil, and finally, terrorism. Hangker wants it to spread slowly from the holy city of Jerusalem to engulf the whole world."

"So, before fixing the problems of the world we need to fix our own," said Joseph. "How can we defeat the Riders? If there is a way, most respected Sanath, please speak now."

"Very well then. This is the symbol of the Gate," said Sanath solemnly, pointing an imperious finger at one of the crests hanging on the wall of the Rittersaal.

"Behold the tricolor lily of Anorhad, the symbol of the second portal of the gate. The blue petal of the lily represents our emotions, the yellow petal our thoughts. These bombard us constantly from the areas of the past and the future. The eternal teaching of the Daskalians, the true masters, is to advance on the central channel of equilibrium, the white petal. Lao Tse, Confucius, Socrates, Mohammed or Guru Nanak all talked about this so that we may access the white petal that springs upwards, the area of the present moment, between thoughts and emotions. The white petal is the path that crosses the gate for, as you see, the blue and yellow petals recoil backwards. It means that those trying to ascend these channels cannot progress farther, they cannot cross the narrow gate.

The white channel is safe: the Riders cannot find the central area; they can only ride our thoughts or our emotions and turn them to darkness. To achieve this, they usually ride together. Let me give you just one simple example.

Two brothers lived in a small village; they were very good neighbors and friends. One had a son who was talented and good-looking, the other one had a son who was not so favored by nature. The first one was a good child but somewhat vain because of his talents and good looks. Here appears the Rider of Vanity. The boys were close friends in childhood but as the second child grew up he became progressively more jealous of the first. But then, galloping along came another Rider: Jealousy. The second boy now made false accusations and complained about the first boy to his mother, who began to see her nephew through her son's eyes. Here comes another Rider: Attachment. Because of the possessiveness and the over-protective attitude of this woman towards her own child, she misjudges the character of the first child. She starts picking on her nephew and becomes increasingly nasty: the Rider of Anger joins the herd. The squadron of Dark Riders is about to break the friendship between two otherwise excellent and united families because the parents of the first child resent the unjust treatment inflicted on their son by his aunt."

Tracy intervened at this point. "If I may, Master Sanath, I would mention a case that is better known. Lately we watched a documentary on the life of H.R.H. Diana, Princess of Wales. It is a heartbreaking story. Her sudden death in a car crash in Paris as she was fleeing paparazzi is so symbolic of this tragedy that it led to an unprecedented worldwide outpouring of grief. The entire British nation felt such compassion for her. Consider the facts: her husband, Prince Charles, was cheating on her with his long-time mistress, Camilla. Initially, it was he who was entirely in the wrong. But she became so jealous and angry that she became completely unstable. She sought revenge and from there, reacting to her own feelings, she made one mistake after another – competing for the attention of the media, picking up lovers, falling deeper into her fear of the British Royal Family and of loneliness. If only she could have forgiven him, she would truly have been and stayed the Queen of Hearts she aspired to be for Britain. In this case the prince made the initial mistake, the princess reacted, and all suffered. How to stop this, how to break the vicious cycle?"

"You are absolutely right, Tracy. I was coming to that," pursued Sanath. "You have just provided the answer. The blessed lily of Anorhad, as I said, contains a miniature cross. The cross contains a weapon in its center: it is the white hole of forgiveness. Listen attentively.

If the white hole at the core of the lily makes it bloom and open, the lily can easily swallow any foul Rider, such as jealousy or resentment, which are forms of anger. If, in my example, the first child could forgive his aunt, her anger will be ineffective and the friendship between the families will not be spoiled. If Princess Diana could have forgiven her husband, she would have occupied the moral high ground and enjoyed tremendous regard from everybody for the rest of her life. Of course forgiveness is not compromise, but it is liberation.

This white hole absorbs the destructive sequences of causality that spring forth under the hooves of the Riders; it reduces their negative impact and minimizes the damage inflicted. If human beings could forgive, the plans of Thanatophor could not progress as they do through chain reactions."

Joseph thought aloud: "The deaths of Sadat and Rabin that so upset the Middle East would not be in vain for this is what they died for: forgiveness between nations. Peace would come at last to Jerusalem. Africans and black Americans would be freed from the burden and memories of past injustices: the load of slavery and colonialism. Yes, it would work for a new world. But how to forgive?"

The assembly was perplexed by the unexpected explanation from the wizard and the implications Joseph had drawn from it. No one suspected forgiveness to be so powerful a weapon. After some time, Lakshmi broke the silence. "Indeed, Master, in my country Mahatma Gandhi freed us from the British colonial power through his non-violence movement, which was a form of forgiveness. But this does not always work. How to confront violence with forgiveness? Violence will win the day if it is not opposed."

"There are cases, yes, where violence must be matched by force. Yet the power of forgiveness is much more subtle. The one who cannot forgive is imprisoned by his pain and resentment. Forgiveness is an act of freedom. And I mean also, of course, forgiving ourselves for the mistakes we make.

If a man who has been initiated in the Deep Way can forgive another who attacked him, forgiveness deploys even greater effects. Being forgiven by the victim, the man who committed the aggression or the injustice is exposed to the justice of the divine power that takes over. Retribution may come to the aggressor in ways that are not expected, but it will come. In the last analysis, forgiveness activates the Law of Maat. He who died on the cross, the son of Adivatar, is indeed the master of the Gate of the Elephant because he opened its second portal through the formidable power of his own forgiveness. Can you imagine, he forgave his own crucifixion, forgiving those who crucified him?"

"But... but," stuttered Joseph, who had spent many sterile years in a college of theology dwelling on such subjects as the meaning of the crucifixion. "It did not work, because he came two thousand years ago and we are still in a mess."

"It did not work because we did not follow him," replied Sanath sternly. "He forgave those responsible for this ignominious injustice. In so doing, he opened the lily of Anorhad in all our foreheads. This spot in our brain is very tiny, a thin passage between the pituitary and pineal bodies. The gate is called the gate of the Elephant because the child god Ganesha that Lakshmi worships defends the first portal of the gate at the root of your body. The child God is within Christ. He is the same as the Christ who died to open the second portal of the Gate for us. He is the child, you understand, the eternal child, and remember what he told us?

He warned us to be like children in order to enter into the kingdom of heaven. We can cross the gate if we can follow their example. Real children are innocent. How many of us can say the same?"

Joseph was opening his mouth to speak again, but Tracy was faster. "Sanath, we respect your teachings but now, I must confess, I am completely lost. What does this mean? How can we become a child again? We are adults and quite complicated." Lakshman nodded in approval. Sanath turned to Lakshmi and said, "Explain to them."

Lakshmi was somewhat hesitant at first, as she did not know what to say, but the words came by themselves. "In the Basin of Vaikuntha, when the Goddess took me in the folds of her sari, I became a child again, completely innocent, pure, resting in the presence of joy, and in the joy of presence, born again, resting in the present. Is this what you mean, Sanath?"

Joseph, who was still carrying the frustration of years of vain theological speculations, continued, "All right, Lakshmi, but exactly how are we to be born again? This was Nicodemus' question to Jesus. You had this experience through a weird and dreamy astral trip. We cannot follow you there, and in any case, you're back to square one anyway. So, what should we do? Jump into a Baptist swimming pool or sing Easter hymns and pretend to be born again?"

This time the Hllidarendi, ignoring Joseph, spoke again. "Proximity to the Goddess gives you the first inkling of essential joy. It is the mother that creates the child. Amazing that we forget, isn't it? Under the influence of their priests, the great religions of the Middle East became amnesic about the Goddess, the sacred Womanhood. The Avasthas saw a secret form as the Lady of the Rock. Yet she has other forms, as John the Aulya could see.

Hear now the meaning of the second prophecy of the Book of Revelation that Ivan read to us. It was announced that the woman clad in the sun, standing on the moon, was to give birth to a child. That child is the divine child within each of us, the restoration of our innocence. Then this child is also the fusion of all of us into one collective consciousness, one new race. This awaits all those who will be touched by her redeeming grace. Thus, the gate will be opened within each of us, will be crossed within each of us. The passage between the Outer and the Inner Worlds will be found again in each of us. The Deep Way will announce the higher civilization of the restored unity."

Ivan intervened, saying, "Thanatophor wants to prevent this and he knows his job well. He rules modernity. Just one example, and forgive me for being so blunt: with many millions of human beings logging on each day to view pornography on the Web, which is, by the way, in this context, an appropriate name for the internet, including even monks in monasteries, how can the human attention turn to a subtler and purer reality? How can the horse of the mind become white? How can the attention turn towards the Deep Way? The devil wants to devour the child and, as a matter of fact, he is quite modern in his approach."

"He has not quite succeeded yet," replied Sanath with great firmness and sudden majesty, "for the Highest One has multiplied in myriads of fragments known as the universe and, in the last instance, all of us, lost in this universe, also belong to Him. Why shouldn't some of these fragments, those who seek the inner truth, merge again back into his Oneness? What came out of unity can return to it: *e pluribus unum*. The Deep Way, my friends, is nothing but the way of the return."

The subject so moved Sanath that tears glistened in his eyes and he said once again, forcefully, "It is the mother who creates the child. When the mother will wash and cleanse the child, innocence will be restored. The gate will be crossed, all these brains purified in the flow of grace, all these horses will turn white and these horses will fuse into one and this is the horse that John the Aulya saw in the heavens."

A silence settled over the room. Sanath's audience was struggling to grasp the implication of his words. Ivan asked shyly, "Why didn't you tell us this before, Sanath? In our village you never explained the meaning of the casket buried under the oak in such detail."

"I speak at this time because the sacred oak is dying. I greatly fear that the dying oak brings tidings of the white rider of destruction; yet, it also announces that the tricolor lily of Anorhad will start opening: resurrection will now come to us, as the Goddess clad with the sun and standing on the moon will succeed and manifest the new birth of the divine child within."

"Yet how does forgiveness of a wrongdoing lead to its punishment? I don't understand," thought Joseph, who had kept this question in his head. Sanath answered aloud:

"As for the relationship between forgiveness and punishment, let me repeat: it is quite simple. If a follower of the Deep Way forgives a wrongdoing, it means he renounces the punishment of the wrongdoer. As a first step, the white hole in the sacred lily absorbs and thus destroys the chain reaction of negativity. As a second step, and this is the answer to your question, a call is placed to the higher power. This connection ensures retribution and justice. Swift or slow, justice shall come."

Joseph asked incredulously, "Do you mean that if we give up resentment and renounce taking revenge, the heavens will do it for us?"

"Provided you are connected through the Deep Way," Sanath smiled. "Yes, it shall be so. Crimes, violence, and aggression will be contained or punished without the need for the victims to turn to violence themselves. Thus, they will avoid drinking the inebriating wine of the cup of hate and revenge. We should seek this connection through which all problems can be solved. Indeed, the time has come for me to reveal the higher world of the Gods. Now listen to this new twist for no one knows about this.

There is an essential aspect of Adivatar, sublime and awesome, beyond all description. It represents both existence and destruction. The proud and gracious figure of this God, with matted hair, stands before the entrance of the fortress of Elnelok." Sanath turned to the cousins and to Ivan and said, "You may remember that he carries a trident as an attribute. This weapon is called the Trishul; the trident is meant to punish wrongdoers. Although the Lord of the Trishul is forgiveness itself, he is well capable of destruction, especially when he comes to the help of innocent victims who are able to forgive, though they suffer at the hands of evildoers. It is at this point that the lily turns into the trident. This simply means that the task of sanctioning the Law of Maat, through the punishment of the wrongdoer, is activated when the lily within the head blooms into forgiveness."

Tracy experienced a moment of eureka, one of those rare moments of insight that remain with someone for the rest of their lives, a vision of how peace and justice could coexist in this world. She felt a surge of confidence and hope and exclaimed: "Yes, that would be beautiful! People would not need to harbor bitter feelings such as sour frustrations, revenge or resentment, and yet, you say, somehow justice would be done. I wish Jonathan were here to hear this. He had been so badly treated by our father that he still hurts a lot. Deep down, he can't forgive. I am glad he is arriving tomorrow morning."

Ivan now intervened, saying "Does this mean that we don't need to unveil the turpitude of the Church and that I can burn my files?"

"The operation of the lily of Anorhad does not mean that this earth will be abandoned to the evildoers. If a base act is witnessed or comes to the attention of one initiated in the Deep Way, its author will in due time be exposed by circumstances. This is because the information is passed on to the central record of the universal unconscious, which is accessed by the Gods; they instruct their collective power, the Parampara, to take charge. Don't waste your energy starting a fight with an institution that has lasted two thousand years, Ivan, but get initiated to the Deep Way. That will be much more efficient than starting a new thirty years' war.

The best of the Anorhadans, in the ancient days, achieved far-sightedness and this is why some human beings called the lily 'the third eye.' They had managed to develop the powers of the tricolor lily of Anorhad in such a manner that negativity could not enter their brains. They could always elude Thanatophor and his minions and this is the reason they were amongst the most feared Avasthas. They constantly practiced the Deep Way and so they never let themselves feel resentful."

"'Forgive us our trespasses as we forgive those who trespass against us' was the instruction given to us in the Lord's Prayer two thousand years ago," observed Joseph. "I understand what you mean, Sanath, but I do not know how to put it into practice: how to forgive?"

Joseph kept coming back to the topic of forgiveness because he had already heard so much about it in the Church but it was only now, for the first time, that he felt close to understanding it. There was a practical mechanism in the brain for forgiveness to work out its redeeming power. Justice would also come, as the lily of Anorhad would turn into the Trishul. Still, he felt baffled at having finally grasped the meaning and scope of forgiveness without being able to use it effectively.

"It has to come from within… " intervened Tracy, who, unlike Joseph, could detach herself more fully from her Catholic upbringing. She had sensed what it was to forgive during Sanath's speech, because true knowledge is more likely to ride a feeling than a thought.

"… it has to come from the heart," continued Lakshmi.

"If Jonathan could feel this love, if his heart could be filled with love, that love would spill over and he would forgive his parents."

Having experienced that kind of love in the Vaikuntha vision, Lakshmi could also relate from within to what Sanath explained. She felt as if the love she had received was eager to flow from her heart to comfort and heal others. She remembered how concerned Jonathan had been about the endless cycle of violence around Jerusalem. Sanath had revealed the potential of a spiritual mechanism through which man could eventually face and defeat evil without violence.

THE ERRANDS
OF THE THIRD DAY

"Hi Seagull! Welcome to the Rhine country!" Tracy, Joseph, and Mike ran towards Jonathan as he appeared in the Arrivals Lounge of Frankfurt airport, clumsily pushing his cart laden with three pieces of luggage. They exchanged loud and cheerful greetings, as was usually the case when the O'Lochans met. There were simply too many things to talk about so everyone started speaking at the same time. They boarded Philip's car, now driven by Mike because Stefan had a bad migraine; he had been feeling weak, affected no doubt by the dying of the sacred oak.

The journey was pleasant and the exchanges lively; Mike told Jonathan about the fantastic battle, about Aliskhan, and the details of past lives that had been revealed. Jonathan, incredulous at first, had to admit they were walking along the borders of strange worlds in which anything could happen. He heard what a wonderful place Schloss Jetzenstein was, and asked for a moment-by-moment detailed description of the epic battle on the first day of the Council of Sanath. He heard too how on the second day, they had learned about the Gate of the Elephant and its second portal, the subtle center of the lily. He also rejoiced at the prospect of seeing his best friend Lakshman and his beautiful cousin Lakshmi again.

In turn, he narrated his own bizarre story about the brawl between the bald eagle and the ravens on the balcony of Mike's apartment in Georgetown and how, since then, he felt much more energetic and confident. Tracy and the younger brothers were quick to point out that the incident had taken place exactly when the Archangels were fighting Hangker and Belzebseth above the Rhine valley.

On his arrival at the castle amid great excitement, more embraces awaited Jonathan as he walked into the glittering luster of the entrance hall. Lakshmi was one of those who rushed forward spontaneously to give him a hug and then, as she pressed against his chest, she felt uneasy and retreated; Jonathan glanced at her with a hint of the same recognition he had felt at Casa della Minerva. Again, he noticed how sparkling and pretty she was. She blushed, which fortunately was hard to discern under her golden-brown skin.

The bouncy young woman had suddenly become quite shy. Lakshmi, well attuned to introspection and with being in touch with her emotions, could not ignore this exchange, however fleeting it might have been. Part of her had felt strange because, as a traditionally raised Indian woman, she was not supposed to hug adult men. However, deep down, she sensed that her embarrassment was connected to a deeper feeling. She remembered at this moment the attraction she had felt for Jonathan at Lorelei's party. This rush of feelings was a bit confusing but she remained playful, happy that Jonathan had joined them and that the group would be complete for the third and last evening of the Council of the Hllidarendi.

None of the others, except Tracy, had noticed anything. She had always been protective of her brothers and it gave her a sixth sense. She had never much liked Jonathan's girlfriends, including Jenny. Yet this time, as she noted the one or two furtive glances that Lakshmi threw at her elder brother, she felt intrigued and strangely pleased. "Wow, I think it could be that Lakshmi feels something for Seagull," she thought secretly. "Naturally this fellow won't notice anything. He has been quite depressed lately since that silly Jenny left him. Serves him right, though. He's broken enough hearts in the past, and being ditched himself should be educational for once."

Sisterly love is not indulgent. As she was musing about this, Lakshmi approached her laughing, "Tell me, Tracy, why do you call Jonathan 'Seagull'?"

"I don't quite know. I guess it's because his mind would rather fly than walk; he doesn't quite feel comfortable on the earth."

"Do you think so?" Jonathan had overheard the conversation and joined in. "I hope you're wrong. At least I know why I accepted the nickname: I always felt a tremendous nostalgia for the sea. Water is my element."

Lakshmi looked at him and knew instantly that this was something important to know. They laughed and joked for some time and caught up with past events, swapping stories about their respective adventures and escapades. Jonathan unbuttoned his shirt and showed the two women the scars on his chest left by the ravens' attack. The day was sunny and invited outdoor activities but he declined to join the group for a horseback ride. He was feeling jetlagged after one full night of work and one night of travel, and he preferred to stay with Philip, Laira, and Sanath for lunch. In the afternoon he withdrew to his room, admiring the stunning view of the Rhine valley from his window, and then fell into a deep and restorative sleep until it was time for dinner.

While Lothar, Lorelei, and Mike went down to the river on horseback, Lakshman, Lakshmi, and Tracy trekked through a nearby forest. Rays of sunlight filtered through the foliage, splashing gold here and there through the light green leaves, caressing old tree trunks and illuminating mossy stones on the earthen path. They could still feel the wonder and the blessedness left in the air around the castle by the victory of the archangels. As they rode along, they chatted gaily and Tracy shared her experiences and aspirations of the Oikos Project with Lakshman.

Sanath had informed her that he had flown to Germany from Bogotá, Colombia where a local member of the Order of the Hllidarendi, an old woman called Marichu, had taken him on a trip to the remote northern area of the Sierra Nevada de Santa Marta, the highest coastal mountain formation on the planet. Sanath had become a close friend of the elders, or Mamas, of the Kogi, Arhuaco, and Wiwa pre-Columbian tribes. These were people who more three centuries ago had fled before the Spanish invasion and taken refuge in this mountain paradise. The Mamas were the custodians of a world view that was similar to the Oikos philosophy. They believed that the area entrusted to them was the key to the balance of the Mother Earth. Under the spiritual guidance of the primordial creator, perceived as the Great Mother, the tribes saw their physical labor and spiritual work as weaving a pattern of balance through their lives, between two extremes, in order to maintain an ecological and cosmic balance in the Sierra. They conducted their farming, harvesting, and cattle-grazing activities with the sense of laying a protective cloak upon the earth.

Yet the elder brothers, as the Indians called themselves, were now deeply distressed by the level of disturbance to their delicately spun ecosystem brought about by the younger brothers, the modern men. The older brothers were now being attacked from all sides: settlers cleared forests, sometimes for plantations related to the cocaine trade. Incursions by leftist guerillas and right-wing para-military bands projected the onslaught of the Darkness into their symbolic regional microcosm. For the Mamas it was an indication of the end of times: imbalance was deadly for their imperiled sacred sanctuary.

"You see," concluded Tracy, "Sanath feels that these Columbian tribes are still, to some extent, unconsciously connected to the Deep Way. He said yesterday that the destruction of their sanctuary is linked to the death of the sacred oak."

Lakshman knew about the Kogi prophecies because the tribes of the Sierra were the heirs to the Tayrona civilization that flourished around 1000 AD. His archaeology teacher had been involved in the discovery in the jungle of the lost city of Tejuna back in nineteen seventy.

Lakshman and Tracy chatted for most of the way, while Lakshmi followed along behind them. "Laksh, I think your cousin is a bit dreamy today," observed Tracy.

"I know, I noticed too. I think it's her Avastha past that's haunting her now. She would have wished to have heard about it from Sanath or somebody else she loves and respects, certainly not from a demon. Think about it: she is supposed to have been Erilie of Eleksim, captain of the Sheravalian Guard, lady-in-waiting of the Lady of the Rock. Yet she has no memory of this. She, the daughter of Ichwaril, high lord of Eleksim, once walked on this earth and yet now she doesn't have a clue about it. I find her exceptional in many ways but she doesn't show any of the special powers Erilie was supposed to have. She is part of the fall of the Avasthas, I guess."

"What about you, Laksh? Weren't you supposed to be someone rather special too? I mean Etakir, leader of the Yuva platoon, who could navigate through sandstorms and direct his arrows to their target with the power of his will? Can you still do that?"

Tracy had asked this in a jocular mood, but she immediately regretted it. Lakshman looked at her with a glance that was both severe and sad. He did not reply. Tracy continued hastily, "I'm sorry, Laksh, I did not mean to make fun of you. You know how much I admire you; I would never do anything that could hurt you. I, I..." She stuttered, feeling completely gauche. Lakshman gave her an arch, distant look – this conversation was not going well. But when Lakshman realized how awkward Tracy felt he mellowed his stance; his expression softened and he came to her rescue.

"I usually love it when you are naughty and tease me but, I trust you have noticed, Tracy dear, not this time. You see, Etakir or not, all this past life business opens an old wound. Somehow, deep inside, I know that I was once much more than I am now. I always have had this feeling, I don't know, it's hard to explain. I feel a bit like a fallen angel. What is my path, what should I accomplish? I am an orphan, and the most poignant image of my entire life, I should say of all my lives, is what I saw sitting in that hotel room in Amsterdam. I was with Sanath the second time we opened the Casket of the White Feather. I saw myself as a pathetic juggler, trying to please the queen, or, should I say, trying to please the mother that I never found and that I never had."

Tracy was emboldened again by his kindness. "I don't care whether you have fallen from somewhere, from another planet or a coconut tree. I think that what matters is what you are, here and now, not as Etakir but as Lakshman. It is Lakshman who will make it and accomplish what must be. It is the man in you that counts now, not the Avastha. Remember the words of the wizard? 'Fate is what happens to you; destiny is what you do with what happens to you.' I don't think you have lost anything, those oranges are still in your hands, and the queen is still blessing you. She loves you."

She had spoken passionately, with all her heart, without even knowing where the words were coming from or what authority she had to make such pronouncements. Lakshman looked at Tracy – she had touched his heart. For her part, Tracy took his glance deep into herself; she was so open to him at this moment that they experienced a feeling of great oneness.

Oblivious to their exchanges, Lakshmi was enjoying the enchantment of the forest, the display of joyous light and the promise of the hour. "So, he likes the sea?" she mused. "What a fellow, this Jonathan. I am sure I have seen him somewhere before." Everything seemed bright and wonderful in the footsteps of the archangels.

Further down the hill, the Jetzlar grandchildren and Mike were having a great time together, enjoying each other's company. Lothar demonstrated his agility and strength in climbing trees like an acrobat, while Mike impressed them with his mastery of Philip's horse, an animal that could normally only be ridden by its owner. The flooding of the Rhine had been brutal but short-lived. The water had receded but had left behind a mess of flotsam and jetsam on Lorelei's favorite sandy beach on the banks of a tributary of the Rhine that marked the border of the estate. They tied their horses to nearby trees and rested for a while on huge boulders in the middle of a brook. Lothar was adept at tickling trout, catching them with his hands, and in what seemed like no time he had caught a few and prepared and grilled them on an impromptu campfire. After enjoying this delicious improvised meal, they relaxed on the grass and spent the afternoon chatting animatedly about the growing revelations that were now unfolding, discussing the lore of Dagad Trikon, and comparing their impressions.

Lorelei shivered at the thought of the demons. The words of Belzebseth had penetrated her mind and she was still trembling with the recollection. Somewhere, deep in her subconscious, lay the pain and the guilt of Esitel, the first fighter of the Sheravalian guard ever to fall into the hands of the enemy; she had been captured through the malefic ophtalir on that fateful day when the emissary of Thanatophor discovered the Triangle Rock and precipitated the end of the Avasthas.

"We don't know how things would have happened without Sanath," said Mike gently, trying to distract her from the lingering pain that still haunted her. "You're right. Still, I feel that something else would have worked out."

"I felt this too," Lorelei exclaimed in a surprised tone. She then shared a dream she had had the morning after the momentous night of the battle.

"I think it has something to do with what we are going through but I don't understand the link. We were in a lovely wood, on the banks of a bubbling mountain stream, a bit like this one, only for some reason I knew that we were in Nepal. There were a lot of children around a woman who was sitting on the ground with us. My heart told me it was the Lady of the Rock. The children, and both of you were among them, were making some kind of pledge to her, praising her and saying, 'We acknowledge who you are.' Then we found ourselves around a large chessboard with somebody saying, 'A fool on the left, a fool on the right, and the queen in the middle.' A big chess game began, with all the children playing against the lady. She turned towards me and asked, 'Don't you play?' I responded, 'No, I am just observing.' After this, the scene changed suddenly into a game of cards. The children had all the aces and kings; the Lady had only the twos and threes. At first I think, 'It's not fair' but suddenly I realized, it's the play of recognition. It was She who distributed the cards so that we could win.' I woke up and I thought: my God, when the Deep Way expands and spreads, I expand. I? Who is this 'I'? This 'I' was immense. It knows no boundaries between the individual and the collective. Is it that? Is it what we are searching for?"

They remained silent as they absorbed the profundity of the dream. Lothar observed gravely, contrasting suddenly with the lighter mood of the last hours:

"I hardly dare believe what is happening to us, but my heart seems to recognize it, in spite of myself. Sometimes, I feel I love all the incarnations so much – Rama, Krishna, Socrates... I feel I was there when Mary Magdalene discovered Christ's empty tomb. Somehow, I feel I miss their company so much; I know I shouldn't. It's weird. My emotions are not quite tuned yet. It's within that love that resides an exquisite flavor of my existence. In some strange way it gives me a sense of my destiny, playing in the game of hide-and-seek. I guess,

Lorelei, it's your card game of recognition." He added more slowly, as if shyly sorting out his own insights:

"When I come near them, then I am real. It's because man cannot live without God that he makes a God out of anything he can grasp, because God means destination and purpose, it means intensity and plenitude, it means identification of destiny and meaning."

Mike responded by saying, "You're right, Lothar, and we have probably been trotting down this road, knowingly or unknowingly, for a long, long time. It bothered me that we heard about our Avastha background from the demons and not from Sanath. I don't quite know the usefulness of knowing about this past life stuff. Of course it's intriguing, but I'm not sure it helps me in my life as it is now: finishing my studies, finding a job, and surviving the mess that is my family. It is now that I need to sort out my life, not through some bygone mythology. Jonathan has had a hard time: he's been thrown out of his job, at which he was hugely talented and highly regarded. Jenny, his fiancée, has left him and he's hurt because he thought she was someone with whom he could finally settle down. So we have not been too successful at anything in the recent past, with the notable exception of this quest, of course, where clearly we have hit upon something really big. Yet, how can we talk to others about all of this? They will think we're mad."

"Did you see the metamorphosis of the white monkey as it dropped down from the tapestry? I only had a glimpse of him before he jumped into the Gothic triptych. And then Gabriel materialized before our eyes. I'm not sure he had a physical body though – did he? How handsome and powerful he was!"

Mike, still incredulous, added to his friend's recollection: "The golden age, the angels… I thought all this was fiction. And then we saw them: the white monkey disappearing into the image of Gabriel, and Gabriel himself emerging. It was magic. But what is magic?"

Sounding thoroughly convinced, Lothar said, "Magic is when fiction, legend or mythology return to reality. It's the passage between worlds, between the known and the unknown."

Lorelei asked, "You mean, like between the inner and the outer worlds, like the Gate of the Elephant?"

"I guess so," intervened Mike. " The passage must work both ways. I think that only those who find the passage can find out that the magic is real too. It's just a name given by ordinary folk to things they don't yet understand."

Lorelei returned to the events of the recent night. "Did you notice how quickly the scene changed? The demons looked stunned and they dropped their sarcasm when they saw the monkey. They just weren't expecting that visitor. The Archangel Michael was awesome. He was, in a sense, frightening – with light coming out of him, his spear, and his glittering armor, yet his appearance was what reassured me most. When the demons entered I was really terrorized, I felt paralyzed and when that horrible specter of Belzebseth talked to me, I felt sick to my stomach. I can't believe we ever had the strength to fight such dreadful devils in the past. If we did, it's sad because it means that we've lost all our powers. Left to ourselves, we would have been finished. But when they saw Gabriel and Michael it was their turn to get scared. Ah, what a triumph! My God, I hope those devils are gone for good. It was the wizard, of course, who somehow choreographed this amazing encounter. Grandpa always told us how great he was, but this was beyond all my expectations."

Mike said, "There is a greater attention that watches over this quest. I sense that it pushes us in a different direction to that which the wizard had expected; indeed, he said as much himself. In some obscure way, the revelations make sense to me. I definitely have the feeling I've known both of you for a very long time, and, well, I feel we were close; we were part of a team. It's great that the team has been rebuilt because this puzzle is too hard for any individual to solve by himself. We must progress together; it's our only chance. We can't move forward toward the past, I mean the past of the Avastha kingdom that cannot be reawakened."

"You're right," added Lothar firmly. "I don't think this magic is the real solution. Personally, I'm not into the business of magic. I'm much more interested in results that I can produce."

"So what about being a Stealthstar?" asked Lorelei, shaking her hair as if trying to clear her head of her memories. "At first I thought it would be exciting to know about our past lives, that it would help us to understand ourselves better. Yet now I'm not at all sure. I don't know what to do with the information we've now been given. The fact that Lothar feels like a brother, the fact that you feel like, well, a friend, this is what remains true, no matter from where these feelings originate. What are we to do with this Avastha legacy? We forgot so much. I feel sorry because they arranged all those caskets for a purpose. They wanted to help us, they wanted us to find something more. I'm afraid we are letting them down but the world is not what they thought it would be. Who's interested in the truth today? Who believes in destiny? People just don't care anymore, do we? Do you, Mike?"

"The magic would be to find out – not as Aliskhan, Esitel, and Hanomkar – but as we are now, as Mike, Lorelei, and Lothar," Mike replied convincingly. "The whole key to the Dagad Trikon prophecy lies with the Deep Way. Have you ever seen a Russian doll? There is one big doll containing another smaller one, and so on, a doll within a doll within a doll. I think it's the same for us. We have been built like that. Mostly we live only in the outer doll and perhaps from time to time we become aware of one or two of the smaller ones. The Deep Way will take us to the secret doll at the core of all the others, piercing through these different sheaths of our being on its way. In the process, we may pick up some of what the Avasthas knew, but it's not as important as Lakshman and Lakshmi seem to think; it's the destination that matters."

"Oh Mike! If only this could work out, it would be so cool," responded Lorelei, a bit dreamily, trying to figure out what her core doll could be. "We would have everything within us and we wouldn't depend on anything or anybody to feel happy and secure, nobody could snatch the treasure from us."

None of them realized that it was precisely because of their Avastha background that Mike had come to a correct conclusion so quickly and that Lorelei could recognize it. Lothar noted a bond developing between his sister and the young American, but on this occasion he didn't mind. Unlike the case of Silvio, the affinity between Mike and Lorelei appeared completely spontaneous and just felt right.

Mike commented, "Yes, the whole puzzle would fit together because it's clear that evil rises with hate under all its forms. The Foul Rift breeds on all the minute moments of hate in our psyche – suspicion, diffidence, envy, aggression, and treachery. At the same time, the world of goodness spreads its love in all its forms – friendship, loyalty, respect, trust, and solidarity. Yet it is difficult for most human beings to express love when receiving it has been effectively denied to them."

Lothar said, "Right! Evil attacks early in life: many children are denied love in their formative years and life becomes difficult for them. The emotional dryness of their early childhood hampers their lifelong capacity to become emitters of love themselves. From the cradle on, so many children receive information about hating others – those who have a different skin color or those of a different nationality or religion. The prejudices of their ancestors are dutifully handed down, generation after generation. Can we now assume that we could, by ourselves, through the Deep Way, access a well of love? Can we discover a connection within us to an ever-flowing source?

It would reverse the negative dynamics of an environment in which love was so scarce. We would never suffer from a shortage again and we could go on giving. Think how confident we would be! Grandma used to quote a Spanish saint who said: "If there is a place where you don't find love, put love there and you will find love." Yes, Lorelei, I think Paradise must be something like that."

They remounted the horses and, enjoying a happy mood, prepared to return to the castle. The day had been spent in the dusty glory of a golden sun that carried the blessings from the assembly of the Gods on Mount Kailash.

While love was shyly blossoming in the woods around the proud fortress, Sanath had asked Philip, Laira, and Ivan to join him on the rose loggia that overlooked the splendid Rhine valley. He explained to them that they would age much faster now that the protection of the sacred oak was being removed.

Philip confirmed this statement. "After the events of the night before last, I feel relieved but also very tired, as if my energy has been sapped. I know about the demons and the Dark Riders, but can you explain in more detail how we have reached this critical point where the specter of destruction is upon us? I have hardly ever seen you upset or scared, but you seemed utterly distressed about the possible consequence of the opening of the Casket of the Cross."

"You may well say so," answered the wizard. "We have reached this moment of catharsis through a slow process of degradation of the consciousness that took us from the former golden age of the Avastha to the present age of Darkness. The hour of reckoning is coming. How did we fall?" He paused and responded to his own question a little later.

"Throughout history, there have been perhaps two mistakes that the human race has committed most consistently. I have finally given a name to these two temptations: I call them the bane of Petrone and the bane of Bonaparte."

"I beg your pardon?" said the Count, puzzled.

"Napoleon Bonaparte was an artillery officer from Corsica who managed to turn his first name into a brand name in world history. He did so because he used a time of crisis and change, when many futures were possible, to shape the future through his own genius and will power. He seized the moment and became, as it were, the instrument of the Weltgeist of his time. Many may try to achieve this position; however, few succeed. This proved that he was connected in some way to the Grand Scheme. Nevertheless, he did not know where to stop and, caught in the momentum of his own linearity, he became the chief artisan of his own fall. Linearity results in rigidity and blindness. The syndrome of Bonaparte seizes all those who are carried by their ego and intoxicated by the fruits of their own actions. They strive for power and control. They may have a vision and lofty goals but they are those whose prayer sounds more like 'My will be done' than 'Thy will be done.'

They do not leave a space for the heavens to help them, and gradually, help that is not accepted is no longer offered. Auspiciousness fades away and failure follows. The West has worshipped these heroic models – Alexander, Julius Caesar, Napoleon – without realizing that, in terms of their personal lives, all three men failed. Alexander died early, his son was killed, and his empire immediately crumbled. Caesar was murdered and so was his son Caesarion – killed on the orders of Caesar's own nephew and heir, Octavius, who seized the throne. Napoleon ended up on Saint Helena, and his son also died an early death. These heroes strayed from the path of balance and the blessings left them. In the same manner, all stories of linearity have left behind the footprints of disasters. Disasters are of course a familiar mode for the progression of history, but there are other ways that are more pleasant."

"All right, I get the idea, and although not everybody is Caesar, all of us certainly have an ego. But what is the bane of Petrone?"

"This is a bit more complicated to explain: it is about enjoying decadence. Petrone was a Roman senator who went from Marseille to Rome at the time of the Emperor Nero. Petrone's receptions, his villas, his pranks, and his mischief fascinated the city. He was the master of fashion, the referee and arbiter of elegance and style. The high society of Rome at the time of the Emperor Nero cherished Petrone's talents and feared his biting wit and nonchalant irony. He was the ultimate dandy, a charming hedonist, aware of the empire's decay and of his own, yet quite determined to take pleasure from it. He had an aesthetic talent for depravity.

The bane of Petrone is about our lack of faith in our potential for ascending and the cynical acceptance of our own corruption. Petrone knew that Rome was falling and that he was too, but he resolved to enjoy the fall. He was shaped by pessimism and epicurean hedonism. Nero finally sent the Praetorians that Petrone had so often mocked to carry out the order for his death. Against the backdrop of the sober elegance of his villa of the jasmines, in Cumo near Naples, Petrone organized a sumptuous banquet to orchestrate his suicide and died as he had lived, like a work of art, with a silky lightness and the pretense that style is more important than substance. And so, my good friend, whether we force our will on others like Bonaparte, or whether we accept that we live for nothing like Petrone, we miss the central path and thus we land ourselves and our world in confusion. This is the jungle wherein people now stumble."

Philip nodded – he had understood.

Thus the time passed until at dusk when they all met again in the Rittersaal for the third night of the Council of the Hllidarendi.

Jonathan was standing in the embrasure of a window, waiting for Sanath and watching the last streaks of another grand sunset over the Rhine valley. Philip came to his side and put his hand on Jonathan's arm. "The Rhine looks different to me now. You know, your bombers destroyed the cities of my country. The cities were rebuilt. The Nazis destroyed the soul of my country, but our soul never completely healed again. The Nazis hijacked the idealism that flew in this nation. World War II was a nightmare of our own making. The Germans used to have big dreams. Now they do not dare to dream any more, lest their dreams turn into nightmares once again."

Jonathan shook his head and replied, "A French writer, Paul Valéry said, 'The best way to make dreams come true is to wake up.' Perhaps we should all do just that and become aware of our actions. The founders of my country also had a dream: it was a dream of freedom. They came from other lands to create a new nation, yet they built it on the genocide of the Native Americans and the slavery of the Africans. One man's dream is another man's nightmare." Philip looked at Jonathan sympathetically. It was not uncommon to find Germans who, consciously or not, felt guilty about the Third Reich, but it was less common to meet an American who questioned the past of his own nation.

The Count continued, "We are still shaken by the news of the impending death of the sacred oak. The world that opened with the incarnation of Christ is coming to an end and the future of this Aquarian age is clouded. For the first time in my life, I saw Sanath afraid. He fears the return of Christ, the Son of Adivatar. However, at the same time I sense he is tremendously alert, as if looking for something… the last piece of the puzzle. As for me, I confess, I feel tremendous hope now. Even if destruction is fated to befall us, I don't think it is a mindless occurrence but that it has its own purpose. What I am trying to say is this: just as we need to die first in order to resurrect, so it is for the age that is passing now."

Jonathan replied, "Death and resurrection, this was, after all, the meaning of Easter."

"Yes, Jonathan, there is a future for those of us who still hope. Death is upon us but perhaps, if we are lucky, it shall only be the death of the cocoon of our illusions. The great ones whom we worshipped in the Middle Ages, Michael and Gabriel, have shown us their splendor – the heavens are stirring! Yet again the Immortals are coming to our help. What a wonder it is! I feel renewal in their footsteps; my country will heal. I feel a tranquil joy rising from the Rhine that I did not feel before. I feel grandeur has returned.

The Avasthas fought for something I still believe in, Jonathan, and so do you. I can see it; you have not given up yet, still believing, still fighting. I know how hard you tried as a diplomat to bring peace to the gates of Jerusalem. We were not born to struggle helplessly in this silly mess only to see violence and stupidity win the day. There must be a way out. Let's have patience, although peace in Jerusalem is not something that I shall see with my own eyes. Sanath made it quite clear: my time is up. Only a few more years are given to the companions of the oak. It will be up to the grandchildren and to all of you to solve the Dagad Trikon enigma. I sense we are very close now."

As the German and the American were bonding, the polished stones of the Falkenlust tower gleamed in the rays of the sunset. A train of passing clouds left behind wisps of what seemed like glittering hairs of copper. Lorelei, Lothar, and Mike, leaning out of the window, admired the magnificent spectacle. This was again the coming of a night of secrecy, full of promises, a night that sparkled as if painted by a magic brush. The great door opened and Sanath entered the hall of the knights. He looked his usual enigmatic self and walked slowly, leaning on his large wizard staff. They clamored to greet him and all sat down around the rectangular table in front of the fireplace; he remained standing. They each sensed that this was a time for mysteries to be unveiled.

"Friends and Stealthstars, I declare open the last session of the Council of the Hllidarendi. This is an evening to harvest the pearls of knowledge. You know me as the heir of the Order of the Hllidarendi but once upon a time, as you may well now consider, I was also Elkaim Ekamonon, the highlander they called as the Sand Keeper under the ancient moon. Yes, indeed, I was the attendant of the High Lady of the Rock."

Sanath uttered a name for the first time, a name that none had ever heard him say before; his audience was electrified. The great hall looked quite different now, friendly and welcoming. They were bathed in a golden light that reminded them of the manifestation of Gabriel and Michael.

Sanath continued, "Wizards, Aulyas, and all men of knowledge are followers of the primordial Daskalians whose teachings are bound by the Law of Maat. Together with the high lord of Dagad Trikon, Aslerach of Anor, I guarded the Triangle Rock under the leadership of the blessed Lady. This makes me the last custodian of the lost world of Dagad Trikon. I arranged the dispatch of the caskets and recently, for centuries I tried to find my folk again. I looked for the Stealthstars and found a few of them, vainly waiting for the time when their powers would mature. I filled the office of the Hllidarendi as a tribute to the blessed Lady and I sense that the time of this service is now running out. I too have my limitations. I could not prevent the dissolution of the Avastha civilization.

In a sense, the Gods have played a trick on me. So, when I met you again, my friends, who were so dear and close to me in the days of the Rock, I did not recognize you at first. And so I entrusted Lakshman with the quest for the Dagad Trikon prophecy that had to be entrusted to a human being, for I thought him to be one. I had looked back into his past, but not far enough to realize that he himself had been an Avastha. It turned out to be correct, however, because Etakir had now become fully human. I reached a turning point when I realized that the world of the Avasthas had gone for good.

And yet, can you believe it? It was Etakir himself who found the Glorfakir and the Sadhan weapons that he had seen buried ten thousand years ago. I see this as a complete proof to all of us that the Master of the Scheme is leading us all and that His grace is now shining upon the race of men.

All the same, as I could not count on the Stealthstars to regain their ancient strength, I had to change my entire strategy. I threw down the gauntlet to the demons, a bold move I must say," he added with a chuckle. "I was lucky they picked up the challenge because it was for them a very stupid thing to do. When the devils revealed your past identities they confirmed my suspicions. It is only now, after the cosmic battle between the Archangels and the arch demons that I finally grasp what happened.

Indeed, in his mercy, the high Lord Hanuman retraced his steps and the blessed form of the white monkey visited me again in a dream last night. He confirmed that the Stealthstars had now become completely human and could not re-enact the Avastha codes. Thus, the human consciousness is now the field of the cosmic battle between Good and Evil. Nonetheless, he brought tremendous gladness to my heart in assuring me that the heavenly powers had foreseen this. He revealed that henceforth there exists a secret method to master the Deep Way embedded in the human race. It can work for the former Avasthas, as well as for all other human seekers who choose to do so. Thus, the glory of the coming golden human age will rival the splendor of the Avastha civilization.

On the third day of this Council, I am authorized to give you some help: I can answer any questions you wish to ask on such matters, one question from each of you. The truth shall be known. You may ask one after the other, following the random order in which you are seated, starting from my left. Tracy, you are the first."

EPISODE 26

THE HOLY
AND THE TRUE GRAIL

Tracy was more than ready; she did not need to collect her thoughts and eagerly asked the first question. "How can we relate to what you are saying and what knowledge will enable us to discover the things you speak of for ourselves?"

Each of the attendees waited for a straight answer. Wizards, however, have their own sense of how straight or curved lines are, be they thoughts or otherwise. Sanath paused for a moment and answered, "Socrates, the epistemic Daskalian of the Occident, warned his disciples Aristotle and Plato that we must not be trapped in doxa, a prison formed by our mental opinions, our subjective beliefs. The Dark Riders operate in the shade of that cave. When the mind is thus sufficiently confused, the witches of Belzebseth spin the web that seals the entrance. We must develop episteme, which would be like walking out of the cave of doxa into the bright light of a cognitive sun. Episteme is a direct knowledge of reality. When the Deep Way bestows episteme, it becomes Samyak, the state of recognition where the brain and the heart become integrated and act as one.

In the same way that small streams must join larger rivers in order to ultimately flow into the ocean, human beings must merge into greater personalities in order to return to the divine dimension. Actually, it is the enlargement of the capacity of our hearts that really matters. Larger hearts that care and give, these are the hearts that can receive the Gift. These are the hearts to trigger the return to the Godhead. In the state of Samyak, the brain can feel, the heart can know: the one who walks out of the cave does not need to fight his or her shadows any longer. Such a person experiences total rejuvenation and is empowered to access Ananya, the great Oneness."

Lakshmi muttered to herself, "Samyak, Ananya, what else?" she pondered thoughtfully. "These philosophers have found so many names for this. In the fold of the goddess' sari, I just called it 'mother's love.' I wonder whether they knew?" The recollection of this blessed moment that she had found outside of time brought tears to her eyes.

Philip von Jetzlar, who was sitting next to Tracy, arose slowly, bowed slightly before Sanath, and asked longingly: "Master Elkaim Ekamonon, you who are the sentinel of the highlands, the Sand Keeper, and benevolent wizard of the ancient order of the Hllidarendi, please enlighten us: the sacred oak is dying and I feel it is also taking my strength away. Before I depart, I wish to ask again the question I asked in Byelorussia, but that you never answered: what is the Holy Grail? What was the role assigned to the Westerners in the Grand Scheme?"

Lakshman and his cousin glanced intently at each other. Philip was right; this question deserved a response because looking backwards into the past of a race was tantamount to crystal glazing to catch a fleeting glimpse of the future. They recalled their own insights and the legend of King Arthur and the Knights of the Round Table: they had discussed it in Delphi. Lakshmi, through a brilliant intuition, had connected this legend to a myth from the East. It was the myth of the Vedic age in which Gods and demons had fought for the elixir of immortality. The cousins had seen the statues of the monumental entrance at the Temple of Angkor Vat in the jungle of Cambodia, depicting how competing Gods and demons churned the ocean of milk using the king of the snakes as a huge rope to obtain the blessed nectar.

Sanath the Sand Keeper pursued the course of his revelations. "It is fit that a knight asks this question, and to this knight I shall respond." He spoke pensively, his gaze lost on a faraway horizon that only he could see:

"True knighthood does not come from birth, it comes from seeking. Indeed, at the origin of Christian knighthood, in the high Middle Ages, there was a code of honor built on chivalry; dedication to the divine Lady; and assistance to the weak, the poor, and the needy. Fidelity to a heroic quest was at the core of this code. Some of those who went on the Crusades hoped to find the ultimate goal of their quest, but most went solely to grab power and territory. Renaud de Cormorant had been initiated in the secrets of the East and was introduced to the full meaning of the prophecy of his mentor, John of Jerusalem. But later, he fell from grace and knew that he could no longer access the blessed condition that was the fulfillment of the true knights' quest.

Thus, the notion of true knighthood faded away over the ages, until finally the French Revolution brutally dismissed a caste that had lost its quality of service to society and that had dissolved into decadence like Petrone. Indeed, the Dark Rider of vanity destroyed those that were supposed to be the best. Today the knights don't know themselves. We recognize those who are left, as they are those who have the courage to seek, true to the heroic quest, no matter what their creed, country, or condition of their birth.

The brotherhood of the Knights of the Round Table was formed in ancient times to defeat evil and to find the ultimate treasure: the cup of the Holy Grail.

The cup is called "Sangreal" meaning the "true blood" of Christ that Joseph of Arimathea collected in a cup as it flowed from Jesus on the cross. Christ was no ordinary human being and the meaning of his "true blood" was not just the blood released from his physical body. Hence the mystical secret of the Grail is not about the cup but about its content: the mystical blood of Christ, the ambrosia, the elixir of spiritual energy and bliss.

Merlin the Hllidarendi was meant to guide the brotherhood of the knights so that they might receive the Gift. He had anticipated the attacks of the Evil One. He studied many possible paths the Dark Riders might follow in their attempt to pierce the defenses of Camelot. Yet he did not foresee the adultery of Queen Guinevere with Lancelot of the Lake and so the Dark Rider of Lust brought down Camelot. Through this fault, the bond between the knights was broken and everything was lost. Only Sir Galahad found the Grail, for he was indeed an ancient Avastha from the house of Anorhad and blessed with innocence. Alas, he vanished without revealing the secret of the Avastha prophecy. All the other knights failed in their quest and so too did the lesser Christian knights who came after them.

The Knights of the Round Table and all those who followed and failed like them were doomed to reincarnate time and again on earth until they fulfilled their quest. In the Middle Ages, some of them came close to discovering the secret of the Gift but the King of France and the Pope destroyed them. More recently, your brother Baldur was one those knights. Baldur von Jetzlar knew that Hitler, Himmler, and his SS were in search of the Grail. Baldur joined his friend Klaus Schenk von Stauffenberg and other officers in a plot to kill the envoy of Thanatophor, Adolf Hitler. When the conspiracy failed, Baldur pretended to be shot by Soviet anti-aircraft fire and crashed his plane on the headquarters of the SS brigade fighting on the Stalingrad front. The Gestapo never found out that he was part of the plot. He and his friends were truly brave and it was an honor for me to take his name."

Philip was shocked at this unexpected revelation, which touched him deeply. The death of his brother was intertwined with the explanation of the most mysterious legend of Occidental civilization. He had always had great admiration for his elder brother. Baldur had been a secretive character and had never told him that he was part of the plot to kill Hitler. Unlike the unfortunate von Stauffenberg, he had managed to keep his family out of the reach of Nazi vengeance. Philip listened attentively as Sanath continued.

"Hear now, my trusted friend, the secret of the Avasthas for which so many died through the centuries of failed quest. Verily the knights of the West and the sages of the East were born on this earth for the same purpose – to find the Holy Grail – although they named it with different words. This elixir of immortality had similar names in India and in Europe. The cup of the Holy Grail, Count of Jetzlar, is at the core of the Dagad Trikon prophecy. Verily, I must repeat, it is not the cup that we seek, but the mystery of what it contains. The Gift is bestowed when the content of the cup is poured onto the human consciousness. When the cup is turned upside down, it actually becomes the human skull at the level of the limbic area on the top of the brain. That is where ecstasy can be experienced, flowing from the top of the brain into the whole body, filling it with an indescribable shower of divine bliss. The search for this elated state and the life of fulfillment that opens with it is the goal of the human quest."

Philip remained silent, trying to absorb the information. The cousins could hardly contain their excitement. Lakshmi felt a quiet jubilation, as she was certain that Sanath confirmed now the condition she had experienced during her mystical trip to Vaikuntha.

It was Lothar's turn now and he rose earnestly to his feet to ask the next question. Once more he proved his maturity as his question went to the core of the matter.

"Respected master, what is the relationship between the Deep Way and the Holy Grail?"

The wizard answered Lothar fondly, "The Deep Way is a training by which we learn how to reach an equilibrium point inside so that we may let things happen – good things, things willed by the Gods themselves. We call upon auspiciousness in our lives through an inner connection with the higher power. Basically, we invite what ordinary folks call good luck. This training is necessary to succeed in the quest. Indeed, the Holy Grail cannot be grabbed. We may, at best, invite the blessing of receiving it from the bestower of the Gift. All those perished who forced their way to find this place of bliss in the brain without being authorized.

It is only the Gift that can reveal the Grail to the seeker. Alas, so many destroyed themselves in the modern age by taking drugs and following other forbidden paths, lured by the false prophets to reach a destination that can be experienced only through gradual progress along the Deep Way. Let me repeat this: the Grail cannot be conquered. It cannot even be found; it can only be received. There are those who seek to acquire higher powers, to overcome the Grail, to take it as the prize of discovery, a treasure or a trophy that is due to the deserving explorer. They fall into the trap of the seventh Rider, the carrier of Pride. They miss the target."

Lakshman was sitting next to Lothar. His train of thought was following a different course and he brought it to the next question. "I am just an ordinary human being, but if I understand correctly, once upon a time I too was an Avastha; I had high powers and I lost them. Why did I fall and how can I regain them or better, simply achieve the state of being that you have been describing?"

"My dear Lakshman, as Etakir, the leader of the Yuva platoon of Dagad Trikon, you were indeed a hero. For some millennia, you couldn't help but be that, lifetime after lifetime, and so it was that you always remained a warrior. Then you went beyond that stage and tried to achieve mastery over your senses, juggling those oranges. I can see that, as success is within grasp, you will become a mentor to others. And now I shall respond. The Stealthstars have been trapped in the world of materialism that Thanatophor and his lieutenants prepared. The Avasthas then fell because they lost faith in their destiny.

As for the second part of your question, I had long discussions about the potential of the human brain with Professor Rahurikar who, in the past, had been a yogic master himself. In his words, there is a biochemical map to the Deep Way. The creator prepared a neuro-endocrinological support for this transformation of the consciousness. Receiving the Gift has a lot to do with rewiring the circuitry of our brains. Base hormones and brain chemicals such as oxytocin, dopamine or serotonin get enchanted by the pouring of the Gift. Brain chemistry and neurotransmission start responding to the influx of the new energy. The effectiveness of the corpus callosum that connects the two hemispheres of the brain becomes magnified; it then bridges the gap between emotions and thoughts. Thus, our very brain has the tools to enjoy Ananya, the great state of Oneness," he concluded dramatically.

Silence pressed upon their ears as their consciousness seemed to soar above their heads somewhere near the high ceiling of the hall. Their awareness mingled in a common elated flight of joy while their bodies, all the while, were experiencing a pleasantly cool feeling of relaxation. It was as if they could taste what was said. Philip looked with admiration at his mentor and friend: this indeed was the magic of the Council.

Lakshmi heard herself whispering: " Then it is all about love, isn't it, Master?" She knew it was almost stupid to venture a question at this point of the revelation. The air around her was still, as if waiting expectantly. Sanath seemed unconcerned. As he continued in a low but vibrant voice they all felt goose pimples in the central part of their backs, around the spine.

"The Gift has more than one form. We already explained how, in some powerful cases, the Gift might cause the release of super-charged bliss chemicals throughout the whole body, what the past saints and seers called amrit or ambrosia. I spoke about it a little while ago. But the very experience of the Holy Grail is a very rare occurrence.

Rahul speculated that it might happen through neural-limbic pathways, involving the cingulated gyrus or the cerebral cortex. But what do I know of such technicalities? Discussing biological factors, hormonal psychology or brain chemistry patterns will only keep scientists happy. Their scientific explanation is just the support for the happening; it will not take us there. Scientists miss the fact that this reality is sacred; it can be unveiled only by seeking purity, not learning."

Sanath added, as if hesitantly:

"This was the mystery of the crucifixion of the son of Adivatar. In dying on the cross, Christ opened the narrow gate of the lily of Anorhad but he did more. As his body was opened and his blood flowed in this divine self-sacrifice, the energy of blessedness that his body contained flowed over the earth. In other words, it was made available for mankind. It is there for them. The next step now is for man to discover how to access the Holy Grail, the elixir or redemption."

"If this was indeed the secret of Christianity, it has not been easy to figure it out," observed Joseph plaintively. "We simply missed it."

"And yet Jesus gave a clear and last hint."

"A hint? What do you mean?"

Out of his fondness for Joseph who was an ardent seeker, Sanath actually broke his own rule and agreed to answer Joseph's second question.

"What is the last thing that Jesus said to John the Aulya when he was on the cross?

"He said, behold the mother," repeated Joseph incredulously.

"That's right Joseph." He did not say, "Behold Simon Peter.

For the mother had the key, not the church."

"Mary? The mother of Jesus? But she is so, how should I say, so… "

"Unassuming?

"Precisely. She is quite in the background. With the exception of Luke, the evangelists hardly mention her. She is so discreet."

"She chose to be this way. She withdrew all her cosmic powers within herself. But she is an eternal personality."

"When I think about it, it is true… I now remember the painting in the National Gallery in London, where Leonardo da Vinci depicted Mary as the Virgin in the painting called The Lady of the Rocks. A beautiful painting it is. Was this a hint also? She looks a bit like the lady in the famous portrait of the Mona Lisa, known in France as La Joconde. It is as if La Joconde is smiling at those who seek and those who pretend to have found."

Laira looked around at her companions, now absorbed in a profound peace. The power of the revelation was slowly sinking in. Turning to the wizard, she whispered softly: " By which power can your words carry the power of the Sao Iambu stone?"

Sanath smiled at her and spoke in the same tone: "By the power of the giver of the Gift, the blessed Lady of Dagad Trikon. She has gathered us here tonight. The Gift, my friend, can give you the mastery over the senses that you could not achieve in your past lives through yoga, meditation practices or attempts at mind control. It opens the moment of an immense epiphany, a stream of existential insights, the transcending of contradictory perceptions. We grasp and integrate the truth of our divine self in the conscious mind. When this happens for the human race, the processing of emotions and feelings in our daily lives will lead to more mature reactions, insightful responses, and loving relationships. The effects of the Great Schism and of the resulting Foul Rift shall be countered, minimized, and eventually, finally abolished. Next question, please."

Did the wizard answer? It seemed to Lakshman that he did and, yet he did not. An essential piece of the puzzle was still missing.

THE HARVEST OF THE
THIRD NIGHT

It was now Jonathan's turn to speak. He was careful to keep his voice subdued, as he did not want to betray his lingering sense of frustration. However, his words sounded shakier than he would have wished: "Master, all this discourse is both extremely remote and strangely familiar. I live in this century; what is in for me? What is my own relationship with this quest?"

"If you put this question, I cannot fail to answer, for all veils before my own eyes have been removed after the battle of the Archangels. You are Jonathan of the Lake, no matter how painful this knowledge may be. In the language of the Byelorussian folk *'lochan'* means 'lake.' All seekers of truth have been their own predecessors and they incarnate again and again to learn from their mistakes and to fulfill their destiny. You were Lancelot of the Lake in one of your past lives and fate was adverse to you. Verily, you sought your beloved more eagerly than the Grail. How then could you find it? You lost the trace of your goal and fell for the wife of King Arthur." He nodded at Jonathan who sank further into his seat, staring at him in sheer disbelief.

"You did not have enough strength to resist her fatal spell; you coveted a married woman and thus you broke the Law of Maat. Both the queen and the first knight were mighty and ancient beings and yet a Dark Rider caught them: they lost their powers as they committed adultery and betrayed their king. The rest of your story became the legend of the fall of the Western knight who cannot resist a woman equipped with the magnetism of lust. Your story was sadly prophetic, for in the following centuries the Dark Rider of Lust wrought havoc on the men of the West."

Jonathan's heart sank. The walls of the hall seemed to reverberate with the damning words: "betrayal," "the fall." He felt his companions' eyes on him, seeing his naked wretchedness and his guilt. The words of the wizard, equipped with the Vani power, were piercing; his eyes filled with tears. The story was both personal and collective and the pain was intimate, personal, and intense. He gasped: "This then was the hidden wound? I should have known."

Sanath continued undeterred: "And you, Jonathan, have had many lives since then, trying time and again to help rebuild Camelot. You sought to repair the harm you caused, always loyal and dedicated, but always to the wrong prince or to a government in decline. Recently, for example, trying to defend the U.S. against its outside foes and always failing, because you could not make out the ways of the subtle enemies, the Dark Riders of Thanatophor. Seagull was always attracted by the vastness of the sea. Indeed, in another life, you were once, my poor friend, the knight Renaud de Cormorant, who knew of the prophecy of John of Jerusalem and the legend of Dagad Trikon but whose blurred consciousness could no longer relate to its content. You have suffered much for having once betrayed your king, but the debt has been paid now. Forget your bitterness and keep faith in your destiny. Verily the white monkey came to you, which indicates that you are forgiven and that the Gods will again be kind to you."

To hide the tears in his eyes, Jonathan looked away. His intimate fault line had been suddenly exposed in a crude light. This was a strange session of the Council, for never had the Hllidarendi spoken so directly before. At the same time, because of the magic of the wizard, his words penetrated deeply. Jonathan realized how, in this lifetime, he had been weakened yet another time, vainly looking for love through various love affairs. As a result, he was losing the subtle energy of innocence that was needed for him to properly pursue the quest. He kept this insight to himself, not raising his head, as if to hide from piercing glances. He felt Tracy's attention, of course; she had not been prepared to see her dear brother in this light although she was aware of his weakness. She had always been the one least prepared to sympathize either with him or with his former girl friends.

Mostly, at this moment Jonathan was aware of the black fire in the eyes of Lakshmi, who was looking intensely at him. What was she thinking? Was she disappointed? He realized Lakshmi's opinion now mattered to him more than he had previously suspected. At this moment he raised his head and looked up at Lakshmi. She was staring at him and whispered encouragingly: "Don't worry, you're fine, you're all right." She was beautiful with her sleek and silky black hair twisted up into a knot at the back of her head. He smiled nervously but his face was no longer on fire.

Joseph did not pay too much attention to his elder brother's dilemma, so focused was he on his own obsession. Bent forward, frowning, and breathless, he asked the wizard, "Master Sanath, can you please tell us what is the point of seeking if we cannot find?" He looked around the group and back to the wizard, as if to seek approval for his concern. "Please understand me: I sat through years of theology classes and was mostly bored to tears. People who talk or write about spirituality think they own the subject. In fact, they are just exhausting us with their own mental opinions. We don't need descriptions or road maps any longer. If there is any truth at all about us reaching a higher consciousness, let's get it. We must reach there, we must attain it. If there is to be any sense in our destiny, I cannot believe that it is to hang forever like a dangling yo-yo, between a Grand Scheme and a Foul Rift."

Sanath smiled happily. He always seemed especially patient with the frustrations of the former priest. "You can be forgiven if you experience a certain degree of uncertainty about the condition of existing." Joseph wondered whether the wizard was being sarcastic but the Hllidarendi went on nimbly, adding a fresh thought:

"The heroic quest is programmed in the brains of men, but they have to learn to separate it from their performance imperative, their drive for conquest.

Look, Joseph O'Lochan, you might try to visualize the human dilemma this way: we can knock on heaven's door but we cannot open it, because it opens from the inside, not from the outside. In other words, we are not on the side of the lock. But there is a code for knocking and if you learn the code, the door will open. I trust you realize that I have started to repeat myself for I started to explain this when I spoke about the lily of Anorhad." Joseph concentrated on not missing a word, staring pointedly at the master.

"By and large, it is hard for humans to keep faith in their deeper destiny. They stop knocking, they become discouraged or cynical. They invest their energy in what they can do, not in who or what they can become. Jobs become their quest and sex their chief investment in love. Naturally, true fulfillment eludes them. To cross the Gate of the Elephant, I dare repeat, we need to reach a balance between yin and yang, as Lao Tse said, future and past, hot and cold, sun and moon, thoughts and feelings. We are bound to seek this synthesis, yet unable to achieve it on a permanent basis. We just get fleeting insights through peaks of silence and joy.

Men and women either aspire to something they cannot reach, or they turn their backs on the quest and lose themselves in instant sense gratification and materialism. This is the paradox of the human condition, indeed the great paradox: Zen Buddhism exposes it,

Taoism plays with it, but the Deep Way breaks it. You are right, Joseph: the paradoxical condition of human beings may feel frustrating but it is only a transition. Now I see clearly that the Stealthstars cannot bring forward the next state of consciousness by themselves, but the Lady of the Rock (unlike me) must have foreseen this. She has certainly prepared a secret path for humans to receive the Gift, which is beyond the reach of Thanatophor. Next question, please."

Joseph frowned at the explanation. He was not entirely happy with the response but it was hard to pin the wizard down and he hoped that someone else would be able to elicit more specific information. Lakshmi had planned to ask a critical question relating to the nature of the Gift but she had been distracted by Sanath's response to Jonathan. An outpouring of powerful feelings carried her away. Casting her shyness aside and overcoming her embarrassment, she stepped in and asked almost plaintively: "Master Sanath, I don't think you have spoken the full truth about Jonathan. Please do it now because I feel it concerns me too." For days afterwards she would, at least in part, regret her boldness. The response came, sharp and incisive.

"You are right, Lakshmi, Erilie, maid of Eleksim who once was the Sheravalian captain, carrying the banner of the three-and-a-half coils. This age of darkness has been hard on you. Your fate has been intertwined with Jonathan's.

The love for the sea is the mark of the Elnorians. Olophon of Elnur, as a young warrior of the yuva platoon, was in love with Erilie, maid of Eleksim. However, he was unable to declare his love because she had never left the service of the High Lady before leaving Dagad Trikon to dispatch one of the caskets. Olophon was to become the last Nizam in Elnelok and he never married nor loved another. Your paths crossed thereafter for many eons, sometimes in happy encounters or, as I have already disclosed, in desperate passion. You caused the fall of the one you loved. The fusion both of you sought through carnal love can only be achieved on a higher plane. Still, both of you may yet achieve your full potential in complementing each other. If you so wish, you may, in this lifetime, taste such harmony. Your relationship shall be remembered as an example of what a successful marriage can be and what a man and woman in love can give to each other."

Lakshmi was stunned, shocked, and amazed, but the words do not do justice to the emotions that cascaded over her; they do nothing to convey the range of feelings and emotions that coursed through her breast. Some of the emotions she had long stored deep within herself were now bursting out. She felt shame creeping across her red hot cheeks. Her curiosity had been great, her heart's intuition had been confirmed, but she had not been prepared for such a public disclosure, or for such brutally direct information. "Serves me right," she told herself angrily. " Whom do I think I am playing with? This wizard is benevolent but his truth is dangerous; Oh, why did he embarrass me so much?" and then she revised that thought immediately, "Why did I embarrass myself by asking the question?" She came to realize that, in the mode of the Council's proceedings for the third day, Sanath, when asked personal questions, had no choice but to disclose a full response to the question. It was her turn to recoil and to look at the ground, avoiding Jonathan's gaze. It was better not to know about the past. In any case, it was not wise to ask personal questions. How would Jonathan react to her now? She should have asked about the Gift. She felt exposed and vulnerable.

However, Jonathan had received the wizard's words with a strange sense of acknowledgment. They had opened a little corner of his heart in which, until now, he had not dared to look. A new peace settled within him. He was happy to hear that the master had given his blessing to a future with Lakshmi. Without a need for deliberation or reflection, he knew the truth of what the master had said, that he and Lakshmi would live a happy and fulfilled life together. Little did he realize that he had been granted the blessing flowing from Kailash that the Goddess Uma had sought from the lord Shiva to help humans escape the Darkness.

Moreover, it was liberating to find at last the nature of the hidden flaw that was embedded in his flesh and in his being. It was as if the Hllidarendi had lifted an ancient curse that had hovered over his history, his peers, and the lost seekers of the West. It had something to do with controlling these famous flying oranges Lakshman was talking about after his vision in Amsterdam.

It was now Michael's turn to ask his question. Although he did so very respectfully, he seemed not to register any longer the subtle lift of awareness he had enjoyed a little while ago. It was as if switching the mind back into motion was quietly erasing the imprint of the secret inner state. As none of them had control over the elated state they had briefly experienced, they had all exited it again without even noticing it.

"Revered master, forgive my presumption, but I wish to ask the following question. Will you help us with words only or is there another way to empower us?"

Sanath blinked benignly at the gathering.

"Always to the point, I see. I shall respond to this question from Michael the Swift at the end. There are two more people who haven't spoken yet – Lorelei and Ivan – to whom, I should think, I will respond with words. Do you wish to ask a question, Lorelei?"

The young woman did not dare to ask about Mike or herself, having witnessed how the unbending light had embarrassed Lakshmi as it was cast on the past relationship between her and Jonathan. Cradling her hands, she answered a bit nervously: "No master, please respond to Michael's question. Mine is the same. We may all benefit."

Lorelei had adjusted well to the previous night's revelations. The growing complicity that was developing between her and Mike

473

was comforting her. She did not want to discuss it, least of all in public, since Lakshmi had been put in a spotlight because of her curiosity. It was amazing that the love that flowed between Avasthas a thousand years ago could still blossom. Lorelei could touch within herself the love between Esitel and Aliskhan and she now felt more clearly her feelings for Mike.

Ivan mentioned simply that he too would ask his question later. Sanath agreed and said that he would now respond to Michael's question. He asked Jonathan to pass him the special item of luggage from Washington. The elder O'Lochan pulled out two boxes from below the table and placed them on the tabletop. Sanath opened them. They contained the two small, elegantly engraved weapons: the Sadhan and the Glorfakir. The time had come to show how to use them.

The wizard closed his eyes, laid his hands on the shield and the sword, and quietly intoned some mantric incantations. He was the one who, ten thousand years earlier, had buried the weapons in the Alwakil fields, having directed the craftsmen to engrave the magic spells on them so that the weapons would serve only Avastha warriors. The plan for the return of the Stealthstars had failed. Sanath needed to unlock the codes for the weapons now so that they become compatible with ordinary men and women.

A long pause followed. After some time he opened his eyes and, looking majestic, he invited the companions to stand next to each other in a semi-circle, to hold each other's hands, and to close their eyes, all in order to facilitate the impact the weapons would have inside them. He asked Mike Aliskhan to stand at the right-hand end of the chain and to hold the Glorfakir sword in his right hand; Lorelei was asked to stand at the left-hand end. As soon as Mike took hold of the Glorfakir, they all experienced a growing feeling of unease. What was going to happen?

This was the process triggered by the magic weapons: there was a perceptible movement in the attention of all those standing in the human chain. It was not that their attention moved from one object to another: rather, their attention became much sharper and alive, taking on a magnified dimension, yet fully under the command of their will power. They felt a keen sense of alertness, without the underlying tension linked to, for example, the use of so-called awareness-enhancing drugs. They were completely in charge and completely at peace. Compared to this acuity, it seemed that their usual state of awareness had been wrapped in a foggy dullness. They heard the voice of Sanath, as if coming from far away. "Your awareness is your sword. The attention is the edge of the sword. Learn the art of Glorfakir fencing and you shall defeat the Dark Riders."

Sanath asked Mike to return the sword to him and he now gave the Sadhan shield to Lorelei. Their attention wavered and melted into a vast space of stillness. Their awareness moved from the sense of mobility that was linked to the alertness of the attention to a deep, gaseous, and motionless state. In this new condition, the notion of time disappeared altogether and they were floating in an energy-giving pool of silence. The feeling was soothing and regenerating. After some time, they heard Sanath's voice coming from far away again. "When the attention stops moving from one object to another but instead takes the self itself for object, the state of true contemplation opens. Meditation is your shield, which stabilizes you in the present moment where the Dark Riders of Thanatophor cannot find you. It is your intimate line of defense."

Then the wizard walked towards Lorelei and took the Sadhan from her. He raised the Glorfakir from the table and brought the two weapons to Lakshman, who was standing in the middle of the chain. He asked Lakshman's neighbors in the chain to touch his shoulders while Lakshman took hold of both the Glorfakir and the Sadhan. Sanath invited them to keep their eyes closed. They entered the third stage of the weapon's initiation.

Movement returned slowly to their awareness. Within the depth of the meditative state, some inner shapes of emotion and desires, traces of doubts and fears, deeper aspects of their inner being, came into focus. These forms of consciousness were presenting themselves, as it were, before an inner eye in their foreheads. Naturally, the manifestation of these shapes presented itself differently for each of them.

Lakshman witnessed how his attention constantly flew outside himself. It was carried away and often lost in the senses: tasting, smelling, seeing, hearing, and touching. These were the escape routes and the paths to constant temptation. He realized, of course, that he could not juggle with the oranges of the senses, something he had tried to master for so many lifetimes, vainly trying to gain control over his own mind. Now he found the way out, the method for the long-sought mastery over the senses as he effortlessly realized that he could control the gravitational pull of the oranges through a combined use of the Glorfakir and the Sadhan, a field of attention and meditation. This was most enjoyable and fascinating.

"I am what I am," he sensed with a silent jubilation. "And whatever that is, it is beyond thoughts, emotions or perception. Wow! This is rock bottom, solid, compact, Being."

From this vantage point, he witnessed how thoughts and emotions could come and go, whirling freely, and independent of his own desire. He saw how some of these thoughts and emotions carried the germs of the Dark Riders – be they jealousy or vanity, anger or attachment. He could equally see how they were galloping to bring his attention to either one of the thresholds of fears or doubts. One such fear was the fear of failing to achieve what he wanted to achieve: selfhood and love. He saw also the doubt in his own destiny and in the intrinsic goodness of the world. Fear and doubts, creeping and insidious, were the chief enemies on the path of his becoming, the first a tool of Belzebseth, the second a tool of Hangker.

The interesting thing was that this inner sight was detached. He recognized these psychological movements with a direct intuitive clarity and without being entangled in or affected by them. He realized that this had nothing to do with psychoanalysis, psychotherapy or other mentally driven processes. His witnessing standpoint was either much higher or much deeper than the normal analytical process that would not be able to bring the same sense of easy obviousness. He was both the knower and the information that is known.

He could not yet realize at this point that his companions, who were holding hands, had experienced a similar expansion of their self-awareness and that they had, in fact, jointly entered into a collective state.

Sanath's remarks had reached their ears, as if the wizard knew what was happening. "Behold the combined action of the Glorfakir and the Sadhan. Attention within meditation blossoms into introspection. Action within inaction shall give you the mastery of the field. Through introspection, the witness stage may be achieved and the inner eye activated, the inner eye that is the core power of the lily of Anorhad. It will catch all intruders – riders of doom, sneaky serpents of doubt, and shadows of fear – meant to take you down from the throne of your self. Introspection shall wash away all shapes of sins and free your mind. You shall embark on the most enjoyable travel, discovering as you go, the landscape of your inner being."

Sanath retrieved the weapons. It was the end of a unique and extraordinary exercise, their first training in the Deep Way. They slowly opened their eyes and looked at each other, their faces glowing. They all stood thus in a tight oneness in which Speech was unnecessary.

They each understood what the Sadhan and the Glorfakir had revealed: the manifestation of some of the deeper powers that human beings had within themselves: attention, meditation, and introspection. The maturing of these powers would bring them to the Avastha levels of mind-effectiveness and expansion that they thought had been lost for good. But nothing had been lost. It was still there, deep within them. They experienced a huge sense of relief. They took their seats and time passed in which they enjoyed the recognition of the beauty and grandeur of the inner world that Sanath had facilitated for them through the magic invested in the weapons. Lakshman, whose voice sounded muffled, muttered something like:

"It just did not occur to me that the weapons were within us."

The wizard, grinning, turned to Ivan and said quickly, "It is for you, my trusted friend, to ask the last question of the third session of my council." Ivan responded, pointing towards the ornamental wall decoration that had been at the center of the epic battle between the Archangels and the demons. "My question relates to the magic triptych of the dove. Before the battle with Hangker and Belzebeth, it represented the Virgin Mary with the dove of the Holy Spirit on Her head, Gabriel on Her right and Michael on Her left. When the Archangels manifested in this room, their image disappeared from the two sides of the Gothic triptych. What remained then was the image of the Holy Virgin with the dove above Her head. I think the dove was still there at the beginning of this meeting but now we can only see the image of the Virgin and the rays of light emanating from an empty place above Her head. I would like to ask why the image of the dove has disappeared now too? Had you noticed?"

Sanath seemed totally surprised and brusquely turned towards the triptych. His mouth opened but no sound came out. He bowed again in the same manner as when calling for the coming of the white monkey to manifest as the Archangel.

"No, I had not noticed. These are great tidings, Ivan Sadaka, and not of my making. What is now happening is far beyond my art and my magic. Perhaps I made a humble contribution to the calling of the holy Archangels, but I have had nothing to do with this disappearance. It announces the calling of the dove. Verily I say to you, the greatest of all powers has announced that it is now at work, here and now on this planet. I did not expect such a rich harvest for the third night of our council. Praise and glory be given to our High Lady, the gentle sovereign, and to the redeeming power that is hidden in the Triangle Rock."

MARRIAGE
AND MOURNING

Whilst most of the members of the Council returned to their rooms at around two o'clock in the morning, Michael and the Jetzlar grandchildren went out into the small French garden that overlooked the Rhine valley. They sat on the earth to meditate. It was a quiet starlit night and a mild wind caressed the hillside on which they sat. They felt humbled by the magnitude of what was happening: all petty worries had been removed in light of the majesty of what they had experienced, the touch of divinity within themselves, and the indication that divine powers were now intervening in human history in order to rescue the human race. If the disappearance of the Archangels from the triptych had indicated their manifestation into the world of mankind, the disappearance of the dove would then manifest the appearance of the Holy Spirit, the third person of the Christian trinity. Yet what could this mean? Only silence, a very deep silence, would answer that question in their minds. When the moment seemed right, they finished their meditation and, without speaking, they went off to their rooms and to sleep.

They were as yet unable to recognize the importance of the depth of inner silence they had touched and did not understand that it was a sign that they were reconnecting with their past Avastha powers. Their channels of connection to the Deep Way were not yet fully open and the perceptive state induced in them during the Council meeting quietly evaporated during the hours of rest that followed.

The following morning during a late breakfast, Lakshman and Lakshmi tried to get some more information from Sanath on the meaning of the miracle that had taken place during his Council – the disappearance of the dove. However, he muttered incomprehensibly under his breath and was not forthcoming in the least. When pressed, he snapped and offered an unusually vehement explanation. "What else is there to say?" he asked curtly. "The Council of the Hllidarendi is closed and the Vani, the power of speech, will not work any more. This power is bestowed to allow the listener to truly recognize what is being talked about. What would be left in your mind if I spoke further now? It would only be more words – words bound to create concepts in your brains. The concept is not the thing and would only bring confusion, not insight."

"Oh please, master," said Lakshmi longingly, "don't give up on us now; you can't leave us in the dark. What does the dove mean, and what is the significance of its disappearance?" The wizard shook his head, looked penetratingly at the young woman and, deferring to her intense sincerity, he changed his mind and spoke slowly.

"Lakshmi, what is happening now is not of my doing. A portent of tremendous significance appeared in the heavens. A great mystery that came from the world above is now moving on this earth. I sense that the prophetic vision of the knight John of Jerusalem is now taking its shape. The dove is the Holy Spirit of the Christian Trinity, which is the symbol of the great Mother Goddess. She might yet grant to mankind the six powers of the Avastha Houses and the seventh awareness in case they also receive the Gift that shall integrate them all. This verily would bring about the Golden Age. Yes, indeed, what matters at this point is the capacity to call up the Gift. I pray, I trust, I sense that it will be vested in mankind, but I do not know how or when." He grinned, as if to excuse himself from further explanation and left it at that.

The cousins spent some time discussing this response. Their brains refused to shut down, combing over the details of Sanath's words on the third night of the Council again and again to ensure that no sliver of meaning was lost. Yet their brains alone were simply not up to the task of retaining this subtle knowledge: they were like clenched fists trying to hold water in their grasp.

Michael and Lorelei spent a lot of time together over the following days, wandering through the local hills, following trails through the woods of the estate, sitting on lichen-covered boulders, and admiring the lofty view over the Rhine. They completely opened up to each other and things that were hidden deep within their hearts were revealed.

Thus it was that they chose to ask Sanath for his guidance and blessings. He had retired to his study in the Falkenlust tower, reading old parchments at a wooden table covered with ancient manuscripts. The two young people spoke completely freely about intimate matters, questions close to their heart. Lorelei evoked her summer affair in Italy.

"You know, Master, I realize how important relationships are for our happiness. After my flirtation with Silvio, Grandpa wanted me to understand something about seduction games and our hunting instincts. To drive the point home, back in Germany he invited us to see Mozart's *Don Giovanni* at the Semper Opera House in Dresden. Grandpa always has so much class! Don Giovanni was a playboy, like Silvio. The pangs of love of Donna Ana and Donna Elvira sounded quite pathetic to me. Both were pining for the same seducer who was already boasting of a hundred and three conquests in Spain alone. I got the point. Don Giovanni was singing *"Viva la liberta"* — Long Live Freedom, but he really meant his own freedom to take what pleased him, to indulge in the sport of stealing hearts. As his valet

Leporello mournfully observed, the heart of the seducer is a heart of stone. We were taken by the manner in which the music of Mozart exposed his fate when the statue of the commander he had killed took Don Giovanni into hell. He was a wretch, not a hero. However, there must be a right way to meet, seek love, and receive it and I wanted your advice on this."

"Yes, yes, of course," mused Sanath. "I am extremely fond of Mozart myself. Precious memories... I was sitting in the salon of the Schoenbrunn palace when he played as a child before Empress Maria Theresa. They understood each other well. Both were ancient Avasthas but did not know it, and there was no way of telling them... Anyway, let's go back to the subject. There is an art for love to really bloom, you know. This art respects subtle rules for a relationship to be mutually energizing and never boring. After all, pleasure is what we all want, isn't it?"

Lorelei nodded eagerly, inviting the master to be a bit more specific. He went on.

"The togetherness of man and woman should be comforting, playful, and free – it should be fun. There should be humor, charm, and elegance; there should be mutual trust and dedication. Such a marriage is like the eternal play of the waves and the shore. They face each other in eternal discovery, never tire of each other, always new, always fresh. Woman is the earth, man is the sea and the waves crash on the beach, again and again, for all to enjoy the evidence of the timeless play. There is no monotony in this repetition, no monotony at all. It is an embrace, a dance of natural energy."

Lorelei blinked. In a brief insight she could recognize the type of bond that wasn't a bond. The bond of Avastha marriage was both exclusive and free because true and deep love gives space to the other. It does not bind, it does not shrink into possessiveness and dependency, nor does it leave space for suspicion, fear or jealousy. She felt the stirring of that deeper love the wizard was trying to describe.

"You speak of marriage" intervened Mike "Is this the only way?"

"It is so. We, the Avasthas, we hold these truths to be self-evident.

Commitment and trust is required for deep love to flow freely, for lovers to be without doubts and fears, and we call this marriage. It seems modern men and women think otherwise but do they find happiness? Do they escape pain and boredom? They throw their love around, this way and that. They eventually marry, mostly soon to divorce, while leaving hurt and damaged children in their wake. Anyway, this is why so few children are born in your countries these days. The streets of many German or Italian villages are now quite joyless."

Lorelei had received her response. Encouraged by the vision of Sanath, she began to speak, hesitantly at first, because she wanted to express her feelings for Michael. However, almost immediately, Michael interrupted her with a direct question to the old man:

"Master Sanath, were you ever married?'

Lorelei frowned; she did not like being interrupted and felt that this was the sort of question that well-behaved people do not ask of a high wizard. However, to her surprise, this wizard burst into a loud and clear laughter. "Of course I have been married! Not in this particular lifetime, however, which I admit, has been extremely long. I never could quite manage it this time for I had to monitor the slow and steady rise of the Darkness. But I was married in my previous lives; I was married for instance when I was the Sand Keeper. In the past, most of the great seers, saints or wizards were married, for they knew that spirituality is about love. Marriage is the public and concrete way to announce love. Then it can spread from man and woman to the family and from the family to the society. It is so simple really. I always have been puzzled that trendy people in developed countries do not seem to understand the benefits of morality.

Nor do they know that romance can exist within marriage. Happy marriages are great blessings of Adivatar and the whole society benefits."

Encouraged by the friendly openness of the wizard, Michael finally asked a question that had been long on his mind. He cleared his throat, not quite knowing how to start.

"This point of balance between yin and yang, thought and emotion, is also surely the equilibrium point between male and female and the space of their intimate relationship. Well, you speak a lot about marriage but frankly, master, today there is an awful lot of sex going on without marriage. People have actually written books to tell us that sex itself is a spiritual ritual. So, when we speak about revealing the power of the feminine side, many think it is about sex and…

"I know, I know." Sanath raised his hand and interrupted him. His voice was calm but perhaps a bit tired. "The tedious repetition of a mistake does not make it a truth. Remember that the Age of Darkness started eight thousand years ago. Much experimentation went on during this long time. The claim that sex leads to the gods was made in Greek antiquity, through the rites of Eleusis, the ritual prostitution of Egyptian priestesses or the tantrika heresy in India and Tibet that left its imprints on many Asian temples, including at Konarak and Khajuraho. I admit that modern writers love it, yet it is a mistake. If sex were the way to the heavens, prostitutes and gentlemen equipped with a generous supply of potency-enhancing pills would be the first to reach the kingdom of God. Doesn't it sound a bit counter-intuitive to you?"

"Quite. But why all the fuss?" Mike was relieved by Sanath's no-nonsense response as he had not been sure how his question would be received.

"I have already partly explained this Michael. The myth of the Holy Grail was about the sacredness of the feminine reality, which is linked to blessedness. But it is completely beyond sex. Two thousand years ago, Mary was the unknown form of the Holy Ghost. The mother of Christ had vested her Gift, the ambrosia, in her son. Similarly, she shall grant it to her other children, the offspring of Eve, or at least to those who shall master the Deep Way.

The Gift is of the consciousness, not of the flesh. But hear now where the tantrikas, the sex worshippers, went wrong. In some cases the experience of drinking from Sangreal, the cup of beatitude, can be so intense that spiritual elation is enjoyed also as an extraordinary physical sensation. Some speak of a shower, some of a fountain. As I said during the Council, the pouring from the Holy Grail is expressed as fluid foam of unbelievable enjoyment flowing from the top of the brain. You must understand: it can penetrate every cell; it can lubricate your entire body with sheer bliss.

That intensity of spiritual elation causes a physical pleasure that is actually more intense than what man and woman can experience during sex. Of course, in the Dark Ages, very few could conceive of such a sacrosanct condition, leave alone experience this highest sacred state. It is the reason for the confusion of the tantrikas; they were failed yogis and this state eluded them. Thus, third-rate yogis reduced the human potential for spiritual joy to sex. You may call it a blasphemy and you would be right. I just call it stupid."

"Stupid? That's all?" Lorelei was surprised by this choice of words.

"You don't know, my child. Stupidity can be deadly stuff. When the humans fall below a certain level, the connection with the messengers of Adivatar are broken. God wants to communicate but he can't. Gabriel cannot help any longer. He too respects human freedom."

The conversation in the Falkenlust library continued for a long time. And so it was that the master Hllidarendi, wandering from the Holy Grail to marriage, finally completed his explanation of the

True Blood of Christ. Lakshmi had unveiled some of this mystery in Delphi thanks to the help of the white monkey.

Michael, reflecting on the difficulties of Joseph with the Church and the family events in Birchwood, realized how much the Christians had missed the point. Celibate priests, who feared sex, and the many Christians turned libertines who were now addicted to it had not understood the proper relationship between the togetherness of man and woman, fulfilment, and spiritual ascent. Sanath concluded with some words on marriage and sex:

"The fire that cooks your food can also burn your house. Marriage is the altar where the fire of sex burns in happiness for couples and families, in the privacy of the household.

If you bring the fire to the house, don't be surprised if it burns down the house. If there is no trust and commitment in such a private exchange, don't be surprised if relationships are upset, families destroyed, and society wounded. This was the wound of Lancelot and Guinevere. Remember, the black horses work together. Now like then, this horse of lust immediately calls for the horses of jealousy and anger. All this is so plain and obvious to me that, I must say, sometimes I fail to understand humans."

The youngsters profusely thanked the older man for his openness and adjourned to their respective rooms for a regenerative siesta. When they woke up in the late afternoon, they heard a commotion in the first floor and were surprised to find Sanath standing in the entrance hall. He looked very matter-of-fact, dressed in his travel clothes and ready to take his leave. Resisting the distressed pleas of the Jetzlars for him to stay a while longer, he told them to have courage.

"Keep heart and faith. These are my parting words to you; verily heart and faith used to be one single power – it was the same thing in the love that the Avasthas had for Adivatar. It is faith that brought the Archangels. Beyond forgiveness, faith and surrender indeed are the great qualities released by the lily of Anorhad, once it becomes all white. These qualities manifest the Avahan, the calling power. To this calling, the heavens always respond, as you saw when I sought the help of the two great Archangels Gabriel and Michael."

Before bidding them farewell, he mentioned that sad but unavoidable events would visit the assembled company. They should understand that he had been unable to intervene. Then the wizard spoke briefly to Jonathan and, now clearly moved, embraced Laira and Philip warmly. As he did so he whispered a few words in the Count's ear, pressing his hands firmly. Philip smiled faintly.

Standing shoulder to shoulder, they waved good-bye in the courtyard of the castle as Lothar took the wheel to drive the illustrious guest to Frankfurt Airport. They were all gripped by a huge sense of loss, feeling somewhat like orphans as they watched him go. They wondered whether they would ever see him again.

The feeling of loss sadly revisited them as Sanath had prophesied. Exactly one year after the battle of Jetzenstein, on a grey morning, Laira tried to wake up her husband but to no avail. Philip Luitwin, sixteenth Graf von Jetzlar, then in his eighty-eighth year, was found dead in bed. The passing of the sacred oak had weighed on him heavily and his health had deteriorated steadily. He had died quietly in his sleep, without apparent suffering, an ethereal smile on his ivory face. The pain and shock were great for Laira and the grandchildren.

On that same fateful day, as if a renewed and ominous challenge of the Darkness was taunting the already shattered inhabitants of Jetzenstein, two neo-Nazi parties made significant gains in local elections in several provinces of eastern Germany. The results of this perfectly democratic process would open for them the door of the federal parliament, sending tremors through the country and its neighbors. It became clear that a victory in the heavens does not translate automatically to a victory on earth.

The battle between the Archangels and the demons had not left Thanatophor powerless. His cavalry continued insatiably to roam the fields of human consciousness. The hoofs of the steed of the Dark Riders resounded through the hills and dales of those European regions affected by a dire return of poverty in the aftermath of the globalization process and the situation in the poverty-stricken parts of the world went largely unchanged. Laira, now helpless, felt that the enemies of her tribe and the ghosts Philip had fought his whole life had gathered strength again. The next night Lothar woke up in a hot sweat, having dreamed of the burning of the Reichstag in Berlin and of asphyxiation by toxic gas.

For two days, Laira walked in the castle and its courtyards, her face often bathed in tears, inconsolably talking to an invisible Philip. The hotel staff feared that, through sheer grief, she was losing her mind. She felt a part of her was gone, was missing. She did not know how to live with this great big lonely hole within herself. The grandchildren were distraught to see her in this condition; they were used to her being a kind, comforting, and protective presence in their lives.

Ivan and Alexandra came hurriedly from Italy and the cousins flew in from India to pay their last respects. Mike attended on behalf of the O'Lochan family. To everybody's dismay, Sanath was nowhere to be found. There was neither a ceremony in the church nor burial in the cemetery. A grief-stricken Laira led a simple farewell ceremony attended by family, friends, and the estate staff.

After the cremation, Philip's ashes were dispersed ceremoniously on the surface of the Rhine in accordance with his will. The river looked sullen and somber, without traces of the enchantment that had visited its shores in the aftermath of the celestial battle. Laira offered flowers to the river and, as she did so, she uttered sacred mantras. At this precise instant, clouds opened and a ray of light beamed precisely on the party of mourners. It was an auspicious sign and it warmed their hearts.

Thereafter Ivan spoke to the widow in consoling tones:

"Come, my beloved sister, remember what the wizard told us under the sacred oak such a long time ago. Death does not exist. Only the earth and water elements are dropped when we die, the material sheath. All the rest remains. During these past days he was still in the castle with you, I agree, but now he is gone. In the beginning of the ceremony, Philip was still around, silently watching, until we spread his ashes on the Rhine. I tell you, I saw flowers falling from high above; your husband waved to us and departed for the heavens. I believe I saw the shape of Sanath, in the Bardo, bidding him a happy farewell. Have faith that he fulfilled his destiny. Do not grieve, please, for this is not what he wants for you. Do not prolong this mourning. Remember Lairouchka: faith brings the Avahan power."

In the days that followed, Laira did not allow sadness to replace the proud legacy left behind by Philip. He had led a noble life through difficult times and had penetrated some of the mysteries of the heavens that most humans only aspire to discover after their death, if ever. So, she regained her composure and became serene. Inspired by the magic that Sanath's presence had previously brought to the castle, Laira decided not to let the gloom of the Count's passing overwhelm Jetzenstein.

Mike and Lorelei had kept in regular contact via e-mail and by phone; indeed, hardly a day passed without them speaking to each other and their closeness had grown steadily. During the year, Lorelei had flown to Washington a couple of times and lived with Mike in the Georgetown apartment that had been vacated by Mike's brothers. Their relationship matured in a rather charming cocoon of shyness and mutual fondness; indeed, the delicacy of this cozy proximity was reminiscent of the days of the Avasthas. Laira had quietly observed the growing relationship and the manner in which it unfolded gladdened her heart. She knew how much her beloved Philip had valued self-respect and had hoped for a rebirth of subtle Avastha values. This would reintroduce the Maryadas of the Law of Maat, the ancient code of righteousness. Thus, Mike and Lorelei further lifted the somber mood still looming over the castle by announcing their engagement, which had the happy consent of Laira.

Laira told the young couple that it had been the Count's clear wish to see the ancient love of Aliskhan and Esitel sanctioned one day by the bond of marriage between Mike and Lorelei. With his considerable foresight, he had even left a generous provision for Mike in his will. Such generosity, in stark contrast with the behavior of the patriarch of the O'Lochan family, touched the boy deeply. The news of the engagement brought great contentment to their friends and well-wishers.

Mike was now close to finishing his postgraduate degree. He decided that they should marry only after he had found a job because he did not want to be obliged to live off the proceeds of the Jetzenstein estate. Lorelei's happiness made her grandmother very happy too. On this happy note, Laira settled her affairs, and legally entrusted the estate to her grandchildren. Lothar and Lorelei took up their managerial responsibilities with the help of the director of the hotel, who was competent as well as loyal to the family.

The next year brought increasing layers of maturity to Lothar as he began to manage the estate while pursuing his forestry studies. Laira proudly attended an official function in the nearby village of Gundelfels, where Lothar was elected the local mayor. He and his sister were busy with the many demands the estate placed on them and were unable to leave Jetzenstein again until beckoned by great news.

Indeed, happy tidings drew them from the stronghold above the Rhine to the shores of faraway India for the long-anticipated wedding of Lakshmi and Jonathan.

November in New Delhi is pleasantly warm during the daytime but there is an invigorating freshness in the evenings. The houses along Pandara Road, hidden behind gates, are mostly painted in a worn creamy yellow that imparts an air of faded gentility. In this warm and defining light one could easily imagine the charms of living in this secluded colony. The area, a residential enclave of the former colonial British administration, with its spacious private gardens and tree-planted alleys is a green oasis of peace in the ever-bustling rhythm of the Indian capital.

Within the walled compound of the house of Shri Chandi Darshan Vani, MP, however, there was a hive of activity. He was the leader of a leftist party, concerned with eliminating rural poverty in the face of the great changes taking place in the country and the wealth that globalization had brought to the Indian middle class. These days, however, another duty kept him fully engaged. The next day would be very special, an occasion for indulgence in great festivity: the celebration of the wedding of his only daughter Lakshmi with Mr. Jonathan O'Lochan. At first, Mr. Vani, an influential Member of Parliament, wanted an elaborate celebration, as is the custom in the Indian capital. Nevertheless, the young couple preferred a more modest ceremony, and managed to persuade him otherwise. After all, Jonathan's parents and relatives would not be in attendance, only his brothers and sister. Eventually, a compromise was reached: a reception with friends and relatives at the Imperial Hotel and a more intimate family ceremony in a large marquee that had been erected in the garden.

Jonathan was in an auto-rickshaw returning bumpily to his prospective father-in-law's house; he was exhausted after a morning's shopping and from coping with the rapidly worsening traffic jams in the metropolis. Normally he would have been impatient but on this occasion he felt light-hearted and content, musing about the happy twist that fate had brought him. "I don't quite believe I am getting married tomorrow; it's not even scary! I can't recognize myself! In the past I was always afraid of making this kind of a commitment. I must say, Erilie, well, Lakshmi is truly a gem."

Peering over and around the noisy traffic, he let his thoughts dwell on some words of the wizard: that marriage sanctified by the protocol of the Avastha fire was a gateway to happiness, an invitation to great souls to take their birth as the children of such unions. Life was wonderful. He chuckled; since the nights of the Council, he thought Lakshmi had become even prettier.

Jonathan had left his Lakshmi in the company of Lothar, Mike, and Lorelei in the Janpath enclave, where Lakshmi had embarked on the gleeful chore of sari and gift shopping. Indeed, as befitted the status of the event, selected guests would be showered with lavish presents. He was glad that Lakshman, Joseph, and Tracy were also coming – they were actually on their way.

Jonathan had been greatly relieved to have been so well received by the Vani family, despite the fact that he had basically lost all worldly status and wealth, matters that are usually of some concern to Indian fathers when they marry off their daughters. It was fortunate that Shri Chandi Darshan had accepted the judgment of his daughter and had himself been able to recognize the qualities inherent in Jonathan. Was there some irony in the fact that an Indian girl should marry a penniless American, when, viewed from an Indian perspective, everyone in the USA, especially in the upper middle classes, was supposed to be rich? "A sign of changing times," he sighed as he pondered yet again on the vagaries of fortune.

His fortunes had recently changed for the better, through a succession of unexpected events. How could he know that the most unexpected twist of fate was yet to come?

WALKING THROUGH THE CURTAIN

L akshmi and her three friends were sitting in a sari shop scrutinizing the merchandise and sipping cool drinks. Salesmen sat on a long quilted bench in front of the clients, next to a colorful mountain of saris spread open at the women's feet. Consultations were unending and opinions flowed freely; there was such a dizzying choice of patterns and designs. The foreigners, as the salesmen called the three young friends, were amazed at the refined artistic sensitivity of these saris, which had been hand-spun in rural India. They had already reduced their choice to a dozen. As Lakshmi was explaining the subtleties of a particular fabric to Lorelei, something strange happened. A young boy of fifteen or so, dressed in red and apparently an employee of the shop, approached them with an invitation, gesturing to a curtain leading to a back room. "Please, Memsahib, Mrs. Daya Devi would like to meet you."

"How odd," thought Lakshmi. "I don't remember anyone of that name and, in any case, who would know that we were in this particular shop? It might be one of the relatives who saw us yesterday at the reception in the Imperial Hotel. Perhaps they recognized my father's car and driver parked outside. Let's check."

The four friends followed the boy, who raised the curtain to allow them through. They entered a back room and as they looked around they found it brightly lit.

"Congratulations, you have found the passage through the curtain." The lady who addressed them was sitting in an armchair before another glittering array of saris. She turned towards them as they entered, removing her spectacles as she did so. She was wearing a white sari with a large red border, and around her shoulders was a cream cashmere jacket. Her black hair was loose and fell down on her shoulders.

Her forearms were adorned with glass and gold bangles and she wore a large traditional mark of red turmeric on her forehead. Her smile lit up her entire face and revealed glittering white teeth with a small gap between the two upper front teeth. Her large black eyes exuded a sparkling joy. Two stunningly beautiful younger Indian women sat on either side of her on the floor. One of them looked after the older lady's handbag. They were also dressed in silk saris, one gold and the other blue.

The three friends advanced hesitatingly, looking at the lady in the armchair with a sense of premonition, and then made room for Lakshmi to move through and greet the three ladies. Lakshmi looked dazed. There was a special ethereal quality in the air of this back room, as if it was shimmering slightly. Mike, Lothar, and Lorelei were thus only half-surprised when Lakshmi prostrated herself on the floor in a traditional gesture of worship. In a voice filled with emotion she repeated, *"Namaste Ma, namaste Ma, namaste Ma."* This unexpected encounter was not happening in the Bardo but in the midst of her own world, in a sari shop in Delhi, and Lakshmi was overwhelmed to recognize the Goddess that she had met previously at the Basin of Vaikuntha.

"Here you are, Lakshmi, you've taken ages to cross this curtain. Congratulations at last and thank you for bringing your friends to me too," said Mrs. Daya Devi in a welcoming tone. Her radiant smile helped to put the visitors at ease despite the strangeness of the situation and her next remark. "I came here to choose your wedding sari."

For some moments Lakshmi found herself unable to raise her eyes; in fact, she could hardly move at all. Eventually, with her cheeks flushed pink, she raised herself from the prostrate position. Still blushing, she rose slowly to her knees. She brought her hands together and folded them before her face, as if to hide herself. Finally, she raised her eyes above the cupped shape of her hands and stared silently. The air was by now positively fizzing with subtle energy. Michael felt awestruck by the contrast between the bustling shop and this enchanting space. He stared in disbelief, incapable of comprehending what was happening around him. Finally he was impelled to break the silence and with due protocol, bowed slightly and said, "Greetings, my lady. My name is Michael O'Lochan and this is Lothar, Count Jetzlar, and his sister Lorelei."

However, Lothar heard none of all this because as he had been looking at the lady, the contours, shapes, and colors in the room gradually began to shiver, melt, and then disappear, to be replaced by an extraordinary vision. The entire space was filled with lights of blinding energy that radiated from the head of the lady. As for her face, he could see only the dark patches of her hair framing an oval space of dazzling light punctuated by the darker shades of her eyes and a third eye on her forehead.

The lady responded to Michael's introduction with a glance that was both inviting and penetrating. "I know that these are your names now, Michael. As for my name, Lakshmi greeted me correctly three times, for I have a triple name, remember?"

At that moment, Lothar's vision melted away. He looked around him, recognizing the room as it was previously, and in amazement, kept silent.

At the same time Mrs. Daya Devi granted Michael the special privilege of recognizing his own past history through a brief revelation, visualized in a series of portraits. Images flashed into his head and he saw some of the same scenes that Jonathan had visited in Cairo and that Lakshman had experienced when he opened the Casket of the White Feather. He saw the entrance of the cave of the High Lady of the Rock in the Gundaldhar Fault, a young woman who looked like Lakshmi holding an unfurled banner and dressed in red armor, and he saw the sacred cobra that kept watch at the gate of the cave. He came to realize how, through the ages Michael-Aliskhan, Lothar-Hanomkar, and Lorelei-Esitel had started their quest thousands of years back in the days of Dagad Trikon. He recognized, with a surge of joy that he had found the mysterious Goddess again, the Goddess that they had been looking for during many ages. Overcome by gratitude, Mike prostrated himself on the ground before Mrs. Daya Devi, who looked very much like the Lady of the Rock.

Lakshmi thought she heard someone say, "Prepare the cup, prepare the consciousness." She was still motionless, silent and adoring. In that condition she felt again the bubbling sweetness of the love she had experienced in the Vaikuntha Basin. However, this time she was fully present in her body and in her wakeful consciousness. That she could be inwardly enjoying the intimate proximity of this love again filled her with a torrent of joy. Lakshmi muttered to herself: "The nectar, the nectar. She is the Goddess."

Lorelei and Lothar sat on the floor, sharing in the grace of this special moment. When the Goddess spoke again, she said, "Forget about this Avastha story, forget the past. It just plays tricks on your mind and gives you false identifications." She addressed the young men engagingly: "No point in seeking to have visions either."

In saying this, she was gently calling them back to the present. She was telling Mike that, yes, it was true that he had had a long connection to this quest. Yet, it was only in the present that real progress could be achieved. She emphasized the point with crystal clarity. "What will you do with visions? For example, sometimes we take a boat to cross a river, but that doesn't mean we should carry the boat on our backs for the rest of out lives once the river has been crossed. It is the same for our past lives and actions. They are just steps that we have taken on the ladder that leads to the heavens. We need to move on. Whatever is to be achieved must be achieved in the present, in the here and now.

The state you are seeking is reality itself. You must experience it, you must taste it. It is neither memory nor theory nor hypothesis. Only the discovery of the beauty and the bliss of the inner Self can help mankind now. This is what the knowledge of the Deep Way brings." This injunction sounded very much like the teachings of Sanath Elkaim Ekamonon, the Sand Keeper. Would the lady now reveal to them what the wizard had kept hidden?

This thought emboldened Lothar to ask, "May I ask, Mother, how are we to discover the Deep Way?"

"There is a way to go beyond the restlessness of thinking that keeps your brains permanently distracted. The Deep Way is the blissful experience of natural, spontaneous living. In this condition, the relationship with your creator is restored, the relationship with nature is reestablished in its pure simplicity. You discover your subtle connections with the elements, the sun, the moon, the stars, and the inner togetherness with each other. Ultimately you become one, a new collective being, the culmination of history."

This was so powerfully said, the conclusion so unexpected, that they remained speechless.

Gently breaking their awed silence, the Goddess served them tea and warmly congratulated Lakshmi on her forthcoming wedding. "He will be an ideal husband for you," she said of Jonathan. "Poor fellow, he has suffered a lot in the past. You know, there are fifty-four specific considerations as to what makes an ideal marriage; you have fifty-one in place. The rest is for you to work out. I am sure you are going to look after him very well."

Lakshmi laughed happily at this unexpected turn in the conversation and was now completely relaxed. An animated conversation followed and the occasion took on the feel of a family reunion. No one noticed how, in only a few seconds, this unanticipated encounter had switched from one of total awe to a close, comfortable, and friendly intimacy. The rich display of saris provided a particularly colorful setting to this unique meeting. No one came and intruded or in any other way disturbed them.

Each of the four spoke in turn about their lives and aspirations, about the legend of Dagad Trikon and their apparent roles in the saga. Mrs. Daya Devi asked them questions, smiling encouragingly but often she did not directly answer the questions they asked her.

Finally, Lakshmi received, from the hand of the Goddess herself, a beautiful deep green-blue silk sari, with a darker border, covered with minutely intricate designs in pure gold thread. There was so much motherly love in this gesture that Lakshmi prostrated herself again in thankfulness. She thought, "This sari looks just like the sea: my Jonathan will love it. It's amazing how She knows everything!"

At this moment, one of the attendants signaled them to open their hands in the direction of Mrs. Daya Devi who was still sitting in the armchair. They felt a cool breeze flowing into their hands and a gradual cessation of mental activity.

After some time, Mike asked, "Forgive me, my Lady, for asking so directly, but are you the Lady of the Rock?" Mrs. Daya Devi looked serious and thoughtful as she responded.

"Evil has launched its onslaught most secretively with all its power and might. Nowadays, no one can make out who is a saint or a reincarnated demon. Indeed, a demon may be a politician, a mullah or a Brahmin. Who knows? The mother would not leave her children alone in a minefield of hidden devils. So she had to respond with the complete integrated form of all these powers contained in the heavens. She more than matched the camouflaging tricks of the demons with the art of her own stealth.

The Christians, for instance, have depicted her under the unassuming symbol of the dove, for she is verily the one who grants peace."

In a flash Lorelei realized that the disappearance of the dove on the Gothic triptych had presaged this very encounter.

Mrs. Daya Devi glanced at her swiftly, as if to confirm her understanding and continued, "Indeed, who could witness or bear her tremendous powers? Who could see a three-eyed face that shines like a thousand suns? Now you will understand the secret meaning of the tortoise that was shown to Lakshman. The Goddess has withdrawn all these powers within herself, like a tortoise hides under her shell. There is no way people can make her out. She is within the world and yet unseen, because she is the great illusion, beyond the grasp of any creature. She is shunya, nothingness, and even beyond shunya."

As she spoke, Lorelei looked at the ceiling of the room; her attention was distracted by what appeared to be small commas of white light that swam and criss-crossed the air in all directions, as if the words of the Lady were themselves beaming particles of light. She refocused on the Goddess who continued, "My children, this was the message hidden in the prophecy that was announced through the secret name uttered in the Gundaldhar Fault: 'Ma treya' means what the early Gnostic fathers of the Hllidarendi Order called the trimorphic protonnoia: the name reveals the triple manifestation of the primordial mother, the one they also call the Holy Ghost in the West. The Buddhists call this power Maitreya, the Buddha who was to return at the end of this time. 'Ma-treya' indeed means the carrier of the power of the triple mother, the one who controls the three areas: blue, yellow, and white. Meanwhile, Shiite Muslims wait for the Mahdi, the twelfth imam."

Ignoring the startled looks of those seated at her feet, she added with the twinkle of a smile in her eyes, "It was further written that the twelfth imam would have no beard." She smiled and Mike noted immediately, "This is indeed the secret name: She refers to the secret name of the Lady of the Rock, Imam Maitreya. And, no, of course women don't have beards."

Michael felt the veins in his temples pulsating rapidly. He dearly wished to connect with the Goddess on his own terms, in a very personal way. He was slightly upset that he was not experiencing the degree of emotional closeness that had so overwhelmed Lakshmi. As if reading his mind, the lady addressed him, looking straight into his eyes.

"As a matter of fact, I am not easily contained in a name, secret or otherwise, for I am neither this nor that." Then, as if realizing the puzzlement on the face of the young man, she suddenly delivered a more precise response to Michael's silent queries.

"The Lady of the Rock is today sleeping within each one of you. It is the Holy Ghost deposited in you, the power of transformation, waiting in three-and-a-half coils to be awakened. This power was sought by the Gnostics of all ages. It is feminine and responds only to innocence and purity. It will counsel, comfort, and redeem men and women of good will."

Lakshmi was fully alert. "This is it, this is it. Now she is going to tell us!"

Mrs. Daya Devi paused for a while as if to ensure that her listeners were still with her. Indeed they were captivated, receiving this knowledge, as it were, from the source. She continued, "The ancient knowledge of divine womanhood mostly disappeared over the millennia. Here in India, this ancient country of saints, the seers who handed over the lore from generation to generation called her Kundalini for this energy is coiled in on herself in the triangular sacrum bone. Today some simple villagers still sing for her awakening, yet no one knows how to awaken her. She is pure undulating energy, symbolized by ancient races in the representation of the sacred serpent. They called her '*Nagakanya*,' the virgin female snake."

At this moment Lakshmi recalled the words uttered by Sanath in the pergola of the castle of Jetzenstein and intervened. "Mother, where are the seven seals that must be broken?"

"They are within you, my child, within your own body. Each man and woman carries wondrous wheels of spiritual energies meant to release divine blessings. But these channels of communication to the heavens are kept sealed. They are constricted and closed as a result of our ignorance and all the mistakes we commit under the evil influence of the Dark Riders."

Lakshmi's curiosity was burning. "Did the Avasthas know about this?"

"Those who mastered the Deep Way had access to this subtle knowledge and the secret instrument within. The six great houses had the spiritual mission of maintaining the cleanliness of the six first centers, so that they would not constrict as a reaction to impurities and attacks from outside. They were ultimately defeated mostly because they did not find the way to unite in the seventh house, the highest house."

"The seventh house? Neither Sanath nor Lakshman spoke about a seventh house. This is the first time we've heard about it."

The lady smiled at them engagingly. "Indeed, the seventh house is hard to reach. Remember, children, the secret room at the top of the spiral staircase?" She paused for a while to let them make the connection and continued. "The seventh house is called the House of Ni. This is the place of mystery where all the powers of goodness, love, and justice integrate. It contains the talisman of Osiris. Osiris resurrected through the action of the feminine power, Isis. In the same way the divinity in you will resurrect in the seventh house.

You will understand the meaning of the fountain of Zem Zem that the prophet tasted in the paradise of Allah once the feminine power of Kundalini is awakened, rising through the six lower houses, breaking open all the seals, granting you your second birth."

This house was described by Buddha as the thousand-petaled lotus on the top of the head and he shall return there as Maitreya. The seventh house is protected by the double Gate of the Elephant and is beyond the reach of the Dark Riders. The seventh house was not supported by a tribe at the time of the Avasthas and it must now be formed as a great new tribe of the human race in a gathering of enlightened souls so that the Golden Age may return. The House of Ni, my children, is your destination: the seventh wheel of a thousand powers in the limbic area of your brain, the refuge of blessedness and home of divinity. Do not try to grasp it with your thoughts, for it is beyond. It shall reveal itself."

Lothar noted that these words echoed Sanath's response when asked in Jetzenstein about the chamber of treasures.

Michael had already been pondering over the words spoken by the Goddess before Lakshmi interrupted with her question on the seven seals. He felt the Kundalini was the key to the secret chamber, the one who could access the Holy Grail in the calyx of the brain. Such was the mystery of Dagad Trikon and of the ancient religions. He asked in a whisper, "In our tradition, the snake is identified with evil. Aren't snakes dangerous?"

"If awakened by the magic of a person equipped with divine authority, she is the gentlest mother. If provoked by those lusting after the inner powers of dominion, she transforms into the dragon of fury, carrier of a burning wrath. I just have to awaken her and she will chase away all enemies and sorrows. Michael, she is bringing you the Gift, the cup of nectar. She is the one who blows the celestial music of Rasa through the seven holes of your magic flute. She is the one to awaken within you the subtle centers within. They store the spiritual qualities that were worshipped by the great houses of the Avasthas. She balances and exquisitely fine-tunes your powers; she teaches and instills right behavior. Above all, she grants true freedom from the attachments that keep the human mind constantly hooked to lower levels from where it cannot rise."

Somewhat to his surprise, Michael found that he just loved it when Mrs. Daya Devi pronounced his name. It was like a soft caress inside his chest and he was so absorbed in it that he did not completely understand her last sentences, but he did not inquire further. Now Lakshmi mustered enough confidence and courage to go back to the core of her curiosity and she asked respectfully in a soft voice, "My cousin Lakshman involved me in a mission we called the Dagad Trikon quest, and, I believe he saw you in the visions of the caskets, in the rock complex of the lost desert, and in the palace of the turtle. I am certain too that I saw you in the Basin of Vaikuntha but it was not like this; I mean, I wasn't seeing you in the real world. Also, Jonathan had been asking about a public function led by a holy woman in a stadium in Saint Petersburg in Russia many years ago. The people there felt the cool wind in their hands as we do now. Mother, was it you?"

"I have been in many places, Lakshmi. I was certainly in Saint Petersburg and I was in Delphi the day you arrived there. I was present in the resort of the Maharashtra Tourist Development Corporation in Ganapatiphule. I saw you as you sat on the sandy beach in front of the Ganesh temple, gazing at the setting sun shedding its light on the sea. My followers, those who have already found me were the people all around you. They had gathered there from the four corners of the earth for the festival of the Great Mother." Her eyes were sparkling and she laughed.

As the impact of these words sank in, Lakshmi felt an emptiness in the pit of her stomach. She was quite despondent. "We have been searching for you over the millennia. How come those people found you when we were still searching? Why didn't we meet you in Delphi or earlier? Why didn't you tell us? Why aren't we your followers? " With tears in her eyes, she was about to add, "It is not fair," but she stopped just in time. The exchanges were so simple and direct by now that it was easy to forget oneself in this atmosphere of cordial proximity.

"Some of my followers think they follow me but they don't. Some who don't know me, in fact, follow me. You should not be sad.

There is only one Gift and only one way to receive it, but human beings attempt to follow many paths to find it. Some shoot like arrows to the target. Some must go around in circles, especially those driven by an inquiring mind; they can become attached to the game of search and discovery for its own sake. Both styles have their meaning and their consequences. You and your companions chose the path of the inquiring mind long ago and for a little while longer you must pursue this quest to its finish. Some distance is still left to cover. At some point you'll find that the inquiring mind does not help any more and that an intellectual approach cannot bring you to where you want to go. It may bring you close to the house of destination, which is your very own home. It cannot make you enter that house. On the other hand, your search will, in time, help others who are searching too, pointing to the right destination so that they may find this cherished abode on the map of their being."

Lakshmi stared at her incredulously, feeling chided at being side-tracked by her intellectual approach, but Mrs. Daya Devi continued, "Be reassured: to have a brain does not mean you don't have a heart. Both must work together. It is through the heart that devotion and love can ultimately take the brain, the knower in us, to the core of our beautiful innermost dwelling. Your heart is very much alive: indeed, it is, as you already know, in recognition."

"Mother of all graces, shall we not also receive the Gift?" asked Lorelei hesitatingly, with an imploring glance. It was the first time she had spoken. There was such a compelling fluidity in their togetherness, such an encompassing atmosphere of trust, proximity, and ease that chatting with this mysterious woman felt like it was the most natural thing to do. They were now thoroughly enjoying themselves. Her question turned out to be very much to the point.

"You have, my child. You have received it already: it is blowing on your hands," she said with a huge smile, as the mystical commas of light seemed now to spring forth from the very top of her head. Lorelei thought she could see a jet stream of white energy rising majestically from the parting in the center of her shiny black hair. In her outstretched hands, she felt again distinctly a cool breeze emanating from the lady. There was no fan or air-conditioning in this otherwise hot storeroom.

The lady continued to unfold the mysteries of their quest in a simple and direct way that was most enlightening and helpful.

"Yes, the Gift is brought to you by the cool wind. But it is still hidden, so to speak, in its wrapping paper. You must unwrap it carefully now through your meditation. In this movement much shall be revealed." They looked at her with great expectation, waiting for her to chart the road ahead. Mrs. Daya Devi continued, "The wind you now feel blows from the infinite sea. You have reached the shores of the great ocean of the Self and the first waves on the beach are gently lapping at your feet. When you shall swim and dive, many wonders will come to you. You shall discover pearls and jewels of knowledge and uncover the secret mechanisms to open the human consciousness. You shall master the working of the Deep Way. Not everything can be revealed now: you must first increase your receiving and storage capacities.

You must also remain in the midst of these confused human beings, not becoming enveloped in their fog of illusion but still sharing their problems with them. In this fashion you shall understand and help them better. You are closer to them when you can still see things the way they do. In this way, you will oblige me." She added these last words with an encouraging nod, a broad smile, and a renewed shine in her black eyes. "I need your help. I cannot do this by myself. The purpose of my brave children, the Stealthstars, is to carry candles of light while walking a little longer in this dark place. For darkness itself has also a meaning: it is in darkness indeed that the meaning of light is revealed."

She closed her eyes, paused for a while, and then added slowly, in a meditative mood: "You shall light your own candle and while doing so, you shall slowly remove the veils that cloud the minds of modern men and women from within yourself. Thus, you and all the others who have been seeking for ages shall now subtly heal the awareness of the human race. All of you shall be able to share the truth, help this earth, and fulfill your destiny."

The peace of a deep silence lasted for a long time. Finally, curiosity returned. "Does this mean that we will recapture our ancient powers?" asked Mike hopefully. "Will we be able to fly in the air, destroy demons or talk to each other telepathically?"

The Goddess responded patiently as if addressing a child who did not quite understand a lesson. "I am a mother. I want to help you to mature properly. First comes the awakening of the Kundalini, granted by an authorized master and not by one of these cheats who tries to make money out of religion. Kundalini grants the experience of Samadhi, the opening of your consciousness. Then you progress. It has to happen step by step: achieving a stable state, settling down to sustain the condition of the twice-born, and then moving on from there. You will come up gradually, with no need for showing off. All these books about mysticism, parapsychology or science fiction will not take you anywhere. By reading books or watching movies you do not become a higher being. The Gift to be granted to your race is something real. You see, a mother must always be a very practical person."

Lakshmi was emboldened by this last remark and she asked, "How is it going to work out, Mother? I mean, we feel the Gift now, you allowed us to feel the cool wind, the experience of Samadhi, but how is it going to work out for all of them, those on the wrong side of the curtain? They are still lost, aren't they?"

"Many charlatans have sold their wares on the streets in the guise of religion and many fanatics use religion to spread hate. This is very different. When you realize the truth of your being, you reach true love and this is what religion is all about. When you reach the abode at the core of your being, you rest – secure at last, in the wonderful comfort of inner peace. Man cannot establish peace in society until he has established peace within himself."

Again, Lakshmi wished Jonathan were there. He needed this advice, preoccupied as he still was with the troubled state of world affairs. The Goddess continued, using the Vani power. Everyone present felt that they were actually experiencing what she was talking about deep within themselves.

"First you become completely integrated inside. There is no compromise on this point. Morality must be part of your life and the Atma, the soul, the divine essence of your Self will then be able to shine through in your behavior. When the Spirit starts acting, you manifest your meaning. You will then have the power to feel happy within and to make others happy too. You'll enjoy one personality, free from contradictions. The joy is not damaged and this is indeed the gift from the heavens: the opening of consciousness brings the splendor of truth at last. In this light, you shall integrate within and also become one with each other in a continuing stream of love." She paused for a while, then added softly, "The whole body of enlightened people will arise and open the path for all men and women."

The silence was sacred. Behind the peace of their closed eyes, they were traveling through time and space into the now, traveling within the mystical shell of their core essence to a glorious place where being is verifiably real.

There was no way of knowing how long the meeting lasted. When they opened their eyes again, the ladies-in-waiting were standing; it was apparent that it was time for them to go. Lakshmi felt her heart become as numb as stone; Mike sensed a churning in the pit of his stomach; Lorelei was just staring through the soft moisture that her feelings had brought to her eyes.

The Goddess took a small, pale blue envelope from her bag and gave it to Michael. "Read this at home," she said. She told them she would always be there for them and that they would indeed meet again. Relieved, they slowly bowed.

One by one, as if spontaneously following some ancient protocol, they walked backwards slowly and respectfully to the curtain and left the storeroom.

They found themselves once again in the atmosphere and bustle of the busy shop, but they remained detached, insulated from the agitation and noise around them by a thick mattress of inner silence and the depth of their emotions.

WHAT'S BLOWING
IN THE WIND?

H alfway towards the shop counter, Lakshmi said suddenly, "Oh, I've forgotten my shawl," and she made her way through the curtain to the back room. Seconds later, she rushed out with shawl in hand, looking agitated. "Where have they gone? Did you see them come out?"

The salesmen looked up at her because of the disturbed tone of her raised voice. Mike asked, "What do you mean?" Lothar checked the back room; it was dark, dusty, and empty except for some cardboard boxes piled up against the wall.

"Where are the three ladies who were in there?" Lakshmi asked the shop owner.

"Which ladies, madam? That room is simply a storeroom. Only our staff go in there, and there is no other exit."

"I really don't understand what is going on. The young man, dressed in red kurta, your attendant, took us to meet Mrs. Daya Devi in there. Where is he, please? He'll confirm what happened."

"Memsahib, I am very sorry but there is no one dressed in red working in this shop. I don't understand what you are talking about. Is something wrong?"

Lakshmi, the Jetzlars, and Mike looked about in complete bewilderment. Mike gathered himself together. "No, Lakshmi, no one came out of the room, otherwise we would have seen them.

It's all right, everything is fine, let's just pay for the saris we bought, and leave."

They paid the bill, collected their purchases in two large plastic bags, and started towards the door. Lakshmi stopped and looked at the small bag that hung from her arm. She took out the sari she had been given by the mysterious lady and showed it triumphantly to the others for it proved that they had not dreamed up the whole encounter. Lothar scratched his head and answered, "I know, I know," and then pointed to the curtain. "Look, we didn't notice the pattern on the curtain!"

The design on the curtain depicted a frieze of small dancing elephants in a warm orange ocher color on a burgundy and pink background. Lorelei looked dreamy as she whispered, "The passage of the elephant? Wasn't that the color of the Gundaldhar fault? Is this the passageway between the two worlds, here, in this shop?"

"C.S. Lewis told the story of children walking through a wardrobe to enter the world of Narnia," commented Lakshmi. "Well, I guess this time it was just a curtain. This specific curtain is wearing little dancing elephants. To me, it looks as though they are guarding the gate of the Mother, just like the child God Ganesha is reported to do."

Lorelei summed it up thoughtfully, saying, "I think this is just symbolic; the passage is in our mind is everywhere, and it opened up for us." They smiled at each other with a lingering sense of disbelief and left the shop under the quizzical glances of the salesmen. They had been good but strange customers.

Back in the heat and the noise of the street, Lorelei breathed in the fragrance of India she liked so much, the heady mixture of heat, dust, and incense. The shop faced on to one side of a green square with a small temple in the center. The square was surrounded on three sides by trees. In front of the temple, an old Brahmin was decorating a stone statue of the goddess Durga with red turmeric powder in preparation for the October Navaratri festival and chanting repeatedly in a raucous growl, *"Om aim, rhim, klim, chamundaya viche namaha."* A couple of monkeys in the trees were watching him, ready to snatch any bits of food offerings, for monkeys were tolerated near the temple. Lakshmi and her friends, still absorbed by the glowing vision they had seen in the storeroom, did not notice that one monkey looked distinctly different from the others. They climbed into the Ambassador car, which resembled an old British Morris Oxford from the 1950's. Back home, they were greeted by a jovial Mr. Vani and repaired to the shady verandah overlooking the garden. Lakshman had just arrived from Mumbai and had already met up with Jonathan. Tracy and Joseph were due to land at New Delhi International Airport in a few hours' time.

After extended and joyful greetings, Lakshmi, Lothar, Mike, and Lorelei glanced at each other because they did not know how to introduce the subject of the encounter in the sari shop with the Goddess; Lakshman and Jonathan would be so disappointed to have missed it. Lakshmi cleared her throat and, not knowing what to say, she just took out the special sari from her bag and put it on the table. "How beautiful, quite extraordinary," said Jonathan. "This is like looking into deep water, like a lake, or, rather, like the sea with golden Avastha sailing vessels navigating its waters." The sari fascinated him the more he looked at it, touching something deep within him.

In a low voice, Lakshmi began to relate the fantastic and extraordinary encounter they'd had in the back room of the sari shop. She ended her account by saying, "The one and only thing that disturbed me as I was at her feet was simply how much I wished both of you could have been there too for you've both invested so much of yourselves in this search."

She was surprised and somewhat relieved when she heard her fiancé responding, "Don't worry, my love, this sari is actually meant as a present for me. I am the one who will enjoy seeing you in it and it is exactly my favorite color." They laughed, relieved to see him in a light and happy mood.

Lakshman had stretched out his hands, and he told them, "Just see: the air is still, not a leaf moves in the trees, yet a cool wind is coming from the sari. I think she gave you one of her own. The workmanship is exquisite – quite exceptional."

They could all feel the breeze coming through their finger-tips into their hands and flowing from their hands into their whole essence. The breeze was taking their attention deep inside. It was rather like navigating through a network of subtle channels into the profound silence of their being. Gradually the rhythm of thoughts and reactions slowed down. Lakshmi, Mike, and the Jetzlars felt they were back on the other side of the magic curtain, in the back room of the shop. After a while Jonathan whispered, "There is no denying it. We all feel it now; it's the wind of Pentecost." The others opened their eyes and look at him.

"What did you say?" asked Mike.

With a movement of the head Jonathan gestured towards the sari. They again spontaneously closed their eyes. The feeling was subtle and easier to perceive when one's attention was not distracted outside. The wind coming on to their hands had a soft, relaxing effect on the entire nervous system. A blissful peace settled into them that was way beyond any thoughts or emotions, a peace that enveloped them softly. It took on a volume that filled their entire being. This lightness of being was delicious, a complete wellness that spread softly, producing a sense of delight within each one of them.

Yet, in a sense, it was almost too much; they could not fully absorb what they were experiencing, like a cup that is too small to contain the water poured into it starts to overflow. They gradually came out of the silence, bubbling with excitement and eager to share their powerful impressions with each other. Thus, they lost the subtle connection with the sacred wind.

Lakshman felt both stimulated and inspired. He started speaking, slowly at first and then faster, as the flow of thoughts rushed to lay bare the itinerary of the secret quest beyond the mind. "It all fits together. Remember the spiral staircase under Sanath's 'Schatzkammer' in Jetzenstein? It was the staircase to the chamber of truth, again the symbol of the mystical serpent power, the one that is coiled in the sacrum bone as three-and-a-half coils, waiting to reach the chamber of truth, which is the limbic area of our brain.

From all over the world, the wizard had collected objects that served through the ages as beacons for the understanding of the Kundalini and stored them in that chamber. He did not reveal this to us, nor did he speak about the disappearance of the dove from the Gothic triptych, for he knew only the Goddess could bring the ultimate revelation. Sanath understood that the word is not the action and this Kundalini can only be revealed by the inner action of its awakening, not by words.

In his *Book of Prophecy*, the knight John of Jerusalem, another templar, clearly states that in the millennium after the millennium, the Great Mother will open the age of redemption and close the age of the barbarians who polluted the earth. My guess is that the templar knights had found out something about the Kundalini in Asia. The sacrum bone had a role in their rites and the knights were accused of kissing it, as the king of France wanted to destroy their Order of the Temple. During their trials, the Inquisition brought charges of sorcery and sexual perversion. The knight Renaud was a survivor of this persecution. It fits. How come we didn't see it?"

"See what?" asked Jonathan, captivated by his friend's intuitive explanation.

"Joachim dei Fiori, an Italian Cistercian monk in the Middle Ages and a seer, predicted that the Age of the Holy Ghost would come after the Age of the Son, the era of the Fish, which is the Christian era. Christians believe the wind carries the energy of the Holy Ghost. Who is the Holy Ghost? Do you remember the Gothic triptych of the dove? The dove was positioned above the head of the Holy Virgin; I now see it was her symbol. When the dove left the Gothic triptych during the last night of the Council of the Hllidarendi, as the Archangels on the Gothic triptych had done before, it indicated to us that the Goddess herself is now at work in our world. Today you had this extraordinary encounter with Mrs. Daya Devi. You had the proof of this hypothesis."

The Jetzlars were staring at Lakshman questioningly; he continued, quite focused. "When you met her, she exposed both the Kundalini and the cool wind, thereby revealing the meaning of the serpent power. Who awakens the Kundalini? The Goddess does! At the same time it is when the Kundalini rises that we can feel the wind. What does the wind mean according to the Christian tradition? It announces the Holy Ghost. So, it is obvious that the Holy Ghost was the Gnostic code word for the Goddess, the Great Mother that was worshipped in antiquity. She controls the Kundalini: this is why Athena and Isis were represented with the emblem of the sacred serpent. This is what the Lady of the Rock stood for at the core of Dagad Trikon, the entrance of her cave guarded by the Ureus, the sacred cobra."

He spoke slowly, as if overwhelmed by the implications of what he was saying. "She is the Holy Ghost. The Holy Ghost is the Goddess. Look at the Christian trinity: A father, a son, and, yes, why not a mother? The Great Mother that, according to John of Jerusalem, will change history in the millennium after the millennium, the third age of Joachim, the third Christian millennium. In the seventies, in the musical 'Hair,' they sang 'This is the dawning of the Age of Aquarius.' Well, it is. Aquarius symbolizes the vibrations, the wind. This subtle energy, the wind of the Holy Ghost, is what we felt coming from this sari, probably just because she touched it. So the power is within her. Christ had this power within him too, which is why those who touched him were healed. Don't you agree? It is so clear now."

Lakshman concluded, "The Holy Ghost first blows as the wind, as the Gnostic fathers knew. If we can absorb more of this energy she will eventually reveal the Gift: the wind flow concentrates, so to say, in a lubricating flow of blessedness within. That is the blissful consciousness symbolized by the legendary chalice of the Grail, contained in the cup of our skull. The Gift is the soma, amrita, the ambrosia. It is, my dear friends, the elixir of eternity, the ambrosia that Parsival sought and Galahad found. We searched for it for many millennia. It all fits together," said Lakshman more slowly, awed by his own insight, "but the plot is bigger than anything anyone guessed before. This is indeed the cornerstone of the Grand Scheme. Eureka!" They kept silent for a while to let the idea sink in.

A servant arrived bringing chai, a sweet Indian tea, and samosas, salted pastries filled with spicy ground vegetables and meat.

Lakshmi's eyes flickered as the insight came to her. "As an archaeologist, you used to say that the fun is in exploring, not in finding. Now I wouldn't be so sure. Do we want to search or do we want to find? Let's be attentive to recognize truth when we encounter it. Remember, Parsival saw the Grail but did not recognize it. Remember how Orthodox Jews are still waiting for the Messiah, two thousand years after his coming? In my opinion the strangest aspect of this Avastha prophecy today is that mankind is still waiting for something, which, actually, if we believe what we just saw, has already begun to happen."

"Yes, it is there. It is working but out there in the world, the picture is quite blurred," interrupted Jonathan. He frowned and with a slight strain in his voice continued, "We can see both threats of destruction and the potential promise of redemption, albeit a very faint one."

"What do you mean exactly? Are you referring to your experiences in the Middle East?" Mike knew the mind of the former diplomat, but Jonathan elaborated convincingly, "The outside world, the international scene, it is all part of the same movement; it is all within the Grand Scheme. Could it be, just as in the title of the movie 'Apocalypse Now'? Just see: violence is spreading around the world from old Jerusalem while some human beings are discreetly building the new one in their consciousness? Jerusalem is linked with Christ who is now slowly opening the narrow gate of the lily of Anorhad after the death of the sacred oak. It makes sense. It does make sense. It explains the Christian prophecies about his second coming."

Lakshman agreed with his friend's explanation. "I confess that after Sanath's explanation of the death of the sacred oak I was scared of the prospect of more conflicts, terrorism, and destruction. In the Oikos scenario this obviously leads to breakdown point. Now, after your extraordinary meeting today with this holy Lady, I am sure this time redemption is possible."

Lakshman added approvingly, probing a collective insight further, "If so, people in the world out there do not know it, and as long as they don't, it does not exist for them. Not yet. Destruction, of course, is well advertised. Usually it has a way of taking care of itself. What about redemption?"

Jonathan nodded vigorously and said with a broad smile, "The point is to tell people about the redemption – but how?" Lothar echoed the doubt: "Who would believe us?"

Silence reigned again; no one attempted an answer. The noise of Delhi's traffic reached them faintly, as if muffled by invisible walls around them.

After some time, Lothar intervened. "Let's recall the words of Master Sanath. For a very long time the sages of the East and the knights of the West were looking for the Gift, the greatest prize that mankind can attain. Many people, including hermits, some knights in the Middle Ages, writers, the Stealthstars, even some pop singers, all of them, in their own way, have been on the trail. Now we know that it is the gift of the virgin Goddess. Moreover, we know that she is within. It's amazing, isn't? She is within each of us. The Lady of the Rock has hidden her redemptive power in the sacrum bone of each and every one of us."

Lakshmi's view of the Dagad Trikon legend story was now crystallizing. From early in their search, she had sensed that the Lady of the Rock would play a central role in the prophecy and that she would reveal the feminine dimension of spirituality and the spiritual aspect of womanhood.

Lakshmi had long been wondering whether Hinduism, her own religion, was right in stating that God is also a woman. Lakshmi had the first confirmation of this through her extraordinary experience in the Vaikuntha Basin. She observed with a bright smile, "Clearly it is the Goddess who controls the mystic serpent. She is already pushing the wheel of history into the new age. And I'd say she has begun to do something about it herself. She showed us that today. Since the Kundalini resides within each one of us, the Goddess invites all of us to join in this transformation. That will close the gap between spirit and matter and reverse the trend of the Foul Rift. Today we crossed the curtain, the gate of the elephant, and rediscovered the passage between the inner and the outer worlds."

"Thus spoke the legend of Dagad Trikon," Lakshman whispered. Mike continued, "We have learned so much. Now we need to do something about it." Lakshmi looked at him fondly and concluded mischievously, "Leave it to us. You guys have made a mess of this world. Let the women now help to fix it."

"What do you mean?" asked Jonathan somewhat amused and slightly vexed.

"I'm just kidding." She paused for a while and with a brilliance shining in her eyes, continued, "The Kundalini is the pure, feminine power. We all have it within, stored, as Lothar just said, hidden in three-and-a-half coils in the triangular sacrum bone; all of us, men and women alike. This explains the shape of the Gundaldhar fault, in the middle of Dagad Trikon: it was a huge symbol offered under the stars of the desert nights. I tell you, my friends, the Kundalini delivers the talisman of Osiris that brings resurrection." She raised her voice joyfully. "We will be called upon to share the knowledge of the Deep Way and the Gift that we felt today in our awakened state. Beauty inside, once revealed, shall transform the world outside. This is the dream of all religions, isn't it? But I hope you'll forgive me for not dreaming about this today," she said, getting up and blowing them a kiss in a playful manner. "See you later, I have a wedding to prepare for!"

Jonathan's eyes followed her as she walked jauntily to the house, and he muttered gratefully, "If God wants to bless a man, He gives him a good woman. Frankly, I am so lucky to have Lakshmi. Yet, I sense, this impending marriage is not the end of our road but a new exploration, a new beginning."

Immersed in his own train of thoughts and with his mind back in the storeroom of the sari shop, Mike said pensively, "It seems we have learned much, but it's hard to guess how much more there is to know. What about the other Stealthstars, for instance? Where is our disappearing wizard now? Mrs. Daya Devi mentioned that 'for a little while you must pursue this quest to its finish.' I suppose it applies to all of us. However, I don't know what it means for each of us individually. I for one would have liked to have met some of the other Stealthstars, Lidholon for instance, who, according to the saga, would be our close friend." Lothar nodded in agreement and Mike leaned forward to drive his point home.

"We must decode the Deep Way, the science within that was known in the First Age of the Avasthas. What about the other caskets Lakshman saw dispatched to the corners of the earth in his vision in Iceland? There are still all these bits of parchment out there. Surely, they also contain revelations for our race. We must find out."

Lothar interrupted him suddenly: "Hey Mike, we forgot about the letter she gave you; why don't you open it now?"

Mike nodded, took the small envelope from the breast pocket of his shirt and opened it slowly. They smelled a strong fragrance of rose and jasmine. The handwriting on the letter was round and childlike. Mike stretched out the letter on his knees and slowly read aloud:

My dear Michael, my son,

I want you to know that each of the six great houses of the Avasthas is the custodian of a prize; the fruits of the tree of life to heal the nations of the earth, fruits that you have yet to discover. Become a child, cross the Gate of the Elephant, go inside: you shall climb the tree and you shall find the fruits accordingly.

The greatest prize beyond them all is the seventh fruit and I have already bestowed its gift upon you and your friends. You shall receive it in your hands and your hands shall speak. The inner secrets will be revealed. You shall achieve the inner conquest of the Self.

Nowadays, they may make movies about Judgment Day but they don't believe in it. Yet, a day is coming that is the day of love and justice. The twelfth Imam, the Mahdi, Maitreya, and the one they call Kalki in this land, have all been announced in the Holy Scriptures.

They are all merged into one great movement of manifestation to reveal the power of the love that acts, the power of the Holy Ghost. I am preparing the way for the white horse of the heavenly rider, he who is the first and the last. Behold the bright morning star.

The water of life shall flow in New Jerusalem and they shall drink of the blessed fountain.

Some who think they know me, in fact, haven't found me. And some who don't even know me, in fact, are finding me. Remember: I am elusive.

To those who are humble, I shall grant the mastery of the Deep Way. Mankind has forgotten me but I have not forgotten them. Tell your friends.

Your loving mother,
Daya

Michael remained silent. The characters on the page were dancing before his eyes. After some time he cleared his throat and said hesitantly, "Well, it's really very nice of her to write me like this. It sounds that there are still many things we need to figure out. I don't really know where to start."

"Jetzt," said Lothar abruptly.

"What's that?" asked Mike, a bit startled.

"He means '*now*,'" responded Lorelei with a helpful smile, translating from German the word that, centuries ago, had given its name to the family and the castle of the Jetzlars. "Remember the teachings of Sanath? Everything to be discovered can be found in the here and now. The Goddess also said so."

They looked at each with a sense of common understanding, enjoying the togetherness, the unique oneness of their quest. Once again, they stared at the sari that Lakshmi had left on the table and closed their eyes. They opened their palms and began to meditate.

How refreshing was that gentle cool breeze. Michael turned to his friends with a grin and asked:

"What's next?"

GLOSSARY

This Glossary has been extracted from the Chronicles of Dagad Trikon written by Alhakim, prince of Golkur, Chancellor of the Avastha University and kept thereafter in the Annals of Dikayoson, the herald of the Chamber of Maat.

ABUZINAL *See Titanosaur*

ADIVATAR *The Highest One, Generator, Operator, Destructor (G.O.D.)*

ABRAHAM *Manifestation of the primordial Daskalian (master) who taught the Jewish people about surrender to the Grand Scheme, the divine will: a key principle of the Deep Way.*

ALHAKIM, PRINCE *Head of the House of Golkur that was related to the House of Falkiliad, Alhakim was the high priest of the fire ritual and, on behalf of the Aulyas, officiated as the chancellor of the Avastha University. His mother was an Anorhadan priestess and he was, of course, well versed in all aspects of the Deep Way.*

ALISKHAN THE SWIFT *One of the warriors of the Yuva platoon identified in the Dagad Trikon saga. He could talk to the flying horses. Together with his cousin Lidholon, he was left behind at the end of the age of the Avasthas because of his desire to help human beings. This compassion was a trait of the House of Elnur to which he belonged.*

ALNYA *Princess from the desert tribe who was the appointed lady-in-waiting of the Lady of the Rock.*

ALWAKIL FIELDS (THE) *Sacred fields in front of the city of Shambalpur where the Avasthas performed religious ceremonies.*

ANANTA QUETZALCOATL *Name given by the Hindus and the Aztec to the cosmic cobra that served as a couch to the Emerald King.*

ANANYA   *State of Oneness with the Whole, fruit of the Deep Way. See also under Gift.*

ANGKURA   *Germinating power of Self-knowledge, fruit of the Deep Way.*

ANOR (HOUSE OF)   *One of the great Houses of the Avasthas, entrusted to be the keeper of the worship of Urakash, the power of the ether. The Anorans raised the flying horses and the best of them could fly some distance by the power of their thoughts. The elders of this House were telepathic. Anor provided the best archers and most of the Yuva platoon was recruited in its midst. It also provided the network of rangers and spies, which helped the Sand Keeper to monitor the moves of the Enemy. Haslerach of Anor was one of the greatest Nizams of Dagad Trikon although he ruled at the time of its decay.*

ANORHAD (HOUSE OF)   *One of the great Houses of the Avasthas, entrusted to be the keeper of the worship of Urtej, the power of the light. Many, through the ages, were initiated in the mystical power of the Deep Way and taught the other Avasthas accordingly. As a rule, only Anorhad could serve in the household of the Lady of the Rock or converse with her. Those warriors of Anorhad who had been initiated in the Deep Way were a terror to the hordes of the Darkness; they were said to use the power of a third eye to blast their enemies.*

ARCHANGELS   *Assistants of Adivatar who discharge appointed tasks to support human beings succeed in the Grand Scheme.*

ASLERACH   *Head of the House of Anor, he was the overlord of Dagad Trikon and Commander of the Avastha warriors.*

ATHA GLAUKOPIS   *High priestess of Atlantis who belonged to the circle of the Aulyas. She witnessed the end of her civilization as the explosion of an island volcano and the resulting tsunami destroyed Atlantis.*

AULYAS (CIRCLE OF THE)   *The Aulyas were the seers of old who could decode the subtlest spiritual meanings and steps in the framework of the Grand Scheme. They provided advice and guidance to the Avasthas. But after the Great Schism the earthlings did not use this knowledge any longer.*

AVASTHAS *Earlier race which ruled the earth long ago at the time of the Age of Truth. The Dagad Trikon prophecy identifies them with their last tribe left on earth, dwelling in the red triangle rock. This is why they are sometimes described as the Rock Avasthas.*

AVATAR *Incarnation in a human form of a deity, that is of a specific aspect of the one Adivatar (God).*

AZURA, AZURIC *or titanic creatures are the chief servants of the Master of Darkness, Thanatophor, and the two demon kings, Hangker and Belzebseth.*

BALDUR VAN JETZLAR *See Sanath.*

BANDHAN *With the knowledge of the Deep Way, external physical gestures can mobilize inner spiritual powers. The bandhan is a gesture of protection around the aura of the subject.*

BARDO *The twilight zone between death and life from where many of the ghosts and creatures of Belzebseth are operating to infiltrate human psyche. Many angels and a few Avasthas are also dwelling in these spheres to protect the humans.*

BANE OF BONAPARTE *Condition associated with the human ego when man under the influence of the ego, pursues a linear action until the impact of that action recoils against its initiator, bringing the ultimate fall.*

BANE OF PETRONE *Condition associated with the human superego when man under the influence of conditioning loses faith in its own inner worth and starts enjoying the process of its own destruction.*

BELZEBSETH *Demon king and the left hand of Thanatophor, he infects the blue channel of desire, feelings, and emotions of the past. He chairs the Dark Council of necromancers, sorcerers, and witches. He devised many methods to ensnare the humans but is known to work mostly through addictions, lust, possessiveness, attachment or jealousy. Most effective when working in combination with Hangker.*

BHAIRAVA *Name given by believers and demons to the Archangel Michael.*

BHARATMA *Name given to the Indian sub-continent by the Avastha geographers.*

BIJE *Seed power*

CAVE OF WONDERS *Residence of the Lady of the Rock and a place of divine enchantments.*

CHANTA *Head of the House of Kalabham who mastered the secrets of earth's fertility and ensured the food supply of the inhabitants of the Rock*

CONFUCIUS *Manifestation of the primordial Daskalian (master) in the land of China who taught the rules of proper behavior contained in the law of Maat.*

CONOSAUR TROLL *One of the primeval forms of brutish negativity of weight and inertia, left over from Thanatophor's earlier works that remained embedded in stone.*

DAGAD TRIKON LEGEND *The departing Avasthas of the Dagad Trikon rock left the elements of the prophecy in ten caskets spread throughout the world. The prophecy was intended to avert the pending destruction of the human race in initiating the quest for the Deep Way and the Gift.*

DARKNESS, DARK COUNCIL *For Darkness, see under Thanatophor. The Dark Council gathered mostly witches and necromancers to plot the downgrading of the human consciousness and the extermination of the last Avasthas.*

DARK RIDERS *see under Deadly Sins.*

DASKALIAN ASSEMBLY *The Epistemic Daskalians are the master teachers endowed with the direct perception of truth and hence pure knowledge. Their successive projections in history guided the world's civilizations and religions. All these forms are successive incarnations of the one primordial master. They are all-powerful but their capacity to lead mankind is inhibited by the fact that, unlike Thanatophor and his lieutenants, they respect human freedom. The Daskalian Assembly is called at the command of the primordial master.*

DAVIDRIEL *First knight of the House of Falkiliad who dispatched the casket of the star with six branches.*

DAYA DEVI (MRS.) *Name given to the ancient primordial Goddess who walks on the earth in a camouflaged form to grant the powers of Angkura and Ananya and unwrap the Gift.*

DEADLY SINS (THE) *Lust, anger, greed, attachment, jealousy, vanity, and the seventh that pervades them all, pride. They appear in the saga as the dark riders, carriers of tendencies that infiltrate and corrupt human awareness, steering human beings towards the Foul Rift.*

DEEP WAY (THE) *Knowledge of the relationship between the Outer and the Inner Worlds that was available to the first-born before the Great Schism. That knowledge entailed connection with the subtle forces of heavens and nature, knowledge and understanding of the deities, and access to higher dimensions/powers of the psyche. The Deep Way was bestowed through a ceremony of initiation. This initiation was reported possible only after the crossing of the Gate of the Elephant. Thereafter, the pilgrim could receive The Gift of Adivatar. The purpose of the Dagad Trikon quest was to rediscover access to this lost knowledge.*

DHULJALAL *Auspicious time in the Avastha stellar calendar that brings the moisture of divine blessings.*

DIKAYOSON *The herald of the Chamber of Maat, where the Daskalians held Council, kept the Annals of the teachings of the Daskalians that contain the principles, knowledge, and practices of the Deep Way. Some chapters relate also to the history of the Avasthas. These records are not normally available to any of the races living on earth.*

DOXA *Subjective opinion about reality springing from limited mental constructs that have the potential to generate diverging views, distortions, and conflicts. Favored approach of Thanatophor.*

ELEKSIM (HOUSE OF) *One of the great Houses of the Avasthas, entrusted to be the keeper of the worship of Urvayu, the power of the air.*

ELEKSIM *Maintained the protocol of the heart and of pure feelings that was at the core of Avastha culture. Its priestess instructed the girls from all the Houses in the arts of the Sheravalian Guard. Eleksim could produce the fierce sandstorms through the rhythmic power of the Rasa music.*

ELKAIM EKAMONON *See Sanath.*

ELNELOK (CITADEL OF) *The great underground citadel of the Avasthas was constructed in a giant subterranean chamber and penetrated deep within the earth through a network of caves and galleries, through many rock layers and ascending floors. The builders from the lineage of Kalabham completed it at the time of the great parting of the Avasthas. They named it Elnelok in homage to Olophon of Elnur, father of Philthalas, who accepted to remain with his swordsmen to ensure the defense of these underground dwellings.*

ELNUR (HOUSE OF) *One of the great Houses of the Avasthas, entrusted to be the keeper of the worship of Urjala, the power of the water. It is this House that contributed most to the wealth of the rock elves. Its members were sea-faring explorers and navigators who trained the Thalassean traders. They controlled the trading routes of the Avasthas at the time of the splendor of Dagad Trikon. The Elnurians were the devotees of the Emerald God. Nizams of the House of Elnur resisted the call of the sea as the outer world fell under the Shadow, and they ruled thereafter in Elnelok. It is not know when and how they departed from the earth.*

EMERALD KING *Represents the operating power of Adivatar. However, if the mystical slumber of this God in the ocean of bliss lasts too long, Evil takes its best chance to strike and take over the world in his supposed absence. When awakened, he travels on Karudas and corrects the sense of history. In his blue form he is known as The Sower, as he plants the seeds of renewal, transformation, and redemption.*

ENEMY (THE) *See Thanatophor.*

EPISTEME *Objective knowledge of reality as the object of knowledge is absorbed by a direct cognitive experience. Favored approach of the Avasthas that is achieved through the Deep Way.*

ERILIE *Maid of Eleksim, who was the captain of the Sheravalian Guard and, first and foremost, a devotee of the Lady of the Rock. Erilie had the power of healing and could call on the Rasa energy while playing musical instruments.*

ESITEL *Sister of Erilie. Her dancing could evoke and provoke the flowing of the Rasa energy. She was retrieved from the grip of Belzebseth by the might of the Lady of the Rock*

ETAKIR   *Leader of the Yuva platoon who kept the full knowledge of his past lives through his reincarnations, a quality that brought him unmatched skills, experience, and wisdom.*

EVENYL   *Sister of Erilie and Esitel. Her singing could evoke and provoke the flowing of the Rasa energy.*

FALKILIAD (HOUSE OF)   *One of the great Houses of the Avasthas, entrusted to be the keeper of the worship of Uragni, the power of the fire. They were masters of artistic expression, guardians of the Avastha science, and crafted most of the Avasthas secret weapons, including the Glorfakir and the Sadhan. The Sand Keeper traditionally came from this house as he drew on the fire to be the master of secrets, creativity, and crafts.*

FOUL RIFT (THE)   *Master scheme of Thanatophor. The disintegration of man has to happen in his surroundings and in his very psyche. At the time Lakshman discovered the casket, the scheme of the Shadow was well on its way.*

FOUR AGES (THE)   *The four ages constitute this cycle of history in which the fate of the Avasthas and the humans mingle. In the first Golden Age the truth is known and Avasthas rule. In the Silver Age misunderstandings appear and righteousness is weakened. In the Bronze Age, confusion and dissent emerge and evil rises; Avasthas are exiled. In the Iron Age, the fourth age of man containing these modern times, the rule of evil spreads wide and deep but Avasthas return unnoticed as the famed Stealthstars.*

GABRIEL   *Heavenly form of the angelic messenger of the gods and assistant of the Emerald King, he appeared in Indian mythology as Hanuman.*

GAIA   *One of the names given to Mother Earth favored by the Avasthas.*

GATE OF BLESSEDNESS (THE)   *Entrance of the cave of wonders.*

GATE OF THE ELEPHANT (THE)   *Mythical passage to access again the Inner World after all access was lost as a consequence of the Great Schism. Access to the Gate was a key initiation to the Deep Way.*

GIFT (THE) *The Gift is of the entry into the blessed consciousness of Oneness and of the nature of Oneness, where absolute truth stands revealed and existence can be enjoyed in the consciousness as the glory of bliss. The bestowal of the Gift means the end of the Great Schism and the return to Godhead.*

GLORFAKIR *Some Avastha craft-smiths initiated in the Deep Way developed magic weaponry whereby special powers were embedded into specific weapons. The Glorfakir, a small sword discovered by Lakshman, was one of them but its operational code remained secret.*

GODDESS (GREAT) *Companion of Adivatar and ultimate bestower of the Gift, she takes many different forms and was known under many different names. She is the mother of the Lady of the Rock.*

GOLKUR (HOUSE OF) *One of the smaller houses of the Rock elves that was however held in high esteem for the quality of its scholarship and farsightedness.*

GORSCHKAK *see Titanosaur.*

GRAND SCHEME (THE) — THE GAME *Adivatar created the universe out of His love, for he wanted to share the bliss of existence. But He can do so only with evolved and conscious beings that are free. Thus mankind has to grow to a level of maturity and understanding where it can receive the Gift. The Grand Scheme led by the Sower is meant to take mankind through the various steps of history until it reaches that level.*

GREAT SCHISM (THE) *The split between the Outer World and the Inner World that breaks the unity of the creation, bringing ignorance, falsehood, and hypocrisy, thus opening the conditions for the Foul Rift.*

HABIMANYON *The youngest member of the Circle of the Aulyas, he was a young knight of great wisdom and immense valor.*

HANGKER *Demon king, the right hand of Thanatophor, he infects the yellow channel of thoughts and action and of the future. He commands the Titanosaurs and leads the raw might of evil hordes to fulfill his master's will to power. He is known to work mostly through pride, arrogance,* selfishness, greed, avidity, anger, hatred, resentment, and belligerency. He is most effective when working in combination with Belzebseth.

HANOMKAR THE STRONG One of the warriors of the Yuva platoon identified in the Dagad Trikon saga. He was from the House of Eleksim and commanded great Rasa powers through the beating of his drums.

HANUMAN Heroic figure of the Indian epic 'The Ramayana.' See also white monkey.

HASLERACH OF ANOR Nizam of Dagad Trikon at the time of the departure of the caskets. He was famed for his brilliance and mastery in the arts of war and devised, with the Sand Keeper, the content of the ten caskets that would be the Dagad Trikon prophecy.

HASARA Name given by the Avasthas to the great desert.

HERMES TRISMEGISTE Perception of the angelic aspect of the messenger of the gods corresponding to the personality of Hanuman that is contained in Greek mythology.

HLLIDARENDI (THE ORDER OF) An offspring of Rasmus the Aulya, who had consigned the principles of the secret knowledge of the Aulyas in mathematic formula. The hidden fellowship of the Order survived through the ages, passing down the initiation into the Deep Way to the next generation of wizards.

HIMAVAT Name for the Himalayas mountains.

ICHWARIL Head of the House of Eleksim, he was splendid and gallant, master of emotions and equipped with the power of conveying the security of love in its many forms.

INDRA (ALSO ZEUS OR JUPITER) Names given by the Aryans to the chief deity controlling the climate whose importance is realized by lesser human beings mostly under scenarios of extreme weather events or climate change.

ISAPREM Head of the House of Anorhad who was reputed to have achieved the exalted state of Sanidya.

IVAN SADAKA *One of the companions. He was a scout and Sanath's bodyguard and became one of his closest disciples. He aged very slowly due to his proximity to the Hllidarendi. He became a cardinal to identify and retrieve the casket of the wheel from the Vatican.*

JALADHAR *Deity controlling the rain and the sea in accordance with the precepts of Indra.*

JETZLAR (PHILIP LUITWIN, 16TH GRAF VON) *Companion of Sanath who was captured by the partisans of Sanath on the Russian front during World War II. He gradually understood and supported the potential of the Deep Way for healing people and nations.*

KALABHAM (HOUSE OF) *One of the great Houses of the Avasthas, entrusted to be the keeper of the worship of Urgaya, the power of the earth. They were the rock elves par excellence, could see in the night, and drew their power from their connection with Mother Earth. They built the dwellings, water channels, galleries, and the festival caves of the Avasthas in Dagad Trikon with the help of some dwarf tribes who had sought their protection. They later built the citadel of Elnelok and many of them married with the nagas after the peace treaty was concluded. They are devoted to the Lord of the Night, who bears the trident. It is from him that they learned the subtle magic of the Rasa music.*

KARUDAS (PRINCE) *Prince of the eagles and vehicle of the Emerald God, the master of the Grand Scheme. His folk are the protectors of the Avasthas and they even followed them underground in the last age of their presence on earth.*

KEM HEIM SAGA *Main scroll contained in the casket of the white feather that Lakshman deciphered telepathically in Iceland and Amsterdam. It is the song of the Return and brings revelations on the inner channel of evolution, both at individual and collective levels.*

KOAN *Riddle containing a hidden truth.*

KRIYAFEL KURION *Head of the House of Falkiliad, he mastered the art of action according to the Deep Way, was the arbiter of aesthetics and Avastha elegance, and supervised all infrastructures and building activities of the Rock.*

KUNDALINI *The secret inner power that represents the pure desire of becoming the Self.*

JONATHAN O'LOCHAN *One of the companions who was fated to enter the Dagad Trikon quest.*

LADY OF THE ROCK *The true ruler of Dagad Trikon, she controlled the power of Angkura and the mystical serpent energy.*

LAIRA VON JETZLAR *Sister of Ivan and wife of Philip, she was initiated as a child into the Deep Way by Sanath but the process did not enter into her conscious mind, so she could not consciously use, recall or explain the subtle knowledge.*

LAKSHMAN KHARADVANSIN *One of the companions who was fated to enter the Dagad Trikon quest.*

LAKSHMI VANI *One of the companions who was fated to enter the Dagad Trikon quest.*

LIDHOLON OF ANOR *One of the warriors of the Yuva platoon identified in the Dagad Trikon saga. He was the son of Haslerach and could have gone with him to the stars but, like his cousin Aliskhan, he stayed behind at the end of the age of the Avasthas because of his love for human beings.*

LAO TSE *Manifestation of the primordial Daskalian (master) in China who brought the teachings of Daoism, equilibrium, and dialectics, relating to the Deep Way.*

MAAT (CHAMBER OF) *'Maat' means The Law of Righteousness or dharma in Sanskrit. The Chamber of Maat hosts the Council of the Daskalians who are the guardians of the wheel of the eternal law of righteousness.*

MAHDI *The twelfth Imam of the Shiite Muslim faith who returns as the liberator at the end of the age of darkness.*

MANTRIC (INCANTATIONS) *Power of the word actualized by the Deep Way. The uttering of specific prayers and invocations activates subtle centers of energy within the human body.*

MARYADAS *The rules of right conduct and morality, spanned by the wheel of law to keep mankind on the path of higher evolution.*

MERCURY *Perception of the angelic aspect of the messenger of the gods corresponding to the personality of Hanuman that is contained in Roman mythology.*

MICHAEL *Archangel that leads the heavenly hosts against the dark forces of Belzebseth, he is the assistant of the God with the matted hair that holds the Trident.*

MLECHAS *Creatures that have been completely enslaved by the six dark riders of the Deadly Sins. Degraded by the action of Thanatophor, they expand his dominion through their depraved or cruel behavior.*

MOHAMMED *Manifestation of the primordial Daskalian (master) in the land of Arabia who taught about the oneness of God and integration, a key principle of the Deep Way.*

MOSES *Manifestation of the primordial Daskalian (master) who came to complete the work of Abraham.*

NAGAS *Race of mutant creatures that could be both human and serpents. The nagas are the jealous rulers of the underworld and never accepted the rule of Thanatophor. They have hypnotic powers and humans cannot resist the seductive spell of Naga girls. Naga females could ensnare even the Avasthas. After the peace treaty of the battle of Elnelok, many warriors of the House of Kalabham married naga girls.*

NIZAM *The secular ruler of Dagad Trikon.*

OIKOS (PROJECT) *Attempt by the international community to identify and address the deeper challenges of the 21st century in establishing a broad basis of understanding of the options opened for the future of the human race. However, as the Oikos researchers came too close to unveiling some of the schemes of Thanatophor, the project encountered trouble.*

OLOPHON OF ELNUR *Defender of Elnelok at the beginning of the dark age and the last known Nizam of Dagad Trikon registered in the annals of Dikayoson.*

OPHTALIR   *Magic object in the form of a binocular conceived to see at a distance.*

ORICHALC   *Fabulous metal found in Atlantis that was endowed with great resilience and secret properties.*

ORPHEAN (ARMOR)   *Special Avastha armor that could completely absorb the reflections of its environment, thus conferring a cloak of invisibility.*

PARAMPARA   *Formless energy of Adivatar also known as chaitanya in Sanskrit. It is projected in the cosmos, invisible, omnipresent, omnipotent.*

PHILIP, COUNT VON JETZLAR   *German officer who became the disciple and friend of Sanath. He strengthened the communication between the Hllidarendi and men, while learning much from Sanath about the Deep Way.*

PHILTHALAS OF ELNUR   *Son of Olophon, First Lord of Elnelok, Philtalas was a disciple of the sea. He retreated within Mother Earth when the age of the Avasthas passed away. He is one of the few elf lords who remained active in the Bardo to carry the commands of the Daskalians for the protection of the human race.*

PUSHPAK CHARIOT   *Magic chariot that could fly at will under the telepathic command of its master. Only specially trained Avasthas could fly the Pushpak.*

PUJAN (FESTIVALS)   *Ceremony of worship of the divinity by which the first-born triggered the inner journey towards truth, consciousness, and bliss.*

RAGHUBIR, HIGH LORD   *King of Ayodhya, Ram Chandra Aryaputra was a great lord and manifestation of the Emerald King; he was an ally of the Avasthas.*

RAJAH JANAKA   *Kingly manifestation of the primordial Daskalian (master) in the area of northern India and Nepal.*

RAKHI   *Small thread symbolizing the mutual bond of love and protection between brother and sister.*

RASA (ENERGY, MUSIC OR VIBRATIONS) *When the Parampara was made accessible to earthlings through a magnified capacity of enjoyment, it was called "Rasa," that is, the juice of blessed energy.*

RETABLE OF THE DOVE *see Triptych.*

ROCK (TRIANGLE) *Refers to the mountain complex lost in the immense vastness of an inhospitable desert. When the Avasthas took it as the last refuge of their waning civilization, they named it Dagad Trikon.*

SADHAN *Some Avasthas craft-smiths initiated in the Deep Way developed magic weaponry whereby special powers were embedded into specific weapons. The Sadhan, a shield, discovered by Lakshman, was one of them but its subtle properties remained secret.*

SALOKYA *First state of proximity to the mystery of the world. Avasthas that were initiated meant it was the capacity to approach the Goddess.*

SAMIPYA *Second state of proximity to the mystery of the world corresponding to the capacity to address or invoke the Goddess.*

SANIDYA *Third and more intimate state of proximity to the mystery of the world that involves receiving the fullness of the Gift.*

SAMADHI *Name given in the Sanskrit language by ancient seers to the Gift. (See the Gift.)*

SAMYAK *Integrated knowledge, that is, knowledge not received only with the brain but also with the heart. The fusion of heart and brain triggers recognition. See also episteme. Samyak is episteme with the added emotional value of love.*

SANATH *Sanath was the heir of the Order of the Hllidarendi, and a key figure in the unfolding of the Dagad Trikon prophecy. He had been sent by the Daskalians to lead the quest of human beings in unraveling the meaning of the Dagad Trikon prophecy. Sanath revealed his secret name during the council of the Hllidarendi at Jetzenstein Castle.*

SAND KEEPER *The chief wizard of Dagad Trikon, master of knowledge, warden of the House of Falkiliad, and Teacher of the Deep Way. Having gone through the seventh level of initiation of the secret fire, he was also a counselor to the Lady of the Rock. He lived with his family as a* highlander. Through his network of spies and the fleet of pushpak chariots, he was the ear and the eye of the Rock.

SAO IAMBU The sacred wind stones, created by Mother Earth, to emit the power of the Parampara.

SERAPIS Counselor of the Nizam, governor of the city of Shambalpur and administrator of the finances of Dagad Trikon, he was a magistrate of great influence but he was said to harbor a secretive taste for power.

SHADOW See Thanatophor.

SHAMBALPUR Capital city of the first-born whose legendary magnificence and wealth excited the rapacity of Hangker for the fame of Shambalpur, in the earlier ages, went over the whole world.

SHEKHINA Expression of the invisible presence of the formless divine power.

SHERAVALIAN GUARD Company of Avastha virgins that formed the Household cavalry of the Lady of the Rock. They were mounted on felines, and were fearless and undefeated in battle. They possessed many mind powers acquired as a result of their devotion to their mistress. When chanting or dancing, the Sheravalian virgins were best among the first-born to call the Rasa power.

SNEAKY WAY (THE) Qualification given by the Rock dwellers to the attack of Belzebseth consisting of possessing the psyche of vulnerable humans.

SOWER (THE) At times when the Emerald King decides to intervene in earthly affairs to lead the Grand Scheme and throw the seeds of change and redemption, he borrows a blue shape of infinite grace and charm that can yet reveal awesome might and grandeur at will.

STEALTHSTARS Avasthas born in the human race without being revealed to others, or more regretfully, without being revealed to themselves. Without becoming aware of their own powers, the Stealthstars would gradually vanish into irrelevance.

THANATOPHOR He is the Lord of Evil, whose origin is hidden to the Avasthas. He is called Satan in the fourth age of men. The Sand Keeper assumed that Thanatophor was generated in the first age when freedom was granted to creatures although they were still under a cloak of ignorance. The greatest strength of Thanatophor is the control of a collective force by which he bound all the servants of the Darkness. His purpose is world dominion.

THALASSEAN NAGIVATORS The Thalasseans are the people of the sea. This ancient race of navigators equipped the transcontinental fleet linking faraway kingdoms and provided, on contract from the Admiral of the House of Elnur, captains and sailors to the Avastha fleet. The mother of Olophon of Elnur was a Thalassean princess.

TITANOSAUR A crossbreed between titans and leading demons of the first ages that lead the hordes of Hangker and execute the sinister schemes concocted by Belzebseth. The four of them control the hemispheres (northern, southern, eastern, and western) and leave behind a trail of lust and violence. In the fourth age of men, most of the Titanosaurs did not take an individual physical shape but operated through the cracks created in the human psyche by the plots of Belzebseth. In this story, only Gorshkak (North) and Abuzinal (South) appear.

TRACY O'LOCHAN Sister of Jonathan and secretary of the Oikos project for the USA.

TRICOLOR LILY OF ANORHAD Symbol of the second portal of the Gate of the Elephant. Human beings referred to it as the third eye. The subtle lily in the human brain opens wider through the power of forgiveness. It can also call on the power of the Trishul, a weapon of retribution that punishes those who break the law of Maat.

TRIDENT OR TRISHUL The Trident is the attribute of the aspect of Adivatar that embodies existence and destruction. This great God was represented at the entrance gate of the fortress of Elnelok. See also under the Tricolor lily of Anorhad.

TRIPTYCH OF THE DOVE Ornamental painting on wood paneling of the late Middle Ages kept in the Hall of the Knights at Jetzenstein Castle. It served as the main store of power and support to the magic the wizard used to call the higher powers from above. (Also retable.)

URAEUS *Sacred pet cobra of the Lady of the Rock that was the symbol of the serpent power she controlled.*

UDURLAN *Younger brother of Haslerach and father of Aliskhan, he was one of the most accomplished warriors of the House of Anor.*

URAGNI *Mystical power of fire endowed with the property of purificaion.*

URAKASH *Mystical power of the ether endowed with the property of communication.*

URGAIA *Mystical power of the earth endowed with the property of innocence and nourishment.*

URJALA *Mystical power of the water endowed with the property of life and regeneration.*

URTEJ *Mystical power of the air endowed with the property of knowledge and light.*

URVAYU *Mystical power of the wind endowed with the property of carrying the messages of the Gods.*

VAIKUNTHA (BASIN OF) *Placed at the center of the Chamber of Maat, the Basin of Vaikuntha gave access to the higher world where the Emerald King ruled.*

VANI *Power of speech, which is developed through training in the Deep Way. It allows the listener to experience directly the state and condition that is being uttered or described.*

VILAMBA *Area of consciousness between two thoughts that connects to the present moment and gives access to the Gate of the Elephant. The practice of the Deep Way widens the space between the waves of thoughts. The Vilamba is the entry point into silence, serenity, and Self-mastery.*

WHEEL (TEMPLE OF THE) *The Temple of the Wheel, hewn out of the cliffs of Dagad Trikon by the best Avastha architects, was meant to shelter the assembly of the Daskalians. Its core consisted in the Chamber of Maat that serves as the hall for the congregation of the Daskalians.*

WHITE MONKEY (THE)   *Master of subtle knowledge, alchemy, and magic, the lord Hanuman is the messenger of the Emerald God. He can change forms at will and travel in parallel universes at the bidding of his Lord.*

WITCHES   *Female followers of Belzebseth, who incarnated in large numbers in the fourth age of men to lure the humans and mostly young girls in the ways of their dark master.*

WIZARD   *Wizards in the days of the Rock were those having passed the higher rites of initiation and authorized by Prince Alhakim to teach the Deep Way. The first wizard of the Avasthas was the Sand Keeper. See also Sanath.*

YUVA PLATOON   *Elite unit of the Avasthan army composed mostly of young archers initiated in the Deep Way after an intensive period of martial training. They could call on the power of collective consciousness so that, in case of danger, any of them could use the power of all.*

ZARATHUSTRA   *Manifestation of the primordial Daskalian (master) in the land of Persia and teacher of the Zoroastrians.*